TAPESTRY

TAPESTRY

J. ROBERT JANES

MYSTERIOUSPRESS.COM

OPEN ROAD

INTEGRATED MEDIA
NEW YORK

copyright © 2013 by J. Robert Janes

cover design by Mauricio Díaz

ISBN 978-1-4804-0077-1

Published in 2013 by MysteriousPress.com/Open Road Integrated Media
345 Hudson Street
New York, NY 10014
www.mysteriouspress.com
www.openroadmedia.com

Acknowledgments

All of the novels in the St-Cyr–Kohler series incorporate a few words and brief passages in French or German. Dr. Dennis Essar of Brock University very kindly helped with the French, as did the artist Pierrette Laroche, while Professor Schutz, of Germanic and Slavic Studies at Brock, helped with the German. A very special thanks must also be extended to Robin Walz for his marvellous *Pulp Surrealism*, to Sarah Fishman for her excellent *The Battle for Children: World War II, Youth Crime, and Juvenile Justice in Twentieth-Century France* and *We Will Wait—Wives of French Prisoners of War, 1940–1945*, and to photographer Alex Waterhouse-Hayward of Vancouver for his very kind assistance with all things Argentine. Should there be any errors, they are my own and for these I apologize.

Author's Note

Tapestry is a work of fiction. Though I have used actual places and times, I have treated these as I have seen fit, changing some as appropriate. Occasionally the name of a real person is used for historical authenticity, but all are deceased and I have made of them what the story demands. I do not condone what happened during these times. Indeed, I abhor it. But during the Occupation of France everyday crimes of murder and arson continued to be committed, and I merely ask, by whom and how were they solved?

TAPESTRY

Tapestry: History's woven moment being spun and dyed, is linked pattern to pattern to design and panorama, hiding truth until unravelled.

1

Each stood in a doorway, out of the rain, and when the slit-eyed, blue-blinkered light from Louis's torch found the blocky faces, Kohler saw that impassive gazes were returned.

Each then evaporated into the blackout, the *click-clack* of the Occupation's wooden-soled shoes earnestly retreating along the *passage* de la Trinité, a lane so narrow and old, water rushed down its centre finding the shoes first and sewers second. Rain, an icy, bone-numbing rain: Paris, Thursday 11 February 1943 at 11.47 p.m.

It gushed from downpipes to fountain across the *passage*, blocking all reasonable access to the *vélo-taxi* that had been crammed into a doorway. A bicycle taxi across whose backside bold letters gave . . . *Ach, mein Gott*, could a better-chosen name have been found? *PRENEZ-MOI. JE SUIS À VOUS.* Take me. I'm yours. And stolen too!

'HERMANN, LET ME!'

Jésus, merde alors, how many times had he heard Louis yell it like that? A rape, another grisly murder probably and they not home more than an hour. Dragged off the train from Colmar, Alsace and now the Greater German Reich, ordered here or else. Two honest cops, one from each side, and fighting common crime when everybody else was in on it. 'She's all yours, *mon vieux*. I would never have found her without you.'

1

'Grab the last of those departing *filles de joie*. Tell her that pneumonia is in the offing and that if she doesn't answer truthfully, I will personally deny her the necessary medical treatment but not the VD checkups she has constantly been avoiding!'

Louis shouted things like that just to keep his partner sane. 'She's already agreed. Hey, her hand's cold, wet and trembling, but I'm calming her.'

'*Bon*. Without a licence she's going to need it. Is that still the *quartier* de Bonne-Nouvelle's most notorious *maison de passe*, madame?' Louis rammed a pointing hand towards a door of no edifying virtue.

'*Oui*,' she grunted dispassionately. Purposely he didn't hear her, so she yelped it again and shrilled, 'MESSIEURS, I KNOW NOTHING OF THIS MATTER. I AM SOAKED TO THE *PRÉFET'S* GOATEE AND CANNOT SWIM!'

The walk-in hotel, one of Paris's many to which the street girls took their clients, asked no questions, took no names and, like the *passage*, preferred anonymity.

'Snow should soon begin,' shouted Louis as he reached to open the closest of the taxi's doors, 'but first there will be the ice pellets.'

Half of him was soon squeezed inside the *vélo-taxi*. From it Kohler could hear the muted, '*Ah, mon Dieu*, mademoiselle, you're safe now. My name is Jean-Louis St-Cyr of the Sûreté, but I'm not like most of those. We'll get the one who did this. We won't stop until we do.'

He ducked out to earnestly confide, 'Hermann, let that one go. This one's not only been savagely raped but brutally beaten. We'll have to take her to the *Hôtel-Dieu* and quickly.'

More couldn't be said, but through the celluloid of the side windscreen, a fever of blue-washed light passed quickly over the victim before being extinguished. 'Easy, mademoiselle. Easy. Please don't try to talk.'

'My children . . .'

'Madame, we'll see to them.'

'My papers. My keys. Our ration cards and tickets. My wedding ring.'

'Please don't concern yourself further. Rest. . . . Just try to rest.'

'She's passed out, Louis.'

'Fish oil, Hermann. That taxi reeks of it. There's grease on the seats and on her neck and shoulders.'

At 1.07 a.m. sleet pinged off the Citroën. They had put the woman, as yet unnamed, into the very best of hands, felt Kohler, had got his little Giselle and his Oona to watch over the children, and would get back to her as soon as possible, but *liebe Zeit* was there to be no rest? Bleakly he gripped the steering wheel and stared through the shrapnel at the silvery darkness the storm and the blackout gave to the boulevard Montmartre. Not another car was in sight, of course, for virtually all of them had disappeared from the city in June 1940, the crowds, too, at this hour, and didn't the Führer pride himself on having war-torn Europe's only open city and the good example it set of all things Nazi?

The *passage* Jouffroy, at number 12, had been built in 1846, thought St-Cyr, but Hermann didn't need a travelogue, not with Walter Boemelburg, his boss and Head of Section IV, the Gestapo in France, breathing down their necks and a telex that had summoned them on the run: return hq immediately / streets being terrorized by blackout crime, and so much for the Führer's shining example of an open city.

Pitch-dark, beyond the regulation dim pinpoint of blue that should mark its far end and exit, the glass-and-iron roofed Jouffroy was much wider than that of the open-slotted Trinité. Secondhand books specializing in photographic equipment most could only dream of in this third and most miserable winter of the Occupation were on offer; secondhand mechanical toys, too, and walking sticks and umbrellas . . .

'Used postage stamps,' grumbled St-Cyr. 'That's not you is it, Agent Bélanger, not the officer I last worked with here on the thirteenth of October 1939, the one who had been wounded in the left shoulder at Verdun in the autumn of 1917?'

To flatter a Parisian *flic* was even more insane than trying to grease one of their waiters without offering cash, but this one, Kohler noted, was a *hirondelle,* one of the swallows with cape and bicycle, and God help him if he tried to ride that chariot he had chained to the light standard.

Briefly Bélanger shone his torch over them. The Gestapo was a draining giant of fifty-five with pale-blue eyes and an expression the torchlight did nothing to alleviate; the Frenchman, a former *boxeur* of the Police Academy, was blocky, chunky, broad-shouldered, of medium height and fifty-two years of age, the big brown eyes noticing everything, the full, dark brown soup-strainer one that should definitely suffer decapitating scissors and a razor, lest the stomach get a hairball.

That terrible scar of the Bavarian's was on the left and ran from eye to chin. Everyone had heard of it. The police, the Sûreté, the SS and Gestapo. Honest . . . these two were not only known for their absolute honesty, that scar was the reward an SS whip had given Kohler for their steadfastly having pointed the finger of truth, the idiots.

'It is this way, Inspectors,' grunted Bélanger.

Besides the truncheon, he toted one of those torches in which there was a dynamo that was activated by repeatedly pressing the thumb down on a lever. No batteries though, thought Kohler, and they did say the things didn't wear out as easily but were a bugger on the thumb.

Au Philatéliste Savant was at the far end and not six steps from the old Hôtel Ronceray. The little blue exit light, mounted high on the wall, was there in its wire cage, but flickered instant warnings of yet another power outage: punishment of the population for the 'terrorist' actions of a few or simply industrial demands elsewhere. Always the power could be cut off.

Now suddenly not even the exit on to the rue de la Grange-Batelière could be seen but the door to this four-metre-wide shop had been jemmied. As Bélanger's torchlight passed over them, banks of envelopes stuffed with collector's 'bargains' appeared. Nothing over five and ten francs and yet there must be thousands of the envelopes, felt Kohler, astounded by the dedicated patience of the years and the musty smell of old, worn-out glue.

'The safe is at the back, Inspectors,' said Bélanger. 'I have touched nothing.'

And did this last need to be mentioned? wondered Kohler, only to hear Louis patently ignore the fact and ask, 'Time of entry?'

The torch went out to give it a rest. 'Inspectors, you must understand that I didn't make my rounds here until forty-five minutes past midnight. Immediately I have called in.'

'As you should have,' said Louis. 'Give us a span, if you think it appropriate, but narrow it as much as is prudent.'

And if that wasn't polite and deferential, what was?

'From twenty minutes past midnight to thirty. Normally I would have been here between those times, but heard a disturbance in the *passage* des Panoramas and have retraced the steps for another look.'

More up-market, though older, that *passage* was right across the boulevard Montmartre at number 11. 'Why didn't the alarm go off here?' asked Kohler.

Pumped torchlight momentarily touched the *flic's* heavy black-rimmed spectacles before swinging aft and aloft to reveal the brass of an ancient clapper pan that was just above the inside of the door and would have awakened the dead had its fist-sized hammer been allowed to continue and not been silenced by a wad of rat-grey clay.

'Which reeks of the sewers, Hermann,' muttered the Sûreté, having beaten his partner to it while under cover of darkness. 'Put in place as entry was gained.'

'The alarm known about?' quipped Kohler.

'You're learning. That's good. Being with me helps.'

The safe, ancient and of cast iron, was hidden behind a faded curtain that had dutifully fallen into place even though the door was wide open. One of its little legs was missing, a half-brick having been substituted years ago.

The obvious had best be given but it wouldn't hurt to use Louis's rank. 'Two medium raps with the sledge, Chief Inspector,' said Kohler deferentially. 'One to knock the dial off and the other with the chisel to punch in the spindle and tumblers.'

Good for Hermann. Together they'd unsettle this *flic*. 'But . . . but, Herr Hauptmann Detektiv Aufsichtsbeamter of the Gestapo's Kripo, the contents can't have been touched beyond a desired item or two? Three thick wads of old francs kept in the faint hope of their amnesty? Folios and envelopes too precious to leave out after hours, the owner's private collection as well? A half a baguette made from white flour, at least three hundred grams of Camembert, which, like the flour, can only be obtained on the *marché noir?*'

The black market.

'An open tin of Portuguese sardines and a quarter litre of milk, these items to be shared with . . .' Louis paused. 'The cat, where is it?'

'Gone to where all such cats must go when released by a sudden noise and an open door,' said Bélanger.

A poet! but horn-rims must be feeling confident. 'Milk,' grumbled Kohler, 'when mothers haven't been able to find it since the winter of 1940–41.' But had used postage stamps been bartered to provision this one's larder? Absolutely! Even among the Wehrmacht's grey-green-uniformed soldier boys, its "Green Beans," there were avid stamp collectors and guess who were the black market's biggest dealers?

Taking hold of the hand that held the light, he lowered it a trifle before reaching deeply into the safe. *'Saucisson de Lyon fumé,'* he said appreciatively. 'Homemade, Louis, and hung for at least ten days in the chimney.'

Now, of course, such a practice could only be done late at night, prolonging the finishing time and keeping the news from neighbours, but possessing smoked sausage was illegal in any case. 'Agent Bélanger, have you notified the owner?' asked St-Cyr pleasantly enough.

'My orders were to await yourselves, Chief Inspector.'

'The *préfet* is being considerate, Hermann.'

The chief of police and an archenemy. *Merde*, were they in for another dose of Talbotte's 'consideration'?

'The owner, M. Picard, has lived in the Hôtel Ronceray for years, Inspectors. If it is your wish, I'll ask the concierge to awaken him.'

Such politeness from a *flic* had to have its reasons and Louis knew it too but said, 'Let him sleep. He's going to need it. Stay here and seal this off and we'll come back when there's no need for the electric lights we could have used. Ah, I almost forgot. Your pocketknife.'

Taken aback as to why such a lengthy trust should suddenly have befallen him, Bélanger dragged out the knife. 'Inspectors . . .'

Ignoring him, Louis scraped a bit of clay from the dial and put it into a handkerchief. 'Rags, Hermann, were used to muffle the sound. Rags still heavy with their mud.'

'And from that same sewer as was used on the clapper, Chief?' Horn-rims was now panicking at being ignored but as if on cue to save him, the bold clanging of a call box started up. Again and again, it shrilled.

'Answer it,' said St-Cyr with a sigh. 'It's all right. You can leave us. I have a torch whose batteries I was budgeting.'

Now only the sound of ice hitting the roof of the Jouffroy came to them. 'The driving will be a bugger, Louis.'

'Especially with the absence of road salt. Wasn't it all requisitioned and sent to the Reich?'

'It's not my fault.'

'Our *flic* is hiding something.'

'The sausage,' retorted Kohler. 'He cut off a thick slice and ate it. You would have smelled it on his breath if you hadn't been so busy playing detective.'

'The Camembert on that breath was overly ripe and there were breadcrumbs glued to the knees of his trousers, Inspector, but if *you* had really been alert, you would have noticed the instant of panic that greeted my telling him to stay.'

'He lifted a little something else from the safe,' said Kohler.

'The bank notes were left untouched,' mused the oracle.

'But our safe-cracker passed up . . .'

'The paper twists of gold louis our M. Picard would most certainly have set aside.'

'And not declared as they should have been?' quipped Kohler. These days everything more than one hundred thousand francs in value had to be registered, if one was fool enough.

'We'll treat the matter with discretion, Hermann, since our *flic* has realized we might well be aware of the absence.'

'But was he left that little something to silence him?' asked Kohler blandly.

'*Ah, bon, mon vieux,* you really are learning. It's a great comfort to me, of course, for Paris has much to teach a former Munich and Berlin detective, though with such a slow learner, I tell myself patience is required. We can leave him entirely in charge. Indeed, I doubt there will even be another mouthful of sausage taken when we come back for that closer look, and I think we will find the proof of what is missing has been returned and no one will be the wiser for its little absence.'

'Inspectors . . . Inspectors,' bleated Bélanger from out of the ink. 'Someone at headquarters has made an unpardonable mistake. You were not to have been assigned to this robbery and are to hurry to the Restaurant Drouant. Another sex attack has been made.'

'Not assigned to this, Louis? Another rape?'

'Are we to only cover those?'

There was no other traffic but why, please, only the rapes? Murder, blackmail, robbery, arson and fraud were their specialties.

The Drouant, at the corner of the rue Saint-Augustin and the rue Gaillon, had opened in 1880 and become famous for its seafood. Though it hurt to have to admit it, Louis had to say, 'The clientele is largely French and most definitely Parisian.'

There'd be several of the 'friends' of those, felt Kohler, but only the *bourgeoisie aisée,* the really well-off, and the *nouveaux riches* everyone else was bitching about, could afford such a place: the BOFs, the *beurre, oeufs et fromage* (butter, eggs and cheese) boys of the black market and other *collabos,* bankers, businessmen, those of inherited wealth and those who had made it, if only recently.

Candles that had all but vanished from the city since that first winter flickered in the sudden draught as they stepped into the foyer to confront an absent maître d'.

In the silence that accompanied their entry, a nearby glass of the *blanc de blanc* was downed in one gulp by a blonde in an emerald-green suit dress and diamonds. Guilt made her lovely eyes moisten, fear caused her lips to quiver. Like every other female in the place, she'd be thinking she could well have been a victim herself. The forty-year-old stud at her side wore the navy blue of a lieutenant in the Abwehr, the counterintelligence service, and didn't she look like what some had come to hate and call *les horizontales*?

The place was packed. Several were dressed for an evening at the Opéra, though the performance would have ended early for those who needed the *métro*, and most here would simply stay the night unless they'd a pass allowing them to be out after curfew.

Embarrassed by his continued scrutiny, she finally lowered her gaze. Twenty-two if that, thought Kohler. A gorgeous figure, beautiful lips . . .

'The oyster bar is superb, Hermann. *Belons, portugaises* and *marennes. Ah, mon Dieu,* the *bouillabaisse* is magnificent, the *filet de sole Drouant* a bishop's sin.'

'You've eaten here?'

'On my pay? People such as myself only hear about places like this. Monsieur . . .'

The maître d' had arrived to shrill, 'Inspectors, why are you not keeping the streets safe? A mugging? A slashing? A groping? This *homme sadique* has ruined the dinners of everyone and has upset the chef and sous-chef, my waiters as well as myself most especially.'

'Monsieur, just lead us to the victim,' said Louis. It was a night for sighs.

'*Victims!*' cried Henri-Claude Patout. 'The hysterics. The splashes of blood on the carpets—how are we to clean them? The oceans of tears and screams? The shameful clutching of a woman's *parties sensibles* as the ring is torn from her finger and she has thought the virtue, it would have to be sacrificed or else the throat, it would be slashed? Yes, slashed! Monsieur Morel, he has been unable to defend her from this animal. Struck down, he has fallen into the gutter to ruin the tuxedo and has been robbed. ROBBED, DID YOU HEAR ME, of the wallet, the gold pocket watch of his wife's father, the silver cigar case . . .'

'Calm down, monsieur,' snapped Louis, stopping him on a staircase whose wrought-iron balustrade curved up from ground-floor ears and eyes to sixteen private dining rooms.

'WHY SHOULD I BE CALM WHEN YOU PEOPLE DON'T KNOW YOUR DUTY?'

'They don't appear to have stopped eating.'

'THE ATMOSPHERE HAS BEEN PLUNGED, INSPECTOR. PLUNGED!'

'Louis, let me.'

'Hermann, a moment please, and then he is all yours to arrest for obstructing justice. Which of the rooms, monsieur? Come, come. Out with it.'

'The Goncourt's.'

The Académie Goncourt had held their meetings here since 31 October 1914 to award the country's most prestigious literary prize. 'Take care of him, Hermann. Scrutinize the papers of everyone. Be sure to take down all the necessary details. One never knows when something useful might turn up. And make damned sure those who are allowed to leave have the necessary *Ausweis* and are not required to stay cooped up in this doss-house of the elite until five a.m!'

Thank God Louis had got that off his chest.

'Messieurs . . . Inspectors . . .'

'It's Chief Inspector St-Cyr and Detective Inspector Kohler of the Gestapo,' said Louis.

'It . . . it is this way, please.'

And so much for not knowing their duty. 'We'll leave the papers for the moment,' said Kohler, plucking at Patout's sleeve and using his best Gestapo form. 'Just see that a little something is sent up from the kitchens.'

Not even an eye was batted, thereby revealing that the house was quite used to such.

'Hermann, we haven't time. Besides, you know the stomach, accustomed to those little grey pills that keep the Luftwaffe's night-fighter pilots awake, will not sit well with such richness.'

The Benzedrine, but still the stomach would like to try.

M. Gaston Morel, victim number three, was not happy. Big in every sense below a blood-soaked bandage, he lifted lead grey eyes from an all but drained bottle of the Romanée-Conti, the 1934 and a superb year, to impassively gaze at Louis first and then at this Kripo.

Grizzled cheeks wore the eight days of customary growth that hid the pockmarks of childhood but served also to make him look like a slum landlord after arrears. The starched shirt collar was no longer tight, the black bow tie having been yanked off in disgust.

'*Ah, bon*, you've at last condescended to show up,' he grunted. 'Considering that the assault occurred at eleven fifty-two p.m. yesterday, and that it is now two thirty-five a.m., we should think ourselves lucky, but please don't bother to claim you were delayed or that the dispatcher fucked up and sent you to the wrong address.'

Compressed, the thin lips were grimly turned down beneath a nose and heavy black eyebrows that, with the stubble, were fierce. Had he been a union buster in the thirties? wondered St-Cyr.

'Monsieur, mesdames, a few small questions. Nothing difficult, I assure you.'

'Don't be an *imbécile*, Inspector. My wife's stepsister was very nearly murdered.'

'And the others?' asked Louis, indicating the wife who sat next to a female friend who was younger than her by a good fifteen years. A former debutante, a tall, auburn-haired, permed and very carefully made-up, sharp-featured socialite who'd be taut when pressed.

'They stayed at our table while I accompanied Madame Barrault to my car,' said Morel.

'You've an *Ausweis*?' asked Louis with evident interest.

'And an SP sticker,' came the dead flat answer.

The *Service-Public* sticker that had to be signed and stamped not only by the Kommandant von Gross-Paris but also by the *préfet*, and wouldn't you know it, this one was a friend of both!

Before the Defeat there'd been 350,000 private autos in Paris

11

and unbelievable traffic jams and smog. Now there were no more than 4,500 and here was one of their owners.

It wasn't difficult to see what was running through detective minds, felt Gaston Morel, but he'd have to ignore it. 'The rear tyres had been punctured but due to the rain, we didn't see this at first. When we did, I sent my driver to telephone for replacements and that is when this bastard struck. First myself, as I was helping Marie-Léon from the car, and then herself to be thrown up against the wall, the overcoat ripped open, the dress down.'

Isolated from the others, Madame Barrault sat in one of the armchairs at the far end of the table. Huddled in a thin overcoat and cradling a bandaged left forearm and hand, she couldn't bring herself to look at anyone, felt Kohler, was badly shaken, but terrified of something else as well.

'See to her, Hermann. I'll deal with the others.'

'Leave her,' grunted Morel. 'She's in no state to answer anything. He used a cutthroat to free her handbag and when she refused to give up her wedding ring, slashed her arm and the back of her hand before ripping the ring off and then grabbing her by the crotch for a good feel.'

'*Putain*. . . . That is what he has called me,' blurted the woman.

Madame Morel, the arch of a well-plucked, heavily shadowed dark black eyebrow sharply cocked, hung on every word as did her companion.

'Madame Barrault's husband is a guest of our friends—a prisoner of war,' offered Morel as a gesture of cooperation. 'Marie-Léon, I'll see that your papers are replaced. Please don't worry. The ration cards and tickets also.'

Had the wife sucked in the breath of 'I told you so'? wondered Kohler. Certainly the companion knew what it was all about, for instinctively she had laid a comforting hand on Madame Morel's.

Louis had seen it too, but wasn't about to let on. 'Can you give us any kind of a description, monsieur?' he asked.

'If I could, I'd find and kill him myself.'

Coffee and cognac arrived—real coffee and real alcohol, a Bisquit Napoléon, the 1903, along with a plate of petits fours, some pâté and bread—nothing ersatz there either. The former debutante poured. The night's victims three and four refused nourishment, Madame Barrault first lowering her gaze out of despair or shame, and then stealing a glance at the petits fours as if guilt and pride had been tempered with . . . what? wondered Kohler. Need, for sure, but not for herself.

'The wallet, monsieur,' said Louis brusquely. 'A few details. They'll not be of much use, but threads we must have if we are to clothe the attack better.'

Was this Sûreté a tailor? 'Bought in Algiers, in a bazaar in 1938 and with me ever since.'

'The leather the usual?' asked the inspector, meaning the Arabic design, Henriette Morel told herself with a curt nod as she waited for the rest.

'Of a soft morocco,' went on Gaston, ignoring her as usual, 'and one I will miss. Loaded with fifty big ones simply because they're easier to carry.'

With 250,000 francs, the leather as soft as a lecher's extended organ, Gaston? Henriette wanted desperately to say but couldn't—the detectives would find out soon enough.

'Any *Reichskassenscheine*?' asked St-Cyr.

The Occupation mark at twenty francs to one. 'Ten thousand.'

'Your papers?'

Again Morel lifted his gaze from the glass and bottle. 'Those I keep elsewhere. He'll be disappointed.'

Everyone knew there was a roaring trade in false and stolen papers. 'Your place of business?' asked Louis.

'It has no bearing whatsoever on what happened. You might as well ask me about the opera I had to endure.'

'Very well, what was it?'

'La Bohème,' gushed Madame Morel. 'It was magnificent, wasn't it, Denise?'

The husband didn't give the former debutante a chance. 'Fucking Italians. A sick whore and a pawnbroker? Duels with coal shovels and fire tongs?' He tossed a fist. 'One hell of a lot of caterwauling I had to pay good money for, Henriette.'

'You were constantly grumbling, Gaston. Several noticed.'

Again the companion rested a sympathetic hand on that of the wife but this time the other victim stole a longing glance at the petits fours and the pâté and bread. Her coat, like the dress that had been pinned up, had been made over. The early thirties, felt Kohler. No silk stockings like the other two would be wearing, but probably none of the leg paint either and brand-new button earrings of enamel from the Bon Marché's bargain bin.

'Place of business?' demanded Louis with more force.

'*Cimenterie Morel*,' came the grunt. 'The company I acquired in '31, and which supplies the Organization Todt.'

Cement hadn't always been good, not in the depths of the Great Depression, but with the Todt's building of the submarine pens at Lorient and elsewhere in 1940 and now the massive fortifications of the Atlantic Wall, it must be a great comfort.

Leaving Louis to it, Kohler pulled coffee and cognac towards him and went to sit down with victim number four. 'Why not tell me what you can, madame? You've a son or daughter and are understandably anxious to get home.'

Much taller than the other one, he'd a terrible scar, Marie-Léon noted, others too. Those of the shrapnel from that other war, but far more recent nicks and cuts as if from flying glass, also the crease of a bullet across the brow like his partner, she wondered, but a little more recent than that one's?

There was a warmth though, to his pale-blue eyes. They couldn't be those of a Gestapo, and yet . . . and yet he was one of them. 'I can tell you little, Inspector. One minute the monsieur was crying out, the next, I was yanked from the car . . .' She glanced at her wounded arm and hand, felt so ashamed, could not stop the tears. 'Please, I . . . People like me never come to places like this. A night out? A little break from the endless days of never knowing when my husband will come home or if he will still feel the way he once did about me?'

Not well off, but well brought up, the stepsister was neither really, really plain nor pretty. *Une jolie-laide*, the French called them. Plain but not so bad after all, age: thirty-four, and a good twenty years younger than Madame Morel. The hair was long and of a deep chestnut shade, thick and clean and worn in a chignon that had come loose, the freckled brow still worried. The eyes were dark brown and normally frank, no doubt, but searching as now, the nose more robust than she'd want, the unpainted lips quite lovely, even if those of a woman who knew she was being assessed in such a manner by such a cop but had her pride.

The chin was determined. 'Where's home?' he asked.

She wouldn't even glance at Henriette or Denise Rouget, Marie-Léon told herself. 'The rue Taitbout, near the corner of the rue la Fayette.'

He'd been wrong about where the earrings had been purchased, but it had been an easy mistake, for the flat wasn't far from the Galeries Lafayette, another of the biggest department stores, not that there was much to find in them these days, but definitely not an up-market address. A one- or two-room flat, no bath, the toilet shared by everyone on her floor. 'We'll see that you get home safely, but first, do those cuts need stitches?'

Hadn't he the evidence such wounds would leave? 'There'll be terrible marks, won't there? Marks that will tell my husband *everything* my stepsister and that . . . that parasite who calls herself a social worker want him to believe!'

Gratified by the outburst, the former debutante condescendingly smiled as did Madame Morel, felt Kohler. Unlike them, though, this one hadn't spent hours with her favourite hairdresser but had done what she could herself. 'Look, do something for me,' he confided, reaching for the cognac. 'Down two shots of this and quit worrying about the petits fours, the pâté and the bread. I'll see that you get to take them home without the others knowing. Now let me have a look at those cuts. We may need a doctor.'

'Fish oil, Inspector. The one who did this stank of it. He was big too. Big in the stomach.'

*   *   *

15

Alone as always, just the two of them, they shared a cigarette in the car, in pitch-darkness as the curfew lifted and the city, with its millions of bicycles and *métro* riders awakened.

'A savage rape, Louis—an example to all females who would run around with the Occupier?'

Hermann lived with two of them: Giselle and Oona, so must be worried. 'A safecracking to which we are sent by mistake.'

'Delaying us from getting to the Drouant.'

It would have to be faced. 'Whoever committed that latest attack had the timing down perfectly, *mon vieux*. He knew exactly when Morel would take the stepsister home.'

'And was watching for it, even to knowing Morel would send his driver in to the telephone.'

'But this time the attack is not so severe. The warning to such wives, if that was it, is more muted.'

Both looked out to what awaited them, a corpse. The rue du Faubourg Saint-Honoré was shrouded in that same silvery darkness. Ethereal, if one was of such a mind; desperate if not. Even the little blue light that should have been above the entrance to the École des Officiers de la Gendamerie Nationale had still not been given the juice it needed.

'That *flic* on duty at the quartier du Faubourg-du-Roule's Commissariat, Louis. Like your friend Bélanger, he had heard the gossip about us and could hardly contain himself as he handed me the lanterns and asked if we were being kept busy tonight?'

A *pédé* that one had said about the victim here and had laughed. A *cucu*, a pansy.

'Why here, Louis? Why at the very place Préfet Talbotte trains his cops?'

The call had apparently come in to the district's commissariat at 11.13 p.m. from the Lido, at 78 Champs-Élysées and not far. A girl in tears and largely incoherent but one who had, in spite of this, managed to blurt that the cows—the cops—should look for something at the school and right under their noses and that she hoped it wouldn't get splashed all over the newspapers because she had already sent those boys to have a look.

'Perhaps the killer wants the publicity,' sighed St-Cyr, but what is of more immediate concern is what has happened to that caller.'

Had they not *one* but *two* corpses waiting for them? wondered Kohler. Making such a call couldn't have been easy at the best of times. Between sets then, the girl a dancer perhaps, the others hurrying to change while she stood freezing in a poorly lighted corridor fumbling first to get the token into its little slot—she'd have had to have a *jeton*. No calls were free, especially not those of chorus girls, even if reporting a murder. Had she dropped it in her panic? Had it rolled away, she thinking that the one who was forcing her to make the call would have to get another from the bar and that maybe, just maybe she could escape?

'But again we have a delay in sending someone to look into things,' said St-Cyr. 'It's been six hours since she rang them.'

'The *salaud* said the girl must have been pissed to the gills and that he had thought her just buggering about. At midnight, the *quartier*'s *sous-préfet* went through the call notes and sent two of his boys to have a look.'

'And since then?'

It would have to be said. 'Spent his time trying to track us down, seeing as our names were on the duty roster Préfet Talbotte had circulated to all commissariats.'

'On purpose?'

'Why else?'

'Just what the hell is going on, Hermann? We arrive, are thrown into the breech and everyone seems to welcome it but us!'

Together, they got out to stand in the sleet. Dark in silhouette and huge—ugly at this time of day and probably always—the 160-bed hospital and hospice that the financier Nicholas Beaujon had had Girardin build in 1784 for the children of the poor impassively waited.

'It's this way,' said Louis. 'I was last here in '32, on the sixth of May when *Monsieur le Président* Paul Doumer was assassinated while holding a freshly autographed copy of Claude Farrère's latest novel.'

'I'm getting not to like your authors.'

'Gorguloff, the White Russian fanatic, succeeded in giving the *président* the *coup de grâce*. Farrère, no slouch, tried desperately to stop him. Myself and four others weren't quick enough, you understand. Farrère was hit in the wrist, blood splashed all over the pages of a novel whose title escapes me since the rest of us had to grapple with the Russian, but by the time we had that one on the floor and bleeding himself, the book was ruined. No doubt there are some who will make a monument of it for tourists to gawk at. We carried the *président* here, though it couldn't have been of any use.'

End of story, but was it still to be a time of truth between them?

'Prior to the presidency, Hermann, Doumer had been the governor of Indochina. Having effectively ended the power of the mandarins, he used brutal taxation to open up the colony with roads, railways and bridges. A new and very well-educated middle class was born that, largely educated in France and rightfully considering themselves French, helped to make the colony what it became. Immensely wealthy and profitable.'

But since 7 December 1941 entirely controlled by the Japanese in spite of still being governed by France and run by its civil servants.

'Gorguloff went early to the widow-maker.'

The breadbasket, the guillotine. Louis would have had to watch the head fall.

'In '36 the hospital became the *préfet*'s school,' he went on as if the travelogue had to be given to keep his partner's mind from what was to come. 'The entrance to the cellars is along here and not easily seen even in broad daylight.'

Or heard? wondered Kohler. The stairs would be steep and coated with ice. 'Hadn't I best light the lanterns?'

'I'll just go down and have a little look.'

At one point Louis very nearly slipped and the beam of the torch shot up over the soot-blackened stones only to begin to feel bottom and focus on the corpse.

Pale . . . The skin was wet and waxy-looking where not scraped, bruised or welted, the legs hairy, with the same across the back of the shoulders and between, the buttocks up, the torso and face down—had he been pitched in there? wondered Kohler. Had he been dead before hitting that doorsill against a corner of which the face was crammed?

'HERMANN, DON'T!'

'I have to. Aren't I supposed to give the orders? Aren't I the one from the Occupier who's supposed to watch over you?'

A former captain in the Kaiser's artillery. Shielding the lanterns as best he could, Hermann started down, the shadow of him reaching behind and back up the staircase.

'I warned you,' said St-Cyr.

'He hasn't just lost all of his ID, has he?'

Not a scrap of clothing remained. 'A broken neck. The shovel that hit him in the face . . .'

'The *spade*, damn it, Louis! Why can't you call it that?'

Many these days spoke in whispers of the torture of the spade, the coal shovel the Gestapo and their French counterparts were fond of using on the difficult, but this one's handle had been much longer, its blade far sharper. The fingers of both hands had been removed. They'd have one hell of a time identifying him.

'His teeth . . .' began Hermann, only to gag, to turn away and throw up. *Merde!*

'Did they crush his balls, Louis?' he wept. 'Was he a *résistant*?'

Sometimes the Gestapo or their friends would dump a victim for others to find, but not this one, not here. 'A *maquereau*?' asked St-Cyr to keep Hermann busy.

A mackerel, a pimp and not a homosexual at all? He'd been young and healthy, maybe twenty-two years of age. Well groomed, thought Kohler, blinking away the tears. In good shape, well fed, the pomade having greased the jet-black hair down and still shedding the rain.

'He's not languishing with all the others in the Reich, is he?' said Louis.

There were one-and-a-half million French POWs in Germany, millions of Allied ones too. 'And not an STO conscript either,' managed Kohler. The Service du Travail Obligatoire, the forced labour call-up, but *liebe Zeit*, how could Louis and he talk like this, as if nothing were out of the ordinary and they'd seen it every day, which they had.

There was no smell of cordite, though, he thought warily. Not even that of broken geranium stems—mustard gas. Nor had the sweetness of rotting human flesh and the stench of erupted bowels come to him yet, or that of mouldy earth with its bits of tattered clothing and blood-shredded arms and legs.

Late autumn 1914, that, and on into the winter of 1914–1915 in Alsace, then later at Verdun, but did it matter a damn now, those dates with Louis firing at him from the other side?

'Hermann, please don't be so hard on yourself. Go and bring us a blanket. Let's make him decent. You know that always helped. Respect we used to call it, you boys as well. Respect for those who wouldn't be going home.'

'The press, Louis. If they've already been here, Boemelburg is going to tear his hair, what little he has left of it.'

Von Schaumburg, too, the Kommandant von Gross-Paris.

'Maybe it was the way he'd fallen to his knees that caused the *flics* to brand him a homosexual,' said Kohler.

One just didn't mention them these days if possible. Invariably they kept a low profile. 'I'll check his temperature, shall I, Inspector,' came the reminder to bugger off. *Lieber Christus im Himmel* how could Louis do it? Shaking down the mercury like that while shielding it; peering at the gradations to make sure he got it right, then easing the thing inside?

Cold weather would speed the cooling but nowhere near what was commonly thought. Each corpse had its own rate—even the time of day and the weather could influence it, but on average a corpse lost heat at a little over two degrees Centigrade an hour—that was the figure Louis often used. And from thirty-seven degrees this one's had fallen to . . .

'Nineteen and close enough.'

Death had occurred at between eight and nine last night, though the coroner would have to confirm it. 'Did the evening's entertainment begin with him?' asked Kohler sadly.

Was it a portent of things to come? wondered St-Cyr. 'And then the girl who telephoned?'

'Was this one her pimp?'

'Perhaps, but for now we must wait.'

One of the lanterns was reached for. Dutifully Hermann started up the stairs to get a blanket.

'I'm going to have to watch over him,' confided St-Cyr to the victim. 'He was forced to witness some terrible things only a day or two ago, was showered with broken glass and has been hating himself ever since when no blame should ever be attached to him. He's not responsible for Hitler and the Nazis, or the Gestapo and the SS, or what the Wehrmacht are doing in Russia and have done elsewhere. As a detective, he had to belong to the Kripo—one couldn't have resigned in protest. He has never had anything to do with any of them, has always been apart and himself and, since coming to France, has become a citizen of the world to whom a little polishing is necessary from time to time.'

At 7.45 a.m., the light was pitiful and the sleet had changed to such a heavy downpour one had to be mindful of the marker that was along the quai de la Tournelle, right where there was a fabulous view of the Notre-Dame on warm, sunny days. Normally the river's level stood at two metres, Kohler knew. At four, all traffic had had to stop before the Defeat, though now that was, perhaps, less of a problem, but anything beyond that level and the city would need its water wings.

'When this quits, Louis, there'll be fog for days,' he grumbled. In war, as in this Occupation, there wasn't any sense in getting sentimental about anything.

The Lido had yielded zero about the caller of last night. No one had mentioned anything about anyone having been forced to telephone the police, nor had anyone gone missing.

It wasn't good. It was terrible, and yes, at least three-quarters of the audience of last night or any other would have been of the Occupier, the rest their friends. And that, too, wasn't good, for both Louis and he knew damned well that the Occupier craved female company and could and did commit murder or any other common crime.

While they'd been there, the *quartier*'s commissariat had found them and now, more than soaked to the skin and freezing, they were standing in the rain, waiting. The warden of the Parc Monceau, one of the city's loveliest and not far from the *préfet*'s school or the Lido, had found freshly dug earth and hastily replaced flagstones under the shelter of an arbour and had let the *flic* on patrol know about it.

'The fingers can't be here, Hermann. The gates to the park would have been locked at the time of the killing.'

Yet chance could and did play a part in things these days. Bourgeois—wealthy beyond mention, some of the *quartier*'s residents—the park was second home to the establishment.

'Financiers, Hermann. Bankers, lawyers, men of commerce but writers too. Proust lived nearby and loved this park. It comes out in what he wrote of it. Old money, new money . . .' Brusquely Louis indicated the surrounding hotels and mansions as if even within *les hautes* there were substrata that did not mingle.

It was tough being a Socialist, thought Kohler of his partner. They were standing near the northeastern end of the park, overlooking the naumachia where frozen, moss- and ivy-covered Corinthian columns formed a horseshoe at the far end of an ice-clad pond atop which water had rapidly pooled. Rose beds in winter's burlap, were to the left. Pigeons—perhaps the few that hadn't yet been trapped and eaten—suffered atop the colonnade. Beyond them, the trees were tall; beyond those lay the fence and some of the *hôtels particuliers* of the very wealthy. Nice . . . it must be nice to live there and overlook the park.

Beyond these residences lay the boulevard de Courcelles and the boulevard Malesherbes.

The warden, in his cape, hat, rubber boots and faded blue coveralls, was watching as two of the underwardens carefully removed the earth. 'Inspectors . . .'

Ten fingers—were all of them here to remind him of the trenches of that other war? wondered Kohler.

The grave was shallow. 'A dog's ear, Hermann.'

There were mutters of consternation. 'I can see that, Louis. A terrier's. Irish probably. Is there a tattoo?'

All dogs with a pedigree, and this was a *quartier* for them, would wear their registration number inside an ear.

The fur was rusty coloured and more shaggy than wiry but still, the ear was long and pointed as it should be and there were two of them and the tail and paws as further proof, and not dead that long, thought Kohler. Maybe a day, maybe two or three, given that it was still winter. 'Number 375614, Louis. Skinned, the pelt sold or kept, but in either case to be tanned for further use, the rest consigned to the stew pot or soup.'

Dog snatching had become rife, felt St-Cyr. Household pets of all kinds were at risk. Notices, posted on walls, warned of the dangers of eating cats, since the vermin they might have consumed would surely carry disease. And hadn't the average family or individual already seen nearly 80 percent of their wage packet's prewar purchasing power vanish? Hadn't those same wages been frozen at 1939 levels? Wasn't the Occupation's horrendous inflation one of its most tragic curses, the consequences being suicide and lawlessness? 'I'll just bag these, Hermann, and we'll be on our way.'

The *passage* de la Trinité, that of the Jouffroy, the Restaurant Drouant and the police academy . . . A *vélo-taxi* theft and the beating-rape of its passenger and purse-snatching, a safecracking with clay from the sewers, a brutal mugging, slashing, deliberate humiliation and another handbag snatch, a violent murder and a missing pet.

'Assignments that are given on purpose and others that are not, Hermann.'

'The stench of fish oil. A man with a gut.'

'Grease, and two wedding rings. It's curious, is it not, that both the Trinité victim and one of the Drouant victims have absent husbands.'

Who were languishing in prisoner-of-war camps in the Reich or farther to the east—they'd found this out when they'd taken Giselle and Oona to the Trinité victim's flat to look after the children. 'Did the assailant or assailants know beforehand where each of the victims would be, Louis?'

That, too, was a good question for which there could, as yet, be no adequate answer.

2

When the boys heard the sound of the Citroën at 8.42 a.m., they knew absolutely who it was. That big, black, beautiful *traction avant* slid to a stop down there at number 3 rue Laurence Savart in Belleville. Antoine Courbet's mother did the cleaning but never the washing-up. Hadn't Monsieur Jean-Louis once said that such a humble activity was the best way of relieving tension and that he'd better keep doing it so long as the pots hadn't burned the dinner. What dinner?

'He's home at last,' said Guy Vachon with a sigh. They'd be late for school.

'It's been ages since we've seen him,' said Dédé Labelle. 'At least a week.'

Together they stood in the rain those two detectives. 'They look exhausted,' whispered Guy. 'Has there been trouble?'

'There's always trouble for them,' whispered Antoine. 'Maybe your *papa* can find them another set of side mirrors.'

They all knew that Monsieur Jean-Louis didn't like using the black market or imposing on the neighbours. Hadn't Antoine been the one to suggest his mother look after the house in the chief inspector's absence and that of the second wife and little son?

'That wife and son having been killed when the Gestapo left a bomb the Résistance had hidden on the doorstep for him,' said

Hervé Desrochers, shaking his head just like everyone else did at the thought. 'A *collabo*, that's what those people in the Résistance think he is because he has to work with a German. The wife hadn't helped either by coming home from the flames of a love affair with one of the enemy simply because the thrusting, it was over, and that one had been sent to the Russian front.'

'It was the long absences,' muttered Dédé sadly. 'She never knew if Monsieur Jean-Louis *would* come home.'

'He only has a Lebel Modèle d'ordonnance 1892 six-shot, swing-out, double-action revolver. The eight millimetre,' said Hervé with a sigh.

'It's *not* the 1892, idiot!' said Antoine. 'I don't think he's *ever* been allowed one of those. It's another 1873. Don't you remember that he was first issued an 1873 by Gestapo stores but that he then lost it in the Rhône at Lyon?'

A case of arson. A packed cinema . . .

'The 1873 uses black powder, low-pressure, eleven-millimetre cartridges,' admitted Hervé reluctantly.

'They're almost as big as those for the British Webley Mark VI, the .455 inch.' said Dédé with a sigh.

'The 11.6 millimetre. He looks as exhausted as his geraniums,' said Antoine. '*Maman* says he needed that second wife and is going completely to seed in her absence.'

'He needs another gun,' said Hervé tartly. 'That old Lebel is no match for the Walther P38, nine-millimetre Parabellum automatic Herr Kohler packs. Eight in the clip, *mes vieux*. Another up the spout and a little pin that sticks out to tell him all is safe but ready. Three hundred and fifty metres a second muzzle velocity and almost double that of the Mark VI.'

'It's a semiautomatic,' said Guy. '*Bien sûr*, you don't have to pull the slide back when there's one in the chamber, but Monsieur Jean-Louis, he can hit a swallow at forty paces.'

Everyone knew swallows were among the fastest of birds but . . . '*Imbécile*,' hissed Hervé, 'a slug like that would blast the bird to pieces. He's a nature lover and would *never* shoot such a thing!'

'But those old cartridges,' muttered Dédé, 'they're so tired sometimes they don't even bother to wake up when struck by the firing pin.'

It was a worry. Ex-champion boxer of the police academy and soccer forward, ex-sergeant in a signal corps in that other war, Monsieur Jean-Louis had been wounded twice, the left side as usual. No medals, no citations—he wasn't a man for those but had never complained of it. 'I always tried to duck,' he had once said, 'but honourably'.

'BOYS, WHY ARE YOU NOT IN SCHOOL?' came the yell.

'THE STREETS, THEY ARE NO LONGER SAFE AT NIGHT FOR OUR SISTERS AND MOTHERS, MONSIEUR L'INSPECTEUR PRINCIPAL. WE ARE PROTESTING AND HAVE GONE ON STRIKE!'

Good for Hervé.

'IT'S TOO WET AND SLIPPERY FOR SOCCER,' added Guy. 'WE CAN'T KICK THE BALL TO YOU.'

'Louis . . .'

In hooded rain capes, the boys waited to see what their response would bring. Hollow-eyed and gaunt, each of the little buggers gazed guiltily up from under shelter.

'Now what's this about a strike?' asked Louis.

'We're late,' confessed Dédé. 'We only wanted to see if you had arrived home safely so that the pretty lady would no longer be distressed.'

'What pretty lady?'

'Your chanteuse.'

'She's not mine or anyone's but her own.'

Natal'ya Kulakov-Myshkin, alias Gabrielle Arcuri of the Club Mirage on the rue Delambre over on the Left Bank, in Montparnasse. 'The one who sings to eight hundred of the Green Beans and over the wireless to all the others at the front?' asked Kohler blithely.

Both to the Krauts and to the Allies, since those boys would also listen in and she had such a fabulous voice. '*Oui*, that one,' said Dédé. 'After your train came back from Vichy and you had to leave for Colmar, she came from the station to stand outside the house of your mother, *Monsieur l'inspecteur principal*. She didn't cry, though I thought she was going to.'

Louis's mother had passed away fifteen years ago yet the house was still considered hers.

'She didn't think you and Herr Kohler would *ever* come back from inside the Reich.'

'Nor did the other two who came to stand with her,' said Guy, watching them closely.

'Giselle and Oona?' asked Hermann of his two ladyloves and saw the boys nod.

'The blackout rapes, Inspectors. Are you working on them?' asked Antoine.

'The handbag snatching, too?' hazarded another.

'*Oui*, especially those if done in daylight,' said yet another.

'All last night and now here just for dry clothing,' lamented Louis. 'Antoine, be so good as to ask your mother to do what she can with what I'm still wearing, but please tell her not to alleviate the dampness by burning any more of my books. Give her the message after school, eh? Now get going. If there's trouble, tell your teacher that you were delayed because we had to question you about the safety of the streets at night.'

'But . . . but you haven't done that?' blurted Dédé. '*Grand-mère*, she is saying things can only get worse and that you both should be worrying about your girlfriends.'

'They'll be found bound, violated, murdered and robbed, she says!' swore Hervé, ignoring his runny nose. 'Their handbags snatched!'

'We've already found one corpse,' muttered Kohler, not liking what the boys had just said but wishing he had ersatz chewing gum to hand out. 'You haven't any cigarettes to sell, have you?'

In unison heads were swiftly shaken and, without another word, the army turned away and headed up the street.

'Has the lawlessness of the black market reached such depths of innocence?' bleated Louis.

'Don't be so naive. I should have asked for underwear and silk stockings.'

*   *   *

Long after the detectives had left the house at number 3, Jeanne Courbet continued to stare across the street at it through the lace of the bedroom's curtain. She knew she didn't have the time to loiter, that one had to be out and about very early if one was to get anything from the shops. Yet I can't move, she silently said. Is it that I've offended God with my gossip about that house and the troubles the chief inspector has had with the first wife who left him and the dead one, too, the one who made the grand cuckold of him, even though he forgave her?

Word was that they had all laughed at him behind his back at the rue des Saussaies. Word was that he and his partner were hated so much for pointing the finger of truth, they would never leave the city alive this time.

Word was . . . But would either of them help her now? Antoine hadn't just been up to mischief but to a crime so serious it jeopardized the whole family. A dirty stub of blackboard chalk had been in one of his pockets—was that not *évidence* enough of scribbled slogans on the walls: *Laval aux poteau*—Premier Laval up against the post; *La guillotine pour Pétain*—the *Maréchal* and Head of State; the V for Victory of Monsieur Winston Churchill; the cross of Lorraine, that symbol of the Résistance and Jeanne d'Arc? *Victoire,* eh? *Liberté*! Antoine knew nothing of such things. He was only ten years old, but that chalk had started her doing something she had vowed never to do in this room of his older brothers. The neighbours wouldn't laugh if the family was arrested. They would sadly shake their heads and later whisper, 'That mouth of hers. That gossip, she got what she deserved,' but one arrest would lead to another and the families of all four would be taken. Didn't that knave Desrochers operate his *vélo-taxi* out of *place* de l'Opéra? Wasn't the stand directly across from the Kommandantur and wouldn't Hervé's *papa* be known to several of those Germans?

A woman's compact had lain under the loosened floorboards beneath the straw mattress Antoine used, a file for the fingernails, too, and a lipstick. A *Kleiderkarte* also, a clothing card and a half-empty packet of cigarettes—Kamels from Berlin, stale but kept as a treasured memento. A matchbox from the Kakadu, on the Kurfürtsendamm, a club or bar. A room key, *ah, oui, oui,* from the Hotel-Pension am Steinplatz and a *liaison sexuelle,* the torn half of a ticket to the UFA Palast, a cinema and hands up this girl's skirt, eh? The silver cigarette case of a virtue lost had been inscribed with the words of all such men. Though she could neither speak nor read the language, she knew they would say, *To Sonja with undying love, Erich, 3 March 1940,* and just before the invasion of Norway.

Four hundred of the Occupation marks had lain beneath that cigarette case, a further two hundred of the Reichsmark. 'And seven hundred new francs, all in one-hundreds.'

If taken and spent, the money would only draw attention to the family. Some would think it pay for watching that house for a repeat of the bomb laying. Oh for sure, stealing from the Boche was not the same as stealing from one's own people and Antoine could, perhaps, be forgiven were the penalties not so severe. His two brothers and his father would be sent into forced labour, herself and Antoine and her girls, his two sisters into . . . But how had her little Antoine come by these things? His share of the loot—was that it? One quarter!

Grey and glued, a crumpled condom had lain alongside the death notice of this Erich Straub, this young man from Berlin who had used it with his Sonja.

'And then,' she said with finality, 'there was this.'

Unfolding a torn page from last Friday's *Paris-Soir,* she read again yet another of the advertisements Herr Kohler placed each week, as did countless others still, and even though he had not been in Paris to receive an answer.

Reward of 200,000 francs will be paid for information leading to the safe return of Johan Van der Lynn, now age eight-and-a-half, and his sister Anna, now age six-and-a-half, son and daughter of Martin and Oona from Rotterdam. Lost to the east of Doullens on the road from Arras, 16 May 1940. Apply Box 1374.

Lost during the Exodus when ten million from the Lowlands and northern France had fled the blitzkrieg to clog the roads until machine-gunned to clear them for the panzers, but why had this Sonja had it in her handbag, or had she? Had Antoine hidden it here earlier, and for what reason, please?

Fool that he was, Herr Kohler wouldn't let this Madame Oona Van der Lynn lose hope, nor would he get rid of her. She was forty years of age, couldn't have good papers and had lost her husband in December to the French Gestapo of the rue Lauriston. A Jew, people whispered, her children only the halves, though such things really shouldn't matter and certainly wouldn't to a Stuka or Messerschmitt.

Herr Kohler had taken the woman in during another investigation, that of a carousel in the Parc des Buttes Chaumont, and wasn't this why the boys loved to go to that park? And yes, yes, he had a younger one and lived with both when in Paris, sleeping with each but in turns as everyone said, herself most especially. 'May God forgive me.'

Giselle le Roy was twenty-two years old and very attractive, though beauty like that would quickly fade and men ought to know this. Half-Greek, half-French and from the Midi, the girl was also from the House of Madame Chabot on the rue Danton, though she didn't work in that business anymore. 'The Lupanar des Oiseaux Blancs!' she said aloud, was filled with hateful thoughts of such 'submissive girls,' as the *flics* were fond of calling them. The brothel of the white birds. *'Fornicatrices!'* she said. 'Leeches who take money that is desperately needed by the families of the men they service!

'Men!' she spat. 'They give you the clap and the chancres because they've been careless and horny. "Seized by the moment," eh? "Unable to control themselves?" '

For the married ones, the occasional lapse was considered both natural and at times necessary and healthful; for the married woman, the gravest of sins and punishable by prison and a fine of from five to twenty thousand francs. Adultery was, it had to be said, a two-faced affair when viewed by the State whose laws were, of course, entirely set by men. Women could, and occasionally did, have husbands arrested but far from being severe, the courts were always lenient. Boys will be boys.

But would these sadists everyone worried about find interest in the advertisement and answer it? If so, those two women of Herr Kohler's would come no more to stand in the street and stare at that house of his partner and friend.

As that one's new girlfriend had done, the wife and little son not dead even three months—Marianne and Philippe St-Cyr—and oh for sure war and this Occupation speeded up such things, 'But honour to a dead wife is honour to one's life, chastity the bankroll of memory and Heaven's cash on deposit.'

Kohler winced when he saw the Trinité victim in the *Hôtel-Dieu*. It wasn't that her nose had been broken, or that the once smooth brow had been repeatedly slammed against the back of the *vélo-taxi's* seat. It wasn't even that her throat had been clenched so tightly there were plum-purple bruises or that, early on in the attack, she had been struck repeatedly.

It was the look in her bruised and deep brown eyes. He'd seen it before—Louis had, too, though he was busy elsewhere.

She was going to kill herself. The disgrace, the neighbourhood gossip, the threat of venereal disease or worse, that of an unwanted child. The shame. The husband a POW in the Reich.

Out of the fug of all such hospital rooms, the hesitant voice of the *interne* who'd been delegated to deal with him started up only to hesitate. Though absolutely nothing would be made of it, he had to wonder if the boy was but one among the many from all walks of life with false papers, a false military discharge circa 1939 or early 1940, or simply suspected of having these?

Such was the undercurrent of bitterness that even battle-hardened veterans from the 1914–1918 war had banded together to demand that only those who had actually fought in this one should be considered as veterans. Not the million or half-million or whatever who, through no fault of their own, had seen no fighting at all but had simply been overrun and rounded up along with those who had actually fought during the blitzkrieg.

'The left shoulder and wrist, Inspector . . .' began Dr. Paul-

32

Émile Mailloux. 'They are badly sprained but fortunately not broken. He must have wrenched the arm behind her back as he . . . Well, you know.'

If the Trinité victim thought anything of this, she gave no indication.

'Scratches?' asked Kohler.

'Of course, but mainly between the shoulders and on the buttocks and hips. The assailant tore a fingernail. We found it lodged in . . .'

'We?'

It would have to be said. 'Dr. Rheal Lachance is the senior physician who oversees such cases. This woman isn't the only one we've had to admit. She's number thirty.'

Lachance, but *ach mein Gott*, so many? 'In how long?'

Had the detective been away from the city or had the matter simply been hushed up even within police circles, the authorities too afraid to admit that such things were happening? 'In the past four months, Inspector. Three so far this week, two last weekend.'

And there were twenty-four hospitals in Paris.

'She's one of the worst,' said Mailloux, 'though we only get the serious cases, of course.'

'Have the attacks been escalating?'

'It's possible.'

'*Verdammt*, either you think it or you don't!'

'Then, yes, especially since the . . . the defeat of your Sixth Army at Stalingrad on the third of this month. Not all were raped, you understand.'

'Robbed of their handbags and papers?'

'Yes. Some were completely or only partly stripped before . . .'

'The hair?'

This one would know all about such things from that other war. 'It was first hacked off some of them before the beating. With others, they were beaten and then it was cut off, and since there is a market for it, the hair was probably stolen and sold.'

'But not all lost their hair?'

'Not all. With this one, perhaps there wasn't time. Punishment, yes, but not continued to that point.'

Though they were all too aware of blackout crime, Louis and he hadn't fully realized the severity of what was now going on, but with so many victims, how could they possibly interview enough to get a clear picture of things? 'Their wedding rings?' he asked.

Had the detective been defeated by the thought of so many? 'The rings, *ah oui*, from those who were wearing them.'

'Meaning that some had deliberately removed them before the evening out, eh? Were all of them married to absent POWs?'

'Not all. Those whose fiancés are prisoners of war did not have such rings to wear, unless the engagement one.'

Which few couples could afford or even give a thought to. 'But fiancées of POWs have also been targeted?'

'That is correct, at least in so far as we here at the *Hôtel-Dieu* are aware.'

'And not others? Single girls, unhappily married nonmilitary wives, those of veterans from that other war or those that simply need the money to feed the kids?'

'Occasionally but perhaps as mistakes. Most of the victims we get are wives of prisoners of war or fiancées of them.'

And targeted, but everyone would be saying the streets were unsafe at night and would be avoiding them if possible. 'Okay. Now tell me about that fingernail.'

'Lodged in the upper right hip. The nail must have been torn or cracked beforehand. Tweezers were used to remove it. There's her blood, of course, and skin, but also some kind of grease.'

A torn, folded corner of newsprint yielded its little treasure. The nail was a good centimetre-and-a-half along the curve, and from two to three millimetres at its widest. The middle right finger, and dirty. Big hands too—a big gut, eh? wondered Kohler but said, '*Bon*. Now tell me why that door was locked and you had to ask the matron for the key?'

Would this one miss nothing? 'The press.'

'What do you mean "The press"?'

'Inspector, let's go into the corridor. They came. Two of them, you understand.'

'I'm trying to.'

Was there nothing for it but to reveal what had happened? 'They photographed her late last night.'

'They couldn't have, not without help.'

Lachance would just have to admit to having failed to foresee such a possibility. 'One of the nursing assistants was bribed, Inspector. Two thousand francs. The girl tried to deny it, of course, and has been dismissed. She'll never get another job in this or any hospital.'

But others would have been bribed and Mailloux set up to take the fall. 'Okay. Now tell me what photos were taken.'

'The back and the front.'

'Then watch her closely. If she kills herself, I'll have you up for murder.'

'I wasn't even on duty when the press got here at three fifteen last night. I wasn't even getting out of bed so that I could catch the *métro* to work at five a.m. I live in Montrouge.'

And not far from the Porte d'Orléans, but one never offered such information these days. At the very least, one waited to be asked. Mailloux damned well knew he had been set up but it would be best to go easy. 'Which paper?'

'*Le Matin.*'

And but one of the dailies, all of which were collaborationist and, with varying degrees, loved to ridicule segments of the populace and to show the citizenry what animals they harboured and that their police needed not only to be strengthened yet again but placed entirely under the competent control of the Occupier.

The headline said it all: RAPE-BEATING NARROWLY MISSES CONJUGAL MORTUARY SLAB OF ÉCOLE DES OFFICIERS DE LA GENDARMERIE NATIONALE'S MAQUEREAU.

Berlin would be in an uproar, the Führer demanding reprisals and deportations, his shining example of an open city badly tarnished. Boemelburg would be beside himself and expecting the early retirement everyone whispered about, the Kommandant von Gross-Paris, Old Shatter Hand himself, utterly unapproachable, Préfet Talbotte bent on revenge and covering his own miserable ass, Louis and this Kripo accused of thoughtlessly letting it all happen or better still, of having taken money from that same press who would be only too willing to admit that they had. And as if that were not enough, Pharand, that arch little Fascist, head of the Sûreté and Louis's boss, would see to it and urge Talbotte on while scheming all the time.

'Get her dressed. Whether you agree or not, that woman has to be with her children.'

The bastards hadn't just taken a simple head-and-shoulders shot. They'd had her stand, had had the smock removed so that full frontal and back views, with the regulation little black triangle in place of course, would hit the page.

And next to them, as if she were in some way connected to him, was the police academy's victim, identified as her pimp and with his bare ass up and all the rest, if not blacked out.

'Moving her today is just not possible, Inspector. Whoever did that to her also used an object.'

The academy's victim had been struck hard on the back of the head, not once but twice, thought St-Cyr. A smooth, blunt instrument, a truncheon perhaps, but a period of time had elapsed between the blows, he was certain.

The pomade was not so much 'greasy,' as Hermann had thought, but oily, sweet-smelling and of sandalwood, giving a reminder of Indochina, a significant source, and the final moments of Président Paul Doumer in this very building.

But had the victim been brought here simply to draw attention to the ineptitude of a police force that now had fifteen thousand *flics* in Paris alone and should have done something to prevent such crimes?

'Hit first an hour or so before he was brought here, Armand?' he asked of the coroner. 'Perhaps thrown into the back of a *gazogène** lorry to lie there unconscious.'

Jean-Louis loved nothing better than a 'good' murder, thought

---

*   a vehicle powered by wood- or charcoal-gas

Armand Tremblay, but had best be cautioned. 'You know it's too early to say. Once he's on the table . . .'

'Yes, yes, but that back of the head was hit again and later?'

Must he always push for answers? '*Oui, oui,* it's possible the second blow followed the first by an hour at least.'

'With death at between eight thirty and nine thirty p.m.?'

'Did I *not* say that was close enough for now?'

'Of course, but if at that time, then he was perhaps abducted as early as seven thirty.'

And near or at the Lido from which the telephone caller had later rung the commissariat? 'Jean-Louis, you mustn't worry so much. Of course we'd both like to save that girl, but by now with so many hours having passed . . .'

The shrug was not one of uncaring but simply of logic. At fifty-six years of age, dark-shadowed and ruddy, corpulent too, though not nearly so much as before the Defeat, Armand had had to deal with successions of *préfets* and knew how best to preserve integrity through hard reason and fact. The dark brown eyes behind spectacles whose surgically taped repairs had yet to be properly mended, were intent. From time to time he tossed his head, gestured or shrugged the rounded shoulders as if in communication with himself.

Again he muttered, 'It's not the usual but all the evidence points to it.' Long ago the cigarette that had fastened itself to his lower lip had gone out. 'It's curious, Jean-Louis,' he said, not looking up. 'The position of the body isn't right, is it? Partly up on the knees, the arms and back stiffly bent—why, please, hasn't he completely collapsed? The muscles should have been flaccid, yet here we have a victim who—oh for sure, rigor is now well advanced— but he's too tense even for that. Was he rigid before being dragged down several of those steps?'

Not thrown from the top of them as first thought. 'Violent exertion?' asked St-Cyr.

'Any such struggle would speed the onset of rigor, making the body almost immediately rigid.'

But this was more. 'The hands,' said St-Cyr. 'Were they so

tightly clenched, the only way the fingers could be loosened was to stamp on the fists?'

'Precisely!'

'As a result of instantaneous cadaveric spasm?'

One didn't see this often, but . . . 'He was strong and in good shape,' acknowledged Tremblay. 'He resisted his attackers. At one point he got away from them but . . .'

'Was brought down and hit again, that second time.'

'The bruising of the buttocks and thighs bear this out, also that of the left shoulder. The scrotum was then grabbed and torn, not crushed. He may well have passed out, though; would have been brought round, dragged up, steadied . . .'

'Held by two men, while a third smashed him across the face with the flat of a long-handled shovel, the neck instantly breaking.'

'A sudden, violent disruption of the nervous system, Jean-Louis, but unlike rigor, the fingers stiffen so much they are far more difficult to open even when compared to the tightly clenched fists of a living person who resists with all their might.'

Had the victim grasped something during the struggle? Had this been why it had been necessary to open the hands, the fingers then removed not so much to hide the victim's identity as to hide the reason for their opening? 'Strands of hair?' St-Cyr heard himself ask. 'A wristwatch perhaps? Some item that could lead to the identity of his killers?'

It wasn't a happy thought, they both looking down at the grille of the sewer. 'There might be a catchment at the bottom of the shaft or a weir to hold back the solids,' mused Jean-Louis who had, it must be admitted, far more experience with such things. 'We could,' he added, 'order up the sewer workers and wait for them to arrive, or go fishing ourselves to save time and further possible loss.'

'Idiot, it'll be freezing. Is it that you would have us toss a coin to see who strips off to take the first plunge? In any case, he must be turned over and moved, and that will help to verify the spasm.'

*　　*　　*

Kohler longed for a cigarette. More than ever he felt Louis and he were on quicksand. Too much bad feeling towards them, the two of them being put on the run like that last night.

Austere in the old Cité barracks, the Préfecture de Police was to his right, overlooking *place* du Parvis Notre-Dame. To the south and directly ahead of him beyond the *quai*, the Seine was mud-grey in the rain, to the east, the main portal of the Notre-Dame accepted a hurrying, umbrella-bearing flock of sisters. Wounded, the eye of the rose window had been plucked to safety in the autumn of 1939. Now its canvas and timber-framed bandage bagged and sagged with accumulated moisture, causing the gargoyles to cringe.

The Trinité victim, Madame Adrienne Guillaumet, age thirty-two, had been a part-time teacher of German for the Deutsche Institut, and hadn't the French, its Parisians especially, flocked to learn the language, and wasn't everything being done to encourage them? But here, too, things were never simple. The Institut had taken over the Hôtel Sagan, the former Polish Chancellory on the rue de Talleyrand and not far from her flat at 131 rue Saint-Dominique, which was in the *quartier* du Gros-Caillou and just to the west of the Invalides, in a very up-market Left Bank neighbourhood.

The École Militaire was immediately to the south of the Gros-Caillou, the Champ de Mars and Tour Eiffel to the southwest. Money there, too, *bien sûr*, but the *quartier* École Militaire was home to retired career officers from that other war and this one too, some of them, and most were nothing more than pompous pains in the ass who would be all too ready to damn an absent fellow officer's wife if she strayed.

She had taught her evening class at the École Centrale des Arts et Manufactures, over on the rue Vaucanson in the Third. At just after 9.30 p.m., or close to it, she must have stood in the rain on the rue Conté to hail a *vélo-taxi*'s little blue light. The college of engineering and manufacturing was popular. Some of those taxis would have been waiting until evening classes were out, but why hadn't she just run the short distance south to the *métro* entrance on *place* Général-Morin? That would have got her home safely.

Though he didn't want to think it, not with her, not with those kids of hers and a husband locked up in the Reich, it would have to be asked: Had she been on her way to meet someone? She had left the children at home, hadn't had the cash perhaps to have hired anyone to come in or hadn't wanted the neighbours to know, yet had had the cash for a taxi.

The *passage* de la Trinité hadn't been far, the time perhaps 9.45 or 9.50 p.m. He shuddered at what she had had to go through, couldn't help but recall other such cases.

When Matron Aurore Aumont of the *Hôtel-Dieu* found the detective, he was staring bleakly down at the square as many must have done in the old days when dragged there to be anointed with oil before being set afire in the face of God. He looked, she was certain, like a *gentilhomme de fortune* who had just seen the ashes of his life.

She had been going to tell this *gestapiste* that there was no soap and little disinfectant, that there had been a 50 percent increase in tuberculosis, wards full of those who had foolishly smoked uncured tobacco, obtained illegally of course, and that appendicitis, ulcers of the stomach and ruptures of the bowel were due entirely to the eating of rutabagas—cattle food! the potatoes having all gone to the Reich. But she couldn't bring herself to say any of it to this fritz-haired giant with the terrible scar and others far smaller but still far too many to count.

'Monsieur, you wished to see me?'

'Has Madame Guillaumet said anything?'

'Not to us. There may be memory loss simply from hunger, you understand. Like so many these days, it's the little things first that one forgets, and not just with the rape cases, which are never easy, as I can see you are only too aware.'

As if it mattered deeply to him, he said that he and his French partner handled only common crime. 'We're floaters,' he said, and that they had been brought in especially to deal with this tidal wave of blackout crime and could use all the help she could give. 'The girl who let the press in?'

'Noëlle Jourdan.'

'How could they have gotten to her?'

'The press, they have their ways. I wouldn't know, of course.'

'But might have an idea?'

Was this one on an amphetamine—Benzedrine perhaps? she wondered. He had a nice grin, not unkind and though the accent, it was harsh to sensitive ears, he *did* speak French and was not like so many others of the Occupier who didn't even bother to learn a few words. 'Inspector, is it that you would shut us down at such a time? Those who must have helped them get to Mademoiselle Jourdan have been set the example of her dismissal in disgrace. Now, of course, they tremble that they'll be next. Is that not enough?'

A wise woman. 'Tell me about the girl. Her age, address, training— give me as much as possible in the limited time you have to spare.'

'Nineteen. The mother's dead. The girl lives alone with her father at 25 *place* des Vosges. Noëlle was very competent. It struck me hard to have to dismiss such a promising candidate. One invests the time, *n'est-ce pas?* One cares deeply, rejoices at each step of progress and then . . .' She shrugged. 'The young, they abandon you.'

'Two thousand francs wasn't much.'

Enough to buy perhaps three days of food, but he'd seen that too, this one. 'Inspector, I simply don't know who paid her, only that when confronted, the girl cried out that she had done her duty. To whom, I ask?'

Her duty . . . 'Was she forced into agreeing, do you think?'

'Did they get to her because they knew they could, is this what you are saying? If it is, the answer must be that I couldn't possibly know.'

There was absolutely nothing else he could do. To offer money to make sure the woman didn't kill herself would only insult the matron who, by one of the pins she wore, had been made a widow by the 1914–1918 hostilities as so many had been: 1,390,000 Frenchmen, with another 740,000 left permanently disabled. 'Take care of her then, madame.'

*   *   *

41

The police academy victim's fingers were stumps. Shreds of skin and splintered bone suggested that in places at least two or even three jabs with the shovel had been necessary; in others, the severing had been immediate.

Anger? wondered St-Cyr. Hatred? Haste? Unfamiliarity with such an action? A new shovel, an old one? These days, obtaining a new one would have been all but impossible. Had the shovel, then, not been used much and therefore not blunt along its cutting edge?

'As sharp as shovels go,' conceded Armand Tremblay. 'There is rust, Jean-Louis. Oxidized flakes of the metal are embedded in the face and will have to be retrieved later, but for now, an old shovel, long-handled, though one not used much and therefore sharp.'

'A killer who doesn't throw anything out or sell it?'

'Or one who has access to such items. Didn't you say one of your Drouant victims was involved with . . . ?'

'Cement. That one couldn't have done it. He'd have used his fists or a sledgehammer, but with this one a thumb and forefinger would be most useful. Was it the killer who stamped on the hands to open them, or one of his accomplices?'

'Whoever it was, he didn't wear rubber boots. Here and here again, there are what appear to be the marks of hobnails.'

Again they both looked questioningly at the sewer. 'Jean-Louis, I really must insist. Who needs a drowned detective or one that's on his deathbed from hypothermia?'

'You sound like Hermann. You worry too much about the wrong things. Haussmann and Eugène Belgrand, his chief engineer, weren't idiots when they put such things in place.'

A hundred years ago . . .

'But is it a lateral for the runoff?' went on Jean-Louis. 'Sometimes Belgrand would have a weir installed to hold back the larger solids, which could then be periodically removed by lifting the grille and using a shovel, a long-handled one, too, at that, I must add. At other times a catchment was installed at the bottom of the shaft for exactly the same reason and also, again, to hold objects that might have accidentally been dropped.'

In an age of pocket watches, wrought-iron keys, flintlock pistols and little leather bags of coins. The end of one era, the beginnings of another.

A glance up the stairwell revealed unabated rain. Out on the rue du Faubourg Saint-Honoré there would be nothing but the hush of hurrying bicycles and the *click-clack* of wooden-soled shoes, the eyes not purposely averted from this scene of horror if the press had indeed brought notice to it, simply gazes that were empty of all feeling.

'Ours is a funereal city, Armand,' he said of the Occupation. 'The sound of laughter is often as rare as that of tears. Instead, there is usually nothing but a numb indifference.'

The area beneath the victim had yielded only the grey granite of the paving stones and iron of the grille. Jean-Louis peeled off coat, jacket, pullover, shirt and undershirt. The thick dark brown hair was pushed out of the way, the bushy moustache tweaked as if he was about to step into the boxing ring.

An iron bar had been obtained to prise the grille open. Lowering it into the sewer, he probed for the bottom and when, perhaps a metre or so below, it was touched, said, '*Dieu merci*, perhaps I've been spared the necessity of holding the breath.'

The force of the water was not great but because of the quantity, there was backup and the lateral full. Reaching down with both arms fully extended, the walls could be felt and gently probed, each brick's outline followed.

'*Ah, mon Dieu*, the things one has to do!' he shouted. 'If Hermann could see me now, I'd never hear the last of it!'

Up he came again, to catch a breath. 'We'll probably have to wait for help,' he said, his teeth chattering.

There were no fingers, there was no weir, no catchment either, it seemed. Repeated attempts failed to yield anything, thought Tremblay, ready with a towel.

'It's not later than Haussmann,' Jean-Louis was forced to admit after a last dip. 'It's definitely not recent. The weir is of cast iron and has rusted through but has held back a little something.'

Like a secretive schoolboy of ten, a frozen fist was opened. Hadn't Napoléon been the one to say men were ruled best by baubles?

'Vanity?' managed Jean-Louis as he rushed to dry off and get dressed. 'Pride? The joys of possession, eh?'

Not just any award, but the thin red ribbon of the Légion d'honneur.

'Was it ripped from the lapel of his killer's overcoat?' he exhaled. 'Caught on the barb of a decayed weir.'

The ribbon was more often worn on the lapel of the suit jacket.

'There's only one problem, Armand. Well, two, no three,' he went on. 'First, of course, it may not have been the killer's, but if it is, he could have been awarded it for honest reasons, either civilian or military, and therefore his arrest might be difficult, especially these days if he's a friend of the Occupier.'

'Or?'

'You know the answer as well as I do.'

'It could have been awarded by a friend or associate for services rendered to that friend or an associate of said.'

'Or associates of both.'

Scandal had also plagued the Légion d'honneur. Hadn't Daniel Wilson, the playboy son-in-law of Président Jules Grevy caused that one's downfall only hours after he had been returned to office for a second term in 1885?

Wilson had sold Légion d'honneur medals and ribbons to retire gambling debts and other loans. 'Yet still we all aspire to it,' said Jean-Louis with a sigh, 'and nearly everywhere it's worn it brings profound respect and a willingness by others to give assistance and even to obey.'

The boulevard du Palais separated the Préfecture from the Palais de Justice. Kohler stood in brief shelter by the main entrance of the latter and under a stone lintel that still carried the carved motto of the Third Republic: *Liberté, Égalité, Fraternité*, freedom, equality and brotherhood, but had been bolted over by a white wooden signboard with black Gothic letters that gave Vichy's and the Maréchal Pétain's *Travail, Famille, Patrie*, work, family and homeland.

Two *paniers à salade*—Black Marias, salad shakers with individual wire cages inside—had pulled in to the kerb. Emptied, girls of all ages tumbled out, raising voices to the rain. Unchained and then linked up again, these 'submissive' girls, who probably hadn't had licences and certainly looked like repeat offenders, were lined up: no hats, all shades of hair now drenched, the dye, mascara, rouge and eye shadow streaming on some, while the open-toed high heels of several were disintegrating. One aged daughter of the night had been pinpricked by cobbler's tacks that had held the red felt uppers to their white wooden soles. She cursed, gestured, shrilled at the *flics*, *'LÉCHE-BOTTES! LÉCHEZ MON CUL, ESPÈCES DE PORCS À LA MANGUE!'* Boot-lickers. Kiss my ass, you worthless pigs. *'Voilà, mon cul!'* she shrilled and flared her bare bottom at them only to be given a clout she'd remember. The stocking seams she had painted up the backs of her legs had smeared.

Herded by their guardians, they were marched along the rue de Lutèce towards him, convicts already, since under French law a suspect was considered guilty until proven innocent and that could take years. The Police Correctionnelle, the small crimes court, wouldn't be in session until 2.00 p.m., a long wait. Afterwards they'd be taken to the Petite Roquette over in the Eleventh on the rue de la Roquette, and wasn't that prison, like all the others, vastly overcrowded? Hadn't one French citizen in every fifty been deprived of their liberty? In November of last year the courts here and all over France, for the whole country had been fully occupied then, had begun to submit copies of every verdict and sentence to the Gestapo. One never knew, as Louis had said at the Drouant, when something useful might turn up, and the Gestapo knew it as well and that even the most incidental thing might lead them to a *résistant* or network of them or to valuables that should have been declared.

The Police Judiciaire, known colloquially as the quai des Orfèvres—Préfet Talbotte's criminal investigation department— was in this massive warren of buildings and courtyards. Detectives were on the third floor, those who kept tabs on visiting nationals on the fourth via Staircase D, if one had a mind to find it. The Bicycle Brigade was in an entirely different building, so if one had to track a stolen bike's owner who had been murdered, one had not just to go from floor to floor, but from building to building. There were almost two million bicycles in the city, the cost of a new one impossible, if one could be found, and weren't *vélo-taxi* licences on file over there, too?

Of course they were. And of course the racket in stolen bikes was huge, but first he had to find the owner of a certain dog.

Records was at the far end of one of the courtyards and in under a stone arch that must date from God alone knew when. The notice board at the head of the stone staircase, whose steps were worn, was cluttered. A reward of one hundred thousand francs was being offered for turning in the names and addresses of those engaged in criminal activities, i.e., the Résistance and those who were trying to avoid the forced labour call-up. Hadn't Louis's housekeeper two sons in that age bracket? Hadn't Yvon Courbet, a veteran of that other war, made damned certain his boys would avoid this one and now that much-hated call-up by finding essential jobs for them in a munitions factory?

Posted dead centre of the notices was an open-fold from the IKPK's* magazine, *Internationale Kriminalpolizei*. Even the Swiss were decrying the explosion of blackout crime:

> *The problem is, of course, not nearly so rampant as in Paris where Gestapo Boemelburg, head of Section IV, blames French decadence and immorality. When asked to comment, Herr Boemelburg has declined beyond saying emphatically that the problem has been blown out of all proportion and that the investigation, though under tight wraps, is rapidly drawing to a successful and gratifying conclusion.*

Horseshit! But even back in September 1940, Boemelburg had known he'd have to have at least one flying squad he could count on to fight common crime and be honest about it. A shining example of law and order in an age of officially sanctioned crime on a horrendous scale.

---

* The Internationale Kriminalpolizeiliche Kommission, the forerunner of Interpol.

The dog registry wasn't even here. Uncovered as he removed the article so that Louis could have a read, a card stated that it was now to be found in another building.

Dry as a bone, Louis was waiting for him. Vacillating, shifty-eyed and dark-shadowed, the clerk behind him was as withered as the apple that one was saving for dessert, once the lunch of thin soup and a half-bulb of garlic had been consumed.

'The *préfet* has been most kind, Hermann. Everyone wishes to assist us but,' he confided softly, 'the offer of ten francs for turning away while I had a look was most appreciated.'

Unknown to the clerk, Louis had pulled and palmed a file card from one of the rotary drums, but even so, had best be told. 'Just you wait, then, until Talbotte sees the newspapers. We're never going to hear the end of it!'

The card was for an Irish Terrier bitch named Lulu. The clerk, whose salary couldn't be any more than his prewar twelve thousand francs a year in this age of rampant inflation and frozen salaries, could easily have taken this Kripo for a thousand, which just showed the difference between Louis and himself.

'It's what the card reveals that's important, Hermann, but for now we'd best find a little peace and quiet.'

'I know just the place.'

'I'm not going there. I absolutely refuse.'

'Don't be an idiot. You're as hungry as I am. Besides, it will give us a chance to tap the street if nothing else.'

He was right, of course. These days *radio-trottoir* was often the only source of information. Pavement radio, gossip but prolific, and what better place to go than the fount of it all? 'Then I had best tell you that though the theft has yet to be set down in stone by Records, that *vélo-taxi* must have been stolen from *place* de l'Opéra. That's where it was registered to work from.'

And with the Kommandantur itself in full view across the square.

3

At noon, Chez Rudi's was packed. Wehrmacht and SS grey-green uniforms were everywhere, Gestapo black too, and Kriegsmarine or Luftwaffe blue, with scattered *petites Parisiennes* and *Blitzmädel* from home, here to do their duty. Beer-hall big under its brightly coloured murals, the restaurant was still such a bit of home, Hermann was forced to swallow tightly.

All talking had ceased, even the hustle and bustle from the kitchens where Rudi had come to stand, poised in the doorway. A fresh apron girded the 166 kilos. Flaxen-haired, his blue eyes small and watchful, the florid, net-veined cheeks round like a burnished soccer ball, this survivor of the uprising of 8 November 1923, the Munich Putsch, was proprietor and owner of this conquering image to a just reward on the Champs-Élysées and right across the avenue from the Lido.

'My Hermann,' he called out, the voice beer-hall big. 'Your table, *mein Lieber*, and yours, too, *mein brillanter französischer Oberdetektiv.*'

They had never had a table reserved for them anywhere in the past two-and-a-half years. The clientele cheered. Embarrassed, baffled and grinning ear to ear, Hermann led the way to the table as Helga, Rudi's youngest sister, her blonde braids and pale-blue work dress tight, hustled through with two overflowing steins.

'The Spaten Dunkel, Hermann,' sang out Rudi. 'Fresh in on this morning's Ju 52.'

From Munich, from home. Well, nearly so.

'*Danke,* Rudi,' managed the guest of honour, what honour?

There was a nod, a, 'I've made *Lederknödel* for you and *Rostbratürste*, but if the Oberdetektiv St-Cyr would prefer, I can also recommend the *Schneckensuppe* to be followed by the *Geschnetzeltes.*' Snail soup and veal slices in cream, or liver dumplings in a clear broth, and afterwards, small sausages with the taste and aroma of the beechwood over whose charcoal they would have been grilled.

Roggenbrot, too, noted Kohler. Rye bread made just like they used to, and real butter, none of that crappy Norwegian fish-oil margarine the troops usually got and the French had to eat when they could get it.

The beer was cold and dark, not too sweet and with the simple lightness of hops.

'Helga, what the hell is going on?' blurted Hermann, as puzzled as his partner.

The girl quivered. 'You're back, *mein Schatz,*' my treasure, she said with tears. 'We are all counting on you, Hermann. All of us girls. Every woman in Paris. The men, too. The real men. Not the monsters.'

They had eaten in silence and eaten far better than most in the country, St-Cyr knew, and certainly if the Résistance were to learn of it, which they would, they wouldn't waste time with this Sûreté, but would shoot first and then ask the questions even though Hermann always seemed to be oblivious to the fact when here.

Conscious of the diners, Hermann had tried not to notice the girls who stole glances at their table while in the midst of conversation. Their trembling uncertainty, their outright fear—some more than others—was all too clear. Bed with the enemy and watch out, eh? he'd be saying to himself. The savage brutality of the Trinité attack, the full frontal and back views, those too of the academy victim. Every one of Chez Rudi's female clientele had seen *Le Matin* or editions of the other papers. While their men friends tried to reassure them, there were those who smirked—SS and Gestapo who must know this Kripo and his French partner had a problem no one else wanted.

'But have we been granted a reprieve, Hermann?'

From the general dislike and the hatred, too, for always pointing the finger of truth no matter where it belonged? 'It looks like it.'

'Talbotte's not just being kind. Our *préfet*'s gone out of his way to forget my having knocked him out and threatened him with grand theft at the Liberation when all such accounts will be settled.'

'But has been told to keep us run off our feet?'

By Boemelburg and the Kommandant von Gross-Paris. 'Perhaps.'

Even Rudi had made certain they would be left alone to discuss things. Cigarettes, pipe tobacco and small cigars had been laid on, cognac too, and real coffee. 'The Trinité victim,' said Kohler, lighting another cigarette as that pipe of Louis's was packed. 'Madame Adrienne Guillaumet must have been heading somewhere other than home when she left the École Centrale at nine thirty p.m. or close to it.'

The lessons in *Deutsch* would have been over, everyone hurrying from the building into the teeming rain and the blackout. 'But had she arranged to be picked up?'

Or had her choice of a bicycle taxi been governed solely by chance? 'She would have had to go to *place* de l'Opéra first if she'd arranged the ride ahead of time. Money paid in advance, Louis, the half down probably and one hell of a lot of trust, if you ask me. I'm not sure she could have afforded it, even though the flat she lives in speaks of money.'

Good for Hermann. He had faced up to what the woman could well have been up to.

'If she did go to *place* de l'Opéra, Louis, was she overheard by her assailant when ordering that taxi?'

Had he prior knowledge of her? Had he been stalking her, the wife of Captain Jean-Matthieu Guillaumet, resident of the Oflag at Elsterhorst, the POW camp for French officers to the northeast of Dresden? 'If so, she couldn't have been aware of it.' But that, too, could mean, as they both knew, that her assailant must have had ample sources of information.

'Isn't that why so many here are afraid, Louis? They've sensed that others have been watching them and that they could damned well be called to account.'

For sleeping with the enemy, but perhaps it would be best to ease Hermann's mind a little. 'There could have been extenuating circumstances. Reason enough for her having hired it.'

Everyone knew *vélo-taxi* drivers, like concierges, were funds of information if for a price. 'The eggs, white flour and sugar, Hermann. The milk also, with which to bake the forbidden-by-law birthday cake of a child.'

And a simple enough reason. 'I don't know if her son or daughter has a birthday coming up. Giselle and Oona might, but I've not been back to see them yet.'

Hermann was not only worried about those two women he lived with, he was blaming himself since, through no fault of his own, he would still be considered one of the Occupier.

'She left her children alone, Louis. Classes would have begun at six thirty p.m. Travel from the flat on the rue Saint-Dominique would have taken a good half-hour, more if she stopped in at *place de l'Opéra*.'

'But did her assailant imagine what she was up to, or had he known of her from before?'

That was the question but still it had to be asked. 'A random attack when there's been so many?'

'Had he been following her, Hermann?'

'There was a fingernail.'

Pipe in hand, Louis looked at that thing, 'Dirt, blood and grease, Hermann, this last no doubt the same as I felt on the seats of that taxi and on her shoulders. Big hands. Strong hands.'

'The Drouant attack. It's not that far a walk from the *passage de la Trinité*.'

That attack had taken place at 11.52 p.m. and with plenty of time to have gotten into position from the Trinité. 'And not random but planned—it must have been, Hermann—the whereabouts of the victims known well beforehand but even more importantly, that M. Gaston Morel would have his driver take his wife's stepsister home early.'

'And that Morel would accompany Madame Barrault to her flat on the rue Taitbout, eh? She's not wealthy, but does live near enough to the *place* de l'Opéra if it was being watched for women like that.'

'Another POW wife, another stolen wedding ring, but condemnation and punishment this time for committing adultery with a Frenchman, the husband of another. I'm certain Madame Morel is convinced of it.'

'As is her friend, Denise Rouget.'

'A social worker.'

'And socialite. A parasite, Madame Barrault called her.'

'From the Secours National?' The National Help.

'We'll have to ask her.' And hadn't Madame Barrault sat as far as possible from Denise Rouget?

'Stamps or some other item are then stolen at between twenty and thirty minutes past midnight and not likely by the same person or persons but that clay, Hermann. Were the sewers used to get there?'

It would have to be said. 'From the *passage* de la Trinité to that of the Jouffroy isn't far by the streets, and this must have been known to Madame Guillaumet's assailant since he damned well knew how to find the Trinité on such a night.'

Whoever was committing these crimes, and there must be several of them, knew the city as if blindfolded. 'But before any of these, the police academy.'

'Which we definitely were to have been sent to?'

'Perhaps. And after that killing, a girl who telephones to let the world know about it.'

A call that had been made from the Lido right across the street from them!

Louis took a moment to glance around at the clientele who now seemed more at ease. Setting his pipe aside, he leaned closely. 'Are we to wonder then what this one has done to that girl?'

Cupped in his palm was the buttonhole silk of a ribbon whose red moiré, a weak shade of scarlet, had definitely been crimped so as to give it a wavelike pattern as always, though now it looked like water spilling down a series of steps.

'Three men, Hermann, at least one of whom wore hobnailed boots.'

'Veterans?'

'Unless we are to be led into believing it.'

'And a dog, Louis.'

'*Ah, oui.* Lulu, age seven. Breeder: the Kennels Bouchard at Louveciennes on the edge of the Fôret de Marly-le-Roi, the dog's owner, Madame Catherine-Élizabeth de Brissac, an old and much venerated family now residing on the avenue de Valois overlooking the Parc Monceau.'

And if that wasn't convenient, what was? The remains would have been buried probably in the late afternoon and just before the gates were closed and locked. The police academy victim had been abducted perhaps from the Lido at about 7.30 p.m., killed between 8.30 and 9.30 p.m. 'But not enough time for any of his assailants to then steal a bicycle taxi, Louis, and ride to the *passage* de la Trinité.'

They were up against it. Doubtless there was another victim— the telephone caller—and as yet they had no idea of what else had happened last night. More victims, further killings. The attacks were escalating, the wives and fiancées of POWs were being targeted, mistakes made, of course, the hair taken in some cases, the handbags in all—identity papers, ration cards and tickets—and wedding or engagement rings, especially if worn.

'Five crimes in one night, Hermann, when invariably we get one or two at most, and certainly these can't all be connected, and yet . . . and yet we are . . .'

'Kept busy as hell but not supposed to have been assigned to the stamps and not to Lulu either?'

Had some overzealous despatch officer been having fun with them? 'Not one assailant but several, and though there is still some question with the Trinité attack, certainly in the academy abduction and killing, the Au Philatéliste Savant robbery and the Drouant attack, information must definitely have been known beforehand.'

Especially as certain things had been left in that safe! 'Noëlle Jourdan, Louis.'

'There, too, for how, please, did the press know she could be tempted and would be on the night shift and looking after Madame Guillaumet?'

'And why did she consider it her duty to let those bastards photograph the woman?'

Rudi, who had been watching them, could no longer contain himself. Surprisingly agile on the balls of his little feet, he was all purpose and swift to it. A plate crowded with *Salzstangen*, the small salt rolls, was in one meaty hand, a tankard of beer in the other.

'*Werte Herren,*' my dear sirs, he whispered conspiratorially as he lowered himself into a chair and spread over the table, 'our *Soldatenheime*, our troop hostels, are being watched, our boys tailed on their evenings out. Pigalle, eh? Those bare breasts they love to get their hands on. The Bal Tabarin with its sacrificial virgins or the Naturiste with its snake charmers. Lovesick boys, Hermann. Boys who are easy to tail since like dogs, they return to those they think are in heat.'

Gossip was like flour to Rudi.

'The *Soldatenkino*, my Hermann. Those are also being watched. After each film, don't the street girls with the sweetest voices troll the pavements even though they know it is *verboten* to approach any man and forbidden also for the men to pick them up and not use one of the licensed brothels that are reserved entirely for us?'

Out of Paris's 120 legalized brothels, 40 had been taken over by the Wehrmacht but . . . '*Ach, mein Gott,* Rudi. Tailed through the blackout? You're being paranoid.'

Stung, the battering ram of a challenging fist was thrust at him only to calm itself and wag a reproving finger.

'This is serious. There are whispers among the brass and visiting big shots that Gestapo Boemelburg is not just due his retirement but beyond it and that someone with far more muscle even than our Walter is now needed.'

He would let them digest that little mouthful, thought Rudi. He would offer each a salt roll and suggest they take two, since it was entirely due to Boemelburg that they had been allowed to continue fighting common crime and hadn't been put up against a wall and shot.

'The French—excuse me, Herr Oberdetektiv—are beginning to doubt us, Hermann.'

A pull at the tankard was necessary, the thick, wide lips pursed, the beer no doubt judged more than acceptable.

'Things are changing,' went on Rudi as he fingered a *Salzstange* before biting into it. 'Some of those who openly supported the Führer and his many legitimate and necessary causes, and saw those as their own, have begun to drift away. *Verdammte Verräter, Kotzscheisser!'*

Damned traitors, nauseating shits. He was really worried. The Battle for Stalingrad had been the Reich's first defeat that had been publicly announced and followed by three official days of mourning.

'The Propaganda Staffel, Hermann. My informants there tell me that they have been ordered to constantly splash news of these black-out crimes across the papers and to emphasize during every wireless broadcast that progress is being made and a favourable solution but momentary. I've warned them that no pictures or interviews are to be taken here. I can't have the restaurant being targeted. I simply will not have it!'

'Rudi, what the hell are you trying to tell us?'

'That no photographs are to be taken here of the two of you, but out there . . .' He indicated the Champs-Élysées and streets too many. 'Out there you are not safe from prying cameras and reporters.'

'Us?' blurted Hermann.

'You, *meine Lieben*. You are to be watched and followed. Tracked—photographed while in action against these . . . these *schweinigein Vergewaltiger und Mörder.'*

These dirty rapists and murderers but thank God Louis understood and spoke the language.

'It's not safe for my Helga, Hermann. You know how sweet she is on you. It's not safe for my Yvette and Julie either, nor for those two women you cannot seem to leave for my Helga. Take care of these *verrückter Sadisten*. Get them by the balls and use the knife. Better still, bring them here and I will give them a fry-up they won't forget.'

The salt rolls that couldn't be refused were again passed. 'If I were you,' said Rudi, 'I would watch in places like that one across the road where, my Hermann, you questioned only the stage doorman when you should have paid a visit during a performance. The Cercle Européen is still being held there once a week no matter what anyone else says.'

A gathering of the establishment to plan and discuss how best to do business with the Reich. Aircraft engines and airframes, synthetic rubber tyres, ammunition, lumber and aluminium and other things like wheat and potatoes, wine and horses, labour also and yes, cheese and submissive girls, cement too, of course!

Rudi didn't even ask if the police academy victim had been trafficking in women. He just took it for granted.

'There's an epidemic of VD among the men, Hermann, and this is preventing them from returning to the front as quickly as needed. These unlicensed girls we're getting aren't clean. The street roundups of women and girls are not working either.'

Housewives, secretaries, shop- and schoolgirls, their teachers and librarians also—any French female in sight between the ages of fourteen and ninety, diseased or not, could be rounded up and carted off for a swab and a look by a doctor they didn't know nor care to.

'The Oberkommando der Wehrmacht estimates that there are between eighty thousand and one hundred thousand illegal prostitutes on the streets,' said Rudi.

The High Command always overestimated such things but still . . .

'Only from five to six thousand have so far been licensed and issued the bilingual cards that show they are *nur für Deutsche*.'

Registered for use only by Germans and how was one to stop

the boys from seizing the moment, especially when forbidden to use the legal, French-only brothels?

'Hospital maternity wards are full of girls having their love children, my Hermann.'

More beer was taken, the salt rolls again passed. 'Not even once-weekly visits by the doctor to each licensed house have lessened the VD plague. I tell you all of this, Hermann, so that should the Kommandant von Gross-Paris raise his voice, you will understand why.'

'But, Rudi, wouldn't the streets being terrorized at night help to lessen the VD?'

'Paris is paradise, is it not? Besides, the Führer in his wisdom made a promise to all of our boys that they would each get to spend a little time here.' Rudi gave it a bit of a pause. 'Also,' he went on, the puffy eyelids with their lashes at half-mast, 'there is one girl, a *Blitzmädel*, Hermann, whose handbag was unfortunately snatched last Sunday at 1247 hours while she was washing up at a restaurant in the Buttes Chaumont Park. Near the carousel, I think. You know the one, of course. "Some schoolboys," she has said. Four of them.'

'Their ages?' squawked the Sûreté as he should.

'Ten. I tell you this, Herr Oberdetektiv St-Cyr, only so that should the handbag and its contents turn up during your investigation, you will know where it came from.'

A salt roll had best be fingered, assessed and then eaten, thought Rudi. 'A reward of one hundred thousand francs has been offered by this restaurant, since she is a secretary for those over on the avenue Foch.'

The SS General Karl Albrecht Oberg, the Butcher of Poland and now Höherer SS *und* Polizeiführer of France, and hadn't chance or fate played its part? No wonder the boys on Louis's street had hung around and been late for school!

'A *Mausefalle*, my Hermann. Your friends in the SS are going to demand that you set one for these criminals and bait it with one of your women.'

A mousetrap.

*   *   *

They had to take a moment, had no other choice and shared a cigarette as the Citroën idled outside Chez Rudi's.

'Oberg can't yet know about the boys, Louis. Rudi will keep that to himself for a while.'

But would he? 'The boys will still be in school, Madame Courbet out lining up at the shops. We'll have to leave it until later.'

Louis was really feeling it and with good reason. 'Rudi sure knows how to threaten. If anything should happen to his Helga or to his Julie and Yvette . . .'

'*Tears,* a girl from *home?*'

The boys *would* steal *that* one's handbag. Louis, who had tried so hard to set an example for them and was their hero, could only feel betrayed.

'If Oberg does find out, Hermann, I'm up against the post and so are you.'

A *souricière* . . . A mousetrap, the floodlights suddenly coming on . . . 'I can't use Giselle nor can I ask Oona.'

'You've used Giselle before and in the blackout too.'

'ARE YOU SUGGESTING I PUT HER LIFE AT RISK AGAIN?'

'Not at all. I was merely reminding you of . . .'

'That time was different.'

'Times, Hermann. More than once you've . . .'

'Face it, I can't ask either of them any more than you could Gabrielle. They both mean far too much to me. It's equal, Louis. I could never choose between them.'

A man with a dilemma. '*Ah, bon,* then let's lose the tail the Propagandastaffel have assigned to us.'

A dark-blue Ford Ten, the 1935 four-door, sat idling behind them, the one at the wheel no doubt the reporter, the other with the flashgun and camera in his lap.

'Let me go and have a word while you take over here, Louis. We can't both be in the same place at the same time anyway.'

'Au Philatéliste Savant . . .'

'Is all yours.'

'The *place* de l'Opéra and the owner of a certain *vélo-taxi*?'

'I'd better do that one and drop in to see Old Shatter Hand.'

'Then please don't forget that once a month he makes a point of inspecting the brothels, the legal ones that are *nur für Deutsche*.' A Prussian of the old school, the General Ernst von Schaumburg, Kommandant von Gross-Paris, was a confirmed bachelor and moralizing prude who hated the French almost as much as he did the SS and the Gestapo, and liked nothing better than to stamp out disorder. It was best that Hermann deal with him.

Kohler grinned companionably as the side window was unwound and a blue fug of Gauloise smoke escaped. Two hard brown eyes gazed impassively up at him from beneath the grey snap-brim of a brand-new fedora.

'Hey, listen,' he said. 'There's been a fantastic development we thought you'd be interested in. A lead, maybe, to the brains behind this whole string of rapes and murders.'

'The brains . . . ?' blurted Jean-Max Privet, taken aback by their luck.

'If you can give me a lift, your friend here can shoot the brass while you scoop the story.'

Was Kohler just ragging them? Could they chance leaving it? 'Hop in, then. Where to?'

'Let's try *place* de l'Opéra first. Protocol. You know how it is.'

The Kommandant von Gross-Paris, and didn't everyone know Kohler and St-Cyr worked quickly?

These two were from *Paris-Soir*, whose aged Alsatian elevator-operator-cum-night-watchman had been the only one left to guard the newspaper on the day the Occupier had marched into Paris and had soon found himself in the boss's chair running one of the city's largest dailies. Decisions by the Propagandastaffel had had to be made quickly. Where else could they have found a man who knew the building better, the workings too? He'd been the man for the job and still was, having easily mastered the art of hiring managing editors and others. Now he just read the articles they submitted and gave advice to guys like these.

'Hector Morand, *à votre service*,' said the photographer. 'It's good of you to cooperate.'

'Isn't St-Cyr going to the Kommandantur too?' asked Privet.

'Him? I'm sending him over to the rue des Saussaies to organize a little backup.'

A Gauloise bleue was offered by Morand and accepted, a light too, and why not? 'This car of yours is nice but not as roomy as I'd like in the back.'

It was really one of the car pool's. 'Move things, Inspector, if you need more space,' sang out Privet with a toss of his head and glance into the rearview as he negotiated traffic.

'Provisions,' chuckled Morand. 'On our way here we had to pick up a few things.'

Two baguettes, one string bag of cooking onions and potatoes, a chain of garlic bulbs, four litres of unlabelled red, one of oil, too, and good by the look, a cabbage, three kilos of carrots and one newspaper-wrapped parcel that had leaked butcher-blood.

'To think that I almost bought one of these cars,' said Kohler with a sigh. 'I was in England on a police course at the time. The British made ninety-seven thousand of them but they were also made in the Reich. *Mon Dieu,* I could have got one for 145 pounds—that was about 10,875 francs or close to it then.' And now only about two thousand francs more than the price of a brand-new bicycle if one could find it! 'Rudi told us the press were going to cover things in detail and that it would be best for us to help you boys, but how did the two of you get chosen?'

'We drew lots at the briefing this morning and our number came up,' said Privet.

They were heading for *place* de l'Opéra now. Long queues for permission, lost IDs and complaints, et cetera. 'Good. I can see that we're going to get along. Don't park too close to the barricades. It's better if we walk a little. That way the sentries won't get anxious.'

The Kommandantur, with its rain-soaked swastika and big white signboard in heavy black Gothic lettering, was in the same building as the leading branch of a bank, behind whose plate-glass windows a forgotten poster with permed mother and saccharine-smiling kids blithely announced, PARTEZ EN VACANCES, SANS SOUCI, LOUEZ UN COFFRE AU COMPTOIRE NATIONAL D'ESCOMPTE DE PARIS.

Go on holiday without fear—rent a safe-deposit box!

'Your papers, press cards and badges, *mes amis*. You'd better let me have them for a moment. That way we'll be able to go right in.'

The poster was big, bright and brand-new, thought St-Cyr, and it decorated Au Philatéliste Savant's window so that one had difficulty looking into the shop. Spaced as though on either side of an open road, *d'après Dorothy and the Wizard of Oz*, long double lines of workmen and women from all walks of life were heading towards the distant smokestacks of the Reich. Above a slender horizon tinged with red, the helmet-and-chin portrait of a stern and unyielding Wehrmacht strong-arm bravely faced the current hostilities.

ILS DONNENT LEUR SANG. They are giving their blood, the thing read. DONNEZ VOTRE TRAVAIL. Give your labour to save Europe from Bolshevism.

Odilon Bélanger shrugged. 'They came this morning, Inspector. Monsieur Picard threatened trouble if I didn't let them hang it.'

'And that one?'

'Reads his newspapers. Sits next to his safe.'

Nearing seventy, Félix Picard was ramrod stiff and thin, all nose, neck and fingers. The hairline was receding, the narrow brow dominant above gold-rimmed pince-nez and intense blue eyes, the shirt collar and tie so tight and out-of-date one had to take another look: 1928 perhaps, 1920 maybe, but definitely a neckband shirt and detachable Argonne collar, the cheapest of the cheap.

L'Oeuvre, that anti-Vichy, pro-Nazi, virulently collaborationist rag of Marcel Déat's Rassemblement National Populaire, was lowered. 'You took your time, Inspector. Am I to be compensated for the loss of business?'

The weekly *Je Suis Partout* was handy. Anti-Third Republic, anti-Semitic, anti-Communist and very pro-German, et cetera. 'Not if you want your property returned.'

'But . . .' He blinked. 'Nothing has been stolen. *Absolument rien.*'

The surprise of surprises, eh? 'Don't be difficult. We already know you've broken enough laws to close the shop and see you in the Santé for a visit of no less than three years.'

'*Merde,* and you call yourself a police officer!'

'Monsieur . . .'

'The safe, it is ruined. The cat, *ma petite* Angèle, has abandoned me, and you . . . you stand here accusing *me* of lying?'

He slammed the paper down, stood tall and swore, '*J'irai le dire à la kommandantur.*'

I'll go and tell the Germans about it. 'You do that.'

'Pardon?'

'You heard what I said.'

'Inspector . . .' hazarded Picard.

'That's better. Now start talking. Two or more twists of gold louis, black-market . . .'

'Only the one. The louis were all I had for my old age.'

'And the illegally obtained rations?'

'The cat . . .'

'Monsieur, what was stolen?'

The louis had been returned—they must have been, thought Picard, and that could only mean the *flic* had taken them and thought better of it! 'An album of firsts. The 1849 to 1850s, among them the twenty-centime black, the blue also, which was never issued because the postage rates were changed immediately after its printing, the pale vermillion "Vervelle" forty-centime, a sheet of which was ungummed, the 1862 reissues complete, the Napoléon IIIs of 1863–1870 . . . Those of the colonies, the 1859 to 1865 Eagle and Crown, the 1877 to 1878 Peace and Commerce, especially the bluish twenty-five-centime, all of those from the French Congo,

French Equatorial Africa, French Guiana, French India, French Morocco, Polynesia and the Sudan, Indo-China also. The 1889 five-centime overprint on the thirty-five-centime *orange* with the surcharge inverted; the 1892 seventy-five-centime *orange* with the *Indochine* absent . . .'

'A fortune?'

'Once in a lifetime such a deal comes along.'

'*Ah, bon.* Now for the difficult part. How did it "come along"?'

'Inspector, must I?'

'It's Chief Inspector and please don't tell me you bought it at the open-air stamp fair.'

Held every Thursday in fine weather on the park benches of the rond-point of the Champs-Élysées and a favourite of the Occupier.

'A girl . . . I'd never seen her before. She had no understanding of . . .'

'The value.'

'She simply said her *grand-maman* wished to sell the collection.'

'And?'

He had best shrug, thought Picard. 'I offered.'

'After some deliberation?'

'A little. One can't always be sure. Stamps, like rare paintings, can be forged.'

'And you were suspicious?'

'Have I not the right to be after fifty-six years in the business, my father before me?'

'Her name?'

'I didn't catch it.'

'Her age?'

'I'm not certain.'

'Hair colour?'

'Brown, I think.'

This was going nowhere. Perhaps if the bracelets were brought out . . .

The handcuffs! 'Inspector . . .'

'Monsieur, you bought on the quiet, *n'est-ce pas*? First, where, really, did the collection come from; second, how much did you pay for it and what was its estimated value to you, the expert with . . . was it fifty-six years of experience? Thirdly, the name and address of the one who sold it to you, and if you gave that one a sex change, correct your little mistake.'

The *flics* had always been shits, the Sûreté far worse. 'The name and address she gave must have been false, though I wasn't certain of this at the time. The price paid was twenty-thousand francs—I've not much for a life's work, as you can see.'

'And its estimated value?'

'I didn't make an exact appraisal.'

'Monsieur, you had a good look as soon as that "girl" left the shop. You closed up and went to that room you've rented for years in the Hôtel Ronceray. Must I ask the magistrate for a search warrant?'

'Between seven hundred and fifty thousand and one million francs.'

The bastard. 'Old francs?'

'Old.'

And enough to retire on. '*Bon*. Whose collection was it? Come, come, the name of the owner would have been embossed in gold leaf on the album.'

'M. Bernard Isaac Friedman.'

'Address?'

'Number 14 rue des Rosiers.'

Right in the heart of what had once, and for so many years, been the Jewish *quartier* of Paris, the Marais, where so many of the immigrants from the east had taken up residence. 'Deported?'

'He must have been, mustn't he? All of those people.'

'The Vel d'Hiv?' The cycling arena, the *grande rafle,* the first huge roundup of last year.

'*Oui.*'

'And now his stamp collection suddenly turns up. It's curious, isn't it?'

'Inspector, I don't know what . . .'

'I mean? Monsieur, dealing in stolen property is a serious offence.'

'I didn't know it was stolen!'

'You most certainly did!'

'To steal from those people is no harm. The more taken, the better.'

'*Ah, bon*, I didn't hear that, monsieur. Though I must still obtain the warrant, please consider yourself under arrest. Agent Bélanger, would you . . .'

'Inspector, the girl came to the shop a few times. Hesitant always and walking the aisles as if to examine the envelopes while studying myself and the clientele. When she had made her little decision, she then arranged to bring me the collection.'

Even though Picard had 'never seen her before.'

'And when was that?'

This one would have to have everything.

'Two days ago, in the late afternoon. About five or five thirty. I remember it clearly. Angèle was thirsty and I'd poured her a little of the . . .'

'Yes, yes. Wednesday, the tenth.'

'She said she was in a hurry and mustn't be late for work or else the *surveillante* at the hospital would be upset, and that . . . that she would take what I could give her.'

A head nurse, a nursing assistant and a bargain but a crime to which they weren't to have been sent.

In the never-neverland of the Kommandantur, where rain-soaked galoshes, mismatched carpet slippers and ankle-deep coal-black dresses waited in line, there was absolutely no sense in pissing around. 'Kohler, Kripo, Paris-Central to see the General on urgent business.'

Rock of Bronze to his staff, but damned dangerous at all times even though well past retirement, Von Schaumburg was still suffering the aftereffects of the flu that had struck him a good ten days ago. A towel was tightly wrapped about the throat, the smell of eucalyptus oil, menthol, camphor and boiled peppermint in the air, positively no tobacco smoke. Even the window he had been bleakly staring out of was open!

Taller than himself, bigger too, across the shoulders and replete with Iron Crosses and campaign medals, he didn't hear at first and only then, as the throat was cleared, did he hawk up a wad of phlegm. 'Kohler, what is this you're saying?'

It was now or never and the look in the watery, fever-ridden, pouch-bagged Nordic eyes said as much. 'My partner, General. He's found something that could well lead us to one of the chief perpetrators of this plague of blackout crime.'

'Something . . . Must I remind you that military men such as myself never like intangibles?'

'The red ribbon of a Legion of Honour, General. You're the first and only one to learn of it other than myself and our coroner.'

'And that's the way you would like it kept?'

In spite of Boemelburg's being the boss of all such Kripo. 'Yes, General. The press . . .'

'Those infernal bastards. I'm going to get them this time!'

Overcome by a coughing fit, he grabbed the edge of the window then pushed the damned thing wide open. 'Air . . .' he gasped. 'My chest. *Verdammt*, Kohler, can't you see what those people have done to me? *Das Stinkt zum Himmel!*'

It's an absolute scandal. *Paris-Soir, Le Matin*—even today's *Pariser Zeitung*—were seized from the desk and torn. '*Mein Kirschwasser*, Kohler.' He flung an arm out to indicate a side table. 'Gestapo Boemelburg was most kind and sent that bottle over as soon as he learned you and St-Cyr were back in the city.'

A cherry brandy from Alsace and a warning should they come here, but there was only one glass, thank God. Boemelburg would, of course, have to be dealt with later. 'The press, General.'

The glass was drained, refilled and drained again. 'Alsace was to your liking?'

The gossip had already reached him. 'Not entirely, General, but a successful conclusion to a difficult investigation.'

Kohler couldn't have put it better. For all the dissipation, skirt chasing and cavaliering, this former captain in the artillery hadn't backed off when challenged, so good, yes, good. 'A ribbon, you said?'

'The killer's, we believe, of the police academy's victim.'

'And the rapist who so savagely defiled the Trinité woman, Kohler? How did the one who stole that bicycle taxi know to take it and no other? *Ach,* don't look so surprised. I'm not without my sources. Was that poor woman seen having a drink over there with one of my officers? *Liebe Zeit, kommen Sie her.* I'll not give you the flu. I've been over it for days.'

Across the rain-streaked wasteland of *place* de l'Opéra, where pedestrians scurried or darted down into the entrance to the *métro* and *vélo-taxis* struggled or parked themselves in line to wait for a fare, the Café de la Paix, on the corner of the boulevard des Capucines, looked inviting. A favourite of the staff here and elsewhere, business hadn't stopped booming since mid-June 1940.

'Was that woman there, Kohler, to arrange an assignation for later last night and if so, which of my officers was she with and did the one who attacked her see her with him and then overhear her lining up one of those infernal machines?'

'She still hasn't said anything beyond a few first words, General. I was on my way over to the café to question the staff and taxi drivers but the press . . . St-Cyr and myself can't have them photographing us as we work. Let me leave the identity papers with you of the two who followed me here. Let me borrow their car since I need it more than they do and my partner is busy elsewhere.'

The grey, bristled crown of that massive head was given an irritated brush with an equally irritated hand. 'Shall I send them to Fritz Saukel's forced-labour office? By evening they could be pouring concrete along the Atlantic Wall or digging bunkers in the Channel Islands, or would you prefer I ask Herr Oberg to consider them *Sühnepersonen*?'

Expiators held as hostages until needed and then shot to atone for some act of terrorism, i.e., *résistance*. Wehrmacht through and through, Von Schaumburg really had little use for the SS and Gestapo. 'Just put the two from *Paris-Soir* to work scrubbing the floors and toilets, General. I know those are spotless but another good scrubbing never hurt.'

And spoken like a true soldier. 'Find the one who wore that ribbon, Kohler, and bring him to me. I want a Wehrmacht solution to this problem the French have created for us.'

All down the length of the rue des Rosiers not a cyclist could be seen hurrying through the rain, not a pedestrian, a hand-pulled cart or barrow.

It's as if the ghetto has become a ghost town, said St-Cyr sadly to himself. Repeated roundups since that of 16–17 July of last year had virtually left the *quartier* seemingly abandoned. Eight hundred and eighty-eight 'teams' of from three to four—Parisian *flics* and students, yes! from the police academy—nine thousand 'cops' in all had hit mainly five arrondissements in the small hours of that night. Arrests had, however, gone on all over the city—12,884 had been taken to the Vélodrome d'Hiver and subsequently deported, among them more than four thousand children. And now, of course, there are empty houses and apartments all over the city and country.

The gilded letters of M. Meyer and Sons Vins et Liqueurs de Sion, of Zion, were still in place but the shelves and counters had been stripped. Alone, a black leather shoe, the left, lay on its side among the rubbish and next to a hastily packed suitcase whose contents had been strewn in the search for valuables.

'Forgive me,' he said, rubbing a fist across the glass to clear it. 'Hermann and myself weren't here when you most needed us and didn't think such a thing could possibly happen in France. But ever since then I've been building a dossier on Préfet Talbotte. He knows it, too, unfortunately, because I was foolish enough to have told him.'

Foreign refugees and naturalized French citizens had been amongst the first taken. Sephardim from Spain, Portugal and North Africa who had fled the Spanish Revolution; Ashkenazim from Eastern Europe and the Reich who had fled the Nazis. Then, too, and since, there had been those whose families had been French for generations. Citizen French.

The house at number 14 was empty. Not a stick of furniture remained, not a wall fixture, lamp or lightbulb, faucet or basin. Friedman and his family could be in any of the camps or already 'up the stack' as Hermann and he had had to hear an SS say at the Konzentrationslager Natzweiler-Struthof in Alsace.

Above the entrance to the house, the curly-haired, ruff-encircled stone head of a smiling young woman from the Middle Ages gave welcome to all who entered. The street was not that of the rosebushes as commonly thought, but of the *ros*, the teeth along the raddle or wooden bar over and through which the warp was drawn as it was wound on to the beam of the loom to keep its width constant and prevent it from being entangled.

Many other houses and apartments in the *quartier* and elsewhere had been emptied just like this of their furnishings and fittings, even the doors and hinges in some cases.

'The Aktion-M squads,' he said. The *M* was for *Möbel*, the *Deutsch* for furniture.

They'd been thorough, those squads of Parisian labourers and their masters. All items thought useful to resettled or bombed-out Germans, especially those of the SS and Gestapo in the newly acquired *Lebensraum* of Slavic countries, had been taken. One special task force, the Sonderstab Musik, dealt only with the musical instruments of the deported. Three warehouses alone just to the north of the city were crammed with pianos; one other, on the rue de Bassano, but a few steps to the east of the Étoile and off the Champs-Élysées in the Eighth and Sixteenth and very close to the SS of the avenue Foch and the French Gestapo of the rue Lauriston, held trumpets, clarinets, violins and violas, et cetera. Last year alone, forty thousand tons of such furnishings had been shipped to that *Lebensraum*, and yes indeed Préfet Talbotte had availed himself of the safe-deposit-box contents of some of those who had been deported and had been threatened with exposure, but had now chosen to be accommodating.

'Because of what it implies, Hermann isn't going to like where that stamp collection came from,' he said aloud and to himself alone, 'but first, the seller of it, Mademoiselle Noëlle Jourdan of 25 *place* des Vosges.'

The Café de la Paix occupied much of the ground floor of the Hôtel Grand, that sumptuous palace of seven hundred rooms that had been opened on the fifth of May 1862 by the Empress Eugénie. A home away from home, the café was busy even though at three forty-seven in the afternoon most should have been working. Wasn't there a war on?

Of course there was, Kohler silently snorted as another waiter brusquely squeezed past him with a heavily laden tray, and everywhere there was the aroma of real coffee mingled with those of expensive perfume and pungent with tobacco smoke. Nice . . . *Ach du lieber Gott*, it must be, but if the Führer only knew. Certainly not all here were with their girlfriends; certainly too, though, among the ranks present there wasn't one below that of a Leutnant, but didn't the Führer desperately need men at the Russian front?

Uniform or not, *Blitzmädel* or not, the Occupier behaved as if he or she had the world by the balls. Here also there was none of that *Nur Attrapen*, that Only-for-Show nonsense on bar bottles of coloured water as seen in the everyday citizen's watering holes, none of those demands for ration tickets or the chalked-up pas d'alcools signs that spelled out the no-alcohol days. Though many of the *Parisiennes* glanced up at him from their tables, their men friends seemed not to notice and were too busily on the make or simply couldn't be bothered even though they damned well must know he was a cop and why he was here clutching a copy of *Le Matin*.

Louis would have said, Look closer still. See how a waiter nods in answer to a male whisper, then gives a curt nod towards a table where someone else's *petite amie* flashes downcast eyes—pimping, are they, some of these waiters? Hasn't a carefully passed one hundred-franc note just been tucked away? Girls and middle-aged women, some with their wedding rings hidden, who hang on every word their companions utter even though some of them can't understand too many and are doing their best to catch up three nights a week—was it three that Madame Adrienne Guillaumet left her children alone in the flat and went to the École Centrale to teach *Deutsch* to females such as these and to older men? Older, since there aren't too many young Frenchman around are there?

Had her assailant known of her? Louis would have asked and said, Oh for sure, that taxi was stolen from the stand out there, but more importantly, from in here one can see whether such a theft was possible and when best to strike.

Had her assailant been watching for her, Hermann, having stalked her for days or weeks only to at last lift his glass or cup in salute and silently say, All right, *ma fille*, it's now your turn?

A regular, Hermann, of this establishment and others, the Lido especially, or had he been one of her students?

Must every possibility be examined, and if so, if some of the waiters were pimping, weren't others betraying those same girls to those who would do them harm? Beyond the heavily draped, plush burgundy curtains that would be tightly closed during the blackout, there were bird's-eye views of *place* de l'Opéra and the white-railed entrance to the *métro* whose subterranean-leading slot opened on to the boulevard des Capucines like an inclined mine shaft. Any female leaving that entrance and heading for the café would be seen well before she got here; seen, too, if earnestly engaging a taxi for later, or had she been sitting here for an hour or more at one of these tables or at one out under the awning and next to the warmth of that charcoal brazier, she smiling shyly, listening intently and maybe, yes, maybe laying a hand fondly on that of her lover? Had she been upstairs first, eh, to one of those seven hundred rooms since officers and *Bonzen* from home were billeted in many of them? Sure the officers, and all others in uniform, weren't supposed to take women to their rooms, but who the hell was going to police such a thing in a place like this? Had her lover been one of Von Schaumburg's men? Had he got up and gone out there to hire that taxi for her and chosen Take Me simply because he had known that's what she wanted or had already let him have?

A child's birthday cake, Hermann, Louis would have cautioned. The flour, the sugar . . .

'MONSIEUR, I MUST INSIST THAT YOU DO NOT WANDER ABOUT AMONG THE TABLES GETTING IN THE ROAD. PLEASE OBEY THE NOTICE AND WAIT IN LINE TO BE SEATED!'

Lieber Christus im Himmel, what the hell was this and from a mere waiter? 'Gestapo, *mon fin.* Kripo, Paris-Central. A few small questions. Nothing difficult unless you want to make it that way. Clear a table. *Ja,* that one will do, and bring me a *café noir avec un pousse-café.'*

A black coffee with a liqueur. Louis would have loved it. His partner playing Gestapo, but only when absolutely necessary. 'Spit in them and I'll not just see you arrested but shot.'

4

Number 25 *place* des Vosges was little different from the rest of the thirty-six arcaded pavilions whose steeply pitched roofs with dormers were sometimes bull's-eye-windowed. Loose slates gave momentarily trapped cascades. Broken, once-painted shutters were open.

'From a swamp to a palace to a horse market, to this,' said St-Cyr sadly to himself. *Grand-maman* had said that to him once, that good woman having dragged him here at the age of six to learn a little history.

He'd been particularly bad, had stolen from her handbag. Just a few centimes . . . Well, five actually. Always, though, the memory would come rushing at him when here, no matter how desperate the circumstance. 'A sliver, Jean-Louis,' she had said. 'A splinter from the lance of his opponent. Who would have thought such a thing possible? A king? Henry II and a bout of jousting? Oh for sure, they didn't have carousels whose operators demanded cash. They were far too busy, but a little fun all the same, eh? A careless impulse? A tournament whose spine of heartwood found the visor slit of his armour to pierce the eye and brain!'

She had given him a moment to think about a life of crime and then had said, 'He died in agony, screaming for his mother.'

Beyond the high iron fence that surrounded the park where

duels had once been fought, the ruins of last summer's community vegetable plots made their graveyards among the severely pollarded plane trees. Lonely on his stone steed, Louis XIII ignored the wet snow that struck him and indicated the plots as if mystified to find them here.

The house at Number 25 was crowded but the presence of a police officer had rapidly filtered on ahead. Gingerly he went up the stairs, keeping as close to the wall as possible. From somewhere distant came the impatient pause-by-pause thumping of wood on wood, but soon that ceased. Even the concierge had broken the law and shut her *loge*, failing entirely to respond to his earnest knock. He'd read the 'flat' number from the decaying list she had posted in 1935, having crossed out names and added others since.

With frozen laundry to his left and a mildewed wall to the right, he came to the room or rooms of the Jourdan father and daughter, the mother having died probably some time ago, Hermann had said.

There was no doorknob, no latch, no lock—nothing but a dirty bit of string to be tied to a nail, no nameplate either, its bronze frame having been unscrewed and sold.

The distant sound of pigeons came, the scrabbling, too, of caged guinea pigs and other livestock. Nudging the door open would be easy, the string having been left to dangle. Knocking with the muzzle of the Lebel would be best.

'*Entrez,*' came the gruff response, exuding, though, both strength and determination, its owner having been forewarned by the bush telegraph. A corridor connected open room to open room, its floor bare but catching the grey light of day from the far end.

Jourdan was sitting at an iron-legged garden table before French windows the constant rain had done nothing to clean. 'Monsieur . . . ' began St-Cyr.

Guiltily the revolver was tucked away. 'It's Sergeant, Inspector. The Fifty-Sixth Chasseurs à Pied under Driant.'

'The Bois des Caures and a key defence at Verdun. The eastern bank of the Meuse and a forest no more than five hundred metres by a thousand.'

'Into which the Boche poured eighty thousand artillery shells.'

'Early on the morning of the twenty-first of February 1916, after days of rain, a little sunshine came to dry the ground and prepare it for the assault but did God really want it to dry, I wonder, though I commend you, Sergeant. We all did, all of us who were at Verdun.'

The red ribbon of the Légion d'honneur was not present and should have been, but that of the Croix de guerre was there and the yellow and green of the Médaille militaire with its rosette in the buttonhole.

'They couldn't kill all of us Chasseurs, could they?' taunted Jourdan.

Falkenhayn's Operation Judgement had met surprisingly stiff resistance when the advance had been launched after that opening barrage.

'The tempest of fire,' said Jourdan, watching him closely. 'Nine out of ten of us were finished in that first barrage, myself among them. Though I've the Boche to thank, I've hated them ever since for having saved me. Now, to what do I owe the pleasure of a visit from a fellow veteran?'

Jourdan was a *grand mutilé* and had lost the left arm at the elbow and the right leg just below the hip. The crutch that had made its sound of wood on wood had all but lost its rubber stopper and was leaning against the only other chair. He was bundled up against the cold and the damp and with writing materials, the prosthesis he used lying ready beside a neat little stack of at least seven letters waiting to be taken to the post.

'When the ink isn't frozen, I write to my friends,' he said, the accent clearly of the east and Nancy. An open packet of Gauloises bleues and a scattered box of matches indicated impatience.

'One of those fucking matches threw sparks into my face.'

They were always doing that. 'At least you have cigarettes.'

'I budget myself. The half, and then a few hours later, the other half.'

And the agony between. 'Sergeant, your daughter . . .'

'Yes, yes, was dismissed from the *Hôtel-Dieu*. Now what are we to do, eh? Am I to send her out on the streets like all those other bitches are doing? She's young, she's beautiful. Certainly she has the urges—what girl of that age wouldn't—but she's mine, Inspector. Mine, and comes from a good home. The two of us would rather starve to death than sacrifice her little capital to one of those bastards from the other side of the Rhine. Some crimes can never be forgiven or forgotten, and a woman's having sex with the enemy is one of them.'

The black hair was thin, revealing patches of shrapnel-scarred skin, the dye job refreshed each day by that daughter, as was that of the full brush of a moustache, which hid its own scars. Others marred the left side of a face that was thin and drawn, the expression given to a wariness that could only make one uneasy.

The olive-dark eyes with their thin brows dropped as that same thought registered. Nothing could be said since pity was the last thing this one would want.

Three tubes of Veronal, one having been squeezed so often it was skeletal, lay next to the pen and ink bottle. Jourdan noticed right away that this Sûreté had seen them and would think the worst.

'I need it, Inspector, for the stumps and the fragments of metal that are still inside me.'

The tubes had been stolen from the *Hôtel-Dieu*. There wasn't any question of it, but neither he nor that daughter of his would yet have found a way of replacing them when this supply was gone: a long-acting barbiturate, of the weakly acidic form, it was rapidly absorbed through the skin, but such continued use dramatically lessened its effects while increasing the user's need. 'Why did your daughter consider it her duty, Sergeant, to allow the press to photograph that poor unfortunate woman?'

'Unfortunate? The slut was selling herself and got what she deserved! The wife of an officer, a prisoner of war? Her throat should have been cut and her *chatte* sliced to ribbons! I told my Noëlle that she had done absolutely the right thing by letting them make an example of the woman and that the hospital should never have accepted such a patient.'

Mon Dieu, such vehemence. 'Old wounds make you incautious, monsieur.'

'It's Sergeant, and I'll say what I please, but obviously couldn't have done it, though I would most certainly have liked to.'

The smile Jourdan gave deliberately invited censure. 'Where is your daughter, Sergeant?'

'Out looking for food and work that won't tarnish her good name.'

The house had begun to crawl back to life. When something fell in one of the garrets above, Jourdan tossed his head up in alarm to desperately search the plaster skies and fix his gaze apprehensively on the supposed source.

He strained to listen. He didn't move and hardly breathed. 'It's all right, *mon ami,*' said St-Cyr, as if still in the trenches of that other war, 'that one missed us.'

'Night is far worse, isn't it? When they come at night, I scream and have to hide my head.'

'*NAME?*' demanded Kohler.

Given in *Deutsch,* the shriek filled the Café de la Paix, making a sweet young thing at a nearby table leap to her feet and drop her cup. Coffee showered over her lover boy. '*Name?*' he asked more reasonably. He'd been getting nothing but the runaround from the waiters.

'*Inspecteur . . .*'

'*VERDAMMTER FRANZOSE, BEFEHL IST BEFEHL!*'

Damned Frenchman, an order is an order, but *Gott sei Dank,* Louis wasn't here.

'Henri-Claude Martel, maître d',' managed Martel.

All eyes were now on them. The lieutenant with the coffee in his lap was furious but afraid to say a thing, so good, *ja gut!* Martel waited as he should. Tall, ramrod stiff, stern and unyielding behind his specs, this lantern-jawed billiard ball on stilts was well up in his sixties and wasn't going to be easy. 'This café,' said Kohler, indicating the crowd. 'I'm surprised the terrorists haven't tossed a grenade into it.'

Taken aback, Martel blurted, 'They . . . they wouldn't dare. It's just not possible.'

'Oh, and why is that?'

'They simply wouldn't. The café is too close to the Kommandantur.'

'And an obvious target.'

'Monsieur . . .'

The things one learned by taking a shot in the dark. 'It's Herr Hauptmann Detektiv Aufsichtsbeamter Kohler. Please don't forget it.'

Give him a moment now, Louis would have said. Let the gravel you've fed him work its way down to the crop. After all, it's the time of the ostriches in France, isn't that so? Now tell him what you've just discovered but don't emphasize the management's threatening the local troublemakers should they have a change of heart. 'Your bosses have quietly paid off the Résistance, my fine one, and have an absolute guarantee that no such thing will happen to discourage business and create costly repairs. No, don't argue. You think I'm not aware of what's been going on under the carpet? Just give me what I need or I'll have the Kommandant von Gross-Paris shut this place down so hard you'll all be heading east for a little holiday.'

Again Herr Kohler paused. He hadn't touched either the *café noir* or *pousse-café* he'd been given. Patting his pockets, he relieved the lieutenant of one of his cigarettes and took time out to light it.

Indicating *Le Matin*'s photo splash, he said, 'I'm certain this woman came here yesterday. You know it; all of your staff do. She sat at one of the tables with a companion, and now you are going to tell me who that companion was.'

'Another woman. One with a young daughter. Not wealthy. Certainly not as well dressed as . . . as that one was.'

That one being the Trinité victim, but the things one learned with a little pressure. 'And?'

'They asked for a glass of milk for the child but as we had run out, the one with the briefcase suggested an *eau gazeuse citron vert* and that was brought instead.'

A lime fizz and ersatz unless the limes had been flown in from somewhere, but let's not forget the Trinité victim had a briefcase. 'Do you mean to tell me you let them sit here, having ordered nothing else?'

'I did, yes.'

But not without good reason. 'And then?'

'The one in the photos went out to the taxi stand.'

'Time?'

'At about five thirty in the afternoon.'

'*Ah, bon.* At last we're getting somewhere. Now tell me, did they come here often?'

Martel shook his head. 'Only the poorly dressed one and not often, but . . . but not always with the child.'

Oh-oh. 'The *cinq à sept*?'

The customary hours from five to seven for *les liaisons sexuelles*. The detective could think what he wished but would have to be told a little so as to get him out of here and quickly. 'Then and earlier. Sometimes the monsieur is busy and telephones to say he can't make it. Sometimes he can only spare a moment to say hello to his wife's stepsister, paying her bill as he leaves. At other times they have the half-hour, never more, so the order is always taken quickly to his table. He presses food upon the woman and she always puts most of it into her handbag. And always he tries to give her money and always she refuses and says, "You know I will only leave it on the table." '

'M. Gaston Morel of *Cimenterie Morel*?'

'*Oui.*'

The finches were gone from the cage, and in their place were gerbils. Handful by handful, Noëlle Jourdan spread wood shavings and sawdust, having saved the soiled for the stove.

'They like to burrow,' she said, knowing that the questions

would come and that there was nothing she could do to stop them. 'They make good company and love to play.'

'Noëlle, please don't get too attached to them,' rasped the father, Jourdan having taken one of the two cane chairs in the tiny kitchen, the daughter having drawn the black-out drapes as soon as she had got to the flat.

'They all know me, don't they, and trust me as a friend, but I won't,' she said, scattering rosehips for the captives, a little treat she had somehow acquired. 'I mustn't, must I?'

Two rabbits occupied the small, screened airing cabinet that had, in better days, held the bread, butter, cheese, milk and meat, et cetera, to keep the flies, the cockroaches and mice from them. A single electric bulb hung above the plain deal table, its height being adjusted by a sliding lead weight along the frayed cord that passed over a pulley whose block was hooked to the wall. As far as one could determine, there were few if any other lights.

Supper consisted of a stew, which had, no doubt, been put to the boil at 4.30 a.m. on the building's communal stove downstairs and had then been placed in the hay box up here to cook all day in its own steam and juice.

She was capable, this Noëlle Jourdan. She was everything a father such as hers needed, but had she any life of her own?

Three rutabagas, some half-rotted cabbage leaves, a scattering of sow thistle roots, a few carrots and a bulb of garlic tumbled from the string bag, the sum total perhaps of the hours of standing in line. A parsimonious bit of sawn soup bone was removed from a pocket, two thin handfuls of macaroni, six Brussels sprouts and a cloth-clad lump of *chèvre* that oozed goats' milk on to the counter. Félix Picard had said he thought she had brown hair but must have been totally mesmerized by the stamp collection.

She was *une belle*. The brow was high, smooth and wide, the eyebrows richly dark and perfectly arched. Modigliani would have longed to use her as a model, Picasso to seduce her. Though the chin was determined, it was soft, the eyes of the darkest Midi olive, their lashes long. Certainly, even after Jourdan's comments about the Trinité victim, the girl must still be a worry, what with the way things were on the streets during the blackout. The ears were free of earrings—had they, too, like so much of the family's things, been sold off piece by piece? The hair was jet black, not brown at all, and worn with a natural wave that suited admirably, the skin of the softest shade of Midi brown, the mother either from the south of France or Italian perhaps, or Spanish. There wasn't a hint of lipstick or eye shadow. Had the father insisted on this?

She was of just a little more than medium height and delicate, yet not delicate, though hiding her thoughts perfectly under such a scrutiny. Bathes regularly, he would have said to Hermann had the two of them been discussing her. Visits the local bathhouse at least once a week. Insists on it even though the cash of such a modest expense is desperately needed. 'Mademoiselle, you sold a stamp collection.'

'Noëlle, what is this, please?'

'It wasn't mine, *Papa*. I found it on the *métro*.'

'And didn't turn it in to the lost property office?'

'*Papa*, I was working the night shift. I didn't want to be late. I . . .'

'Sergeant, a moment, please. Am I correct in concluding that you didn't know about this "grandmother's" stamp collection?'

'What grandmother? Noëlle, what is this one saying?'

Clearly the father hadn't known of the stamps or even of the grandmother and just as clearly the girl felt trapped, she looking to this Sûreté for help when, of course, none could be offered, or could it? 'Mademoiselle, when, exactly, did you find the collection?'

Had he believed her? 'About three weeks ago. The *métro* is always crowded these days. I was tired, you understand. Suddenly a seat became available. Others didn't see this at first. I squeezed past them and dropped into it and . . . and only then realized that there was something on the floor at my feet.'

'A package.'

'*Oui*. I thought to leave it—one never knows if touching such a thing might bring trouble. In the end, I . . .'

'Picked it up.'

'*Oui.*' Would he now ask if anyone had seen her do so?

'And at the hospital you put it into your locker?'

'*Oui.* I didn't even know what it was. I swear it. All night I was run off my feet. Pneumonia, babies, the flu, the epidemic we've been having of appendectomies due to those damned rutabagas. In the morning, I forgot all about it and . . . and hurried home.'

She should have been an actress. 'You left it in your locker under lock and key.'

Ah, merde, was this Sûreté on to her? 'That is correct.'

Now to give her a little more line. 'Day then passed into day, shift into shift, until you realized you could no longer turn it into the lost property office without explaining the delay.'

'That, too, is correct. I . . . I sold it instead.' Confessing to such a thing, even though he had known of it, was still a gamble but sometimes if one didn't take a chance, one didn't get anywhere.

'*Chérie,* I know things haven't been easy, but to sell something that belonged to another . . .'

'*Papa,* I couldn't control myself!'

How many times had he heard that same excuse from unlicenced prostitutes? wondered St-Cyr, sighing inwardly, but he'd have to lie a little to keep the fish on the line. 'For now we'll leave the press photo session, mademoiselle, as I wouldn't want your dinner to get cold. Please be prepared, though, to offer clear and precise answers when next called upon. Sergeant . . .'

'Inspector . . .' began Jourdan.

'See that she tells you everything, *mon ami,* then when we next meet, if she's out, you can relay it to me.'

Three weeks . . . to keep a collection like that under wraps for even that length of time had to imply control and/or fear, but at the door, he said, 'Mademoiselle, your father has corroborated the matron's statement to my partner that you willingly allowed and then went out of your way to assist the press in photographing last night's Trinité victim.'

A hardness entered, a breath was taken and held. 'I did and don't deny it.'

'Two thousand francs wasn't much.'

The shrug she gave was curt. 'I did what I had to for *Papa*'s sake.'

That, too, would have to be entered into. 'And now, what will you do?'

'Me? Do like everyone else. The *système D*.'

From the verb *se débrouiller*, to manage. 'And write letters to relatives in the country?'

'Ours are all dead. *Papa*, he . . . he writes to old comrades-in-arms.'

The 'grey' market, the using those one knew, even if in but the remotest of ways, for help. 'A ham, a chicken, some potatoes . . .'

'Yes, yes!'

'And do they send him such in the post?'

Like everyone else was doing if they could. 'Sometimes.'

'And what is offered in exchange?'

'Tobacco . . .' *Ah, Sainte-Mère*, he had made her so edgy she'd let it slip, and he had known she would!

The father had been desperate and had had to budget himself, but had he lied and was he also spreading that hatred of his towards those women who were having sex with the enemy, their husbands and fiancés being absent as prisoners of war? 'Cigarettes have become the preferred currency, haven't they? You cleaned out your locker at the *Hôtel-Dieu*, did you?'

This one was trouble! 'My locker . . . ? Why . . . why, yes. Matron stood over me while I did. "Quickly, quickly," she said. I was in tears, you understand. I could hardly see. I . . . I just grabbed my handbag and things, changed into my street clothes and left.'

Having then been escorted to the door. 'Tears. Yes, I can understand those. Your father's *Légion d'honneur*, mademoiselle. Why doesn't he wear it?'

'He misplaced it. I've looked everywhere. One of the kids in the building must have been in and taken it. I'll get it back. I know I will.' *Merde*, why had he had to notice it was missing? 'I . . . I've just lost my job, Inspector, haven't yet had the time to ask around.'

'But will, and you'll get another.' But had she been forced to give up the ribbon and to then let the press take those photographs?

He walked away from her, this Sûreté, the brim of that shabby fedora yanked determinedly down, the collar of an equally shabby overcoat turned up. He didn't look back until he had reached the bottom of the stairs. Only then did he see her standing here at the railing, hands on the laundry that would never dry completely but always remain a little damp and frozen.

It wasn't far to the *Hôtel-Dieu*, especially not if one had a motorcar, and this she heard starting up, as did everyone else in the building.

When opened by an attendant and carefully searched by this Sûreté, especially along its metal seams, the locker yielded three pale green tickets bearing dates of the fifteenth and twenty-third of December last, and as recently as the seventh of January, all from Ma Tante, 'My Aunt,' the *mont-de-piété* of the Crédit Municipal de Paris, the pawnshop at 55 rue des Francs-Bourgeois.

Kohler gripped the Ford's steering wheel. The rue Laffitte, which wasn't far to the east of the rue Taitbout, threw up the faint blue firefly lights of its bicycles and bicycle-taxis. The slit-eyed headlamps of a *gazogène*-powered lorry nudged into the stream only to find two petrol-driven Wehrmacht lorries hungering after it for half the load of black-market goods, the usual tariff.

A rare *autobus au gazogène* burped in rebellion, the sodden line of stragglers impassively boarding, while here and there the glow from cigarettes was hardly noticeable due to the extreme shortage of rationed tobacco and the *verdammter Frost!*

Parisians were in misery and this Kripo was definitely among them. Madame Marie-Léon Barrault, Victim Four, hadn't been home. The concierge of the former mansion on the rue Taitbout, that droopy-shouldered *salaud* of a now run-down tenement, had let him waste valuable time climbing five flights of lousy threadbare stairs and then had let him come right back down.

'But, monsieur, you haven't asked it of me? Normally when one gives the floor and flat number, one expects such a request, especially if from one of *les Allemands*.'

And now? he had to wonder, the car idling at kerbside, he staring up the ever-darkening slot of the street to the Église de Notre-Dame de Lorette and beyond it.

High on the butte of Montmartre, the white dome of the Sacré-Coeur caught the last of what had passed for daylight, dwarfing all else as it frowned upon the church he sought that had offered succour to the demimondes of this once virulently bohemian *quartier*. But that had been in the mid-1800s when the owners of these former mansions had had to accept all tenants, and that, of course, had led to the district's increasingly being used in the last half of that century as a dormitory from which the girls could pound the pavements of the *grands boulevards* and the Champs-Élysées until, in turn, the quality of those girls had degenerated to the common. And hadn't the Église de Notre-Dame de Lorette given the name *lorettes* to those girls because it had become their church as well as that of others, but was all this still ancient history, that was the question?

'Madame Barrault must feel the need to confess,' the concierge of her building had fluted. 'That one comes and goes, Inspector, and often leaves the child alone.'

Had he been so wrong about this Drouant victim? wondered Kohler. He had had to wait for more from that concierge. 'Many times my wife has had to calm the child whose refusal to unlock the door to that flat of theirs has always led to my having to use the spare key of this office.'

The shit! but had Madame Barrault refused the offer to look the other way when she went out alone if only she'd give him a bit on the side? Had she come here to confess?

Cop registered in made-up eyes, and as one they sat immobile, now wondering if there'd be a roundup and they'd all be taken for the swab and locked up if failing to have a proper licence.

Maybe one hundred and fifty sat about. All ages from sixteen to seventy. Fur coats and fur-trimmed hats on some, and money there; blankets made into overcoats on others, the church not large, its interior *d'après* Louis-Philippe perhaps. Relax! he wanted to shout at them but knew it would only lead to an immediate exodus and that it would be best to say, 'Stay put or I'll blow my whistle.'

'*Vipère!*' muttered one under her breath, '*Cobra!*' another, '*Couillon!*' yet another, she hastily crossing herself as this 'asshole' searched over the lot of them, noting family medals on some: a bronze for five children, a silver for eight, a gold for ten and how the hell else were they to feed the kids these days?

Madame Marie-Léon Barrault, stepsister of *Ciment* Morel's wife, was sitting at the far side nearest to the open door of the confessional. The woman had already had her turn. At a nudge, the daughter, a child of eight, rose to silently protest but was hurriedly given the firmest of shoves.

Reluctantly dragging off her toque and flinging her braids about in rebellion, she crossed the intervening space. Timidly the door to the confessional was drawn shut. A copy of this morning's *Le Matin* was clenched in the mother's fist. Tears were splashed, the head bowed, the woman blurting, 'Why did that have to happen to Madame Guillaumet or to any woman, Inspector? I only did as she asked. The taxi I sent her to was then stolen. Stolen! She's going to die, isn't she? Her children have no father because he's in a prisoner-of-war camp. Her children . . .'

Marie-Léon looked away towards the confessional and said, 'Please, God, spare her.'

The child or the Trinité victim? one had to wonder.

'Father Marescot knows the name of my husband, Inspector, as he does those of all of us here. Always he asks if I've done anything for which my husband would be ashamed. My René-Claude. My Claude!'

'*Allez-y doucement*, madame.' Go easy, eh? 'Whisper.'

'Haven't I had enough of whispers? *Une roulure, une salope*— isn't that what others are saying about me, Henriette most of all?'

A slut, Morel's wife was calling her but . . . 'Calm down and tell me where your husband is.'

'In Poland. At Stablack.'

To the east of Danzig. A *Stalag*. A camp for common soldiers. 'And Madame Guillaumet's?'

'The Oflag at Elsterhorst. It's . . . I think she said it was near Dresden.'

'That's close enough but given your differences of home and address and husband's rank, how is it that you . . .'

'Our differences of class, Inspector? Of course we didn't walk the same paths, but found ourselves with the same needs and social worker.'

And wouldn't you know it, the parasite. 'Denise Rouget?'

Was it so surprising? *'Oui.'*

Again she looked to the confessional, as others must now impatiently be doing. 'Annette,' she hissed. 'Annette, God has listened long enough! Father, there are others waiting.'

'Let them wait, my child. Please don't interrupt!'

'Annette, don't you dare say anything you shouldn't!'

'Trust is sacrosanct, Madame Barrault, belief absolute.'

'Father, *please!*'

They waited and they waited. And finally the child, subdued and ashen, emerged to look first at her mother and then at this Kripo.

It had to be said, but had best be given with a sigh. 'Come on, then, and I'll give the two of you a lift home.' Louis would be certain to realize that his partner, being the gullible one, had made a mistake about the woman and would never let him live it down.

The Trinité victim was no better, no worse, and when this one from the Sûreté gave her a nod, Aurora Aumont switched off the light and softly closed and locked the door.

'She has said nothing yet, Chief Inspector.'

'But will she live, Matron?'

'Only she can tell us. Now if you will excuse me, my shift has been over for some time and I must get home.'

'A moment, please.'

Must he be insufferable? 'Well, what is it?'

'Noëlle Jourdan.'

'I've told your partner all I know.'

'Of course, but we often work independently. What happened to that girl's mother?'

Why was he asking such a thing? 'She died when Noëlle was five years old.'

'And ever since then the father has raised her?'

'It was that or the sisters. Ah! he was behind her letting the press in, wasn't he?'

A nod would suffice.

'Then it's as I have thought. My one concern was always that the girl could be intolerant at times, particularly with those who had been attacked by these . . . these monsters of the streets and needed our every consideration. When cautioned, Noëlle was careful, though not solicitously so, you understand, and as a result I was forced to have reservations, but only in that regard.'

'And the mother?'

'Noëlle never spoke of her. "She's dead," was all she would say if asked. To have no memories, no photographs is not good, Inspector. There's a vacuum in that girl's life that desperately needs to be filled.'

'And the father, did she say much about him?'

'Only that he was constantly in pain and that she had to look after him. Always she was on about the cost of things and how difficult it was to find enough to continue, yet she always seemed to manage. Never late, usually here before six in the morning or six at night. A willing worker who not only knew she needed the job, but sincerely wanted to become a fully qualified nurse and did everything she could to demonstrate it.'

'Except for that one mistake.'

'Even now I ask myself why it had to happen and if she could have been forgiven. These times, this Occupation, they're putting far too much stress on everyone, especially the young.'

'Could the press have known she would let them in?'

'Why, please, would they have been told such a thing and by whom?'

'I'm only fishing for answers. Was she obligated to anyone?'

'That I wouldn't know. Now, please, I have my son's two boys and their mother at home. If I'm not there on time, they'll worry about me.'

'Did Noëlle Jourdan have any friends?'

'Male or female?'

'Either or both.'

'That I wouldn't know in any case. Because she was a trainee and had a father who was a *grand mutilé*, the girl was allowed two hours off every other midday when she was on the day shift, you understand. It was little enough time in which to queue up for food and other necessities, but her circumstances would have been known to the shopkeepers she frequented, since most of us must shop only with those who have us on their lists. Sometimes Noëlle could bypass the line-ups, so long as it was done on the quiet. Sometimes she would tell the other shoppers that she had to make a delivery. Her shopping bag would appear to be heavy and their hopes would rise so that they would let her go ahead. At other times she would say her dear *papa* was having one of his bad times and that she was desperately needed at home.'

And so much for the Veronal this one must have known was missing. 'Are those shopkeepers she frequents veterans?'

'Why, yes, some of them. They must be, mustn't they? *Mon Dieu,* how many fought in that last war?'

'Too many, myself among them.'

'My husband also.'

But had that girl purposely left a full shopping bag somewhere safe outside the flat when she had returned today? If so, there had been no evidence of previous such forays.

'Noëlle always managed a little, Inspector. Indeed, there were those here that I had to caution about being envious. The girl was *très jolie*. The figure, the complexion, those eyes of hers, the way she walked . . . They all saw these, of course, and some wanted to think the worst when she would come back loaded with a cabbage or, better still, a few potatoes or a small cut of beef most could only imagine.'

'But did that happen often and did those "veterans" you spoke of help her in other ways?'

'Not often, only enough to engender envy. She always knew the prices and would complain about the inflation, like everyone else. She could be kind, too, Inspector. Once she gave me two eggs for my grandsons; once a chocolate bar they were to share. "Sharing's something that must be learned," she said. "It will help them with their mathematics also." Swiss it was and very good, though my daughter-in-law and I only had the aroma of it and the pleasure of watching as it was shared one square a day for each until gone. Other things, too. Shoes . . . Where or how she managed to get them, I'll never know, but when I spoke of their need—small boys will keep growing no matter how skinny—that girl found a way. Five hundred francs they cost me for the two pairs but a bargain. A positive bargain!'

A *sainte*. 'And the means?'

'Pardon?'

'Come, come, madame, had she something to give in exchange other than the cash?'

'That I wouldn't know, Inspector, nor would I have asked.'

Nothing among the contents of today's shopping had indicated any advantage beyond being adept at scrounging, but sometimes she had had success, and sometimes she hadn't. 'Wood shavings and sawdust . . .' he muttered. 'Where would she have got them?'

'Where but from the maker of the coffins that are used for those here who have no known relatives or names.'

Those coffins were made of spruce, not oak or mahogany, or teak and walnut—had there also been rosewood and birch? he had to wonder, but would have to wait until he could ask the gerbils.

Herr Kohler hadn't just driven them home from the church, thought Marie-Léon. He had driven to *place* de l'Opéra and had let the car sit a moment opposite the Café de la Paix, which had appeared, of course, to be all but in total darkness, the *vélo-taxi* stand also, but lots of traffic, lots of coming and going. Shielded torch beams had flicked on and off to save on the batteries few could find even if they had the cash to spare. Cigarettes had glowed, there'd been laughter—that of girls, that of their men friends, all of them out for a good time.

Without a word, he had then driven to the École Centrale, where Madame Guillaumet had taught night school and in front of which she had stepped into that taxi totally unaware of what was to happen or even that its driver wasn't the same as she had spoken to earlier.

He had taken herself and Annette to the *passage* de la Trinité where the only light was from the cigarettes of the women in that place and the dim blue bulb above the door of a *maison de passe*. *Dieu merci,* he hadn't insisted on taking her to the *Hôtel-Dieu* to be confronted with the sight of that poor woman. Would he save that for later?

Now they sat in the car, in the darkness of the rue Taitbout, he having wisely parked some distance from her building, but she had to wonder if he would insist on coming up.

'I don't condemn,' he said, but in spite of this, there was a sadness to him that could only mean he thought the worst of her. 'I just need answers.'

The ignition was switched off, her heart sinking. Annette sat very still between them and yes, it was as if she could hear her daughter swallowing. 'Inspector . . .'

'Annette, there are some things in the backseat that you and your mother could use.'

'I can't accept them, Inspector. I mustn't. Please . . .'

'A few potatoes, some onions . . .'

'If you give me *anything,* or even come up to the apartment, Monsieur Aubin, the concierge, or that wife of his will report it. His brother-in-law is a file clerk at the Préfecture.'

'I am the police.'

'That won't matter, not with them. It will only be sauce to the goose.'

'Then start by telling me why you went to confession?'

'Was I sexually intimate with Gaston? *Ah, mon Dieu,* you're just like my stepsister and everyone else! My husband is a prisoner of war. I deliberately offer temptation and am lonely, aren't I? Vulnerable, *ah, oui, oui,* and am also having a hell of a time making ends meet!'

Cringing, shuddering at such an outburst, Annette tried to make herself as small as possible. If she'd had magic dust, she knew she would have showered it on herself to vanish, but would have sneezed!

When Herr Kohler didn't say anything, *Maman* knew she must.

'You needn't worry about my speaking of such things in front of my daughter, Inspector. Annette has had her ears scorched by that priest.'

'MAMAN, I DIDN'T TELL HIM YOU WERE SLEEPING WITH ANYONE OTHER THAN ME. I DIDN'T!'

'Then what *did* you tell him, *petite*?'

'I DON'T HAVE TO TELL YOU. THE CONFESSIONAL IS PRIVATE.'

Oh-oh.

'Hate it or not, private or not, you had best let me in on it. Silence is by far the hardest of punishments, is it not, especially when one is forced to sleep in one's bed in another room and it is terribly dark and there is no one to talk to.'

Tears wouldn't help, but the rain of them couldn't be stopped. The car would fill up, Annette knew, and then . . . then this Gestapo who had such a terrible slash down the face, would have to open the door and flush them all out on to the street!

'Annette . . .'

'Father Marescot says *Papa* is holding steadfast and that you should also do so and not be tempted.'

'I'm not. How dare that priest . . .'

The nose was wiped with the fingers, a hiccup given. 'You are, *Maman*. I have heard you!'

'Heard what?'

'Must I confess to you?'

'Most certainly!'

Again the nose had to be wiped, the Boche trying to find a

handkerchief she wouldn't have used even if taken before the firing squad! 'You . . . you touch yourself. At night, in our bed. You catch your breath and . . . and then you cry out through your teeth so as not to waken me. Sometimes it takes a long, long time and you only sigh; sometimes the sigh, it is given at the last, after the . . . the tooth-cry and the gasp.'

Ah, Sainte-Mère, Sainte-Mère! '*Chérie,* listen to me. I only do that because I miss your father. I . . . I think I still must love him, but no longer know if he'll feel the same about me.'

'Father Marescot says that what you've been doing is a sin and that you're going to burn in hell. *Papa* and I will never see you in heaven when we die. Never, *Maman.* Never!'

Ach, du lieber Gott, what was the matter with that priest?

'*Chérie,* have you said anything about it to Agnès or Josiane? Her school friends, Inspector.'

'And neighbours, *Maman.* No, I haven't. Not yet.'

'Then don't. Promise me you won't. They wouldn't understand. No one would. They and their parents would only think the worst as some of them already do.'

The tears were wiped away, the forehead kissed and held. At last *Maman* said, 'There, you see how it is, Inspector? For warmth and comfort, Annette and I share the bed her dear *papa* and I once shared, she to have his pillow always, we both asking God to bring him home and quickly. Since I'm a victim of our streets, I wanted Father Marescot to hear from me that I had done absolutely nothing to warrant such an attack, nor have I ever done such a thing.'

A breath was sucked in and held by Herr Kohler. There'd been the absences from the house, and certainly the inspector must be wondering about those, but all he said was, 'And did he believe you?'

'Obviously not. René-Claude was baptized in that church, though not by that . . . that priest who only came to us in the autumn of 1939 when Father Bouchard felt he had to volunteer again and is now a prisoner of war himself. We attended regularly, as did and still do, my husband's father and mother. When René-Claude was taken, where else was I to have turned? Days pass, months come and go, a year, two years and now more than the half again and still he's not home. Inspector, my husband must be well aware of what some of the prisoners' wives in Paris and elsewhere are doing to combat their loneliness or make ends meet, and when he insisted in a letter that I let Annette take confession *after* myself, I . . . I felt he must need that reassurance and said I would see to it, as she has now for almost a year.'

There wouldn't have been any argument, not in France. Here a wife was to do as told by her husband, no matter what. 'Is Father Marescot in touch with the Stalag?'

'He's in contact with as many as possible. He takes it upon himself as a "special duty," and has fought this battle twice, he says. First during the Great War, and now again.'

A fag was desperately needed, but searching the glove compartment only turned up one stick of ersatz chewing gum. Unwrapping it, Kohler found Annette's hand. 'Orange,' he said. 'It'll help us think. Let's share.'

She had better get the division right, thought Annette. She had better not make a mistake!

'*Merci*, monsieur,' came the faintest of responses with a shudder, but the job had been done perfectly, a good sign.

'In the old days, Inspector—the really old ones—there used to be a special early-morning Mass for those who lived in this district and worked the streets. Father Marescot has insisted on reviving it, but also offers one in the late afternoon for those who can't make the other.'

And are too dog-tired and hung over, but they'd heard of the Mass and had come from all over the city. 'Was he a veteran of that other war?'

'How, then, could he have held his special Masses?'

She had a point but it was freezing in the car. Kohler knew he was tempted to give them everything the press had left in the backseat but mustn't. Nor could he speak on her behalf to that concierge of hers or threaten the bastard. Even at the end of this Occupation, and it would come some day, she could well be accused of consorting with the enemy, though she hadn't done anything of that nature, or had she? 'Those absences of yours from the flat, madame.'

He had remembered. 'Are a private matter, if anything in that building of ours can ever remain private, but are nothing much. I have a part-time job as an usherette in a cinema. I make myself available, you understand, and beholden, yes, by checking in with its manager who thinks he may get more out of me. If there's work, I go there in the evenings, but only until closing at ten. I don't stay a moment beyond that and never have.'

A pittance and only the tips she'd receive. 'Does your husband know of it?'

'If he did, he would order me to stop. He's the provider, isn't he, the one who brings home the money even though the wages he is paid for his work in that camp are in *Lagergeld* and can't be sent home? Annette and I must make do on the thousand francs a month the government of the Maréchal Pétain in Vichy doles out to families like ours.'

The *Lagergeld* was less than a pittance in any case. Common soldiers weren't paid much even when fighting. 'What about *Ciment* Morel?'

'Gaston? He's among the kindest of men and sincerely wants to help.'

'*Papa* used to drive one of the monsieur's big cement lorries,' said Annette, momentarily having parked her chewing gum. 'The monsieur says that it's among the most difficult of jobs and that skilled men like *Papa* are very hard to find and should be sent home. He . . . he has asked for this many times.'

'In 1933 I went to my stepsister, Inspector, and begged Henriette to see if Gaston could give my husband a job. We'd been without for more than two years.'

The Great Depression.

'The Café de la Paix is convenient for both of us, since Gaston must frequently call in at the Kommandantur on business.'

'And the driver of the taxi?'

Take Me. 'Gaston pointed him out long ago and said that if ever I should need anything, I was to go to that one only and he would see that I got it. Inspector, when Madame Guillaumet asked if I knew of a reliable *vélo-taxi* driver, I instinctively pointed him out. We're to help each other, aren't we, us wives of prisoners of war? We're in the same boat and now . . . now are both victims!'

'Don't cry.'

'I will because I must! I have seven stitches in my arm, three in the back of my hand, and will have terrible scars!'

'*Maman* . . .'

'*Chérie*, you are all I have!'

A moment was needed. Kohler knew there was absolutely nothing he could offer. Cash would only raise eyebrows, but as sure as they were sitting here and he was feeling utterly useless, Denise Rouget, their social worker, must have brought the two women together.

'Until yesterday I didn't even know of Madame Guillaumet, Inspector, or that the wives of some of the officers who were in the camps could be having the same difficulties as myself.'

'Did she tell you why she needed that taxi to pick her up after school?'

'Only that she had to go somewhere. One doesn't ask of such things, isn't that so? Instinctively one understands the need for privacy and doesn't condemn.'

They came through the pitch-darkness and the rain of the rue Laurence Savart. St-Cyr could hear them as he got out of the Citroën. They knew this street he loved, didn't even need a single light.

'*Monsieur l'Inspecteur,* a moment, *s'il vous plaît.*'

The caller was Antoine Courbet's mother. 'Madame, please don't get drenched. Quickly, quickly, inside the house.'

Last to enter was Hervé Desrochers's father, Lucien or Luc, who stopped him in the darkness of the tiny foyer. 'A moment, Inspector. The one whose *vélo-taxi* was stolen has sublet mine for the evening so that I could be present to tell you about my Hervé. He's a good boy, you understand, but a bit of a follower. Those other boys, that Antoine . . .'

'Yes, yes. Later, I think, after I've heard from them.'

The St-Cyrs had always felt themselves better. This one was no different, thought Desrochers as they crowded into the kitchen. The vacuum flask of soup was opened by that tongue, Madame Courbet. A plate and spoon were produced, the woman knowing the house and having free run of it, a napkin smoothed and *two* chunks of the grey National set beside it.

'Sit, please, Inspector,' he interjected quickly. 'First the soup and the bread, as we have all agreed, and then the . . .'

'The confessions,' countered Jeanne Courbet, daring him to say another word in his son's defence.

They stood and watched from the other side of the table. They dripped water on the floor, but wasn't that what kitchen floors were for, and Madame Courbet would see to it anyway.

The soup, a purée of leeks and potatoes—how had they managed them?—was not only excellent but exactly what he needed. Each family would have contributed an equal share. Madame Courbet would have seen to that. A powerhouse.

Not until the flask was drained and the plate wiped clean with the last morsel of bread, would he let the proceedings of this little court begin.

Judge, lawyer for the defence, the plaintiffs, too, and the prosecution's attorney were all present, but a court secretary was needed to read out the indictment, a jury too, of course, though that could be dispensed with. 'Madame, would you . . .' he hazarded, setting the spoon aside at last.

'Inspector, first the *évidence*.'

A practical woman who was really worried and with good reason. Go on, she motioned to her son. 'You first,' she whispered.

One by one they would approach the bench. Drained of tears, Antoine's expression was that of the condemned who knew only that the blade awaited. Item by item, and there were several of these, the boy laid out his share of the loot. The torn half of a ticket to the UFA Palast, a room key, a cigarette case, a half-empty packet of Kamels—would temptation gnaw at this judge? wondered St-Cyr.

Lastly, at a severe nudge, Antoine unfolded a newspaper advertisement, torn from *Paris-Soir*. It was one of Hermann's many appeals for help in locating Oona's children.

Monsieur Louis lifted gravely troubled, questioning eyes to her—he couldn't help doing so, Jeanne Courbet knew—but he said nothing as he fingered that clipping, wondering as she had and still did, why this German girl had had it in her handbag. 'Antoine, he and the others, didn't tear it from the newspaper, Monsieur Louis.'

A nod would be best, but Luc Desrochers was watching him closely. Behind the mask of worry there was the light of temptation in Hervé's *papa*. Could the document be used to his son's advantage and that of the family? These days nothing was sacred.

'Fräulein Sonja Remer,' said the judge he had become. 'The name is on her clothing card.' He mustn't hesitate, mustn't be struck down by this . . . this scrap of newsprint. Not yet, but Rudi Sturmbacher had told them to find and return the girl's handbag complete with its contents or face the consequences. He'd have to tell them something, couldn't avoid it.

The look he gave would never leave them, Dédé knew. It was like that of a priest before the condemned.

'*Mes chers amis*, she is an employee of the SS on the avenue Foch, a secretary, a *Blitzmädel*, one of the grey mice.'

Had God deserted them entirely? cried Jeanne Courbet silently but wouldn't let tears fall. She wouldn't!

When they did, Monsieur Louis looked not at her but at each of the boys and then at Hervé's *papa*.

It was that one, Jeanne knew, who said, 'Hervé, please return to the inspector your share.' To give the knave credit, his voice was that of one before the firing squad.

'Yes, Papa,' came the faintest of responses but Hervé couldn't find the courage to look at the inspector. 'Forgive me, Monsieur Louis. It . . . it was my idea to steal the German lady's handbag. I . . . I persuaded the others. I know we have all let you down terribly and that you will never kick the soccer ball back to us again but . . . but will let it roll down the street to where it will be stolen by the other boys or flattened by a German lorry!'

There was no money. There were no stale cigarettes or spent condoms. There was only one thing and when he saw it, Monsieur Louis lost all colour, the throat constricting tightly, he letting escape a breath of despair before silencing himself.

The barrel was shiny and grey, the grip mat black—of Bakelite? wondered this judge he'd become. Not crosshatched as most were, but with parallel ridges closely set and extending the length of the butt.

A date was clearly stamped 1936, the weapon's number: 20524.

'A star,' he said and there was a depth of sadness to him that couldn't be plumbed. 'Russian,' he went on, the detective in him taking over. 'A Red Army Tokarev TT-33, 7.62 mm semiautomatic. The TT stands for Tula Tokarev, Tula being a city to the south of Moscow that's known for its artisans, the designer's name Fedor Tokarev, but this gun's history goes back well beyond 1930 when it was first produced. You see, the Russians and their czar bought up lots of Mauser pistols from the Germans before the Great War, and far more ammunition than was needed.'

He paused. He gave the weapon the look of one whose life was lost.

'So much ammunition that they then found they had to have pistols and submachine guns of their own just to use up the leftover cartridges. The 7.62 and the 7.63 of the Mauser are interchangeable, the TT-33 being adopted by the Red Army in 1933.'

He touched that thing. He said, 'This isn't a lady's gun. The recoil, the kick, is similar to that of a much larger calibre weapon—the American Colt .45 perhaps—and as a result, it's not a comfortable gun, especially for a woman.'

The question of why she, a mere secretary had it, was written all over him. 'The boys didn't disarm it, Inspector,' said Luc Desrochers. 'I did when I discovered it in Hervé's school briefcase.'

Out from a clenched fist tumbled the cartridges, all eight of them, and then the broken words from the son. 'There . . . there wasn't one up the spout.'

'Good. The Russians are often quick to action, so this thing doesn't have a safety, beyond that of the half-cock.'

The Parc Monceau was utterly dark. Elsewhere bicycles and bicycle-taxis were about, pedestrians too, but if he stopped someone to ask directions, Kohler knew they would only send him on a wild goose chase. That social worker, Denise Rouget, lived at home with her parents and he had to talk to her, but where was home?

Ach, he'd best get out and walk but would he be able to find the car afterwards? 'Hey, you. *HALT! IHRE PAPIERE, DUMMKOPF. SCHNELL!*'

He grabbed the bike. The *vélo-taxi* jerked and skidded to a stop. The street became deserted, its scurrying little blue lights and cigarettes vanishing. 'Look, guide me to this address and I'll let you go.'

A light came on to read the scribbled page of this one's notebook. 'The judge?' asked Didier Valois, owner-operator of the *maréchal*'s Baton, taxi number 43.75 Butte-Montmartre.

'What judge?'

Did this one not realize who he was about to arrest—was the judge to be arrested? wondered Valois. *Ah, merde,* the loss of the fares, the late nights and carting that one home well after curfew, but an end to the monster—was that it, eh? '*Monsieur le juge* Rouget.'

Oh-oh. 'Judge of what?'

'*Président du Tribunal spécial du département de la Seine.*'

Hercule the Smasher, the Widow Maker's Companion, Vichy's top judge and hatchet man in Paris. Not only did he preside over some of the trials of black-market violators and send the little guys, never the big boys, off to the Reich and into forced labour or to the Santé or Fresnes prisons, he presided over the night-action courts, those in which the 'terrorists,' as Vichy and the Occupier were wont to call them, were tried and convicted. The Résistance hated him and he was as stark a son of a bitch as Vichy could have found. Arrogant, Louis would have said in warning. Positive the police were incompetent and not doing enough. Quick to make up his mind and quicker still to take offence. Suspicious and with a mind that forgot nothing, even that this Kripo protected and cohabited with a Dutch alien whose dead husband was Jewish and whose papers weren't good, but who also lived with a former prostitute who was far less than half his age!

Louis must have known who Denise Rouget's father was but hadn't said—had he really been too busy to think of it at the Drouant or even at Chez Rudi's, or had he hoped and prayed it would simply go away and they wouldn't have to deal with the bastard?

5

The judge was far from happy. Even from a foyer where oil paintings worth a fortune could easily have been snatched in a smash-and-grab, the hiss of his voice was clear from beyond closed doors.

What do you mean, 'There's a Gestapo detective asking to interview my daughter'?

The reply from the maid of all work could not be heard, though Kohler strained to listen.

Denise, what is this, please?

Again nothing could be heard, even from the daughter.

How dare the couillon *invade the sanctity of my home? I'll show the* salaud! *Out of my way, Denise. Out, I tell you!*

Papa . . .

Don't you dare stand in my way!

The Roman statuettes and vase of white silk lilies on the Louis XVI gilded entry table vibrated. The carpet beneath leaking boots was a Savonnerie . . .

'Inspector, how dare you come here like this without an appointment? I'm speaking to Karl Oberg about this. I'm speaking to Walter Boemelburg and to Ernst von Schaumburg. I will *not* have my privacy invaded!'

A tornado. 'Kohler, *Monsieur le Juge.* Kripo, Paris-Central, here on orders from that very Kommandant von Gross-Paris.'

'WHAT?'

'You heard me, Judge. That daughter of yours arranged for two of last night's victims to meet beforehand at the Café de la Paix. As far as I can determine she didn't join them, but since she may well have been involved in what subsequently happened, there are things I need to ask her.'

'Involved? That's preposterous. What things?'

'Things like, How did she know Madame Barrault was even familiar with the café, seeing as the woman hasn't any money to spare and works the odd evening as an usherette?'

'The slut should not be working. She's a wife and mother with an eight-year-old daughter!'

'*Papa . . .*'

'Denise, did I *not* tell you to let me handle this?'

'Your daughter's their social worker, Judge.'

'And are not all such matters held in the strictest confidence?'

Liebe Zeit, was he going to have to threaten the bastard? 'Look, it's only routine.'

'No, you look. The wives and fiancées of our prisoners of war are playing around like rabbits in heat. The one asks for a taxi driver she can trust to pick her up *after* lessons; the other dines at the Drouant with Monsieur and Madame Morel and at Morel's insistence? The Opéra for one so poor? The Drouant? Both attacks have to suggest the obvious.'

'Judge . . .'

'Gaston Morel is known to take his mistresses where and when he can find them and they can't give trouble even if he flaunts them in front of that wife of his, but if I must tell you this, the epidemic has become a plague. Our dear boys in the prisoner-of-war camps in the Reich, necessary as those are, do *not* have the pleasures of using their wives. Others do!'

'*Papa,* your heart.'

'Fuck my heart! Disappear. You are *not* to talk to this one!'

'Then let me ring up Gestapo Boemelburg's office, Judge. You've a telephone—men in positions such as yours have to have one, rare though they are. Let's let the Gestapo's Listeners know

I'm here and wanting to question your daughter on a police matter.'

The *salaud*! 'How dare you?'

'You leave me no other choice.'

'*Papa,* the fewer who know of my involvement, the better.'

'Hercule, Hercule,' interjected Madame Rouget. 'Denise is right. Be your gracious self. I know you've had a very trying day and desperately need a rest. Brigitte, don't stand there looking stupid. Take the inspector's things and put them to dry in the kitchen by the stove then bring some coffee and cognac. The Vieille Reserve . . . no, no, the Louis XIII. The Rémy-Martin and the cigars. Yes, yes, those too. The El Rey del Mundo Choix Supreme.'

An angel, but that very cognac and those cigars had been encountered in Vichy but a week ago. The Maréchal Pétain himself had enjoyed that brand of cigar and still did but that could only mean the gossip was circulating and Madame Rouget would put it to good use if necessary, and had let him know.

Louis should have heard it.

Road Racer, Boot Saver, Comfort's Partner, the *vélo-taxis* waited in the rain and darkness outside the Café de la Paix. The last of the charcoal smoke from the outdoor braziers brought faint thoughts of warmth and dryness that couldn't be dwelt on. 'A Tokarev,' St-Cyr heard himself grimly mutter as he searched the darkness for the little light he needed. 'A TT-33. There can only be one reason why this Sonja Remer could have had it in her handbag.'

Last Sunday the woman had taken a decided interest in the Parc des Buttes Chaumont's carousel and had asked its operator about a certain two detectives and a murder there in December. She had had a clipping of Hermann's advertisement in her handbag, must have been told of Oona and Giselle, would know of the home address, had kept the pistol loaded.

An assassin? he had to ask. A girl? A *Blitzmädel* they would never have suspected?

The boys had overheard her asking the carousel's operator if

Hermann always kept their guns until needed and if this chief inspector had a girlfriend who was the chanteuse at the Club Mirage. Gabrielle would have to be warned.

The boys had held a little conference and then had followed this Sonja Remer. She had gone into the toilets at the restaurant. Guy Vachon, having lost at straws, had snatched the handbag. She had shrieked and cried out, had chased them, but they had run to the carousel, had passed the bag from hand to hand, vanishing into the park as delinquent boys will who know their territory.

'And now?' he had to ask. 'Now we must solve the matter or face the consequences.' Arms weren't regulation issue for *Blitzmädel*, not unless they had first been assigned a special duty and then trained for it. The Fräulein Remer had spoken French fluently. 'Her accent was good,' Hervé Desrochers had said. 'She wanted to know how well you and Herr Kohler worked together, had heard lots of stories, but wanted to hear it from a Frenchman. The operator of that machine, you know how he is. A mouth like a pipe organ.'

'A storm,' Antoine had said. 'We had to find out who she was, Monsieur Louis.'

'It was intelligence work,' Dédé had added. 'Information you and Herr Kohler would need.' There had been a fully loaded spare clip among the boy's share of the loot, but no time to take the matter further. The handbag had been quickly restuffed and now lay in the Citroën under the front seat with their guns, the car locked, of course, though that in itself was no guarantee against theft and he would absolutely have to find Hermann and quickly.

'There was a chocolate bar,' Dédé had added, 'and . . . and a small tin of *bonbons à la menthe* from the Abbaye de Flavigny. These, they are missing.'

And hadn't there been an explosion of juvenile delinquency? Hadn't the number of serious cases before the courts tripled since 1939? Didn't Hercule the Smasher preside over the worst of these cases in the département de la Seine? 'Hercule Rouget . . . Ah *merde, merde*, I should have thought of it when questioning that daughter of his but spent the time with Gaston Morel.'

When Luc Desrocher's *vélo-taxi*, the Red Comb of the Magnificent Cock, rolled in, he was ready. 'Monsieur Albert Vasseur? Sûreté. A moment, please.'

'Time is too precious. How the hell am I supposed to pay the evening's rent for this shit box when you people refuse to release my taxi for repairs and claim it is needed evidence?'

'I'll see what can be done.'

'Have I not heard that before?'

'Calm down.'

'Or you will have me arrested? HEY, OO-OO, *MES AMIS*, HELP! It wasn't my fault the taxi was stolen. Georges, tell him. Henri, you too. Martin, you also, and Jacques.'

They had all climbed out from the shelter of their respective cabs, rain or no rain.

'They will vouch for me, Inspector. One pedals and pedals and cannot piss one's trousers, can one?'

There was definite agreement on the matter, tobacco smoke too.

'I came in and hardly made it to the watering trough.'

'You must know how the Germans are for cleanliness, Inspector,' insisted one. 'If they catch us pissing into the boulevard des Capucines, they have a fit and give us three years forced labour in the Reich or the same but of idleness in the Santé.'

'The *vespasienne* is over there in the darkness,' said another. 'Albert, he has . . .'

'Yes, yes. Please let him tell me himself.'

'We're only trying to help,' grumbled one.

'No one asks our opinion,' said another.

'Blackout mugging and rapes are bad for business yet the law refuses to listen. Come on, *mes amis,* let's go.'

'Wait! I'll listen to each of you but first . . .'

'I stepped into the urinal, Inspector, and up to the trough,' said Vasseur. 'I hurried with the buttons, one of which popped off, and there's no light in those damned things anymore, so it's gone forever. Who the hell's going to bomb them anyway, a little pinpoint of light like that and seen from five thousand metres or more? Others came in behind to rub shoulders. *Jésus,* save us, what was

I to have thought on a night like that or this? The weather brings on the flood. The one to my left said it was a bitch; the one to my right sighed with relief.'

'And then?'

'The one on the right finished up. The one to the left took longer but stayed to let me finish and didn't go out the other way as he could have, so I was forced to retreat and went out as I'd come in.'

'With that one right behind you.'

'That is correct. When I got here, the boys were already chasing after my taxi.'

'Height?'

'Both medium.'

'Weight?'

'The first broad-shouldered like a wedge, the second with the gut of a barrel. I had to throw up a hand to stop myself from kissing the metal as he went past me on entering to relieve himself.'

The urinal's walls were concentric shells with standing room only between. 'Those two sandwiched you.'

'It's possible.'

Hermann, if he could, would always share his cigarettes at times like this, but there were none. 'The accent of the man with the gut?'

'The Butte.'

Montmartre. 'Anything else?'

'The smell of sardines. I'm sure of this.'

Even so, it would have to be said. 'Those urinals reek.'

'Of course, and I can't understand why I should have smelled such a meal. Perhaps it was simply because I was hungry. It's been years since I've had any.'

'Inspector, I smelled them too,' interjected one of the others. 'The son of a bitch who stole the taxi shoved me out of the way. I slipped as I grabbed him. I struggled to get up and he clobbered me. Hands . . . He had big hands, this much I do know also.'

'*Oui, oui,* but sardines . . . ? Could it have been Norwegian fish-oil margarine?'

'To keep out the rain?' exclaimed another. 'He'd have needed more than the tickets give.'

Considered muttering followed, then passive agreement. 'Oilskins and old ones, Inspector. Grease on the shoulders, upper arms and hat, but, of course, a supply,' said the one who had been shoved.

'*Ah, bon,* now we're getting somewhere but, M. Vasseur, how did they know you would return here and not go directly to the École Centrale to pick up Madame Guillaumet?'

'Tell him, Albert,' said one of the others. 'You're going to have to.'

'Earlier I'd picked up a fare here. He asked to be taken to the intersection of the rue Réaumur and the boulevard de Sébastopol . . .'

'And all but to the *passage* de la Trinité and close enough to the École Centrale.'

This Sûreté had understood. 'But when we got there, he changed his mind and asked to be brought back.'

The timing then; three men also. 'And that one? Come, come, remember.'

'How am I to do so? They come out of that café full of food and wine and smoking good cigars or cigarettes, and they shout, "Hey, you. Taxi," as if they owned the world and had the right to order people around. Do you know where my beautiful Peugeot 301 is? A 1933 and cared for like a baby? They took her away in July of 1940, and when they discovered she had a thirst, brought her back minus the tyres and battery!'

A cigarette was offered in sympathy, a drag being inhaled and then another. 'I took him where he wanted to go, Inspector. That's my job, isn't it?'

'Of course, but didn't he ask how much the fare would be?'

'Like most of them here, he couldn't have cared less, even though he was French, and if you know anything, you will know what I mean by that.'

'Tall or not?'

'Not so tall that he reached the clouds like the one in London.'

Général Charles de Gaulle. 'The accent?'

'A *bac*.'

The *baccalauréat* and entrance to higher education.

'A former military man, perhaps. These days the mothballs shouldn't try to roll around so much in the armoire they get in the road of the mice and disturb them.'

The Résistance invariably wanted no part of such officers who, now that the war was turning, increasingly wanted to command them.

'Though it was dark, Inspector, I could see that he stood like a soldier,' said Vasseur.

'Was he wearing his French army greatcoat and cap? You'd have smelled the wool.'

'And the aftershave and tobacco, but he had asked me to hurry, and by the time we reached the intersection, I was worn out.'

'One can't argue with such, Inspector,' said one of the others. 'His boots, Albert. Tell him.'

'Were hobnailed. What else would one have expected?'

'And?'

'The red ribbon,' admitted Vasseur. 'When one sees it, one obeys, isn't that so?'

'You shone your light at him?'

'Briefly, but not in the face. The ribbon stopped me from lifting the light further and when he asked me to bring him right back here, I didn't argue.'

'The times, please, as close as possible?'

'Times?' arched Vasseur. 'I don't have a watch. I had to sell it to one of our "friends" to make ends meet.'

'Then how could you possibly have known how to be on time when picking up Madame Guillaumet at that school?'

'I ask others. I have to. I asked him too. We got back here at seven thirty-eight.'

Leaving lots of time for the urinal and the first of the others to steal the taxi and get to the École Centrale, but not enough for the one with the red ribbon to reach the police academy unless he had had a car and therefore friends in high places. 'Where did Madame Guillaumet arrange for you to take her?'

This Sûreté wasn't going to like the answer. 'Fifteen place Vendôme.'

'The Ritz?'

Was it so surprising, given what many of the wives of prisoners of war were doing, even those of officers? 'It has no other address, has it?'

One of several homes away from home for visiting generals and others of high rank from the Reich. 'Were you to have waited there for her?'

There would have been plenty of other taxis she could have taken after her little liaison, but this one must know the stepsister of Gaston Morel's wife had sent the woman to him and that he would have had to wait. ' "The half-hour, the three-quarters of an hour," she said. She didn't know exactly how long it would take, but felt not too long. She was worried about leaving her children alone at home and said, "I've never done anything like this before."'

But had she? Didn't the wife who was having an illicit love affair often worry about her children? wondered St-Cyr. His wife had, his Marianne.

Hermann wasn't going to like what had turned up but where was he?

The judge was still not happy, the rise in blackout crime due entirely to the ineptitude of the police and a total lack of moral fibre among the citizenry in the face of hard times. The salon and adjoining study, however, were draped in the tassels of a cushioned *fin de siècle*.

'Delinquents, Kohler,' he went on. 'Girls as young as thirteen.' He gave the daughter a stern glance. 'Boys of ten. Not a week ago the savage mugging of a *Blitzmädel* in the Parc des Buttes Chaumont. Four of them attacked her. While the one shoved her back on to the toilet, another snatched her cap away, another the handbag, the last one darting in to pummel her breasts and yank her hair. Bruises, I tell you. Bruises, Kohler.'

Mein Gott, Rudi hadn't been the only one to know of it!

' "Boche pig," they shouted,' continued Rouget. ' "Fascist scum! Communist-killer! Go home where you belong." '

He'd take a breath now, decided Rouget. He'd show this Kripo how lawless the city had become. 'I ask you, Kohler. What, please, would you do if you were me, when these boys were brought before you? Understand that when cornered, one of them brandished a knife.'

Louis's boys . . . The cognac, normally long in its breath, burned the throat, the Choix Supreme offering no comfort. The judge, wife and daughter were all watching him closely. Madame Rouget—Vivienne, he reminded himself—having taken command of things had suddenly lost it with the judge's opening barrage and now sat so tensely, she was unaware of constantly picking at her fingernails, the daughter sitting like a harried little mouse, but something would have to be said. 'Judge, my partner and I haven't yet been briefed on the assault. We've been kept busy ever since we got in last night.'

'We'll come to that.'

'Was this *Blitzmädel* able to give the investigating police accurate descriptions of the boys?'

Had it been a plea for extenuating circumstances? 'Surely you must be aware, Kohler, that in such cases everything happens far too quickly. The girl was in shock—*mon Dieu,* who wouldn't have been? Her stockings were ruined.'

'Yes, but . . .'

Was it clemency Kohler wanted? 'They will be caught. They will definitely be brought before me along with their parents. Communists, are they? The Höherer-SS and Polizeiführer Karl Oberg is insisting on the severest of sentences and will expect it of me. A uniform has been disgraced. It's no small matter.'

Uniforms were sacred and, yes, Oberg did have designs on taking over the French police, but . . . 'Judge, just how sure are you that the girl was threatened with a knife?'

'Very. Two days ago I was in Karl's office to discuss another matter. He had the girl brought in to tell me herself. He's being considerate, I must say, and doesn't want the case publicized until it's settled. Now what, exactly, was it that you wanted to ask my daughter?'

'Yes, please do ask,' breathed Vivienne.

Whereas the judge was corpulent and big-boned, the wife was delicate and definitely one of *les hautes*, yet defiantly wary and absolutely under that one's thumb—was that it, eh? The soft auburn hair was worn swept up and back. The eyebrows were perfect, the eyes not mud-brown like the judge's but azure, the lips tight as a quick breath was impatiently held, the chin defiant under a scrutiny she didn't appreciate.

'Inspector, I asked you to tell us,' she said.

'*Ah, bon*, madame. For some reason your daughter, having arranged for two of last night's victims to meet in the afternoon at the Café de la Paix, chose not to be present. I'd like to know why.'

Had Hercule not put him in his place? wondered Vivienne. 'There was no reason for her to have been present. Madame Guillaumet needed a *vélo-taxi* driver she could depend on; Madame Barrault knew of such a one.'

But was it as simple as that?

The judge, as if deliberating in court, had bowed his head to study knitted hands that could well have been those of a plumber. The double chin and jowls drooped, the forehead was wide and high, the jet-black, greying hair well oiled and combed back to frame the grimmest of countenances, the full lips drawn into a pout, the eyes half-closed, so deep was he in thought and waiting for detective questions.

'Madame, how was it that your daughter even *knew* Madame Barrault would be familiar with that café or know of the taxi driver?'

'Henriette . . .' began the daughter, like a frightened little mouse.

'Denise, let me,' said the mother firmly. 'Madame Henriette Morel has many times informed my daughter of that woman's "familiarity" with the café, Inspector, and the company that stepsister of hers chooses to keep. It seemed the most suitable of rendezvous.

Denise merely put forward the suggestion to both women during each of their respective counselling interviews.'

'I'm with the SN, Inspector. I'm . . .'

'Denise, offer nothing. Your mother is before the bench.'

'*Papa* . . .'

'Daughter, hold your tongue.'

'Hercule, *please*,' said Vivienne. 'I must be allowed to continue. Denise has advanced degrees in social work, Inspector, and is employed by the Famille du Prisonnier, which is now under the Secours National, the National Help, whose Maison du Prisonnier is on *place* Clichy.'

The *maisons*, though few and far between, were one of those rare places where the wives of prisoners of war could go for help they invariably wouldn't get, but what the hell was bothering this little family other than the immediate presence of an uninvited Kripo?

'I have my office there, Inspector. Madame Morel drops in from time to time.'

'She makes a nuisance of herself and is not of our class,' said the mother, raising a forefinger to silence the daughter. 'Her stepsister is a good twenty years younger and quite naturally the woman is concerned.'

'Marie-Léon Barrault hasn't been sleeping well,' offered the daughter stubbornly.

'Worried about her husband, is she?'

Would Herr Kohler really understand? wondered Denise. 'They all are. Certainly those who have been . . .'

'Running around?'

'Denise, did I not instruct you?' demanded the judge.

'Judge, leave it,' said Kohler with a sigh, and then . . .

Vivienne waited.

'Just how certain are you, mademoiselle, that Madame Barrault and Madame Guillaumet were really up to mischief behind their husbands' backs?'

'Denise thinks . . .'

'Let her answer, madame. You, too, Judge.'

'Adultery is a very serious crime, Kohler, for which the *maréchal* and our government in Vichy have seen fit to strengthen the law.'

They had done so in 1942 and had made it stiff for the delinquent wife, not nearly so for the husband even if he wasn't away on holiday in the Reich, but would nothing shut the judge up?

'Please do not forget that there are more than one-and-a-half million of our boys in your prisoner-of-war camps, Kohler. Fully sixty percent of them are married; most between the ages of twenty and forty, so their wives are also young but have urges they can't seem to control.'

'Urges . . .' muttered Vivienne, only to silence herself.

'Forty percent of them have children,' managed the daughter timidly. 'Sometimes six, sometimes as many as ten. Madame Guillaumet . . .'

'In the département de la Seine alone, Kohler, the number of *clandestines* on the streets has tripled to nearly six thousand. Oh for sure there are the card-carrying *putains* as well, about four thousand. The figures vary from day to day.'

'But not the demand, Judge?' There were at *least* ten thousand streetwalkers in Paris alone, to say nothing of the girls in the legalized brothels.

'Kohler, this interview is over.'

'Not yet. And Madame Guillaumet, mademoiselle? You were about to enlighten me.'

Papa was going to be very angry, *Maman* not happy with her response, but Herr Kohler and his French partner had found the woman and must have seen what had happened to her. 'I'm not really certain about her, Inspector. Though there has been some evidence, I would like more before judging her so harshly, but with Madame Barrault . . . Henriette—that is, Madame Morel—is certain her stepsister and her husband are having an affair.'

There, the disgraceful filth was finely out, sighed Vivienne inwardly, but had Herr Kohler been convinced of it?

'Many times Madame Morel has spoken to me of her concerns, Inspector,' went on the daughter, having gained a little self-confidence. 'I really had no other choice but to look into the matter and did so.'

'*Ah, bon*, and how was that looking-into done?'

'Denise had the woman followed,' grunted Rouget.

And wouldn't you know it. 'That can't be in the mandate of the Famille du Prisonniers's social workers, Judge. Who paid for the *détective privé*? I assume one was engaged?'

'Madame Morel,' managed the daughter. 'Cost, it . . . it was no object.'

And wouldn't you know that too. 'And the recipients of this largesse?'

'Kohler, this has gone far enough. My daughter has done nothing wrong. She has only acted in the best interests of a wife who is being subjected constantly to the infidelities of a husband who should know better.'

'Be that as it may, Judge, just let your daughter answer.'

'Or you will attempt to take her in for questioning?'

'You said it, I didn't.'

He would have to be told, decided Vivienne, but it had best come from herself. 'The Agence Vidocq de Recherches Privées, Inspector. A Monsieur Flavien Garnier, but only after repeated offences and at the insistence of Henriette Morel.'

Vidocq, a convicted criminal among other things, had been the first to head up the forerunner of the Paris Sûreté, itself preceding the Police Judiciaire, the criminal investigative branch. An arch blabbermouth, he had then founded the first agency of private detectives and had published his memoirs and made a fortune. In 1840 he had moved his agency to the Second Arrondissement and near the Bourse and the Bank of France, and not far from the Opéra, and into posh headquarters in, yes, the Galerie Vivienne, and if that wasn't a coincidence, what was?

'And the address of this agency now?' he asked.

Should she pause and bait him with the silence? wondered Vivienne, especially as it was another coincidence, he having digested the first of them. 'The Arcade de le Champs-Élysées.'

The Lido had an entrance off that arcade and hadn't the press blabbed on and on about a call having been made from there about a murder at the police academy, and hadn't Madame Rouget known all about it?

'M. Garnier has often seen Madame Barrault leave the table first at the Café de la Paix, Inspector,' said the daughter, her voice one hell of a lot firmer now that the news was out. 'She doesn't always go home, you understand, but often into the Hôtel Grand to take the lift.'

'Gaston Morel then pays their bill and follows,' added the mother tightly. 'Time and again it's the prisoner-of-war wives who are conducting themselves in such a shameful and disgustingly unclean manner, Inspector. Madame Morel had every right to be alerted and have the proof of it. Disease is rife, is it not? Disease!'

'Vivienne, control yourself. Denise had no other choice but to inform the woman that her suspicions had been verified, Kohler. Far too many of these prisoner-of-war wives don't just need lessons in how to care for themselves and their families and manage the finances while their husbands are absent. They need a damned good lesson in morals and should have their heads shorn and breasts bared in public. Madame Barrault has told you she works the odd night as an usherette, but has she also admitted to having stayed well after closing not on one or two such occasions, but on at least three?'

And so much for a social worker's sense of confidentiality.

Denise would have to be spared the embarrassment but one had best be positive about it, thought Vivienne. 'The regular usherettes have informed M. Garnier that the woman is most definitely having sexual relations with the manager of that cinema, Inspector. They have caught the two of them at it in his office and even up on the stage behind closed curtains!'

But when the lights were down and after hours. 'The cinema?'

Had Herr Kohler not believed her? 'The Impérial.'

On the boulevard des Italiens and right around the corner from Madame Barrault's flat.

'Father Marescot, the priest of the Notre-Dame de Lorette,' said

Vivienne, 'has sent a letter of complaint to the Scapini commission in Berlin.'

That organization, the Service diplomatique de prisonniers de guerre, first received all such complaints. The names of those judged serious enough by the Vichy government's Berlin office were then forwarded to the Kommandant of each husband's prisoner-of-war camp, who then called the poor bastard in to let him know what was going on at home.

'Father Marescot is worried about Madame Barrault,' said Denise uncomfortably. 'In no uncertain terms he has told our *détective privé* that she is just like the others.'

Louis would say it never snows but it rains. 'I'd best find my partner then, hadn't I, Judge?'

'Do finish your cognac, Inspector. You've hardly touched it. Take the cigar. It must be cold outside,' said Vivienne, having retreated into herself already. 'I hate the cold. It makes me feel as though I were poor and didn't deserve a fire.'

At 8.40 p.m. the old time, 9.40 the new, the rue Saint-Dominique was pitch-dark. One found direction purely from memory, St-Cyr knew, the silhouettes of the buildings having been lost entirely to the downpour, and when he reached the little square with its delightful Fountain of Mars still unseen, he drew the Citroën in beside it. The *quartier* had, for the last century and more, been definitely an entrenchment of an educated upper middle class. Though virtually nothing could be discerned, the arcaded walks of the surrounding buildings would have arched entrances, the first-storey balconies, their Louis Philippe ironwork railings.

The building at number 131 was heated and that could only mean that at least one of the Occupier had taken up residence.

'Monsieur, what is it you desire at this hour?'

There were concierges and concierges and this one with the reading glasses and volume of Proust was not only well dressed and well read but a war widow from the 1914–1918 conflict. '*Ah, bon*, madame. The Guillaumet residence. Sûreté.'

'Inspector, what is going on? The other tenants . . . There have been complaints. Madame Guillaumet has done nothing here to bring offence. There have been no visitors, no such men friends, you understand, none that I have seen and I assure you I would have, but . . .'

'But what?'

'Some of the tenants are demanding that I serve her a notice of eviction, others that it is not right for us to be having detectives coming here at all hours asking questions about her.'

'What detective? What questions?'

'The other one from the Sûreté.'

'What one?'

'The one with the heavy black-rimmed eyeglasses, the Hitler moustache and the new fedora and overcoat. The one who constantly smokes a pipe, "His little friend." I didn't ask to see his ID. I . . .'

'Just answered him?'

'*Oui.* One has to, doesn't one?'

'And?'

'Four times he has been here. The first, a month ago, then two weeks later, then a week more and . . . and lastly three days ago.'

On Tuesday, then. 'And did you reveal this to Madame Guillaumet?'

She would shake her head, Francine Ouellette decided. She would tell this one exactly how it had been for he looked far more trustworthy. 'Each time I've told him I have seen nothing to condemn Madame Guillaumet in the eyes of God or anyone else. Her life is her own, is that not so? Who am I to question what she does away from here? I checked on the children when she went to her teaching job, but always refused to take payment, since at present she has none to spare, but . . .' She would shrug now. 'What else is one to do?'

But make allowances.

'Inspector, has Adrienne died? What, please, is to become of Henri and Louisette? The father's parents won't take them in. His was a marriage of which they didn't approve and now they've been making her life very difficult, since the son's wages go to them, not to her.'

'She's holding on. I saw her only a few hours ago.'

'But did she speak? Did she describe the one who did that to her?'

'Not yet. Look, has my partner, Herr Kohler, been in?'

'Not today or tonight. The girl named Giselle has gone out, though, and has not yet returned. The other one—Madame Oona Van der Lynn—is alarmed, you understand, and rightly so, what with these . . . these criminals still at large and the curfew nearly upon us and always threatening to be moved ahead without notice. The girl will become lost, Madame Van der Lynn has said, if she tries to find her way back here in the dark. She doesn't know this *quartier* or any other than the one in which they live.'

The quartier Saint-Germain-des-Prés. Though they seldom if ever did, and he had never heard them do so, it had to be asked. 'Did they argue down here in the foyer?'

'And in the lift. The one named Giselle . . .'

'Mademoiselle le Roy.'

'*Oui, oui.* That one has said she could no longer stand being cooped up and that she was going to find Herr Kohler and tell him what he'd done. It's a tragedy, is it not, Inspector? Madame Guillaumet at death's door and Madame Van der Lynn finding not just two children of the same ages as her own would have been but *exactement* a boy and then a girl? I have heard them comforting her. Shouldn't it be the other way around, or has God forsaken us all?'

The Line 3 métro entrance at *place* Malesherbes had been permanently closed just like every other alternate station to save on the power. Bicycle taxi, licence 43.75 RP18, the maréchal's bloody Baton, couldn't have been spending the night picking up fares here. *Ach*, where was he to be found? wondered Kohler. Pedestrians blindly felt their way through the rain, narrowly colliding with him. Other taxis squeaked past, heading up the boulevard

Malesherbes to the Wagram entrance at *place* du Brésil and not that far: eight hundred metres, maybe a thousand but on a night like this and without a torch?

He'd have to do it, would have to leave the Ford where he'd left it back on the rue Henri Rochefort, mustn't terrify anyone. Denise Rouget had said she'd not been certain the Trinité victim had been fooling around, though there'd been 'some evidence,' and that could only mean she'd had the woman followed.

So how was it, please, that a social worker had not only known where to look for a firm of private detectives but had hired one that was right next to the Lido? Vivienne Rouget had been far too uptight, even to letting him know in advance that she had heard the Vichy gossip about Louis and himself and would use it if necessary.

When Didier Valois pulled in to the stand outside the Wagram entrance, several clamoured to hire him, but only one person succeeded. 'Inspector . . .'

'Take me back to my car. I must have lost my way.'

The door to the Guillaumet flat was answered, hope registering and then dismay. They'd been expecting Giselle and, like children the world over whose hopes have been dashed, their expressions fell as they thought the worst.

'Jean-Louis . . .'

'Oona, I'm not here about Giselle.' The eyes were red and swollen, the fair cheeks pale and strained. There was none of that calmness one had come to expect of her, none of that willingness to accept things, hard though they were. Hermann's unthinking act of getting her to look after the Trinité victim's children hadn't been good. 'We'll find her, I promise. These must be Henri and Louisette?'

A slim, warm hand was taken and formally shaken, man to man, the boy tall for his age, the dark brown hair still curly but newly trimmed—Giselle would have done that. The eyes were brown but not so large or deep as the sister's, harder, more instantly accusative—those of the father? he had to ask. Each child was different, exactly themselves of course, and yet . . . and yet he knew with a certainty he couldn't understand that the girl must be more like the mother. Their faces were pinched and drawn, they, too, fighting back the tears even as Oona, tall, willowy, blonde, blue-eyed and everything Hermann would need in a woman had he but the sense to see it, fought for control to softly say, 'It's as I have thought. Giselle has stayed the night at the house of friends. She must have.'

The House of Madame Chabot on the rue Danton.

'Or at the flat on the rue Suger which is just around the corner,' said Henri gravely. 'Are you really a chief inspector?'

'I'm even armed. This is my gun, this one, that of my partner.'

'And that?' asked Oona tensely of the glossy black, regulation-issue handbag under his arm.

'A little something for Hermann to return to Rudi Sturmbacher as soon as possible.'

They didn't ask further and that was a good sign. Louisette hesitantly took his fedora, Henri more assuredly the overcoat and overshoes, Oona the handbag, she mastering the shock of its weight and knowing only too well what it must contain.

'The kitchen,' she said, 'or would you prefer our room?'

'Our *petit salon,*' said Henri.

'Our very own,' said Louisette, whose hair brushed her shoulders every time she tossed her head. '*Maman* has helped us with it, you understand, *Monsieur l'Inspecteur principal.* There it is warm and there we are allowed to keep the things we love and to have adventures.'

'Then that's where we'd best go,' St-Cyr heard himself saying. *Merde,* was he, too, about to burst into tears?

'*Maman* would not have done what they are saying in the papers or on the stairs and in the halls at school,' said the boy.

'She didn't need to be punished,' Louisette added with, she felt, the necessary amount of severity. 'She is a good woman, *Monsieur l'Inspecteur principal,* not a bad one. A tramp!'

'A slut,' muttered Henri. 'A *paillasse*!'

'Henri, Louisette, *mes chers*, make the inspector some tea, please. The camomile . . . do you think that would suit him best?'

'*Et pour toi?*' asked the boy, using the familiar.

'*Moi aussi, merci.*'

'But first our *salon*,' said Louisette. 'Our very own place of magic.'

The room was all of that and more. A clutter of flea-market gleanings, paintings and drawings by the resident artists, a puppet theatre *d'après* Guignol, brass urns, candlesticks, mushroom-shaded lamps, carpets, divans and pillows, a library, too, and wireless set.

They watched him closely, the two of them. They saw him tear his gaze from the dial and he heard them sigh with satisfaction and whisper to each other, 'Just like Herr Kohler, he has looked to see if we have been breaking the law and listening to the BBC Free French broadcasts from London or the Voice of America's swing music of Messieurs Goodman, Dorsey and others.'

They had their tea. They apologized for not having tobacco and acknowledged that they knew he preferred his pipe, 'his little friend,' to cigarettes.

Each in their turn said that they were sorry to learn of the loss of his wife and little son. 'And of Herr Kohler's two boys at Stalingrad,' Henri said.

'*Mes amis,* a moment, please. If Hermann and I are to find the one who hurt your mother, I must get to know her better. First, the rest of the flat, and then the desk she keeps—the place where she writes to your father. Photos of her, all such things.'

'Messages?' asked Henri.

'Certainly.'

'There are none,' whispered Louisette darkly. 'She took it with her.'

'It was from one of her students, I think,' said Henri. 'Madame Ouellette, our concierge, gave it to *Maman* last Friday before the lady from the Maison du Prisonnier came to see us.'

'The Mademoiselle Rouget,' said Louisette distastefully. 'The one called Denise.'

'It was sealed, you understand, and *Maman* told us not to say anything of it to that one, and only that it was something she had to do for . . . for us all.'

'Jean-Louis, you must understand that Adrienne—Madame Guillaumet—had had trouble paying the rent. Her in-laws . . .'

'They receive the three-quarters, in total, of *Papa*'s military pay, Inspector,' said Henri, 'but from that deduct nothing for our rent.'

'And give her absolutely nothing for the children or herself, or for the parcels they send to him each month. Her sole source of income has been the two francs a day the government in Vichy provides towards the cost of the parcels and . . .'

'Her pay from teaching,' said Louisette, watching him closely. 'One thousand a month. It is not much, so messages have to be received from time to time, is that not so?'

'Show me the flat. Come on, you two. Help me to build a profile of her.'

They took him from bedroom to bedroom, all but one of which, it appeared, hadn't been in use since before the Defeat. 'We slept with her,' Louisette said. 'She read to us just like Oona does.'

'And the Mademoiselle Giselle,' said Henri, 'but she slept on the floor beside us. It was like camping, she said. She's very beautiful and lots of fun, as . . . as is Oona, of course.'

'Certainly,' said Louisette, taking Oona by the hand to place it fondly against a cheek.

The *salle de séjour*, closed off and never used, not since the husband had gone off to war, appeared just as that one must have wanted it kept: totally undisturbed by the children or the wife, except when dusted. A mastery of Art Deco into which had been fitted several gorgeous pieces of Biedermeier, it had a chaise longue from among the earlier of such pieces: 1825 by the look—Josef Danhauser's workshop in Vienna? St-Cyr wondered. Of walnut, though, not of the South American hardwoods, which had first been used. The British naval blockades during the Napoleonic Wars had forced a return to native woods. A vitrine and matching cabinet were of birch, with a black lacquered ormulo clock and tasseled candlesticks to perfectly set off the latter. The pear-wood fauteuils were from 1845 perhaps, the maple side table and breakfront bookcase also, everything exuding that clear, clean and uncomplicated line so characteristic of the style, and of Art Deco too, the name coming, of course, not from any furniture maker but from Gottlieb Biedermeier, the much-loved character of a novel whose bourgeois opinions were those of his readers, *bieder* meaning honest, worthy, upright or just plain simple.

It was only later that the style, admired at first by the Prussian and Viennese aristocracy, began to be appreciated by the bourgeoisie and no longer thought of as ridiculing them.

In the dining room the Biedermeier was Russian and of birch wood, the room exquisite but also off-limits and kept closed. Had she been a prisoner of this husband of hers? he had to wonder but couldn't ask, though Oona intuitively knew what he was thinking.

'Her desk, Jean-Louis. It's there that she has faithfully kept every postcard they have received from the prison camp.'

'But only the one letter she was going to send back,' said Henri.

'*Maman* hadn't started it yet,' confided Louisette. 'We're not allowed to keep any of *Papa*'s letters. They must all be returned to him for safekeeping.'

'Idiot, it's because *Maman* has to write on the back of them,' said Henri.

'Two are received each month and two of the postcards,' said the sister, ignoring her brother. 'Unless, of course, *Papa* sends them to his mother and father.'

Because Madame Guillaumet was a career officer's wife and not that of a common soldier like Madame Barrault, the allowances the Government in Vichy paid, even though only to wives whose incomes were below five thousand francs a year, wouldn't have been available to her. Having a salary would have helped, since she would then have been eligible for the family allowance and social security, but unfortunately career officers' wives had never been allowed to take full-time jobs outside the home, and the part-time teaching wouldn't have counted.

Trapped again? he had to ask. In Paris alone there were more than thirty thousand POW wives whose incomes were below ten thousand francs a year and who were in desperate circumstances.

'Her desk is in the bedroom, Jean-Louis,' said Oona, knowing she should tell the children to tuck themselves in but that she couldn't bring herself to do this without joining them.

Reassuringly Jean-Louis reached out to her. His, 'Please don't worry. Hermann and I will see to things,' was meant to be comforting. The desk was nothing but a plain table. To Jean-Louis's right, there was the lamp she had switched on after the children and Giselle had finally fallen asleep. There were only sixteen postcards in that little pile, there having been a good four months at the first when no mail at all had come through to anyone. Eight of them had also gone to the grandparents.

To his left was February's five-kilogram parcel the woman and the children had been making up to send to the camp. No extra ration tickets were ever provided by Vichy for this purpose even though there were so many men locked up. Everything that went into that box, and everyone else's, had to come from the family's own supplies.

There were some cubes of Viandox, once the nation's most popular brand of beef tea, prewar of course and obtained on the black market. Some packets of camomile and of mint tea followed—not much yet, she knew Jean-Louis would be thinking. A pair of heavy woollen socks that had been knitted from the leavings of an unravelled sweater, two drawings . . .

'Cartoons,' Henri said. 'My latest.'

'And one of mine,' his sister added. 'It has been marked with my kisses.'

Though her words would sound hollow, Oona knew she had best say, 'The package won't be sent until the end of the month, so there's lots of time yet.'

'Time for *Maman* to come home to us,' said Louisette.

'We add a bit each day, Inspector. Sometimes once every two days. It depends,' said her brother.

Though heavily censored—blacked out first by the German

censors at the camp and then by Vichy's at the frontier—each postcard held only seven lines, often reduced to four-and-a-half or less; each letter, written on the regulation return that would fold itself yet again into an envelope, held only twenty-seven lines, reduced usually by the censors to twenty or less.

'One can't say much, can one?' said Oona. 'Repeatedly he writes as though she will do everything he says and expects; she, in turn, as though she has.'

But had she? Hadn't she arranged to be taken to the Hôtel Ritz where at least two hundred francs would have been received for a simple pass, four hundred for the half-hour, six for the hour? A steady income? She was handsome—a framed photo taken before the Defeat revealed her to have been a little on the comfortable side but she would have lost all that, would have had the figure trimmed down hard by all that walking if nothing else. The hair was of shoulder length and parted in the middle, swept back to expose droplet earrings of great delicacy that framed a look that was steadfast, serious, and wanting what? he had to ask. To be understood, to be treated as an individual of some worth? Had she been trapped even then?

All over the city and the country it was happening. 'She's lucky her assailant didn't kill her,' he said. '*Mon Dieu*, forgive me, children. I only meant . . .'

They looked at him with moistening eyes, rightly feeling betrayed by the harshness of his judgement but had the life of a detective not forced him into a prison of his own?

'Come on, you two, let's go into our room,' said Oona. "Let's snuggle up and leave the chief inspector to think a little more about what he says.'

'Oona, I'm not like Hermann. Certainly he constantly reminds me to mend my ways. It's only that the policeman in me sometimes forgets. Once a cop, always a cop.'

'And the gun in that handbag?'

'Is another matter but not entirely.'

*　　*　　*

The Ford's heater was throaty, Didier Valois, owner-operator of the *maréchal*'s Baton, less than cooperative. Kohler sighed as he hauled out the bankroll and, in the feeble light from the judge's cigar, counted them off. 'Five hundred . . . No, let's make it a thousand.'

'Two. Things are expensive these days and *Monsieur le Juge* will have my balls put on display before the blade falls if he ever finds out that I've spoken to you.'

An interesting comment Louis would have appreciated. 'Two thousand it is, but with the offer of a bonus.'

And didn't the Boche have all the money and think they could buy everything? 'Sometimes the judge has me pick him up just to make sure he gets home.'

It was a start but one had best go carefully. 'Under the empire of alcohol is he at such times?'

'He's not an alcoholic, only sometimes takes a little too much. It . . . it depends.'

On whom he'd been with, but that had best not be asked just yet. 'The Folies-Bergère?'

'Inspector, I'm not the only one he hires. There are others,'

'Of course there are.'

Pressure was needed, otherwise this Kripo was going to dig a grave that would hold them both. 'The Cercle de l'Union Interalliée.'

That private club of clubs and better even than the Cercle Européen since everyone who was anyone had to be a member of both but only some of the latter were allowed into the former. Men like Gaston Morel, no matter how useful they might be or how hard they tried, would never be welcomed into the Interalliée. It was just that simple. Located on the rue du Faubourg Saint-Honoré at number 33, opened in 1917 and counting that arch supplier of cannon fodder, the Maréchal Foch, as a member, now deceased, the *hôtel particulier* was sumptuous in all regards and had a history that went back a further two hundred years to Louis Chevalier, président of the Parliament of Paris, and his sister, Madame le Vieux, but Louis would have said, Go easy, Hermann. Don't be rash.

The Interalliée, the union of the Inter-Allied, had been started as a place for, amongst others, American aviators to stay when in Paris on leave, and when that other war had ended, this use had continued but been expanded to include others, especially now with the club's military reputation and the Defeat.

Herr Kohler was thinking the matter over and that was good, thought Valois. The judge had stated most clearly on a number of occasions the names not only of the club's most illustrious members—pillars of society—but more especially those of the new ones, among them the generals Karl Albrecht Oberg and Ernst von Schaumburg.

'The Casino de Paris?' hazarded Herr Kohler, but had he asked it so as to distract from the other?

'The Apollo,' said Valois levelly. 'Sometimes the judge likes a little change.'

I'll bet he does, snorted Kohler silently. Both were on the rue de Clichy in Pigalle where lots of those delinquent prisoner-of-war wives trolled the music halls, bars and pavements before lining up outside the nearest *maison de passe* with their clients. 'The Naturiste, the Chez Ève and the Romance?' he asked.

Sister clubs on *place* Pigalle. 'The Bal Tabarin also.'

Number 36 rue Victor Massé and in the area, an old style can-can that always showed lots of leg and frilly-clad crotches. A man of many tastes. 'And after a good feed at the Lapin Agile or some other such trough, the Boeuf sur le Toit, eh, at its new home in a wing of the Hôtel Georges?'

An SS and Gestapo trough! 'Inspector, *Monsieur le Juge* has many contacts he must consult on the business of the courts. Who am I to . . .'

'Entertains them, does he?'

'Is it not necessary?'

'Régine Trudel's La Source de Joie?'

Why had he asked if he knew all the answers? 'There, also.'

The Fountainhead of Joy on the avenue Frochot in Pigalle and definitely better than those who trolled the streets. '*Ah, bon, mon ami,* out with the rest. That wife of his is scared to death of his contracting a heavy dose of the clap. That daughter of his knows all about it too, and may well have a hidden life of her own for all I know at the moment, so give.'

Perhaps if nothing else, this would stop Herr Kohler. 'La Maison de Plaisir du Maître.'

The House of the Master's Pleasure, the SS brothel on the avenue de Wagram. 'Your judge has an interesting after-dinner life, doesn't he?'

'I . . . I wouldn't know. I simply do as I'm told.'

'So tell me where you picked him up last night and don't lie to me.'

'Inspector, as I've already told you, he gets rides from other taxi drivers, from friends, too, among those he entertains. He must.'

'Has a blanket pass to be out after curfew, does he?'

An *Ausweis*. 'Of course.'

Cigar smoke filled the car. Herr Kohler fiddled with the windscreen wiper switch and checked to see that the blades were not frozen fast. He didn't say, I'm waiting. He merely implied it. 'The Lido. *Monsieur le Juge,* he . . . he likes to watch the girls there.'

'While they bathe topless in the swimming pool and sometimes, if the law's not looking, completely bare the rest for the tips they're bound to receive?'

'That is correct.'

'And now for the hard part, since there's room for two in that contraption of yours.'

'He didn't take anyone from there. The girl hadn't been feeling well. The headaches—perhaps the onslaught of the flu.'

Oh-oh. 'What girl?'

Did this one always insist on digging his own grave deeper than necessary? 'The one he often takes to the flat he keeps on the rue La Boétie.'

Scheisse, a *petite amie*! 'Her name?'

'He'll kill me if I tell you. Madame Rouget might find out. She's a . . .'

'Very jealous woman? Surely the judge has told you that?'

'Élène Artur. She's . . . she's an *indochinoise,* you understand, but her skin is almost white and I think her father must have been French, the mother the half if not a little more.'

And so much for racism. The generals and the boys who flocked to the Lido would have been fascinated, but had she made that telephone call and, if so, why? 'Keeps her at the flat, does he?'

'There are also others he uses it for. The judge doesn't stay the rest of the night, you understand. Only the hour or two unless he . . .'

'Falls asleep?'

'*Oui*. She . . .'

'Élène.'

'*Oui*. Élène comes down to the cellar, to the furnace room to get me, and . . . and together we put him into the taxi.'

'Pretty, is she?'

'*Très belle*.'

'Come on, there's no perhaps about it, is there? Twenty-two, is she? Twenty-four?'

'Twenty.'

'Leaves by the side entrance, does she, in the morning after she's rested up?'

'Leaves it at five, when the curfew ends. She has a child her mother looks after.'

A child. 'Whose?'

'This I don't know since she doesn't wear a wedding ring and I've not asked.'

The stage doorman at the Lido had said that all its girls had been accounted for but he wouldn't have said anything of one who had had to leave early, especially not when he'd have known of the judge's interest in her.

St-Cyr was certain the photos on the Trinité victim's desk revealed far more of the husband than of herself and the children. Captain Jean-Matthieu Guillaumet had spent time in the colonies. The first tour of duty had been in French Polynesia. After that, he had had a lengthy stay in Indochina, then in the Sudan and, more recently before the 1939 call-up had summoned him home, French West Africa. Like his *papa* before him, he'd been a graduate of the École Militaire and a career officer.

The wife had, apparently, been left to fend for herself. *Bien sûr,* the husband would have come home on leave—six months perhaps, though three or four were more usual. There were no contraceptives amongst her most personal things—she'd been a good Catholic. There was, as yet, not one hint of her having strayed in all those years. No silk stockings but, like so many women had to these days, had they been sold on the black market? Among the rest, there were no seductive undergarments. One garter belt was neatly to the side of four pairs of plain white cotton briefs. There was not even one pair of the latter for each day of the week. Two slips, one of satin, had seen their wear, an extra brassiere also, but nothing fancy. All of these things were prewar and most of them had been mended, but had she worn the last of her finery? He couldn't ask the children. Perhaps *Madame la Concierge* would have noticed?

Attempts at writing the next letter to the husband had been done on thin notepaper first and then scratched out. *I must tell you. I have to tell you. I tell you I have no other choice.*

On the back of that slip of paper: *If only you would ask your parents to accept me as I am and not continue to prejudge.*

And on yet another piece of notepaper: *If only they could bring themselves to help us a little. They've plenty. They don't need what the government allows of your wages. We do!*

Each page had been tightly crumpled before being thrown into the wastepaper basket in despair and left ready for the fireplace.

It was on another piece of paper that he found: *Why can they not forgive my one indiscretion? I was young. You were away for months on end and didn't seem to want me anymore. You could have taken me with you—at least for a little. It wouldn't have cost that much, but when you did come home, and we did go out, I knew from the looks your fellow officers gave me that you had been with others.*

All these efforts had had to be scrapped—for one thing the

censors would have played havoc with them, for another, there simply wouldn't have been enough space.

Oh for sure, I went to Deauville for a little holiday when you were in Indochina. It was only for a few days, as I have told you many times and, yes, I didn't ask your father's permission since you were unavailable to me, but why must he and your mother continue to hold it against me and believe the worst? I did nothing wrong. I kept to myself. I walked along the beach in my bare feet or sat in the sun, or watched others as they played tennis or danced in the evenings while I sat alone at my table.

Trying to get a grip on her life—he knew that's what she'd have been doing, just as Marianne must have done during the constant absences of this detective husband of hers.

Then Madame Guillaumet had had a son, and then a daughter, the cement of them making things all the harder, and then the Defeat had come.

He'd have to ask the concierge and went downstairs. Madame Ouellette had switched to Victor Hugo's *Notre-Dame de Paris*.

'She wore her street clothes, Inspector, but as always, tried to look her best, particularly as she had to spend two hours or more in front of her class. One of her students brought the message from the Ritz where he's employed as a doorkeeper. I don't know his name, only that when he came here early last Friday, he was wearing his uniform, so there can be no mistake in that regard.'

And weren't all such doorkeepers suspected of being procurers? Francine could see him thinking this as a detective should.

'If my partner shows up, madame, please tell him I've gone to find Giselle. First to their flat, then to the House of Madame Chabot and then to the Club Mirage, unless he catches up with me beforehand. Let's hope he does.'

And then to the Ritz? she wanted so much to ask but knew she mustn't, that they would go there soon enough. Adrienne had had to sell the use of her body but should never have been condemned. Many had had to do it during that other war, though many had also resisted, herself among them, but each day the loneliness had become harder to bear. Then in 1918, on 4 October, a Friday, and right near the end, the notice had come and she had found that the waiting, it had all been in vain and she was a widow.

And afterwards? she asked, still finding it hard to resist not being bitter. Afterwards so few men had remained, God had left no one for her. Two casualties: the husband and the wife.

6

One by one the girls came down to the viewing room at the House of Madame Chabot. Some wore slippers and a flimsy chemise or see-through negligees, one a dishevelled schoolgirl's tunic. They didn't cry as friends should over Giselle's not being found. Their expressions were hard and watchful, the odours of them mingling with the ever-present fug of Gauloises, the acid of *vin ordinaire* and the perfume each had chosen as her own little signature but Hermann *hadn't* come by. 'I want answers, damn you,' rebelled St-Cyr. 'Giselle is not at the flat, as Madame Chabot has claimed!'

That one, that fifty-eight-year-old with the made-up eyes, blonde wig, round rouged-and-powdered cheeks, vermillion lips and double chin who still insisted on *claiming* she was thirty-eight, gave but the swiftness of a green-eyed gaze that would have startled a cobra.

'She has said she would spend the night there, Inspector. Who am I to . . .'

'It's Chief Inspector!'

Ah, bon, he was now shouting. 'That's a *zéro* to me, you understand. The police are the police, but the girl came to the house asking of Herr Kohler and expecting—yes, expecting, I must emphasize—to pass the time of day with friends? What friends?'

'Now, listen. Giselle le Roy was one of your girls. My partner . . .'

'Decided to make a *petite amie* of her and rob the house of one of its top earners? Rented a flat around the corner to constantly remind me of my loss and to tempt others into giving up the profession and moving in with another of *les Allemands*? Pah, *quelle folie!* When spring comes, the Résistance will strip her naked and cut off that jet-black hair your partner loves to rub his fingers and other things through.'

And never mind Hermann's sex life, interesting as that might well be. 'When spring comes' meant the Allied invasion. It could be years away and yet . . .

'That is,' she said tartly, 'if the blackout sadists who prowl the streets in search of such women don't get to her first!'

'She'll try to hide in the darkness of a *passage* like the Trinité,' muttered one of the girls.

'He'll ram a table leg up her for good measure,' said the brunette called Gégé.

'But first, he'll give her a terrible beating,' said Bijou.

'He'll not stop until her throat has been slashed,' said another, clasping her own as the cat wandered in to lift its tail and rub against her legs before arguing with a pom-pom.

'I can't afford to have the house endangered, Inspector,' went on Georgette Chabot. 'This house—any such house—must always guard its peace. The girls move around enough as it is and are subject to temptation that needs no further encouragement.'

'Giselle didn't encourage us to leave, madame. I swear it,' blurted Didi.

'ARE YOU TO PACK YOUR BAGS OR DO YOU WANT ME TO PUT YOU ON THE STREET WITHOUT THEM?' shrilled the woman.

'Madame, please! I only meant. . .'

'SEE THAT YOU MAKE UP FOR IT! Here the house and the licence are French for French, Inspector. Citizen with citizen, patriot with patriot, and that is all there ever has been or ever will be. When that Le Roy person showed up late this afternoon, I told her to get lost and not come back. I can't afford to endanger my girls.'

'You did what?'

'Are your ears not sufficient?'

Threatening her would only prolong the agony. Oh for sure, two of the German military police often paid prolonged visits and the house was heated, its larder sufficiently supplied at a cost, no doubt, to feed the girls, but . . . 'Look, Madame Cliquot, the concierge of that building where Hermann insists on renting a flat, has said the girl never went there today.'

'That woman would say anything,' chided Georgette. 'Frankly, she doesn't want your partner and his women as tenants and is determined to have the owners cancel their lease. She doesn't want trouble either, does she, a French girl who offers herself entirely to one of the enemy?'

'Since when was Hermann ever considered one of those?'

'Since June of 1940, I think. I do know, also, you understand, that Irène Cliquot is intelligent enough not to want such scores settled in her house.'

'And Hermann?'

'Isn't welcome. The law is the law, isn't it? Who am I to challenge it?'

At 10.37 p.m. the little blue lights that dimly marked the most important street corners suddenly went out. The last trains of the métro would have begun their runs at ten and maybe the most distant ones still had a ways to go.

One thing was certain. The Occupier had again ordered that the plug be pulled. Kohler stood a moment at the corner of the rue La Boétie and the Champs-Élysées. Louis must have known who Denise Rouget's father was, but Louis wasn't here.

'I have to do it,' he breathed, the street suddenly damned lonely. 'Either I'm finished as a detective and ripe for the Russian front, or I'm not. That *petite amie* of the judge's may have made our phone call.'

Feeling his way in the rain, he started up the rue La Boétie. Through the hush of the city, sounds came. The throb of a distant motorcycle patrol, the squeal of Gestapo tyres, the *clip-clop* of high heels with their hinged wooden soles one hell of a lot closer, the heavy scent of too much perfume mingling with that of fresh tobacco smoke.

A lonely car, an Opel Tourer by the sound, turned off the rue de Ponthieu to begin its pass as a figure darted from the shelter to urgently rap on a side windscreen. 'There's some bastard lurking around here,' shrilled the girl as she scrambled in, and didn't the Occupier drive virtually all the cars, and wasn't that one just as capable of attacking her?

A cigarette was accepted and a light. The blinkered headlamps went out. The engine continued wasting petrol. Kohler left her to get on with the client's little moment and went along the street thinking of Giselle and how he had saved her from just such a life. No matter what Louis said, she'd be perfect for that little bar on the Costa del Sol, but the sooner they were out of France and into Spain, the better. 'False papers,' he muttered. 'Cash, too, and plenty of it.' The lament of the damned.

When he came to what must be the rue d'Artois, he back-tracked. Each of these former mansions was cloaked in darkness but at one, the concierge had lit the stub of a candle and that could only mean one thing, of course. The house was warm, too. Though this last didn't surprise, it did raise a note of caution, but once committed, always committed.

'Monsieur . . .'

He would have to say it firmly, couldn't waver, not with a tenant or tenants from among the Reich's most privileged. 'Kohler, Kripo, Paris-Central. The flat Judge Rouget leases. Gestapo HQ have ordered me to take a look around. Lead me to it, then wait down here. Lend me that torch of yours and forget you ever saw me.'

'Inspector,' said Laurent Louveau, concierge of this building and with some authority of his own, '*Monsieur le Juge* hasn't been in for some time.'

'Don't get difficult. It's Élène Artur I'm interested in.'

Louveau tossed his head. 'Has the girl done something she shouldn't?'

'Was she here last night?'

'Why, please, would she have been if *Monsieur le Juge* wasn't?'

Logic was one of the finer points of the French, their brand of it anyway, but there was no sense in arguing. 'That's what I'd like to find out, among other things.'

'Then I must inform you that the girl wasn't here either.'

'Good. You've no idea how relieved I am. We'll take the stairs. I don't trust the lifts.'

Had this one not even noticed? 'It shall be as you wish, Inspector, since the electricity is off in any case. The flat is on the third floor.'

'And easy to a side staircase and entrance?'

Sacré nom de nom, what was this? '*Oui*, but . . . but there's a little bell above that entrance and I would have heard it, had that door not been locked as it was and is.'

'*Aber natürlich. Ach,* sorry. I keep switching languages. That means, of course.'

'Monsieur the Lieutenant Krantz sometimes also forgets, as does the Mademoiselle Lammers. They make a big joke of it and tell me I'd best learn a proper language, but . . .'

'Krantz . . . Isn't he one of those who oversee the Bank of France?'

'Ah, no. He is at the Majestic.'

The offices of General Heinrich von Stülpnagel, the military governor of France. 'And the Mademoiselle Lammers? Thesima, was it, or Mädy?'

'Ursula. She's also at the Majestic. A translator, as is the lieutenant.'

And probably working for the Verwaltungsstab, the administrative staff that dutifully subordinated every facet of the French economy to those of the Reich. Fully five hundred million francs a day in reparations and payments had to be coughed up for losing the war and housing one hundred thousand of the Wehrmacht in France, along with lots of others. Converted from its hotel rooms, there were now more than a thousand offices in the Majestic alone, and wasn't it on the avenue Kléber at the corner of the avenue des Portugais and but a short walk to the avenue Foch and the SS, and hadn't von Stülpnagel and Oberg served in the same regiment during that other war?

Of course they had, and yes, Von Stülpnagel left all 'political' matters, like the retaliatory shooting of hostages, to Oberg, thereby disassociating himself entirely from the extremes of the latter.

No one could have brought the Lido's telephone caller here last night. They wouldn't have dared.

The Club Mirage was a crash of noise. Packed to the limit with German uniforms, there wasn't even standing room for one lone Sûreté, the bar impossible to approach.

Up onstage, all-but-naked girls, some nearly fifty, one sneezing at the ostrich plumes they wore, presented a shocking tableau of the boy-king Tutankhamen's spate of pyramid building. Whips cracked. Those being punished cringed. Cymbals reverberated as a bleary-eyed sun began to set but faltered and the guards in their pleated loincloth-skirts stood sentinel with spears if not otherwise employed.

Merde, a tableau such as this could go on for hours! Even those at the bar had stopped attempting to quench their thirst.

'St-Cyr, Sûreté, *meine Herren. Entschuldigen Sie, bitte.* I have to see if my partner's here. It's an emergency.'

Excuse me, please? *Ach,* what was this? 'Piss off, *Franzose.*'

'But . . .' Nefertiti had turned to face the audience and raise her arms. The politically correct albino Nubian began to sponge her naked back while the sun threatened to drop right out of sight behind the screen of a rose-red horizon but decided to hesitate.

'*Verfick dich!*' came a Wehrmacht hiss. Fuck off.

Jumping and waving a desperate arm to signal the bar was useless, but something must have been said, for as Nefertiti's pseudo-Nubian sponged her ankles and calves, Remi, with the face of a mountain that was all crags, clefts and precipices, motioned.

A pastis, a double, had been set on the zinc, the Corsican adding a touch of water to cloud it green as if by magic. 'Down that, *mon ami*. And another. You're going to need it.'

'Hermann . . . ? Has something happened to him? To Gabrielle?'

That massive head with its thick, jet-black, wavy gangster's hair gave an all but imperceptible nod to indicate the dressing rooms as the crowd erupted into cheers through which came calls for the slaves to pluck their feathers and for the guards to drop their spears and loincloths.

Torchlight pierced the darkness of the judge's flat. Briefly Kohler shone the light over a chinoiserie panel of leaves, vines and exotic birds before letting it fall to the Louis XVI table where Rouget would have left hat, walking stick and gloves. Judges were way higher up than detectives; judges had friends and friends of friends. *Lieber Christus im Himmel,* why did it have to happen to Louis and himself? The building had given no hint of warning. From somewhere distant, though, came the metallic clunking of a hot-water radiator.

There was no dominant smell except for that of the mustiness of old buildings and antique furniture. 'Please use the candles, Inspector,' the concierge had earlier said. Candles weren't common anymore. Even in the South, in the former Free Zone, they hadn't been seen by most since that first winter of 1940–1941.

Torchlight found her dark-blue leather high heels. They'd been soaked through last night but were now dry and needing a good cleaning and bit of polish. 'Louis,' he softly said. 'I don't think I can go through with this.' Questions, Hermann, Louis would have said. You must concentrate on those. The time of entry? That call she made from the Lido last night didn't come in to the quartier du Faubourg du Roule's commissariat until 11.13 p.m. There would have been lots of time for her to have joined the judge at his table between sets . . .

Lots of time for others to have seen her sitting there with him. She had a child—was she married to a POW? She hadn't been feeling well, had gone home early, the stage doorman said, but when, damn it, when? Early in a place like the Lido could mean anything up to midnight at the least.

Torchlight shone into the *salle de séjour* to settle on a gilded sconce. The cigarette lighter on the glass-topped coffee table was heavy. The matching cigarette box with its tortoiseshell repoussé hadn't had its lid completely replaced. Had her assailant dipped into it?

He knew she was here. Instinct told him this. Detective instinct.

Resting on the mantelpiece behind glass was a framed poster: *Une Nuit à Chang-Rai, 7 Mai 1926* at the Magic City. Had the judge had a taste for showgirls even then?

Deep blue irises encircled soft pink roses that surrounded a scantily clad eighteen-year-old pseudo-*indochinoise* dancer. Slender, upraised arms crisscrossed above the coolie hat she wore. The look was squint-eye, the black lashes long and straight, the short hair curled in about her neck, and wasn't the thing a parody Élène Artur must have definitely not appreciated, the judge a hypocrite? The dark-blue heels were every bit the same as those he'd just found.

'Élène Artur,' he said again, and weren't names important? Hadn't all the dead of that other war had names that had counted for something?

A vitrine held enamelled boxes, spills of jewellery, strands of pearls and beads, Fabergé eggs, Sèvres porcelain figurines, a Vénus, a marchioness . . . Had Hercule the Smasher used them to tempt his girlfriends into doing what he wanted or to pay them off by letting them choose some little memento as they left, one that said in no uncertain terms, *Ferme-la, chérie*? The kitchen was hung with copper pots and pans, Judge Rouget, *Président du Tribunal spécial du Département de la Seine,* immune to the scrap-metal drives that demanded everyone else cough up such items. The copper-sheathed zinc bathtub hadn't been used to hold her corpse but the bidet had cigar ashes floating in it. A Choix Supreme? he demanded. Had Vivienne Rouget chosen to offer this Kripo one of those *not* because the Vichy gossip could be used if needed to shield that daughter of hers, but because she had damned well known or suspected this might happen?

Clothing clung to the open doors of an armoire whose mirrors threw back light from the candle in his hand. A necklace of sapphire beads had been broken. A dark-blue velvet off-the-shoulder sheath lay crumpled on the floor with a blue lace-trimmed silk slip and brassiere, silk stockings, too, that were scattered and had been yanked off—two men, had two of the bastards done it? The garter belt was entangled with the stockings and her step-ins.

Everywhere things had been broken, everywhere things torn or thrown, he waiting for the shakes to come, knowing, too, that that damned Messerschmitt Benzedrine he and sometimes Louis took to stay awake, wouldn't help matters, but Louis who would, just wasn't here . . .

The hush that enveloped the Club Mirage was every bit as deep as that first time St-Cyr had seen Gabrielle walk out onstage, a mirage of her own. Always she would have to sing 'Lilli Marlene,' and always that voice of hers would be carried over the airwaves by Radio-Paris and Radio-Berlin to be picked up by the Allies who avidly listened in, and wouldn't being such a celebrity damn her in the end when finally France was freed? Hadn't she best be got out of the country? A *résistante*!

Her dressing room was at the end of the corridor and right next to the stage door and stairs that led down into the cellars or up to the Rivard living quarters and storerooms and from those, down other sets of stairs to independent exits or up to the roof and from there to others.

Certainly Gestapo Paris's Listeners had bugged that dressing room and just as certainly Gabrielle had left those bugs in place. Apparently, though, she had taken to keeping a bicycle handy. Unlocked, this shabby, third-hand instrument leaned against a wall, facing the exit and ready at a moment's notice. Age and wear gave it a little less chance of being stolen, and wasn't a bike by far the best means of travel these days? Didn't it allow one to avoid the checkpoints and roundups that increasingly plagued the métro? Didn't it also give advance warning of street controls since one could often see well ahead and reroute if possible or walk the bike up into a courtyard as if one belonged?

The dressing room was starkly Spartan, the more so from when he had met her during the investigation of a small murder, a 'nothing' murder Hermann had called it, only to then find otherwise. 'Standartenführer . . . ? Forgive me, please. I didn't know Gabi . . . the Mademoiselle Arcuri had someone waiting for her.' Remi Rivard *had* tried to warn him. Remi . . .

'St-Cyr, Sûreté—am I correct?'

Schwaben . . . Was the accent from there? *'Jawohl,* Colonel. I'm looking for my partner.'

'Then you'll be disappointed.'

Were the SS hunting for Hermann? 'Gabrielle might have heard from him.'

St-Cyr hadn't moved from the doorway and looked as if to bolt. 'She'll not have heard unless within the last ten minutes. *Ach, bitte.* Close the door. Though I love the sound of her voice, the shouting and applause I find disturbing. Would you care for one of those?' The cigarettes were indicated. 'I'm sure Madame Thériault won't mind.'

Her married name had been used as a definite hint to that 'nothing' murder. As then, there had been Russian cigarettes, but had the case been purposely left open on her dressing table in defiance of this SS since the Russians were now getting the better of the Reich?

This Sûreté couldn't help but notice the other items the 'Arcuri' woman had left out: a glass of the Château Thériault's *demi-sec,* the vineyards near Vouvray, a wedge of *chèvre crottin* with a dusting of herbs and dill, some slices of a baguette, these last forbidden by law and therefore subject to both a fine and prison sentence or forced labour.

Everything registered clearly in St-Cyr's expression, including concern over why she had been so foolish as to not have anticipated a visitor from the SS.

'*Standartenführer* . . .' blurted this *Schweinebulle* who placed honesty and truth above all else, as did Kohler, the two of them having incurred the wrath of so many of Paris's SS and Gestapo, especially for what had happened at that same château.

'*Bitte, mein lieber französischer Oberdetektiv*, Hjalmar Langbehn *à votre service.*'

The heels were smoothly brought together but hardly a sound from the jackboots was heard, a slim hand extended and taken since it had to be. 'Colonel, what brings you here?'

A certain *Blitzmädel*'s handbag, was that what was worrying St-Cyr? 'A little supper—oh, not those.'

The glass of wine he had wished for, St-Cyr knew, when Gabi had shared the repast with him at the Château Thériault's mill on the Loire.

'Those have, I gather, been left for yourself in welcome on your return from Alsace, but . . .'

He would leave a little pause, thought Langbehn. It always seemed to unsettle those who did not wish to reveal more than possible, and St-Cyr was definitely one of them. 'Mademoiselle Arcuri has kindly agreed to be my guest at Chez Francis.'

The Alsatian restaurant on *place* de l'Alma had long been a legend in its own right, but before the Defeat several of its waiters and sous-chefs had been spies and fifth columnists for the Reich. Now, of course, they owned and ran the restaurant.

A cardboard suitcase—nothing so fine as from Vuitton or Hermès—lay tucked behind the colonel's chair, but had he noticed it? Did Gabi now keep it packed and ready to take into hiding at a moment's notice—had things become that desperate for her even within the past ten days?

One might never know. Such suitcases had come with the disappearance of leather to the Reich, but they had one great advantage: so common and identical were they, few among the Occupier could differentiate and they could, if confronted by a control, be casually slid in amongst others at a railway station and left behind.

'These blackout crimes,' said Langbehn. 'Brief me on your progress—I trust such has been made?'

Had Oberg ordered this one to look into the matter? Fortunately Sonja Remer's handbag was still hidden under the overcoat. 'I'll just go out to the courtyard to see if my partner might have finally arrived. Hermann often chooses to come in that way but has trouble closing the doors.'

'*Gut,* then both of you can brief me. I understand that Judge Rouget's daughter was at the Drouant last night with Gaston and Madame Morel when he and the stepsister of the latter were attacked.'

'Give me but a moment. I'll be right back.'

Outside and standing in the rain, St-Cyr knew that the colonel might well look around the dressing room and find things he shouldn't. There'd been an Eisernes Kreuz First-Class at the neck of that uniform, and from that other war, Wehrmacht wound and flak badges too, and the 1939 clasp and bar with Nazi eagle and swastika in silver gilt, the double braiding and skull and crossbones on the cap, an SS-Dienstauszeichnungen also, the long-service award with SS runes and ribbon signifying twelve years of absolute loyalty.

But now . . . now the Standartenführer wasn't simply a soldier but an administrator, one of the Totenkopverbände who ran the concentration camps, and hadn't Hermann and he had to visit the camp at Natzweiler-Struthof in Alsace not three, or was it four days ago?

A granite quarry whose cruelty had been matched by the harshness of winter in the mountains of the Vosges.

The rain was icy when he lifted his face to it. There was, of course, absolutely no sign of Hermann who knew all about this courtyard and stage door but would have blithely roared in through the front entrance to chat up the coat-check girls before taking in a bit of the show and making his way through to the bar.

But where was he when most needed? Had he found Giselle?

The bed was Empire and of mahogany that gleamed but Élène Artur wasn't in it. She had spun away to the far side, had been caught by an ankle, had kicked, scrambled up, run to the dressing table and seized something—a letter opener. Had she defied her assailants with it? She had knocked over a perfume bottle, the toilet water, rouge, talcum powder, face cream and other things. A hand mirror had then been thrown. Where . . . where the hell had she got to? Had she managed to get away?

They had caught her by the hair and had thrown her down. One had pinned her head and hands against the carpet, but she'd bitten his left wrist or hand, had bitten deeply—there was blood on the carpet, not much, but enough.

The door to an adjacent room was all but closed . . . 'Go on, you must,' he said aloud. Louis wouldn't expect it of him. Louis would say, *Hermann, leave this to me!*

But Louis wasn't here and all the sounds of that other war were coming at him now, the stench, too, of cordite and of mouldering earth and entrails. The blast had been so loud the ears had been stunned and they hadn't heard the humming of the shrapnel as it had filled the air. Young Heinrich—Grenadier Oberlan and one hell of a shot, age eighteen who had never been with a girl, let alone the one whose photo he carried—had run blindly through the deep snow among the shattered, decapitated fir trees at Vieil Armand on that mountainside to the west of Colmar in Alsace in that first winter of 1914–1915, his hands desperately trying to contain the guts that were spilling from him.

Heinrich had tripped on them and had lain there blinking up at the one who had always told him, Hey, *mein Lieber,* don't worry. I'm going to look after you.

His legs had still been moving. 'You promised,' he had managed. Nothing else, the bright red, grey to plum-purple, net-veined, sticky tubular coils slithering flaccidly from between slackening fingers, the heart beating and then not, the uniform in shreds.

'Louis . . . Louis, they cut her open and let her run.'

'Giselle . . . ? She hasn't been to the club, Jean-Louis.'

Gabrielle struck a match, the sound of it reverberating throughout the dressing room, she to fix him with a gaze that said, as the match was extended to light the cigarette she had given him, Look after my René Yvon-Paul. I don't know what this one wants of me.

Her son was only ten years old and lived with his grandmother at Château Thériault, but Langbehn was watching closely.

A wrap was found, the Standartenführer putting it about her shoulders then taking her overcoat from its peg, she slipping into it as that one held it for her, she knowing there was little she could say, not even, Jean-Louis, how I've missed you, only, 'I understand from the colonel that you and Herr Kohler are working around the clock.'

Herr Kohler, not Hermann. 'As always.' They couldn't signal to each other, nor could he warn her of just how desperate things had become.

Alone, St-Cyr budgetted the cigarette. She didn't use them often, but when she did, the tobacco was invariably Russian. There was, of course, a phial of Mirage on her dressing table. In the old days, the good days between the two most recent wars, Muriel Barteaux, the source of that perfume, had been a regular patron of Gabi's, listening to her at the Lune Russe and others of the chanteuse clubs, but then there'd been a long hiatus: marriage and motherhood for Gabi, and then the Defeat and widowhood had come and, miracle of miracles word had spread, and there that voice was again, so much so that Muriel had created Mirage for what had appeared on the stage of this club.

Muriel and Chantal Grenier were old and dear friends, well into their seventies, their shop Enchantment on *place* Vendôme— exquisite lingerie and perfumes, bath soaps and salts and much, much more but always crowded with German generals, et cetera since the Ritz was right next door. Had the location meaning for Hermann and himself, especially as the Trinité victim had planned to go to that hotel?

Though he had spoken often of the shop, Giselle wouldn't have sought refuge there. She didn't even know her way across the Seine from the Sixth into the First. The river was like a moat to her.

Sonja Remer's handbag haunted him and he unbuttoned his

coat, took it out, held the Tokarev, checked it as one always should and wondered again where it all must lead. No note or word of warning could be left for Gabrielle, lest it be found or heard by others. The Standartenführer's little visit could mean nothing or everything. Hermann might know something but where had he got to? Had he found Giselle safe?

The girl would have been distraught. Being banished couldn't have sat well with her. She'd have gone in search of a friendly face— some of the nearby shops specialized in magic and the reading of fortunes. A realist, she liked at times to kid herself but wasn't overly superstitious, as were many prostitutes, and why must the cop in him never forget where she'd come from? She was far too intelligent for such a profession anyway, far too sensible but of her own mind always. She would have found those other doors just as shut to her in any case, since the House of Madame Chabot serviced the neighbourhood and what that one said, others obeyed or else.

It would still have been daylight. The café Les Deux Magots was a little to the west but she could easily have gone there, it being on the corner opposite the Église de Saint-Germain-des-Prés. One of the largest Soldatenheim, the troop hostels, was on the rue Saint-Benoît and just around the corner. Lots of friendly faces, lots of interest in her, or had she gone into the church to beg forgiveness for having slept with one of the enemy, only to then catch the métro and try to find her way back to Oona? Had she impulsively caught a *vélo-taxi*, been followed, been taken into one of the air-raid shelters to be beaten, raped, murdered—terrorized first? There'd been no *alerte* but those doors were never locked. She was street-wise—*mon Dieu*, she'd have had to be. Hadn't Hermann used her in more than one investigation?

Had he gone to the rue des Saussaies to see if she'd been picked up and taken there? Was he even looking for her?

'Giselle . . . ?' It couldn't be her, thought Kohler, and yet the feet were as hers, the small of this one's back, the shoulders, the way she had run, had suddenly stepped up on to the chaise longue and then had stepped down to the carpet on the other side, all in a hurry, all in terror, she then tripping to fall to her hands and knees, to pause, to try to understand . . .

'Giselle,' he heard himself saying again as if dazed and wandering among shell-shattered trenches and through the acrid fog of no-man's-land. 'Giselle?

'It's Élène Artur, damn it.'

Pale and flaccid, glistening still, net-veined, dark-red, blood-red, grey-white and blue—pale yellow where there was a little fat—intestines were coiled about her left ankle. At first, on being disembowelled, she had tried to catch herself, to stop the viscera from spilling from her. In shock, some sense of what was happening must have come but then she had collapsed on to her left side, the legs fully extending only to be drawn in and up.

Faeces and urine stained the carpet to mingle with the blood and other fluids that seemingly were everywhere. 'Élène Artur,' he said again, the voice a broken whisper, for the jet-black hair he mustn't touch was that of Giselle and so like hers, the image of her kept coming at him.

Rigor was still present. The eyes were wide and clouded—dust would have collected. Blood had erupted from both nostrils. The teeth, what could be seen of them, were very white and straight— she'd not used tobacco, couldn't have drunk much coffee, real or ersatz, or black tea—had been gagged by a silk stocking that had been forced between the jaws and tied behind the head. Tied tightly—too tightly. They'd done that after she'd bitten one of them. After.

Semen had trickled down the left thigh to be smeared as she had run, but there were only traces of this that could be seen, hidden as it was by the rest, but definitely rape beforehand.

'Élène Artur,' he said yet again. She'd been dead for about twenty-four hours, would have been brought here from the Lido at about what? Eleven forty? Twelve midnight, maybe? The call to the district commissariat had been made at 11.13 p.m. She had first been forced to contact the press. Here, then, at half after midnight, or maybe 1.00 a.m. at the latest, the concierge sound asleep. Had they known this too?

The face was swollen, livid and blotchy. There were deep bruises on the neck where she'd been held during the rape, showers of petechial haemorrhages under the eyes and across the bridge of the nose and the cheeks. Some of the slate-blue to reddish-purple blotches on the lower parts of the left buttock, thigh and calf were due to postmortem hypostasis and would have to be sorted from the bruises. There were abrasions and scratches—several cuts as well, the flesh having been laid open, the assailant darting in with a cutthroat?

'A knife—but what kind of knife, damn it? That was no cutthroat.'

The right breast had been cleanly and deeply sliced open by one slash that extended down through the nipple. That shoulder had also been opened and then the forearm as she had managed to pull free and had tried to fend him off only to have that arm grabbed again by the other assailant, the one who had come up behind her. The knife had been pulled away after she'd been cut open. Blood had shot from its blade, lots of blood that had, only at the last, dribbled from it.

Had the bastard known how to butcher? Had he *been* a butcher?

'That knife, it's not the usual.' Louis and Armand Tremblay would have to see her just as she was, but Judge Rouget wasn't going to like what had happened in his little nest. Hercule the Smasher would have to run to Oberg to beg that one's help in hushing things up. Oberg would love it, since the judge, the judicial system and the night-action trials would then be even more within that grasping fist, the police too, and wasn't that really what Oberg wanted most?

Yes, Oberg would have to hear of it but first from this Kripo. There wasn't any sense in trying to avoid the issue or prolong the agony. It would be expected of him and he had best do that, but first, a little look around so as to have the background needed to save one's ass if possible.

'But what sort of knife would leave a spurt of blood that long when withdrawn?' he asked. 'A blade but not like butchers use even for the smaller cuts, since the thing must have collected one hell of a lot of blood in a groove or something to have had it spurt off the end like that when removed.'

The washbasin was clean, the floor as well, but one had to ask, Why so tidy when one had left such a mess? Why not simply flick ash on to the floor? Impulse, had that been it? One of long familiarity and care?

They hadn't taken her handbag. One of them—the one with the cigar—had dumped it out on a side table in the *salle de séjour* and had dropped a little ash, which had been quickly but not completely wiped away. Again a tidy man. Well dressed? he had to ask. One who knew the judge and had used the flat before and perhaps often?

ID, ration cards and tickets had been taken as with other victims but also to slow identification, though here there had been just too many holes in the sieve for them to have plugged and they hadn't figured on Didier Valois forking up the address and name of the judge's *petite amie*, had thought instead that Hercule the Smasher would have found her first. Not Louis or himself, but Rouget who would then have run to Oberg—had they known that's what he'd do? Had they understood him and the use of this flat so well they had counted on it and felt supremely confident and safe from honest detectives who might just start asking questions?

But why empty the handbag, why not simply take it as with other victims?

When Kohler found her wedding ring, he instinctively knew it was one of those little breaks every detective longed for and that her killers must have wanted it as proof.

The ring had fallen to the malachite top of the table and had bounced on to the carpet, there to roll out and across the parquet before hiding itself under the far corner of the radiator.

Opening the valve, Kohler bled off the entrapped air to silence the radiator's pinging he must have been hearing all along. 'I haven't any other choice, Louis,' he said. 'I'm sorry but I'm going to have to go to the avenue Foch and might just as well do so now and get it over with while I still have what it takes.'

But first, he would have to take a look in the toilet. That, too, couldn't be avoided, especially as the parquet had been mopped but not completely.

Numéro 11 rue des Saussaies was as blacked out as the rest of the city at seven minutes past midnight, now Saturday, 13 February 1943—how had Hermann and himself lasted this long? wondered St-Cyr. Leaving the Citroën at kerbside where it could be more easily located if in a hurry, he avoided the front entrance. Heading up into the courtyard, he felt his way by running a hand along the inner wall, all the while listening to the streets and to the rain.

The cellars were ice cold. Water lay in pools. Dimly lit at the best of times, the corridors ran every which way. The first cells were starkly empty. Scratches gave names and dates—one couldn't help but notice. A poem—sometimes beautifully composed; a message, if but brief; a curse that could only have made things more difficult. A 'reinforced' interrogation brought its echoes. Cringing with each blow, he hurried—Hermann and he had agreed to spend as little time as possible in the building, in that 'office' of theirs on the fifth floor.

The women's cells were at the back, down yet another corridor. French or Occupier, did it matter who was in authority here? Often the former liked to show they were better at it than the latter, but would they really have to answer for their actions when spring came? Wasn't Pharand, head of the Sûreté, a past master at blowing the smoke screen and hiding behind it? Wouldn't those such as himself and Hermann, too, be left to answer for the crimes of others?

Blood, pus, human waste and vomit made the air rank. Suddenly a man shrilled a name. Other names rapidly followed, then a penetrating silence, then a sickening blow to which the whole of the cellars would have listened.

Upstairs, on the ground floor and above this, there was much activity. Questioning the duty sergeant brought nothing more than a knowing smirk and then an uncaring shrug.

There was no mention in the docket of Giselle's having been picked up. The morgue then? he had to wonder. If so, how could he possibly break the news to Hermann? Hadn't it been hard enough having to let him know of the deaths of his two sons? Hadn't Boemelburg deliberately left that duty to this partner and friend of Hermann's?

Walter's door was closed but never locked since none would dare enter without being asked and the duty sergeant was keeping an eye on this Sûreté.

But not long enough.

Quickly letting himself into the spacious office Pharand had had to vacate after the Defeat, he closed the door and listened hard to this place he'd once been proud to be a part of. The blackout drapes had been drawn—Walter often worked late. The green-shaded desk lamp he'd brought from a distant past as a salesman of heating and ventilating systems would be sufficient. Before making the career change to detective, Walter had worked in Paris in the twenties and had learned the language so well as Head of the Gestapo's Section IV he spoke it like a native of Montmartre.

Boemelburg and he had liaised on IKPK matters before the Defeat and on that infamous day no surprise had been shown at finding this Sûreté upstairs in Records destroying sensitive files the Gestapo and SS wanted. He had merely wagged a reproving finger and had said to cooperate or else, since some appearance of fighting common crime, no matter how limited, would be useful in calming the public. 'But I'll delegate someone to watch over you.'

Questions . . . there wouldn't even be time for those when the end came and the Occupier had to leave. Hermann and himself wouldn't have a chance. There were only about 2,400 German Gestapo and SS in the country but there were more than 50,000 working for them: the French Gestapo of the rue Lauriston—gangsters who had been let out of prison and put to work; the Intervention-Referat, the Bickler Unit and other gangs, and as if these were not enough, now there was Vichy's newest paramilitary force, the Milice française. Then, too, the Sûreté and the Paris police—all 15,000 of these last—and every other police force in the country, even the *gardes champêtre*, the rural police. Certainly not all were bad—ah no, of course not—but orders were orders and often the only choice a *flic* or village cop had was to follow them to varying degrees, some more than others.

But civil war would erupt when the Occupier pulled out. Caught up in things—trapped—Hermann wouldn't have a chance, never mind himself.

A metronome drew his attention—such a lovely thing conjured thoughts of childhood piano lessons that had been hated until, wonder of wonders, *Grand-maman* had stopped having earaches.

Next to it was a phial of bitter almond, the smell like that of potassium cyanide. Walter was now constantly searching for improvements: the incessant *tick-tock* of the one during an interrogation, the smell of the other in a war of nerves that was only going to get far worse.

Sonja Remer's name had been written and encircled on an otherwise blank sheet of paper beneath which there was a telex from Gestapo Muller in Berlin but prompted, no doubt, by an enraged Heinrich Himmler. *ACHTUNG.* IMMEDIATE END TO BLACKOUT CRIMES IMPERATIVE OR FACE RECALL AND COURT-MARTIAL. HEIL HITLER.

Berlin were seldom happy. Though Von Schaumburg might be counted on, Walter was really this flying squad's only supporter. By his word alone did they continue to exist.

In the top drawer there were blank identity cards, blank ration cards with next week's colour-coded tickets, blank *laissez-passers* and *sauf-conduits*, all rubber stamped and signed not only by Préfet Talbotte but also by Von Schaumburg. Lots and lots of them, each type bound by an elastic band. French-gestapo plainclothes and others often had to go under cover to trap *résistants* or to locate hidden works of art and other valuables.

Five sets would be needed, but Gabrielle could never be persuaded to leave her son, so six would have to be taken. Giselle, if still alive and safe, simply wouldn't want to step off her little corner of this planet. 'And I know I'm not a thief, not even now,' he breathed. 'It's far too dangerous anyway and I really must stay.'

Behind the desk there was a large wall map of Paris. Immediately apparent from the colour-coded flags and their brief notations was the fact that Hermann and this partner of his had merely scratched the surface. Not only had there been a huge increase in the usual sort of blackout crimes, there had been this other aspect.

While some of the sexual attacks would have been against females simply because they had cohabited with the Occupier, one group, as they had discovered, definitely had been targeted: those who were married to, or engaged to, prisoners of war.

There were close on three hundred of these flags, but the earliest of them dated only from 1 December, so the numbers would be much higher. Of those who could be interviewed, all had lost their wedding rings if they had had these with them. Some had lost their hair and/or their clothes. Not all had been raped, some only threatened with such, others beaten but not severely, still others savagely, some even to death and . . . and recently. *Ah, merde!*

Female, age 20–25, no identity papers, hair jet-black and glossy, colour of eyes not possible. Beaten, raped and kicked to death. Died of a massive haemorrhage.

The attack had taken place in the *passage* de l'Hirondelle, a narrow lane off the rue Gît-le-Coeur in the Sixth, and so close to Hermann's flat and the House of Madame Chabot it sickened.

Pinned to the left side of the map, Walter had noted many of the things they, too, had discovered or been thinking.

1) Violence escalating?
2) Attacks not random but chosen so as to give that impression?
3) The work of a gang whose sources of information yield potential targets that are then followed up on?
4) Targets selected by a committee or by one individual? If so, could information be leaked about Giselle le Roy

so as to put into action the Höherer SS Oberg's astute suggestion that we use the girl to bait a trap?

5) Won't these criminals already have had access to that information? If so, is it their intent to use it before we do?

Had they already done so? St-Cyr had to wonder. Was Oona to be next?

6) Are the press being notified only when felt useful?

A hastily scribbled notation revealed just how desperate things must be.

7) Could the *Terroristen* be contacted and convinced to help in return for lenience and an end to the shooting of hostages or given the offer of treatment, when captured, as prisoners of war under the articles of the Geneva Convention?

The Résistance—had that been behind the Standartenführer's taking Gabrielle to dinner? To sound things out?

She would not have gone along with anything, and Langbehn wouldn't have asked. It was total war and everyone knew it, Walter as well.

Beneath Sonja Remer's name and the telex, there was a slip of notepaper dated 1610 hours, Thursday 11 February and signed by Oberg.

Informants advise possibility of assaults being committed this evening in the passage de la Trinité and outside the Restaurant Drouant. If confirmed, advise assigning Kohler and St-Cyr to those.

There was no mention of the police academy attack or of the robbery at *Au Philatéliste Savant,* nor was there any of Lulu.

7

Venetian chandeliers gave light, deep Prussian-blue velvet drapes hid the crisscrosses of sticking paper on the windows. Paintings still hung, but there were now so many, some leaned against others on the carpeted floor: a Dürer, a Frans Hals—all of them stolen, of course, but why had Hermann decided to come here, to Number 72 the avenue Foch? Why hadn't he met up with his partner first, if for no other reason than to let him mention Sonja Remer's being assigned such a pistol, any pistol?

Dejected, the spirit totally beaten, Hermann was staring at those big, once capable hands as if he had done something terrible. Ashen, he didn't look up, not even when this partner of his, caught between two SS Teutons and hustled by them, was suddenly jerked to a halt before him.

In spite of the presence of the guards, one had to blurt, '*Mon Dieu, mon vieux*, what has happened? Is it Giselle?'

'Giselle?' arched Hermann, flinging up his head.

He couldn't have known of the *passage* de l'Hirondelle attack—mustn't be told of it yet. 'Not Giselle.'

Was it a lie? the look he gave asked, he ignoring the two SS.

'Here, down this, and have one of these,' said St-Cyr, 'then tell me all about it, eh?'

The proffered cigarette wasn't taken . . .

'Rouget. You *didn't* tell me who Denise Rouget's father was!'

'*Ah, merde*, I honestly didn't connect the two. Now toss off the rest of this.'

'Is it the Rémy-Martin Louis XIII? Am I to enjoy an El Rey del Mundo Choix Supreme?'

Sacré nom de nom, what was this? 'Not at all. Of course the bottle isn't the Molotov cocktail these two felt before roughing me up. It simply contains the last of the marc we had in the Citroën's boot.'

'What the hell are we to do, Louis? Our telephone caller, Élène Artur, was nearly four months pregnant. You know what that *belle-époque* plumbing's like on the rue La Boétie. Her killers tried to flush the evidence but the cord got caught and I had to pull it out so gently. A boy, Louis. I know it's hard to tell at that stage, but you *can,* can't you? A son. She'd been beaten, raped . . .'

Out it came in a torrent of French the orderly, an Unterscharführer, and his Sturmmann couldn't understand—even Oberg, head of all of this, couldn't speak a word of the language. 'Leave us,' said St-Cyr in *Deutsch*.

Unterscharführer Bruno Pruetzmann wasn't happy. 'You can't stay here alone.'

'Then back off to the other end of the room. This is private.'

They didn't move, wouldn't move.

'We weren't supposed to find her, Louis. The judge was, but Élène Artur's killing may not have been done by whoever's been terrorizing the streets.'

'Chez Rudi's, I think. We can't talk here.'

'I'VE GOT TO LET OBERG KNOW! If I don't . . .'

'Of course, but it can wait since he's not likely to come in at this hour. Besides, I've got a few things to tell you and something in the car that Rudi wants.'

'Sonja Remer, age twenty-four years, seven months and five days,' breathed Rudi—had he felt they wouldn't be able to retrieve the girl's handbag? wondered St-Cyr.

'Mädelscharführerin at the age of ten; leader of a *Gruppe* at eleven, a *Ring* at twelve. When a Bund Deutscher Mädel such as this comes along, others take notice.'

He'd give these two a moment to digest the lump they'd been fed, but would the regurgitation of it sink into Hermann? The *idiot* looked like death in a greatcoat and should, for he hadn't only stolen a car from two of the Propagandastaffel, he had had them consigned to scrubbing toilets! 'Not for her the *Glaube und Schönheit,* Hermann.'

The Faith and Beauty brigade of the BDMs—girls selected not only for their physical attributes as examples of Aryan Nazism but to be trained further in the arts of homemaking or made to tease secrets from high-ranking civil servants and captains of industry.

'Untergauleiterin at that same age,' went on Rudi.

A leader of five or six *Ringe.*

'Only when young Erich Straub was about to leave for his *Heldentod* did she break down and reveal what she'd been up to with that boy whose family her father couldn't tolerate.'

'The happy couple became engaged,' said Louis with a sigh. 'The third of March 1940, and on the twenty-ninth of April she and the boy's family received notice of the hero's death.'

'*Kommen sie,*' urged Rudi. 'Sit, *ja.* Helga, *bitte*, the soup first and then the *Eintopf.* Your Hermann needs nourishment. We're offering the Reichsführer SS *und* Reichskommissar Himmler's one-pot meal at noon today and nothing else but the soup, the same as is on the menu at Horscher's.'

On the Lutherstrasse and central Berlin's famous restaurant, it having apparently escaped the RAF's nightly bombing raids.

'Red cabbage from home, *meine Lieben.* Pieces of roast meat— I'm using sausage with Charolais beef and New Zealand mutton that was taken off a freighter bound for England but captured by one of our raiders. Potatoes, of course, and onions and beef stock. The trick is to let the meat marinate in wine and not be impatient. A full day if possible. A decent Bordeaux, a Château Lafite perhaps, but I have used a Mouton Rothschild, the 1929. Baked in individual casseroles to preserve all the flavour and juices. Served with chunks of crusty bread—those French sticks I have to make for the curious from Berlin are suitable enough and will have to do since there are extra and they shouldn't be wasted.'

To be forced to listen to this with Hermann so upset and needing answers was hard enough for a French patriot, and Rudi knew it too, which could only mean he had more in mind. 'The soup is excellent, Herr Sturmbacher.'

'Ich Linsensuppe mit Thüringer Rotwurst.'

Lentil soup with Thuringian sausages. Rudi was giving them time, but for what? Kohler had to wonder. 'The Tokarev, Rudi.' It lay all but hidden by the still opened handbag.

'Ach, einen Moment, bitte! First you must see with whom you're dealing. Helga, bring your big brother what he has borrowed from the library of the Propaganda-Abteilung, which is so close its staff are among my most valued customers.'

And if that wasn't warning enough, what was? wondered Kohler.

Photo magazines made life easy for readers in the Reich, seeing as they'd just been introduced to full mobilization. The cover of one of last autumn's *Die Woche*, The Week, revealed a very determined blonde *Mädchen* tying barley sheaves. The Nazi Party's *Illustrierter Beobachter* gave an even more heroic stance, facing into the morning sun, standing with a sheaf under each arm and all of Russia before her, though she couldn't possibly have seen it.

'On the death of her Erich, Hermann, the girl needed time to gather herself and then, after the blitzkrieg's dust had settled in the west, volunteered for duty with the *Landvolk*. She was sent to Vresse in the Semois Valley to supervise female Belgian farm labourers.'

'An admirable ambition and location, Rudi, but shouldn't she have been harvesting tobacco?' asked Hermann.

A good sign felt St-Cyr, not because the area was famous for that crop, but because the comment had come from the old Hermann. 'She looks healthy enough, Herr Sturmbacher, which would seem to indicate sufficient time for her to have come to peace with her loss, but did she learn French while among the Walloons?'

'*Ach, mein lieber Oberdetektiv,* how is it, please, that you even knew the girl could speak such an inferior language?'

One mustn't react. 'I didn't. I just assumed.'

'You did neither. The boys who stole that handbag and roughed her up told you.'

'Rudi, listen,' urged Hermann. 'They were only boys. *Mein Gott,* my Jurgen and Hans might have done the same under similar circumstances.'

'But would have been punished, isn't that so?'

'She wasn't beaten up,' muttered Louis.

'NOT THREATENED WITH A KNIFE?' demanded Rudi.

'Is that what she claims?'

'That and other things, Louis,' said Kohler with a sigh. 'Oberg had her into his office to tell Hercule the Smasher all about it, but I don't think she was asked to bare the breasts she claimed had been badly bruised.'

Sickened, the Oberdetektiv St-Cyr was at a loss, Rudi knew, and couldn't lift his gaze from the soup he had been trying to enjoy, but what was this about Hercule the Smasher? Was the judge in trouble?

One had best continue and not let on. 'So, it's serious, *meine Lieben,* and now you know a little of why.' He would flick a glance at each of them, would check out the customers before taking Helga's hand to fondly kiss it, since the girl still dreamed that Hermann would someday realize what he was missing and fall madly in love with her. 'The Höherer SS saw this photo spread in late October and, needing a listener to the *Mundfunk,* Hermann, asked for her to be reassigned to the Paris office.'

The city's mouth-radio, its *radio-trottoir.* The girl's left knee was firmly pressed on that sheaf, her skirt rucked up, she grasping the braided tie as if a hawser.

A regular little Nazi. Slim-waisted, tight-breasted, firm and shapely from all that exercise and something for the boys along the eastern front to hunger for. A classic and exceedingly capable Fräulein, but why did that God of Louis's have to do this to them?

'And when the blackout assaults began to heat up in December?' asked the Sûreté.

There was no avoiding it, Kohler knew. 'He realized he had to do something. That's why the target shooting, that's why the gun, isn't it, Rudi? He assigned her to also work on this little *Mausefalle* of his.'

'Eat a little, please. You're going to need your strength. The Höherer SS wishes a truly SS settlement to this problem the French have created for us. The Fräulein Remer is an excellent shot—oh please don't get the wrong idea about this girl. It has definitely been understood and accepted by all that her body is hers alone, even in the service of the Führer *und Vaterland*. The mother was French from the Lorraine and a devout Catholic. Having sinned once, the girl has accepted that she must do penance and remain true to that one love, if for no other reason than to set an example to the French and to other *Blitzmädchen*. The father, a POW you understand, in that other war like yourself, Hermann, thought the language might be useful to her, as did yourself, isn't that correct, since we had lost that war but won't lose this one, will we?'

'Rudi, what is it you want?'

'Of you? Well, there is a long list, but your undying loyalty to the Führer and Party must come first. The blood oath, I think, and then . . . why then you could start paying sufficient attention to Helga. Dinner twice a week when you're in Paris—slow things down a little but not the current investigation, of course. With others it's not necessary that you solve every crime in a matter of minutes. Try to leave a few. And no more of these other women of yours, Hermann. It doesn't look good. A film—she loves them. Dancing . . .'

'It's illegal both here and in the Reich, but *ja, ja,* get on with it.'

'Be patient. You'll cooperate in all matters, especially by taking the Fräulein Remer and myself fully into your confidence. Knowledge is power, Chez Rudi's by far the best source of all gossip, but to maintain such an enviable reputation—and I do have one—that gossip must be founded on the cement of absolute truth.'

Gaston Morel was that cement, of course, and Rudi must know

of him but was fishing for something else: the judge. 'And if Louis and I agree?'

'Then I can help you with this handbag and its owner. Helga will simply tell the Sicherheitsdienst* that it was thrown on to the doorstep by the driver of one of those bicycle taxis. The Red Cockade or Rooster's Tail, isn't that *korrekt*, Helga?'

'It happened so quickly, Rudi.'

'But between four thirty and five in the afternoon. Not earlier and not later.'

'Yes, Rudi.'

'The licence had an RP, of course, but you can't possibly be certain if it was followed by a fifteen or a ninety-eight.'

And definitely Luc Desrocher's The Red Comb of the Magnificent Cock, owned and operated by Hervé's dear *papa* but leased last night to Albert Vasseur whose Take Me was still in police custody.

'The boys who stole this handbag, and their families, could then rest more easily,' went on Rudi. 'Otherwise I can tell you duty calls, and that should word of what I know get out, I have it on good authority the Höherer SS will not turn the other cheek. He will seize the opportunity to make an example of them, one the French will not forget.'

'Mont-Valérien,' blurted Louis, aghast at what had been revealed.

'Or the rue Laurence Savart, outside of number 3,' said Rudi, watching them closely.

The execution ground of the fort in the industrial suburb of Suresnes and just across the river, to the west of them. It was that or outside Louis's house, in his beloved Belleville.

'Now eat,' said Rudi, getting up to leave them to think about it. 'Enjoy—don't waste a morsel. Helga, a glass or two of that stuff we used for the marinade. We're about to accomplish the impossible. We're going to make a good Nazi out of this *Landsmann* of ours. That, too, is something the Höherer SS demands, and that, my friends, is not gossip.'

---

* the Security Service of the SS and Nazi Party

*   *   *

The restaurant had grown quiet. Rudi did bang pots in the kitchen and hum the *Horst Wessel Lied*, the marching song of the Nazi Party, but Helga had gone off to dream the dream of dreams.

'God always extracts a price, Hermann, and then squeezes a little more.'

'I'm going to have to tell Rudi something.'

'But only a little. You can't be perceived by Oberg as wanting to protect the boys and their families, nor can you go to that one without first reporting to Boemelburg. The chain of command, *n'est-ce pas?* Offend the one and you offend the other. Besides, Walter can perhaps find a way to cushion the theft of that Ford, especially as Himmler is demanding his recall should the perpetrators of these blackout attacks fail to be immediately apprehended.'

'You've been busy, but I'm not going to let them use Giselle. I can't. Not anymore. You've seen her, haven't you? She's okay, isn't she? She's with Oona and the kids . . .'

'Hermann, listen to me. I did what I could but obviously needed more time. There are still places where she . . .'

'Could have holed up? Madame Chabot's?'

'Not there. Not at the flat either. Look, I'm sorry. I was going to tell you.'

'You were going to break it to me when convenient, eh, like Rouget?'

'Sit down. *Please!* Giselle is probably fine.'

'Safe is the word you want, *mein Lieber*. Safe!'

Even Rudi had stopped humming, but Hermann mustn't be told of the rape and killing in the *passage* de l'Hirondelle and all the rest of what this partner of his had yet to impart. He must be shielded from it, had had enough for one evening, had already forced himself to do the impossible. 'Oona may have heard from her. Giselle might simply have been delayed by a film. You know how she is. I didn't stay. I only checked in briefly.'

'And then tried to find Giselle. What's happened to her, Louis?'

'I don't know but wish I did.'

Louis wasn't telling him everything.

'We'll leave the Ford out in front of the Propaganda-Abteilung, Hermann, but will have to siphon off what's left of their petrol.'

'And take the food. I'm not leaving that. We'll drop the keys in their tank so that no one will try to steal the car unless they smash a side windscreen first.'

The sound of a carrot being crunched was followed by that of another. St-Cyr opened his eyes but otherwise told himself not to move.

More of each carrot was taken. They were standing in their pyjamas, woollen socks and pullovers, staring curiously down at him: Adrienne Guillaumet's Louisette to his right; Henri to the left. The curtain of the puppet theatre had been opened.

'Did you put the coffee on?' he asked.

'The acorn water. I told you so, Henri,' whispered his sister, cupping the carrot to hide it.

'We had to move you in here with me,' went on St-Cyr. 'Hermann . . .'

'Needed to be with Oona,' said Henri severely.

'We heard him, *Monsieur l'Inspecteur Principal*. He was very distressed.'

'Giselle,' said the brother.

'Is she dead?' asked the sister.

'Don't say that. Never say it until certain. We'll find her. Don't worry. Ah! help me up. These cushions, this rug, that left shoulder of mine, the left thigh . . . Old bullet wounds, you understand. I slept, can you believe it?'

They hadn't cut into the baguettes from the Ford, had valiantly resisted that temptation. Potatoes were sliced thinly, onions diced. There were no eggs but there was a sprinkling of dill, some oregano too.

'Add some of the meat,' said Henri.

'Just a little,' said Louisette. 'A taste.'

'Don't forget the garlic,' said the brother.

It was nearly noon.

'You should have gone off to school. It's still Saturday, isn't it? And don't tell me you're on strike. I've already heard that one. I'll just have a wash. There isn't a razor, is there?'

'*Papa*'s extra one,' said Louisette. 'We were not allowed to send it to him. Prisoners of war are not allowed such weapons.'

'Good. Take over here. Turn the hot plate down in a moment. Add more oil from time to time. It's good, isn't it? From Mouriès in Provence, I think. The village is close to Arles, which became Caesar's number-one city, even better than Marseille. There's an amphitheatre that would seat more than twenty thousand. Bullfights are still held. Well, they were before this Defeat of ours. I'm not sure since, having been too busy.'

'And the wine?' asked Louisette.

'First take a sip and tell me what you think.'

'It is thin,' she said.

'It's been watered, idiot!' said Henri.

'It's a village wine, a blend of Pinot Noir and the Gamay. A Clos Saint-Denis. The vineyards are not far from the tiny village of Morey-Saint-Denis in the Côte de Nuits and perhaps twelve or so kilometres to the south of Dijon where our mustard used to come from. You are both right, though, but since it's all we have, refill my glass. I won't be long.'

'He's nice, isn't he?' said Louisette when she had Henri to herself. 'He has lost his little son and wife. Everyone in this house of ours has lost someone.'

'*Maman*'s not lost. She's just waiting to get better.'

'Of course, but I was thinking of *Papa*.'

From the rue Saint-Dominique to the quai d'Orsay wasn't far. Once there, they would follow the Seine upriver to the Pont d'Austerlitz. Hermann hadn't insisted on driving, a bad sign, nor had he asked where they were going. Clearly he was still worried about Oberg, the judge and Giselle, but miracle of miracles, the sun was out. Those in the endless queues outside the shops had taken heart. One old woman had even allowed a young mother to step to the head of the line, obeying the rule from Vichy. A twenty-year-old cyclist really did walk his bike, forgetting entirely that the STO thugs could immediately grab and transport him into forced labour, but was it all some sort of sign God wished to give, wondered St-Cyr, or was He merely getting the hopes up so as to make the crunch all the harder?

'Hermann, I'll just have a quick word with Armand, if he's here. If not, perhaps his autopsy on the police academy victim will have been completed.'

'Oona, Louis. Giselle's become like a sister to her in spite of their both living with me when I'm here.'

A clipping, hastily torn from some newspaper, was smoothed out. It was the notice Hermann had repeatedly placed in *Paris-Soir*.

'I found it under the pillows. She'd been clutching it.'

To say, 'I warned you Madame Guillaumet's children would remind her of her own,' would do no good. To say, 'Wait, let me be the one to find out about Giselle,' wouldn't suit either.

'Oona's convinced her children are dead, Louis. I can't shake her thinking on this. I wish to hell I could and now what have I done but made certain Giselle will be . . .'

He couldn't say it, was blaming himself for what could well have happened.

At the confluence of several arteries, and near the Gare de Lyon, the place Mazas and its adjacent streets were busy—there was panic, though, at the sight of the car, *vélo-taxis* and bicycles turning away. 'I'll park on the quai Henri IV, Hermann. It'll be warmer there and you won't have to keep the engine running.'

'Stop mothering me. You know damned well Giselle could be in there under a sheet. Just go in and find out for me.'

Louis pressed cigarettes into his hand but held on to them. 'When we get to Walter, you're definitely not to take any of these out. Walter has marked them.'

'Don't tell me we've a petty thief at HQ, other than myself?'

'Apparently, but I've yet to determine how the head of Gestapo Section IV marked his pipe tobacco and these.'

Identity cards, ration cards and passes . . . *Ausweise, laissez-passers* and *sauf-conduits* . . . Five sets, only five? Not one for Giselle—was that it, eh, or was Louis not planning to join them?

There were tears in Hermann's eyes. His hands shook but he realized the dilemma too, for if Walter Boemelburg had marked his cigarettes, had he not also marked and counted these?

'You really have been busy, haven't you?'

It still wasn't the moment to let Hermann in on everything but a start had best be made. 'Rouget, *mon vieux*. Give me a little on that flat of his.'

The cigarette was passed. Hermann was always best when kept busy. Out came his little black notebook. Pages and pages—how had he written them, knowing what had happened?

'Concierge Louveau says that the judge let others use the flat from time to time. "Important people." Some older than the judge, some younger, but none in the past five weeks—he was certain of this because the last one, a retired general smoked a cigar on the way up at two thirty p.m. on a Wednesday and also at six thirty p.m. on the way out and both times with the same brunette. She'd a nice, if timid smile and "he wore leather gloves, real ones, and had a beautifully trimmed, snow-white moustache and hair just like the Maréchal Pétain's." '

'A general.'

'In a French army greatcoat with ribbons and medals. Do you want more?'

'Give me something on Élène Artur, if possible.'

'Half Indochinese and not permitted to use the front entrance for fear of upsetting the other tenants. Had a key to the other entrance. Wasn't to take the lift, either. Used the side staircase. Never came with, or left with, the judge. Had a key to the flat. Both keys used by her assailants who must have known of them.'

Merde, how had Hermann done it? 'And?'

Kohler took a deep drag, though God alone knew what Vichy's state-run tobacco company was using now to cut the tobacco. Last autumn's oak leaves, pine needles perhaps . . .

'Entry at between 0030 and 0100 hours Friday. Dead by 0130

hours at the latest. It can't have gone on for much longer but they took their time and knew they must have been able to. One of them a butcher, or former butcher—he sure as hell knew how to gut. The knife not the usual—it spurted blood a good metre and more when he withdrew it. A week ago the girl showed up around midnight, but the judge didn't. Louveau was positive about this. His *loge* is only a few steps from the lift, so he definitely would have heard it, especially as he claims to have stayed awake listening for Rouget.'

'Why?'

'Because a week prior to that Friday evening, the judge had done the same thing—not come—and on the following Tuesday and Thursday, and this Tuesday as well. The girl hung around after that last visit to ask Louveau if he thought the judge had been acting strangely. "It's not like Hercule to pay me in advance and not want me." '

' "In advance"?'

'Apparently Rouget had taken to slipping her the money at the Lido, but it definitely wasn't his usual way of doing things. "Always after he has finished with me," she said. "Never before." '

'Had she a pimp?'

'The concierge didn't think so. "She was too independent," he said, and claimed she "wasn't like a woman of the streets or houses." '

No pimp could only mean, as Hermann must have realized, that the academy victim definitely hadn't been hers. 'And on the night of her murder nothing was heard?'

'Not a thing. Earlier though, on the previous visit, the girl "thought she might have done something that had offended the judge." She couldn't understand how Rouget could possibly have found out about it. "He's too busy," she said to Louveau. "He never goes there. Not anymore and certainly not with me, not since last October and only once then. Others would have seen us together." '

'What others?'

'She didn't say.'

'But where? The location, Hermann?'

'I couldn't establish that either.'

'But others must have seen them. Others who went to the same place regularly . . .'

'And guess who must have discovered she was carrying his child?'

Another cigarette was needed. *Dieu merci,* it was like old times.

'She would have had to tell the judge, Louis, but who else found out? Rouget isn't just a member of the Cercle Européen. He also belongs to the Cercle de l'Union Interaliée.'

God had definitely not smiled at them. 'Your Pétain-look-alike general could well be a fellow member, as could, perhaps, the former captain I may have uncovered in the taxi theft, if indeed he was a captain, but let me hold that one in reserve. Please continue.'

'Are you sure you want more?'

'You know I don't like to be kept in suspense.'

'Good. At the repeated insistence of Henriette Morel who believes that husband of hers is having a torrid affair with her stepsister, that one's social worker hired a . . .'

'Permit me, *mon vieux.* A *détective privé* who impersonates a Sûreté and who calls the pipe he is fortunate enough to constantly smoke, his little friend.'

'Monsieur Flavien Garnier of l'Agence Vidocq?'

'The Arcade de Champs-Élysées. It's a small world, isn't it? Adrienne Guillaumet had asked the owner-operator of Take Me to drive her to the Ritz.'

And more generals but definitely not French. 'Did Garnier find this out?'

'He must have. Three men were involved in her assault. One to set it up and get the timing down—that's my "captain" who is the same, I'm sure, as was at the police academy and who lost his little red ribbon, though it wasn't his to lose, and two to carry out the taxi theft, one of whom made certain that the other did. These last two were of medium height, the other almost as tall as the General de Gaulle, the Trinité rapist having broad shoulders like a wedge.'

'And the one with the gut and smelling of fish oil?'

'Our Drouant assailant, no doubt, and from Montmartre, but both likely wearing worn oilskins that must have needed a little help on such a night. A supply of Norwegian margarine, Hermann, that obviously didn't need its ration tickets.'

Quicksand, were they stepping into it? 'Now tell me why not this "captain's" own Légion d'honneur ribbon?'

'Because I'm all but certain I've encountered the owner of it in Noëlle Jourdan's *papa*, but for now the judge's flat, Hermann. Let's stick to that.'

'Two assailants, one of whom must have been to the flat often enough since he was tidy even after what they'd done. When he went through her handbag, but didn't take it, he spilled cigar ash and took time out to try to wipe it away but failed entirely to find her wedding ring. I did.'

Ah *grâce à Dieu*, this was definitely the old Hermann. 'Do you want me to have a look at the flat? We're pressed for time as it is.'

'Aren't we always?'

This, too, was the old Hermann, hedging his bets but still, one had best be cautious. 'Wait for me. Have a stroll. It'll do you good. That sun should be with us for a while.'

'Then let's hope Giselle is alive and looking at it and that Oona doesn't try to join her children by throwing herself in front of a train.'

'Oona didn't say that. She's far too level-headed.'

'Well, maybe she is, but I thought it and that's enough for me.'

'St-Cyr, Sûreté, to see the *passage* de l'Hirondelle victim. Hurry.'

'There's no hurry where that one's going.'

'Is it that you fancy working in the salt mines of Silesia? That is where Gestapo Boemelburg usually threatens to send me if I don't work fast enough. Ah! I'm late as it is for our meeting. *Merde!* Shall I tell him you delayed me and that, as a result, I might get lonely unless I had some company?'

'It is this way, Inspector.'

'It's Chief Inspector, and I know the way.'

'Clothing—do you want to look at it first?'

'Was any of it taken?'

'Scattered, I think. No boots or shoes. No ID, no handbag either, or jewellery of any kind.'

It had been raining hard in the late afternoon. Though darker in the *passage,* there would still have been sufficient daylight. Giselle would have known of the route as a short cut through to *place* Saint-Michel from the rue Gît-le-Coeur. Rapes, muggings, murders, births, deaths from old age, the plague or other natural causes—sex by the moment and paid for or not—the *passage* had seen them all and yes, her native instinct would have caused her to dart into it, though it was also one that could easily have been blocked off at its other end. Trapped, she would have had to turn to face her assailants.

Giselle's dark-blue woollen overcoat, with its broad 1930s lapels and flaps over the pockets, had been thin and a little threadbare. Hermann would never use his position as one of the Occupier to better the state of his household or himself. Stubborn . . . *mon Dieu*, he could be stubborn.

Folded, the coat had lost four of its buttons and had obviously been torn open. The soft grey tartan scarf that had set off the colour of her eyes was wet and cold, the grey-blue knitted mittens also. The angora cloche she had been particularly fond of was drenched and filthy.

A girl with short, straight, jet-black hair, half Greek, half Midi-French.

'Is there nothing else?'

'Apparently not.'

'Time of death?'

'Late yesterday afternoon probably.'

Friday. 'Found when?'

'At just after eight last night, the new time. Someone tripped over her.'

'Who?'

'It doesn't say.'

'Witnesses?'

'None.'

'Examining *flic*?'

A name was given but it meant nothing. Paris's police force had expanded so much and now there were also 'auxiliary police' and 'order police,' neither of which needed the full qualifications of the first.

'Leave me. If Herr Kohler comes looking for me, don't let him in. If you do, I'll hound you until you die.'

Mud-grey to brown, the river moved swiftly. Upstream there were no barges; downstream it was the same. *Der* Führer, in his wisdom, had had them all taken in the early autumn of 1940 for the invasion of England that had never happened. Now, of course, they lay rotting in the north, cluttering up the harbours unless dragged away and beached or sent to Belgium and elsewhere, and the citizen-coal that should have come to Paris, didn't. Even the compressed dust of its poorest briquettes.

Louis wouldn't be able to identify Giselle, not if they'd done what they had to the police academy victim. She'd a thumbprint-sized mole in the small of her back he wouldn't know of, a blemish she had constantly worried about.

'Giselle,' he said, looking off across *place* Mazas to the morgue. Louis was taking far too long and that could only mean . . .

Irritably he lit another cigarette only to fling it away. This war, this lousy Occupation, the terrible loneliness and the shortages that should never have happened, the runaway inflation, too, all of which could and did put decent mothers and wives or fiancées down on their hands and knees or backs and made others hate them.

And if it isn't Giselle, the detective in him had to ask, then have the bastards got her?

Telephone calls were always listened to by others, but . . . '*Allô? Oui, oui, c'est moi,* St-Cyr. Once pierced but definitely closed up? The Madame Van der Lynn was certain of this?'

She was. '*Ah, bon. Merci.*'

Replacing the receiver was not difficult, tearing his gaze from it somewhat harder. The call to the commissariat of the *quartier* du Gros-Caillou had been by far the hardest he had ever had to make, the waiting for its return a positive agony.

They had sent one of their staff to the residence of Madame Adrienne Guillaumet, there not being a telephone in that building, up-market though the district was.

'Please tell Coroner Tremblay that he's to look for the marks of hobnails and to compare the *passage* de l'Hirondelle's victim with that of the police academy killing. No one else is to examine either victim, is that clear?'

'No one. Do you want to see the loose dental fillings?'

It would be best to shake the head. 'Put what clothing was found with her out of sight in the lockup and don't release it to anyone other than Coroner Tremblay or myself. Not to Herr Kohler, you understand. Definitely not to him.'

Fifty francs were found in a wallet that had been mended with fishing line, the cash a sacrifice, but would it help to cement the bargain? These days one had to pay for everything.

Hermann had been impatiently waiting but had best be steadied. 'Not her,' said St-Cyr, taking him by the arm. 'This one had pierced earlobes. Age perhaps twenty. Jet-black hair, what was left of it. Now listen, Giselle may have gone to ground.'

'Not taken? Not abducted and held in reserve?'

He was really rattled. 'This one was wearing Giselle's overcoat, cloche, scarf and mittens.'

'And they followed the wrong one?'

'They must have.'

'Then they made a mistake and it went harder on the girl they caught?'

'Harder, yes.'

'Rage?'

'Uncontrolled. Hermann, the sooner we meet with Walter, the sooner we can get back to work.'

'You leave Denise Rouget to me, then, Louis, and that mother of hers.'

'Walter, *mon vieux*, but first a little stop en route. Now give me one of those cigarettes. It's not like me to steal things. Usually you are the one who does.'

'Not Giselle . . .'

'Hermann, Oona will have understood this from what was relayed.'

'She and the children won't go out, will they, or open the door to anyone but us or Giselle?'

'That, too, was relayed.'

'Then I'll drive. We'll get there faster.'

The rue des Francs-Bourgeois was busy, the queues in front of the *mont-de-piété* of the Crédit Municipal de Paris among the longest Kohler had ever seen. The wealthy, the poor, the middle class, all had come to pay homage to that great leveller of humanity, Ma Tante.

Four staff cars, their drivers waiting with engines running, were in a line of their own, their officers inside as prospective buyers of what had been left beyond the required length of time. Six months, was it, or now three?

'Four,' came the intuitive reply, Louis not liking what they were seeing, but where else were those who had no firm contacts in the black market supposed to go, if not here?

'You'd better let me come with you,' said Kohler. 'You know how shirty those bastards behind the wickets can be. Muscle is the only thing they understand.'

'And is it that you still don't think I've got what it takes?'

Three pale-green tickets were dug out of one of those bottomless overcoat pockets. Always Louis was collecting the bits and pieces of each investigation.

'So often, Hermann, it's the little things that count. When I found these in Noëlle Jourdan's empty locker at the *Hôtel-Dieu*, I knew I couldn't resist a visit here.'

'You're enjoying yourself. Admit it.'

'That girl has much to tell us and now we are about to pry the secrets from her but . . .'

'Boemelburg will insist that we not bother wasting time with the robbery at Au Philatéliste Savant.'

'And that's precisely why I'm making certain we do, especially as we were definitely not to have been assigned to that one.'

'Noëlle Jourdan didn't pawn the collection.'

'But it's curious, isn't it? Why pawn other items and not that one?'

'Familiarity. Too frequent a visitor to this place?'

'Perhaps, but then . . . *ah, mais alors, alors*, Hermann, was it that the girl realized how little Ma Tante was given to charity and wished to better herself?'

'Or knew those tickets could be used to identify her.'

Good for Hermann. 'But did the robbery of those stamps really have nothing whatsoever to do with the murders and assaults or has chance played its part by sending us to it?'

Chance could sometimes mean everything these days. 'I'm waiting, Louis. I do know that for the lousy two thousand francs *Le Matin* paid her, the girl gave up a very promising career.'

'One that obviously allowed her to acquire the Veronal her dear *papa* needed.'

'A *papa* who should have been wearing his Légion d'honneur. And now what's she to do, eh? Try her hand at making artillery shells or lorries and aircraft here for the Reich, or get on a train to there and leave that father behind?'

'Or find some shopkeeper who'll be willing to hire and not insist on getting into her?'

'There has to have been a reason.'

'And we have to find it, even if the theft of those stamps is totally unrelated to the rest.'

'Which it can't have been, can it?'

'Not unless I'm very wrong.'

The tureen, of Augsburg silver circa 1770, was magnificent. Brought out to be laid on the counter of despair, its design incorporated the heads of several *Chrysanthemum leucanthemum.*

'A priceless heirloom for such a poor household, Hermann. *Mon Dieu,* there was hardly any furniture in the flat and never a trace of anything like this.'

'And that one?' asked Kohler, still shouldering the curious out of the way.

'A pilgrim bottle in Augsburg silver-gilt.'

'Late seventeenth century,' offered the mouse in the bow tie behind the wicket.

'Engraved, Hermann. Peasants at table in an orchard. The mark of its maker, that of?' asked Louis pleasantly enough.

'Johann Christoph Treffler,' swallowed Jérome Godet. These two were going to insist on confiscating the items. Monsieur le Directeur Ducasse, who had still not come back from lunch, would be furious and bound to dismiss him.

'And the last?' asked the one with the dueling scar who was still toying with the pistol he had lain on the counter.

'Meissen, Herr . . .'

'Don't tell me you've already forgotten? Louis, can you believe it? Tell him my name.'

'It's not necessary. Now please don't argue, Herr Hauptmann. We haven't time. An urgent meeting with Gestapo Boemelburg . . .'

'Meissen, Inspectors. The work is most probably that of Heinrici, the date perhaps 1750.'

'A gold-mounted, *Commedia dell' Arte* double snuffbox, Herr Detektiv Aufsichtsbeamter Kohler. The funds released to hold such objects, Agent Jérome Godet?'

Ah, merde! 'One hundred francs for the box; one fifty for the bottle, and . . .' It would do no good to lie. 'Three hundred for the tureen.'

A fantastic bargain.

'Pay him, Hermann. That way he'll be certain to remember your name and not mine. Sign for the objects, too, of course, and tell him that they'll be returned unless it's discovered that they've been stolen, in which case, by having accepted them and not notifying the proper authorities, he'll face a charge of compliance perhaps or even complicity.'

Out on the street, back in the Citroën, Hermann sighed as he fondly gripped the wheel of a car that wasn't even his. 'I enjoyed that, Louis. It was like old times. I stopped worrying about everything else.'

Newspapers littered the antique limewood desk that had been made larger by the addition of pine planks. *Bien sûr, Le Matin* and *Paris-Soir* were there, but also the *Berliner Zeitung* and *Das Schwarze Korps*—that of the SS—*Der Angriff* as well, The Assault—Goebbels's Berlin afternoon paper. All were splashed with the news from Paris and all were, no doubt, demanding that the crisis be settled and the streets made safe again.

'Walter . . .' hazarded St-Cyr. The *Herein*, the Come in, had been brutal.

'*SCHMETTERLINGE*, LOUIS. *DIE KLEINE SCHLAMPE* WAS CAUGHT PUTTING THEM IN *MÉTRO* CARRIAGES. HAND-COLOURED PAPER STICKERS THE SIZE OF MY THUMBPRINT. RAF BULL'S-EYES ON THE WINGS, THE CROSS OF LORRAINE ON THE BODIES. *VERDAMMTE HURE*, SHE'LL HAVE TO BE SHOT!'

Butterflies were what these little stickers were called, though not always done in the shape of such but, 'Walter . . .'

'*Putain de merde*, what is wrong with you French? *ORDNUNG MUSS SEIN!*'

Fucking hell . . . order must prevail. The big hands were thrown out in defeat, the all but shaven, blunt grey head shaken in despair.

'Ten hostages are not enough. Twenty will have to be chosen and she'll have to be one of them. The Höherer SS will insist on it. I'm sorry, Louis. It can't be helped. Not this time.'

'Walter, who was the girl?'

A name was searched for but couldn't be found. The Nordic eyes, bagged by overwork and worry, were ever angry. 'It was an ATTACK!' came the shrill response. 'WE THOUGHT WE HAD BROKEN THE BACK OF THE FTP IN DECEMBER. INFILTRATED, BETRAYED, WE HAD THEM ALL.'

But not quite. The Francs-Tireurs et Partisans . . .

'COMMUNISTS. IMMIGRANTS—ROMANIANS, ITALIANS, JEWS, POLISH *UNTERMENSCHEN*!'

Subhumans.

'At ten this morning, when you two were no doubt still asleep, one of them tossed a grenade into a lorry on the boulevard Haussmann and close enough for the avenue Foch to have heard the blast. French driver killed, French assistant killed, windows shattered, blood and glass all over the street and everyone rushing in to grab what meat they could and let the bastard get away.' A breath was caught. 'Chickens . . . Alive but a moment beforehand.'

And a black-market lorry, sighed Kohler inwardly and still standing behind Louis but towering over him as the chief would too. Fifty percent of those chickens would have already been removed by the boys on the controls, and as for the FTP, unlike other *réseaux* if they even existed, and they did, their whole policy was one of armed resistance, hence the hostages that would have to be shot.

'Now sit down. Kohler close the door. Louis, have a cigarette. Go on. Take one.'

'*Merci*. Hermann, would you . . .'

'I didn't offer him one, Louis.'

'Forgive me, then, if I save it for later.'

'All right, Kohler, you may take one, but only one.'

'The butterflies, Walter. Let's have that, so that we can fully comprehend what has upset you so much.'

That bit of paper was finally found. 'A schoolgirl. Age seventeen. Geneviève Beauchamp. No previous record but juvenile delinquency has become a problem, hasn't it?'

Oh-oh, the boys. Antoine and the others, thought Kohler. The squeeze.

'Walter, the Fräulein Sonja Remer's handbag was returned by me via Rudi Sturmbacher,' said Louis.

'And not thrown there from a passing bicycle taxi?'

'Not thrown.'

'But without its chocolate bar, Louis, and tin of bonbons,' said Boemelburg.

'That couldn't be helped, given the shortages and the necessity of returning it as soon as possible, along with its Tokarev TT-33, which was fully loaded.'

Such sang-froid in the face of the inevitable was admirable. '*À beau jeu, beau retour,* then, Louis.' One good turn deserves another.

'Kohler, you and Louis will take the Fräulein Remer fully into your confidence. You will involve her, work with her and use her to fullest advantage. Is that understood?'

Rudi had been right. Giselle was to have been the bait. '*Jawohl,* Sturmbannführer.'

'*Gut.* Now these murders, muggings and rapes. What have you got for me?'

'They're the work of more than one individual,' said Kohler. *Gott sei Dank,* Louis had been in and had read the chief's note, pinned to the left of the map.

'The level of violence is escalating,' said St-Cyr.

'Well planned, Louis?'

'Exceptionally so.'

'Good sources of information?'

'Excellent,' interjected Hermann. 'We have a probable source but would like to hold that for the time being.'

'A gang?' asked Boemelburg.

'Most certainly,' said Louis, 'though they might not wish to refer to themselves as such.'

'Terrorist links?'

'None that are known, but . . .' went on Hermann.

'But what?'

Louis gave a nod. 'The mothballs are a possibility,' said Kohler. 'One of them, or two, or more.'

'Ex-military types, Walter. This was found at the site of the police academy killing.'

'The ribbon of the Légion d'honneur. Some honour, eh? I want him, you two. He's to be made an example of.'

And hadn't the General von Schaumburg said the same to Hermann? 'There is one thing that has yet to be clarified, Walter.

Whoever wore this may not have been its owner. That is to say, he may have worn the ribbon to . . .'

'Facilitate things,' sighed Boemelburg, 'since the very sight of it still opens doors and commands respect. Now give me the identity of the police academy victim?'

'We're working on it,' managed Hermann. 'There's . . .'

'A connection with another killing, Walter. A delicate matter we felt it best to discuss with you first.'

'How delicate?'

'Very,' breathed Hermann. 'The rue La Boétie. A dancer from the Lido, half-*indochinoise* and mistress of Judge Hercule Rouget, *Président du* . . .'

'*Ach, mein Gott,* what is it with you two? The Höherer SS is going to have to be informed of this but have either of you any idea of what he'll say to me, and it is to me who will be left the task of telling him?'

Calm was necessary. 'Walter,' said St-Cyr, 'her murder was quite possibly done in the judge's flat so that her killers could hide behind his close association with the Höherer SS.'

'Rouget would have had to inform him of it so as to hush things up—is this what you're saying?'

It was.

'Two men, Sturmbannführer, one of whom was familiar with the flat.'

Kohler had found her then, not Louis.

'The girl's killing is definitely linked to that of the police academy,' said St-Cyr.

'Though she was not, in so far as we yet know, present during that killing, the girl was most likely taken from the Lido after first having been forced to telephone the press and then the police.'

'And not killed until last night, Kohler?'

'Killed at between 0100 and 0130 hours Friday, Sturmbannführer. The child she was carrying was deliberately removed and an attempt made to hide it from investigating officers.'

'Uncontrolled rage, Walter, was evident also in the earlier killing at the academy and . . .' Louis paused. 'In that of the *passage* de l'Hirondelle of yesterday afternoon, a girl who was wearing the overcoat and hat of Giselle le Roy.'

'Who must have discovered she was being followed, Sturmbannführer.'

'Oberg's choice of bait, Louis?' blurted Boemelburg.

'We don't yet know where Mademoiselle le Roy is, but are working on it.'

'There's something else,' apologized Hermann. 'The Trinité victim, and both of the Drouant victims, were being investigated by the Agence Vidocq, a M. Flavien Garnier.'

'You two . . . Are you both so blind? The avenue Foch and ourselves use them from time to time. Garnier is one of ours, as is his employer.'

'The Intervention-Referat?' managed Louis. It had had to be asked.

'That I can't, of course, answer, but I didn't know the *agence* was keeping an eye on unlicenced *horizontales*. You watch yourselves with this. Don't, and see what happens. Now get out. You have twenty-four hours and, Kohler . . .'

Boemelburg stubbed out his half-finished cigarette. 'Don't steal any more cars. It doesn't look good for me in Berlin. It can't, can it, especially when the Kommandant von Gross-Paris has to telephone me about it?'

'That girl, Walter? Geneviève Beauchamp . . . That misguided teenager?' tried Louis, a patriot to the last.

'I'll see what I can do but is it that you want me to have the boys in your neighbourhood arrested and their families?'

Instead of executing the girl? 'Walter, we'll solve this matter for you. We're almost there and only need a little more time.'

'Good. See that you do but don't forget what I said about the Agence Vidocq.'

Again they shared a cigarette. Consulting others who must be working on blackout crime would be useless. There was simply too much hatred, too much jealousy. 'Blitzkrieg is the only thing Walter understands at the moment, Hermann, what with Himmler and the rest of Berlin breathing fire down his back and Oberg no doubt fanning the flames.'

Oberg. 'I'm waiting.'

'*Ah, bon.* While we were on the train home, Oberg sent Walter a note advising him to assign us to the Trinité and Drouant should attacks be committed there.'

As they damned well had been. 'And when was that written and sent over?'

'Time 1610 hours Thursday, but there's something else. Gabrielle was taken to dinner last night by the Standartenführer Langbehn. I think now, that in addition to wanting us to look out for her son should anything happen to her, Gabi may have been trying to warn us, but we didn't have a chance to discuss anything.'

'And now you tell me! We're to take this Sonja Remer fully into our confidence so that she can report everything to this SS colonel?'

'Who then . . .'

'Uses Giselle, if found, in Oberg's little *souricière*?'

'Ostensibly to trap the very ones we're after.'

'And us, Louis. *Us.* Admit it. Oberg hates our guts and would like nothing better than to be rid of us but he can't do that without Boemelburg's help, and that one still needs us, so that one doesn't quite know what's up and has to go along with things anyway.'

Hermann always *would* grasp at straws, even that Walter would continue to back them. 'Oberg must have known we were not only on that train but that Walter was planning to assign us to the investigation.'

'That little *Blitzmädel* of his is one hell of a shot. Rudi wouldn't have said so otherwise. Not Rudi. SS floodlights will make night into day in some stinking *passage*. That girl will be right behind us and guess who'll come out of it smelling of roses?'

'Informants, Hermann. *Indics* gave Oberg prior notification of the locations of those two attacks.'

'The Agence Vidocq?'

'We shall have to ask them.'

'Oberg can't have let the chief in on it, can he?'

And stubborn to the last. 'We're deliberately assigned to two assaults that give us examples of what's been happening. Then later on in the evening are found because we are on Talbotte's roster for the evening and fun is fun, so are sent to the academy for a further example.'

'Only to then find that Giselle was to have been taken, Louis. She wasn't to have gotten away.'

'But ourselves conditioned to the severity of the problem and all too willing to go along with Oberg's using her.'

'Knowing that we couldn't refuse, that an order was an order.'

'Let's go back through things. Let's get it all straight if possible. The academy victim is taken at . . .'

'You're forgetting Lulu.'

'*Ah, bon.* Madame Catherine-Élizabeth de Brisac, whose *hôtel particulier* overlooks Parc Monceau, loses her beloved terrier. The dog is held for a time that must be determined, but then has its scant remains hastily buried on Thursday afternoon at just before closing.'

'The academy victim is then abducted at about 1930 hours, but we still don't know from where. The Lido maybe.'

'He escapes but briefly and is killed by 2030 or 2100 hours.'

'Three assailants. His fingers, Louis. What did they do with them?'

'The Seine most probably.'

'Here, give me a drag and I'll light us another. And at 2313 hours Élène Artur—it has to have been her—is forced to put in a call to the commissariat, having first tipped off *Le Matin*. The academy victim may or may not have been a pimp, but she most likely didn't use one, and beyond those two phone calls there is, at present, only two connections with this earlier murder.'

'The killers must have been known to each other, at least in part, and the one who wore the red ribbon was involved in both it and the Trinité assault. Earlier he took a taxi ride to size things up from the Café de la Paix, and then must have hurried to get to the police academy which implies he had an SP sticker and an allotment of petrol.'

'Élène Artur must have been a distinct embarrassment Oberg could well have decided had best be removed, Louis.'

'And where better to do it than in the judge's flat.'

'But with him finding her, not us.'

Such things were always done behind the scenes and the Intervention-Referat were very much a part of them. Hardened criminals but also men drawn from the ranks of the Milice now, and still others, especially here in Paris, from among the Parti Populaire Français, the PPF of the fiery orator and would-be Hitler, Jacques Doriot.

'But well before the rue La Boétie killing, Hermann, Madame Adrienne Guillaumet finishes teaching her night class at the École Centrale.'

'And is taken to the passage de la Trinité.'

'Time 2145 to 2150 hours. No later.'

'The Drouant attack then takes place at 2352.'

'With plenty of time for the one with the gut to have got there from *place* de l'Opéra but perhaps not enough beforehand for that one to have been involved in the academy killing.'

'The break-in at Au Philatéliste Savant is then committed at between 0020 and 0030 hours.'

'But with insufficient time for the Drouant assailant to have got there from the restaurant. Not on a night like that, but plenty of time for the Trinité assailant, if needed.'

'Mud from the sewers.'

'Fish-oil margarine, but an ample supply from where, Hermann?'

'The black market probably. In any case, none of the killings and assaults are thought to be related to the stamp robbery, and that's probably why we weren't suppose to have been assigned to it.'

'Perhaps. And early on Friday afternoon Giselle leaves Madame Guillaumet's flat to find you. She pays Madame Chabot a little visit and . . .'

'Was turned away, wasn't she?'

'Banished.'

'Somehow she discovers she's being followed.'

'And switches her coat . . .'

'She would never have done a thing like that had she known what would happen.'

'Of course not, but that victim is then discovered in the *passage* de l'Hirondelle at around 2000 hours.'

'Was it bad?'

'I couldn't identify who it might be beyond taking a look at the earlobes. Oona confirmed that Giselle had had her ears pierced some years ago but that they had become infected, no doubt due to wearing fake silver wires, and that she had sworn off wearing such earrings.'

'And the little scars had then grown in place.' How had Louis forced himself to find them?

'Perhaps the hobnailed boots of our Légion d'honneur wearer are the same, Hermann. Armand may be able to confirm but I don't envy him the task.'

A deep drag was taken and held for the longest time. 'And Giselle, Louis? Was the rage shown in the *passage* de L'Hirondelle meant for her, or because it wasn't her?'

It was a good question but caution had best be used. 'I . . . I don't know, *mon vieux*. I wish I did and that she was safely here between us.'

8

All along the Champs-Élysées, right to the Arc de Triomphe, the last rays of the sun were caught among the naked branches of the chestnut trees. Kohler eased off on the accelerator. Hadn't Louis marched down this avenue in the Armistice Day parade of 1919 and in every one of them since until the Defeat? Didn't he love the view?

'Hermann, hurry up!'

And never satisfied! 'I thought you might need to see it.'

'A last time? Don't taunt a patriot. You know the view's been spoiled.'

They passed the Hôtel Claridge whose *belle-époque* façade welcomed generals and holders of the Knight's Cross, especially its U-boat captains. *Vélos* and *vélos-taxis* were everywhere, but there were more cars here, of course, for hadn't the Occupier a love of the avenue too?

'We'll hit the Arcade together, Hermann. You into the Lido after those who try to avoid us, myself into the office.'

And so much for his having backup. He was out the door before the engine could be switched off. He was into the Arcade, moving through the foot-traffic. 'Louis . . .'

'Quit dawdling. This is Sûreté business.'

And hadn't one of those been impersonated?

A café, a sugar-cake from that same *belle époque*, formed an island in the Arcade and even though this partner of his knew of it, Louis jabbed a finger that way and said, 'An entrance to the Lido is in there,' as he hit a glass-and-oak-panelled door with gilded lettering, went in and momentarily disappeared from view.

The Agence Vidocq.

'St-Cyr, Sûreté, mademoiselle. Your director first and then a Monsieur . . . Come, come, Herr Hauptmann Detektiv Aufsichtsbeamter, since you don't obey orders, what the hell was the bastard's name?'

'M. Flavien Garnier, *Monsieur l'Inspecteur Principal.*'

And given like a parrot or a mouse. 'Well, mademoiselle?'

The girl at the desk behind the stand-up counter with its little bell in brass had wet herself. Embarrassment flushed the peaches-and-cream complexion under a delightfully made-up pair of the bluest eyes Kohler had ever seen.

'Find your voice, mademoiselle, or I'll find it for you.'

'Louis . . .'

'Colonel . . . Colonel Delaroche has gone to pick up Petit Bob. Monsieur Garnier is out on an investigation and not expected back until Monday at the earliest. Noontime, I think.'

A lie of course. Sweet of her though, to have tried, thought Kohler.

'Messieurs Raymond and Quevillon are . . . are busy elsewhere.'

Another lie.

'I'll bet they are,' breathed Louis. 'I'll just have a look around and then you can tell me everything I need to know. Hermann, put the lock on before going to find . . . What was his name, mademoiselle?'

'Colonel Delaroche.'

'*Ah, bon,* she's recovered her voice, but before you go, I'd better ask her where this Petit Bob is?'

Blue eyes looked at what she'd been typing. She thought to take it out and hide it, then thought better of doing so. 'The . . . the *toilette pour chiens.* Madame Mailloux. Chez Bénédicte. It's . . .'

'Just up the avenue, Hermann. It's been years since I last had to stop in there. Say hello for me. If that doesn't open that one's trap, use your Gestapo clout.'

'Giselle, Louis.'

'We'll find her. Don't worry. Just be yourself. That's what we need.'

Petit Bob was magnificent. Though gentle, he made some of the other dogs nervous. He didn't like having his nails clipped in front of them but understood that it was required. Dutifully he held the left forepaw absolutely motionless. Gazing up at his master who stood by but didn't have a hand on him, he gave that one such a sorrowful look, another half carrot stick was warranted.

Tall, suave, handsome, fifty-five to sixty, with deep brown eyes and immaculately trimmed silvery-grey hair and sideburns that served to emphasize the burnished, cleanly shaven cheeks and aristocratic countenance, Colonel Delaroche wore a knotted, mustard-yellow scarf and charcoal-black woollen cloak with the air and confidence of a thirty-year-old on the hustle circa the seventeenth *siècle*, but his words when they came were something else again. 'It's all right, Bob,' he said, the tone carefully modulated. 'There's my soldier. The hind paws will soon be done and then we'll go for a walk and when we come back, I'll take you in and you can say hello to all the girls. Bénédicte loves you like I do. We'll only be a moment more. Good, Bob. Brave, Bob. We can't have nails curling in on themselves, now can we?'

The voice, definitely of the upper crust, patently ignored the fact they'd a visitor.

The ears were lovingly caressed, the jowls touched. Bag-drooped eyes, of exactly the same shade as his master's, engendered an ever-mournful look. The short-haired coat, of black and tan, gleamed. The fine touches of white on Bob's forepaws, chest and tip of the tail were the marks of an aristocrat. Four years old, maybe five, and absolutely b-e-a-utiful.

Hair dryers of the kind used by *coiffeurs et coiffeuses* were going full blast as two Schnauzers basked in post-bath warmth but eyed

Bob with what could only be a cruel intent. A terrier, though being stripped and plucked, felt no differently. The poodle that was being given a designer hairdo watched them all, as girls in blue *sarraux* dutifully clipped, brushed, groomed and swept up the hair that even from here would have a market.

The blanket of a heavy cologne dampened everything but the sounds. 'Kohler, Madame Mailloux. Kripo, Paris-Central.'

Copies of *Pour Elle* and *L'Illustration* were lowered out in the waiting room, for this . . . this Gestapo had deliberately left the curtained doorway open. 'I'm too busy. Even such as yourself could not help but see this.'

The hair, dyed a wicked blonde, was piled in curls that might last the week out under the bedtime net if one didn't toss and turn too much. The cheeks were of high colour under their rouge and powder, the lips vermillion, the eyes made up and of the swiftest, darkest grey.

'Well?' she demanded, tightening her grip on the clippers, a nail flying off.

'Of course, but like yourself, time is short and the work just keeps piling up. We've another rape and murder to deal with.'

'We?' snapped *Madame la patronne*, heaving rounded shoulders as she gestured with both hands to indicate the crowd and stood as tall as himself and Delaroche. 'Is it that you don't know why there's such a rush at this hour, Inspector? No girl or woman dares be out after dark, my clients, my girls and especially myself!'

'Herr . . .' began Delaroche only to think better of it as Bob questioningly lifted eyes to this intruder.

'It's Inspector.'

'Certainly, but could you not hold off for a moment? Petit Bob is almost done.'

'WE?' demanded Madame Mailloux again while taking off a nail.

Empty Kripo eyes met hers. 'My partner, Jean-Louis . . .'

'St-Cyr.' She let a breath escape. Had her number come up again? wondered Bénédicte. The years had slipped by, as they will. The winter of 1937 had been and gone, with him barging in here just like this 'partner' of his to demand answers to his infernal questions, but that had been after too many other years had passed, the *salaud* having arrested her for not having had a licence to walk the streets. 'I heard he was in Lyon,' she said.

'A case of arson.'

'And then in Vichy, was it?' she hazarded. Everyone was listening, of course.

'We get all the easy ones but that was later.'

'And Alsace?' she asked, pleasantly enough. 'Colmar, was it not?'

The gossip had reached here. 'That too.'

'What is it you want?' Even Miya Sama, the Pekingese warlord in Madame Jeséquel's lap was listening.

'A few small questions. Nothing difficult,' said Kohler blithely. He'd fish about in his pockets and finally pull out the notebook detectives, Gestapo and otherwise, were supposed to fill with all those things that meant so much. 'Ah, here it is. Registration number 375614.'

'Lulu.'

The tears that welled up were genuine.

'Madame de Brisac's Lulu, Inspector. Have you found her? Never have I seen one so distressed. Every day the questions. Constant telephone calls to the Société Protectrice des Animaux to beg them not to put any Irish terriers down, especially since it is now long past the one-week period of grace. The Cimetière des Chiens has been contacted, a mausoleum designed by Lenoir, descendant of the architect Le Roman himself, the one who did the reconstructions at the Royal Abbey of Saint-Antoine-des-Champs in 1770. The stones have already been carved, the inscription done by a poet—I can't remember which, but . . .'

'No remains having been found, she waits in hope,' said Herr Kohler. Petit Bob, Delaroche knew, was watching this Kripo with interest, having got his scent while licking detective fingers. Sugar . . . Had Kohler slipped Bob a few loose grains?

'*Oui, oui*, it's a tragedy,' said Bénédicte. 'Bedridden, Madame de Brisac depended on Lulu to brighten each day. Denise Rouget and

Germaine de Brisac, Madame's daughter, are constantly on the lookout, but each day brings only its new disappointments and what is one to do when a love such as that is so deep no other dog could ever take her place?'

'Bedridden?'

'Cancer. The lungs. The cigarettes. Have you found . . . ?'

'Rouget . . . ? Haven't I heard that name before?'

'You must have.'

'And Germaine de Brisac? Is she also a social worker?'

'That I wouldn't know, Inspector.'

'But you're sure of it?'

No answer was needed and none would be given!

'Then just tell me from where Lulu was snatched and when.'

'Kohler, if you don't mind, I'll take Bob and leave.'

'I do mind, Colonel. Stay put. When I'm finished with this one, I'll deal with you.'

The Cimetière des Chiens, that private last stamping ground of dogs and other pets, was on the Île de la Recette (the "takings") in the Seine. Tombs and mausoleums, rows of little headstones, wreaths of artificial flowers in winter and more than twenty thousand graves at last count* but formerly the island home of those who had been paid a pittance to drag corpses from the river.

'Lulu had just been given a tidy up, Inspector. Three times a week. The Monday, after her walk in the park . . .'

'Which park?'

'The Monceau, of course, so that Madame de Brisac might hear her cries of joy and catch glimpses of her from the bedroom window.'

'Continue.'

'Then Thursday, the school holiday—that is when the Mademoiselle de Brisac's children are home and could play longer in the park with Lulu, sometimes even letting her have a run.'

The park warden and his underwardens wouldn't have liked that, French parks being what they were. 'Not married?'

---

* There are now well over 100,000 graves.

'The husband was killed during the invasion.'

'The daughter taking back her maiden name?'

'They were to have been divorced.'

'Wasn't divorce almost as hard to come by under the Third Republic?'

This one was like a barracuda after its dinner! 'There were family problems. Perhaps the husband wasn't suitable. Who am I to . . .'

'Husband fooling around on her?'

'I didn't say that, Inspector.'

'Kohler . . .'

'Be quiet, Colonel. And on Saturday?'

'Lulu came for the bath and the grooming so as to look her best for Mass, and then . . .'

'Her Sunday run in the park.'

'*Oui.*' He would tell her nothing of Lulu.

'And on which Saturday was she snatched from the park?'

It would have to be said. 'She wasn't. Mademoiselle Germaine de Brisac, coming straight from work, had the car, of course, and had put Lulu safely into the backseat. Mademoiselle Rouget had gone into the Lido to see if her dear *papa* was spending the evening at home and would like a lift.'

And nicely put. 'Time five twenty or six?'

'Six thirty.'

'And Lulu was taken from the car when Germaine de Brisac went to find Denise Rouget in the Lido?'

Dieu merci, he hadn't asked her the reason for such a delay, which could only mean that he'd find out elsewhere. 'That . . . that is correct. Monday, the eleventh of January. It was bitterly cold. I . . . I went out with my torch to wrap the shawl I always wear at such times around Lulu so that she wouldn't catch a chill.'

'Shawl taken?'

'I had clients to attend to. Lulu was safe. I swear it. I shut the car door and checked to see that it was secure as always.'

'Describe the shawl. One never knows.'

Must he sigh like that? she wondered.

'Kohler . . .'

'Be patient, Colonel. Take a leaf from Petit Bob. Listen, since it can't be helped, but don't make a sound. Have a half a carrot stick and give him the other half. He's earned it.'

'I can't. They make his stools loose.'

'And that troubles him, doesn't it?'

'As much as it does those who might inadvertently step in them.'

Petit Bob looked questioningly from one to the other but *grâce à Dieu*, he hadn't let out a moan. 'Inspector, the shawl was of hand-woven wool. Russet, crimson and gold, the colours of a Canadian autumn, for the man who gave it to me when I was a girl of seventeen, was one of those and French too. There was a brooch of my mother's, a shield in silver with the cabochons of banded ironstone like one of my rings. This one.'

A real knuckle-duster. 'Louis and I'll see what we can do. Dog snatching at about six thirty, Monday, January eleventh. That right?'

Serpent! she said silently, sucking in a breath as he wrote it all down. *'Oui, c'est correct.'*

'And Denise Rouget and Germaine de Brisac went to school together?'

Why could he not understand that one had to be so careful these days, that everyone was listening as they watched and that among them were those who would quite willingly, if encouraged, write damning letters to the authorities while hiding behind the innocence of anonymity? 'I did not say that, Inspector. It's not my practice, or that of any of my girls, to divulge information of any kind about my clients even to such as yourself, but since you demand it before reliable witnesses, then, yes, they did.'

'The *bac* and after that the Sorbonne or whatever?'

'Those, too, of course.'

'Kohler . . .'

'Now it's your turn, Colonel, but let's go into the Lido so that Petit Bob can say hello to all the girls and you can buy me an *apéritif*.'

*　　*　　*

To the muted sounds from the Arcade came the urgency of some-one's trying the door to the Agence Vidocq. Was it Monsieur Raymond or Monsieur Quevillon? wondered Suzette Dunand. Chief Inspector St-Cyr was still perusing the papers in his hand. Monsieur Garnier would have shaken the doorknob and then banged a fist against the door. He would have silently cursed her, thinking that she had left before the 7.00 p.m. closing, a thing she had never done but now that door was no longer being tried, now the steps were receding, and why was it, please, that Colonel Delaroche wouldn't allow any of his *agents privés* to have a key, even the most trusted of them?

Monsieur Raymond had tried that door—it must have been him, she decided: M. Jeannot Raymond who had been with the colonel since the very beginning and well before the Defeat. Though he seldom smiled, M. Raymond always saved the best of those for her but never tried to get too close. Not once. He wasn't like M. Hubert Quevillon who always knew the nearness of himself filled her with revulsion but that she would have to tolerate it in silence.

M. Quevillon enjoyed her despair. Secretly he laughed at her—she knew he did, whereas M. Flavien Garnier could as easily have had one of his 'fifty-year-old boots' behind this machine for all the attention he paid to her.

'Inspector . . .'

'A moment, Mademoiselle Dunand.'

'Have you the magistrate's order?'

'At your age it's hard to put force into such words. I wouldn't try, if I were you.'

She coloured—could feel her cheeks getting hot again. 'I HAVE A RIGHT TO DEMAND THAT YOU SHOW ME THE SEARCH WARRANT! I MUST GO AND CLEAN MYSELF UP!'

'In a moment.'

Salaud, she winced. Tears would streak her mascara—Well, let them! He *knew* she had peed herself. He *must* know she was but the latest of the secretaries the colonel had employed, the fifth in the past two-and-a-half years of this Occupation, and that she desperately needed to keep the job or else the STO would come and take her away to Germany to work in a munitions factory and she'd be blasted to pieces by the bombs of the British RAF. Hadn't *that* been what M. Hubert Quevillon had whispered into her ear the last time he had caught her alone and found her cringing at the nearness of him? Wasn't that why so many other girls had left the agency?

Or was it, perhaps, that Colonel Abélard-Armand Delaroche had let each one go before she had found out too much?

'This statement of invoice, mademoiselle.'

He had yanked it from the machine. Stricken, she had stiffened and he had noticed this, as he did everything.

'It . . . it is simply Madame de Roussy's account. On the fifteenth of every month she is . . .'

'*Oui, oui,* but . . .'

'But *what,* Inspector?'

'Twenty-five thousand francs? For what, please?'

'I only do as I'm told. Here . . . here is the invoice in pencil, as Colonel Delaroche has written it for me to type up.'

'The investigation is continuing?'

'I . . . I think so, yes. I . . .'

He'd say nothing of the rue La Boétie killing, decided St-Cyr. He'd try to calm her but only a little. 'You really don't know what it's all about, do you? *Ah, bon,* relax. Forgive me, too. You see, my partner and myself are desperately trying to put an end to this plague of blackout crime but now have yet another savage killing to deal with—the *passage* de l'Hirondelle, mademoiselle. A girl a little older than yourself whose face was kicked in and trod on so hard all the bones were smashed, both eyes as well. Bruises . . . never have I seen such bruises.'

He would give her a moment to digest this. He would watch her like God did a sinner. When he said, 'The *passage* de la Trinité's victim is still in hospital,' he let the words sink in and only then added, 'That one is not expected to live.'

'*La toilette, s'il vous plaît*, Inspector. I know nothing of these. NOTHING, DO YOU UNDERSTAND?'

A handkerchief was found and pressed into her hand. 'The De Roussy investigation, mademoiselle?'

'A . . . a round-the-clock.'

'On Monsieur de Roussy?'

'*Oui.*'

'The file, then. Where is it? Which drawer?'

There were banks and banks of oak filing cabinets, most of which were empty and only for show and not like those the colonel kept locked up in his office, but if the inspector should look, he'd find this out. 'There . . . there isn't one. The investigation's progress reports are given by . . .'

'Word of mouth,' came the sigh. 'It's a puzzle, though, that there's even an invoice.'

'Taxes must be paid; income must be reported.'

'Sometimes.'

Again he gave that sigh. Undoing the shabby overcoat with its buttons that hung by their threads and understandably gave no evidence of a woman's touch—what woman would *ever* put up with such a one?—the chief inspector dumped his fedora on to her desk and took off his coat, preparing to stay for as long as he wished.

'We'll see that you get home safely,' he said, the trace of fatherly concern bringing a sickness of its own, for he'd soon add, and he did, 'Where is that?'

'A flat. It's not far. I'll be perfectly safe so you don't have to worry.'

And given bravely, but a flat, not a room. Had Colonel Delaroche set her up or had someone else since the rents in this *quartier* were prohibitive? Probably one or the other but best to leave it for now. 'Madame de Roussy's husband, mademoiselle. *Bien sûr*, Alexandre de Roussy is on the board of directors of the Renault car company and important, since they supply the Occupier with all sorts of things, but . . .'

Again there was that pause!

'But it always takes two to commit adultery, doesn't it?'

'The wife of another, yes.'

'That of a prisoner of war?'

The girl bowed her head and crushed the handkerchief. Tears were splashed on the desk, her voice like that of France on the day of Defeat. '*Oui*, the . . . the mother of three young children. Monsieur de Roussy sees her twice a week, sometimes more if . . . if necessary.'

'And pays her how much a visit?'

'Five hundred. I . . . I really don't know. It's . . .'

'Only a rumour, that five hundred, isn't it?'

'*Oui.*'

Steep, dark and narrow, the side staircase from the Lido's stage plunged to the dressing rooms, bare flesh and bare of privacy, the girls fabulous, thought Kohler. *Gott sei Dank,* the colonel had hustled him right past the Agence Vidocq, right into the restaurant and down the stairs to the club.

Gold and tinsel were everywhere, see-through pearly water wings on some. High heels, of course, headbands or tiaras, bracelets and earrings, and there was the toddler of one sucking on his soother and looking up at his dear *maman* who was changing too and just as naked as he. Joy in her heavily made-up eyes, ostrich plumes still on her head and Bob having a hell of a time resisting the impulse.

Background noise from the club above them filtered down. The colonel didn't say a thing. Bob waited, watching the girls and hearing the babble of them as, in single file, a robe or some other flimsy bit of costume tossed over a shoulder, they came down the stairs ready to change for the next act but were momentarily more worried about taking a tumble and crashing into the others. Legs . . . beautiful legs . . .

Pungent on the air came the scent of talcum powder and cigarette smoke, *eau de Javel* and chlorine, too, for didn't the Lido have a bathing pool up there? Of course it did, with nymphs *en costume d'Ève* who swung back and forth on swings above the audience before throwing their arms straight out or up to take the plunge.

Perfume, the cheap and the expensive, was on the air with body odours of all kinds, those of clogged drains, too, and of blocks of limestone, for these last made up the cellar walls. Garlic, Louis would have said. Onions, *mon vieux,* and the *vin d'ordinaire,* the *rouge, n'est-ce pas?* The sulphur of freshly struck matches as cigarettes are lit and quick drags taken.

'Bob!' shouted one. '*Ah, mon Dieu, mon petit brave,* you've come back to see us again.'

'No more worries, eh, Bob?' shouted another. 'No more thoughts of Lulu?'

Bob didn't bark. Bob didn't wag his tail. Bob waited.

'Come to Martine,' urged one with open arms, bare breasts, bare everything. 'Colonel, let him come. You know how he likes to see us. You've been keeping him away too long.'

A smile was given, not a grin, for a man like Delaroche never grinned. Bob's lead was unclipped but still he stayed until the colonel softly said, 'All right. Go and say hello.'

Still he didn't bark or bay. Nose to the floor, he went into the lights, to mirrors upon mirrors and gowns and scattered or unscattered female underthings and lots and lots of loving.

Bob said hello to every one of the thirty or more that were crowded into the two long rooms. He didn't play favourites. They laughed, whistled, clapped, called, cuddled, told each other not to be greedy and urged him to come to them, competing totally for his affection.

He didn't run and knock the children over. He was careful. The baby, nestled in its bassinet and asleep after a quick snack, was given but the gentlest touch of his muzzle, not even a lick; the four-year-old who had constantly sucked her thumb, had to pull it out to timidly pet and then hug him dearly. A hero.

But then, puzzled, he looked around for someone else and couldn't understand why they weren't also present. He started to hunt, and no amount of the colonel's calling him back, not even a muted curse, could stop him. He went out into the foyer at the base of that staircase. He sniffed at two or three of the steps, went right up them and came back. Satisfied, he hurried along the dimly lit corridor that led, probably, to one of the club's many storage rooms, only to stop when he reached the wall telephone. Standing, he got a whiff of that too, then headed right back and into the dressing rooms to look about and try to decide what was still missing.

Under the chintz skirt of one of the dressing tables—bare knees had to be quickly swung aside—he worried over something, gave a throaty growl, angry at first, the hindquarters up and tail ready.

'Lulu's b . . .' said one, only to stop herself as Bob dragged it out, worried at it with a paw, then laid it at his master's feet.

An India rubber bone. Well chewed by the look and a constant comfort, but no comfort at all? wondered Kohler. Delaroche had thought it best to distract this Kripo with female flesh and keep him from going to the *agence* but was now thinking better of it.

Back Bob went for more, and when he had that item, he dragged it out by its handle and the one who had swung her legs aside blurted, 'Élène's case.'

No one moved. Not Bob, not any of the girls.

'Where is she, Colonel?' asked another. 'What's happened to her?'

Merde, something would have to be said, thought Delaroche. 'We're working on it.'

'That makes two of us, Colonel.'

'Kohler, we'll discuss it later.'

'Of course, but I'm glad to know the *agence* is involved.'

All thirty-two or -six of them stopped whatever they'd been doing. They waited for answers. They damned well wanted them. 'Well?' said a forty-year-old with the stretch marks big babies invariably leave for one to hide.

Bob nudged the fitted case, pushing it across the cracked linoleum until it rested not at the colonel's feet, but at those of this Kripo. Sorrowfully he looked up and waited, too, for an answer. A missing dog and a missing showgirl.

That answer was not long in coming. It couldn't be, if only

partially given. Reaching into a jacket pocket, Kohler took out the girl's wedding ring—*Ach*, he'd wrapped it in a pair of white pongee step-ins he must have taken from the judge's flat, but had no memory of having done or even of where, precisely, among those rooms he'd found them, but . . . 'This is it, eh, Bob?' he heard himself asking, heard the collective gasp, saw lips part, despair enter the gazes of some, tears those of others.

'Élène's,' said one. 'I knew she was for it. I had a feeling.'

'Kohler, where the hell did you find that?' hissed Delaroche.

'Maybe Bob had best tell us, Colonel, or is it that you already know?'

Not a feather moved. Cigarette smoke trailed.

'Would I even be asking if I did?' asked Delaroche.

'Lulu's gone and Bob's no longer worried about her, Colonel,' said one to break the impasse.

'They had a fight. Bob's ear was badly torn,' said another.

They looked at each other, these girls, and nodded at one of their number.

'Élène took her, Colonel,' said the forty-year-old den mother. 'We knew Madame de Brisac had hired you to find Lulu. We weren't going to tell you but now . . . now that Élène hasn't come to work, we'd best, since that one has her ring.'

'Lulu was causing Élène lots and lots of trouble,' said another. 'Madame Rouget *would* insist on bringing that damned dog of her friend's down here to see us.'

'And do the same when we were up onstage.'

'Now wait a minute,' said Kohler. 'Was Madame Rouget asked to do this by Madame de Brisac?'

The girls threw glances at one another. 'It's possible,' said one, 'but not likely.'

'It wasn't Élène's fault, Inspector. You are a cop, aren't you?'

'I am.'

'I thought so.'

'I did too.' 'So did I . . .' *'Et moi aussi,'* came the chorus. 'One can always tell with those.'

Heads were nodded.

'Lulu wasn't a regular like Bob, Inspector. Oh for sure, she was friendly enough but she hated *Monsieur le Juge* who had savagely kicked her in the park last October.'

'The Parc Monceau?'

'How is it that you know this, please?' asked the den mother suspiciously.

'Never mind, but why did Élène Artur ask to meet the judge there? That's not the usual sort of place for a girl like that, is it?'

They all shrugged. Some looked away, others stared right back at him. Pregnant, wasn't she? he wanted to ask but didn't need to and had best not since the colonel was taking a decided interest in things. 'Continue.'

'*Ah, bon*, since you ask it of me. Lulu could be very friendly with Élène, too, you understand, but hated *Monsieur le Juge,* and when Lulu smelled him on the girl after those two had been together during the *cinq à sept* or even earlier in the day, she just went crazy even though the judge was no longer present.'

'Angry,' said one.

'A real hothead,' yet another.

'Would bite and bark and sometimes even tear at Élène's coat or dress when she came in.'

'Irish terriers are good with most people but can be . . .'

'Bitchy,' said another, 'especially with big dogs like Bob who was only trying to defend Élène from attack.'

'Madame Rouget also had her daughter Denise bring Lulu in to see us, Inspector. Twice, I think, or was it three times?'

'Four. Poor Élène didn't know what to do.'

But she did.

It wasn't wise of her to leave the chief inspector alone in the outer office, Suzette told herself, but she absolutely had to get cleaned up. He would go through the papers on her desk. He'd see beyond a shadow of doubt that Madame Henriette Morel was being billed ten thousand francs each this month for the Barrault and Guillaumet investigations, as she'd been billed last month. He'd find M.

Garnier's files on Madame Barrault and Madame Guillaumet, files that were to have been locked up in the colonel's office had that one come back from Chez Bénédicte's or not have left the door to his office locked as always when he was away, and sometimes even when he was here and in there with a particularly beautiful client.

The inspector would see that on her desk there was also the invoice she had typed for the parents of Captain Jean-Matthieu Guillaumet, who was in the officers' POW camp at Elsterhorst. Twenty thousand francs they'd been billed this month alone for the *agence*'s finding 'conclusive evidence' of Madame Guillaumet's plans to commit adultery. The Ritz, no less!

'And then?' whispered Suzette to herself. 'Then he will discover that the Scapini Commission in Berlin, the Service diplomatique de prisonniers de guerre, have requested an estimate of the cost of just such a "conclusive" investigation of her and that this estimate has been placed at between forty thousand and fifty thousand francs.'

It would do no good for her to stand here stupidly and cry. She must get back, but he would also find that that same commission, at the insistence of Madame Marie-Léon Barrault's husband, who was in the camp for common soldiers at Stablack in Poland, had demanded that such an investigation of his wife be done. Cost: ten thousand francs a month, but that since Corporal René-Claude Barrault had no money of his own, Madame Henriette Morel had willingly volunteered to cover that cost as well. Thirty thousand francs then, this month alone to Madame Morel: ten for Madame Barrault, ten for Madame Guillaumet and ten for the Scapini's request.

'*Un gogo,*' M. Hubert Quevillon had said of the woman. He had flashed some of the photos he used from time to time to convince prospective customers that their husbands were indeed fooling around behind their backs. Totally naked girls.

'A sucker,' she swallowed, glancing accusingly at herself in the mirror that was above the washbasin. Madame Morel was being billed *twice* for the Barrault investigation and once for the Guillaumet, whose in-laws were also forking over twenty thousand francs for that one, and soon it would be the Scapini Commission also, whose cost those same in-laws would gladly pay since the Scapini could recommend to the courts that charges be laid and a divorce granted.

A racket, that's what it was. She knew the chief inspector would find out all of this from her desk alone—Madame de Brisac's invoice was there too, the search for Lulu, a lost dog: no charge at all. Nothing. *Absolument rien* simply because that one was not only an old friend but had recommended the firm to Madame Rouget who in turn had recommended it to her daughter Denise and to Germaine de Brisac, the daughter of the other one. The things one did for business. But having scratched the surface, would the inspector not want more?

Hurriedly she took off her slip and underpants and, rolling them into a tight ball, tucked them into her bag. She would put on her overcoat to hide the skirt's dampness, had best get ready to go home—*oui, oui,* that is what she'd do. Lock the door and lock him out of the office.

'Inspector, I must close up now. *Grand-mère,* she will worry. Always it's the same with her, you understand. She watches the clock, poor thing, and worries especially now with . . . with all of these terrible attacks.'

A lie, of course, but had he believed her? He gave no indication, hadn't been standing anywhere near her desk, had been sitting—yes, sitting patiently by the door—and said, '*Ah, bon*, mademoiselle. It's best my partner and I come back in the morning.'

'Sunday . . . It will be Sunday, Inspector. The *agence* will be closed.'

'Ah! I've completely lost track of the days. Always the work, never the rest. Monday, then.'

Throwing on that overcoat, he took that fedora of his from her desk and said, '*Aprèz vous,* mademoiselle.'

'I . . . I must switch off the lights, then put the lock on.'

'Of course.'

As she did so, he didn't take that gaze of his from her, but held the door, then watched as she pushed the little button in and let her go first, he pulling the door tightly closed behind them and testing it to make certain it was, indeed, locked.

'Perfect,' he said. 'You needn't worry.'

No one was taking any notice of them. No one! Not M. Raymond and not M. Garnier . . . *'Merci,'* she heard herself saying.

'I'll just walk you to the entrance of the métro. That way I'll not worry either.'

Ah, merde! 'There . . . there's no need, Inspector. The flat's just along the way.'

They reached the avenue, which was now in total darkness. The glow from occasional cigarettes was as if that from fireflies in the night and not yet a moon. *'Bonne nuit,* mademoiselle.'

And never trust a police officer, said St-Cyr silently as he gave her time to lose herself in the crowd. That pin tumbler, mortised lock of the colonel's, with its bevelled bolt and dead bolt above, allows you to 'put the lock on' the former but not the latter, which needs its key. Delaroche must always come by to put the dead bolt on, but with the other there are two little buttons mounted on the lock face just below the bolts. Pushing in the one as you did, activates the bevelled bolt, pushing in the other as I did, deactivates it.

The colonel, like any *détective privé* worth his salt, felt Kohler, had a table exactly where it should have been. Right at the back, tucked into a corner in full view of the coat check and entrance and with the whole club spread before him, including its tobacco-fogged horizon.

Bob sat on two of the chairs nearest to that master of his and watched the girls from this distance. He didn't bark, seemed oblivious to the brassy racket from the orchestra and that from the crowd, was mesmerized apparently by the lights and the action.

Wehrmacht boys were everywhere, several with their *petites amies*. BOFs, too, and other black marketeers and *collabos*. Maybe a ratio of eight from home to two of the French, the club filling up fast and no different than any other in this regard.

'Bob has impressive control, Colonel. You've trained him superbly.'

Just what was Kohler after and where the hell was that partner of his? wondered Delaroche, though he'd have to smile and affably say, 'You've no idea how good Bob is for business. Prospective clients, especially the women, take one look at him and are not only reassured but convinced. The younger they are, the harder they fall—isn't that right, *mon vieux*?'

Bob agreed. Husbands would fool around; wives would demand answers, or vice versa. 'A fortune, that it, Colonel?'

'Hardly. A good living, though. Surely you must have thought of going into business for yourself?' Delaroche turned to a waitress. 'Angèle, *ma belle,* would you be so good as to bring Herr Kohler a little something from Munich? The Spaten Dunkel. It's fresh in today, Kohler.'

'*Et pour vous, mon cher* colonel?' brown eyes asked.

'The usual.'

'*Un double de* Byrrh. Is that not correct?'

Jésus, merde alors, those bedroom eyes of hers would have melted butter.

'Bob, give Angèle her little gift. Now don't be stingy.'

A five-hundred-franc bill was gently teased from a bankroll that would have impressed even the wealthiest, the girl taking it between her teeth, too, as she set her tray down to mother Bob, modestly tidy her halter straps and tuck the bill between her breasts.

'It pays to keep them happy, Kohler. You've no idea the things girls like that can tell you.'

Cigarettes were offered and why not accept a couple? A light too.

Kohler blew smoke towards the ceiling and sat back to enjoy the show as if a regular without a care in the world but surely Boemelburg had let him know the Gestapo and the SS employed the *agence* from time to time and had been very satisfied with the results?

Oberg must have told the agency to work with Sonja Remer and to tail Giselle, thought Kohler, but had they found her, or had this one simply vented his rage in the *passage* de l'Hirondelle because they hadn't? 'Tell me about Lulu, Colonel.'

There was still no sign of St-Cyr. 'Catherine-Élizabeth de Brisac is an old and much valued friend. Her husband, Paul, and I were at Gallipoli. The Corps expéditionnaire d'Orient. Kum Kale on the Asian shore, April twenty-fifth, 1915, a diversion that, though the only successful venture of that whole campaign, fooled no one. We then withdrew and went to assist the Australians and New Zealanders on the Peninsula. Brave boys, all of them, but a debacle. An absolute cockup. The damned British High Command let us down as they then did in 1940. One simply can't trust the bastards. Pigheaded, incompetent, arrogant and dishonest. Undermanned and under-supplied, the Turks were savage, Mustapha Kemal Pasha absolutely brilliant. Paul de Brisac didn't come home. I caught him as he fell.'

Their drinks came. '*Salut,*' said Delaroche, raising his glass. 'Byrrh had become our national *apéritif* even before that other war, Kohler, but do you know why?'

'The colonies. The malaria and a need for quinine to be sweetened, else it wouldn't be taken. Hence a dry, vermouth-style drink that caught on. Let's cut the crap and the old soldier bit, Colonel. Élène Artur kidnapped Lulu.'

'Such things happen all the time these days, don't they? Leave one's pet off the lead for a moment, or let the cat out, and *voilà*, it has vanished into the oven or the stew pot of another.'

'Or the soup pot, given her *indochinoise* background and that of her mother, Colonel, but didn't you realize Élène had taken her?'

Kohler had yet to mention the judge. 'I didn't. I did know of the trouble Lulu had been causing. Bob wasn't the only dog to have suffered defending that girl and certainly Lulu could have benefitted a great deal from further training. Spoiled, *oh là, là,* but . . . Ah! what is one to do when asked by a friend of long standing who is in great distress? I immediately offered help. The Agence Vidocq was, as I have already stated, working on it.'

'But not too hard. Élène must have kept Lulu alive until very recently. Maybe a guilty conscience, maybe she sincerely felt the dog was desperately needed by its owner.'

'We haven't charged Madame de Brissac a sou, nor will we. I had kept Bob away from the girls because of the fight he'd had down there with Lulu. Damn it, Kohler, Lulu had challenged Élène and had bitten the girl twice at least. Bob simply leaped in to defend her as he would have done for any of them.'

A real ladies' dog but at other times, at least some of them, Élène, must have got on quite well with Lulu. 'Now what are you going to tell Madame de Brissac?'

'Nothing until it is absolutely clear to me.'

'Lulu hated Judge Rouget, Colonel. Vivienne Rouget hired you to tail that husband of hers and not only find out who her Hercule was fucking but how serious things were.'

'Where did you find that girl's wedding ring?'

It couldn't hurt to tell him, might even help to shake the son of a bitch. 'Under a radiator.'

Out in the Arcade de Champs-Élysées the shoppers took their time, as Germans on leave would, while others hurried homeward, using the arcade as a short cut. Alone in the *agence*, St-Cyr waited beside Suzette Dunand's desk. He had been about to switch on her lamp, had heard something against the foot traffic . . .

Ah! there it was again. Ever so gently the door was being tried. The bevelled bolt had come free . . . yes, yes, that lock had been successfully picked but now . . . now whoever it was discovered that the dead bolt had been engaged and since Colonel Delaroche had not returned to lock up, that could only mean the *agence's* security was in the act of being breached.

There wouldn't be time to do what had to be done, but there had to be something more than the *agence* just sharking the clients. Whoever it was might leave. There'd been no cries for a *flic* to come running, no pronouncements of a robbery in progress, simply a waiting for himself to try to slip away, but was there more than one of them out there?

Retreating, he felt his way through the pitch-darkness until he got to the corridor the girl had taken to the washroom, was hurrying now, found gold-rimmed porcelain cups and saucers and a coffeepot—Sèvres? he wondered—under the light switch. Everywhere he looked in this room he'd entered, there was a tidiness that troubled, a décor that didn't fit the usual image of *détectives privés* but was clean of line, the furnishings very of the *nouveau riche*. A large desk with Lalique pen-and-ink stand, bronze figurines from the twenties. Several oil paintings hung on the walls—landscapes but also family portraits, some dating back more than a century. Surely these weren't of relatives of M. Flavien Garnier or of M. Hubert Quevillon, whose names in bronze were apparent?

Everything spoke of money. There was none of what one would have expected, none of the stale tobacco smoke from endless Gauloises bleues, none of the sweat of the unwashed, the garlic, the cheap toilet water or cologne such individuals were wont to splash on themselves when in the urgency of plotting to seduce some suspecting or unsuspecting female client.

Conclusion: The office was seldom used and then but briefly and really for show, since those passing by on the way to the washroom would be bound to notice, especially if this one's door was left open. Messieurs Garnier and Quevillon were foot soldiers kept on the move by the colonel.

Garnier was also a veteran of that other war, a member of the sometimes ultraconservative UNC, the Union Nationale des Combattants. A former sergeant, wounded at Verdun, but one with ties or leanings to Action française? he had to ask. Fascist anyway, and definitely pro-German and *collabo*.

The in-tray held requests, notes, thin file folders on investigations one of the others must have handed over to Garnier but not yet collected to be stuffed into jacket pockets on the run; the out-tray, the dossiers of Adrienne Guillaumet and Marie-Léon Barrault.

Suzette Dunand had typed up the following for the Scapini Commission and must surely have been worried this Sûreté would find it:

Madame Adrienne Guillaumet, wife of prisoner-of-war Captain Jean-Matthieu . . . et cetera.

Thursday, 11 February 1943: Subject leaves residence at 131 rue Saint-Dominique on foot at 1410 hours. Couple's children are left alone, but Concierge Ouellette reluctantly reveals that she checks on them from time to time and that this is not the only such occasion but one of many.

Proof positive of marital infidelity, eh?

Subject walks to the Deutsche Institut on the rue Talleyrand, entering it at 1430 hours.

And not far from the flat.

Subject pleads for an advance on part-time wages. Said advance denied. In distress, subject hurries from the building and makes her way on foot to bathhouse on the rue Las Cases but decides at last moment to go into the Église de Sainte-Clotilde.

Behind which the bathhouse, serving the *bourgeoisie* of the quartier des Invalides, was located, but why the need to pray, why the *douche chaude*?

Subject is forced to wait for shower bath and doesn't leave until 1610 hours.

And always the delays in such establishments. Though her flat, unlike so many, had had a bathtub, there'd been no provision for hot water since the Defeat. She had obviously wanted to be as presentable as possible, even though it must have cost her a good fifty francs she didn't have. Five it would have cost before this lousy war. Five and no more!

Subject takes métro to place *de l'Opéra and enters Café de la Paix at 1655 hours where she meets and conspires*—Why not confers?—*with subject Marie-Léon Barrault and that one's daughter Annette. On recommendation of the Barrault subject, Madame Guillaumet hires vélo-taxi Prenez-moi. Je suis à vous, which is to pick her up outside the École Centrale after classes at 2115 hours and drive her to the Hôtel Ritz, there to wait until again needed. Wait estimated at from two to four hours. 'As long as is necessary,' subject stated to driver.*

A half-hour to three-quarters becomes such a different length of time?

Subject then leaves Café de la Paix at 1756 hours, catching the métro to the École Centrale where she arrives at 1827 hours in time for her classes to begin.

There was nothing else. It was as if the rape, the vicious assault on her person, the savage beating had never happened.

The signature was firm but hasty. *Salauds*, that is what this gang were. Shark to the woman's in-laws, shark to the husband and the Scapini, shark to Madame Henriette Morel, too, and the 'subject' no matter what but he was racing now. Marie-Léon's 'dossier' was thicker and there were photos. One of Gaston Morel and the 'subject' at a table in the Café de la Paix, his expression one of deep concern or, as implied, one of, Don't worry, *chérie*. Go on up to the room. No one will ever know we've been together.

Another of the photos revealed her waiting for the lift at the Hôtel Grand.

There was a shot of the manager of the Cinéma Impérial who grinned, leered and sucked on a damp fag end: 'Of course I took what she offered. When it is presented in such a package, one cannot be impolite. Pay . . . ? What is this you're saying? She came to me often.'

How much had Garnier bribed him? Five hundred?

A copy of Father Marescot's damning letter to the Scapini Commission was enclosed, even a photo of the priest, and one of the 'subject' entering the confessional at the Église de Notre-Dame de Lorette, and another of those who were waiting to do exactly the same thing, including Annette Barrault, who looked to be all but in tears.

Still it wasn't enough to link the *agence* to any of the attacks and if he heard about the break-in here, as he well might, Boemelburg would hit the roof, as would Oberg. Where was what was needed? Something . . . there had to be something more than these.

'Forged tobacco cards?' blurted St-Cyr, having opened the desk's central drawer, that catchall of things detective and otherwise. 'Fifty of them at least. Evidence . . . I'd best take a few.

'A tube of Veronal . . . ?' Now why would Garnier have such a thing? Old wounds? A girl, a woman he used regularly? So many *filles de joie* would use drugs of one kind or another if they could get them to dampen the discomfort of too much sex, but . . .

'Noëlle Jourdan,' the whisper came. 'Sergeant Jourdan of the Fifty-Sixth Chasseurs à pied, and from one old soldier to another.'

To compound their troubles, beneath the desk's green blotting pad there was a list, in pencil, of names with lines through some to indicate that they had already been executed at the Fort du Mont-Valérien or sent east to camps. Beside these, and still others, though, there were also ticks. M. Flavien Garnier had been busy nailing *résistants* at one hundred thousand francs apiece, the going rate as advertised by the Occupier, but was there still more?

Ignoring the lights, the girls and the action, Bob laid his chin on the table's edge, his mournful gaze on this Kripo as the wedding ring spun itself to silence. ' "*Louis-Maurice Artur, Colonel* and *Élène Nadine Lemaire*." ' Two hearts cut in gold to overlap till death do us part. ' "*Paris, 27 September 1939*." '

Kohler had found her. There was even the mist of sentiment in his eyes, or was that merely the effects of too much Benzedrine? wondered Delaroche. Too little sleep in any case, or simply those beers from home and a clap-sized dose of nostalgia.

'She would have been sixteen,' Kohler went on as if lost to it. 'Probably didn't know her mind or heart—a shop girl most likely, and feeling damned desperate, wouldn't you say; the boy eighteen, who knows? Off to war in a hurry anyway and maybe glad to be avoiding the financial responsibilities of a pregnant wife, but as one old soldier to another, Colonel, it wouldn't have been the first time for that to have happened, would it? Must have lied about his age, though, since twenty-one was usual for France then and now two metres down or in one of the POW camps. Which is it?'

The mist was gone. There was nothing but an emptiness in that gaze, but why hadn't St-Cyr shown up? Why hadn't Jeannot or one of the others sent someone to the table to warn him? Were they all after St-Cyr? 'I know nothing of this, Kohler.'

'Then how is it you knew of the ring?'

'I didn't. Not really. I only assumed.'

'A connection with the other killings and rapes? The beatings and handbag snatches—the mugging of men like Gaston Morel?'

'Now look here . . .'

'No, you look. You're a regular at the Lido. You've seen that girl with Judge Rouget plenty of times, have sat at his table, had him to this one. A beauty, wasn't she? *Très charmante* and with all that it takes, eh? Places like this don't hire girls unless they have it.'

But were Kohler and St-Cyr looking for veterans of that other war?

'A pillar of the establishment runs around with a racially tainted chorus girl, Colonel, when everyone these days had better be more careful, but *mein Gott,* you don't even notice? The lonely wife of a POW—wasn't that what she was?—and there's Judge Rouget going on and on about how Vichy has toughened the adultery laws and that such women . . . *Ach,* let me find it for you.'

The Gestapo's little black notebook was hauled out, its pages thumbed.

'Ah, here we are. That those errant POW wives "need a damned good lesson in morals and should have their heads shorn and their breasts bared in public." '

Hercule . . . how could he have said such a thing in front of Kohler?

'And this from a man who has definitely been breaking those laws.' Kohler found another page. ' "Time and again it's the POW wives who are conducting themselves in such a shameful and disgustingly unclean manner." '

Vivienne had said that. Kohler had been to the house. *Merde,* why had Hercule not stopped him? 'Kohler, where did you find . . .'

'The judge. Let's stick to him for a moment, eh? A fellow member of the Cercle Européen that meets here at least once a week over dinner . . .'

'I'm not a member. That's only for . . .'

'Of course you aren't. You don't need to be. It's for business-men, bankers and others of the establishment whose private lives you and that agency are paid to pry into and they know it, too, some of them, probably. Hey, it's good for business to sit here, especially over the *cinq à sept.* Don't try to tell me it isn't. While you've been keeping an eye on me and another on Bob, you've been nodding to friends and acquaintances, male or female, and worrying over what they might be thinking or might have over-heard. You've been taking in the whole of this place, especially its entrance and coat check. Who's with who, who's leaving a little early or hasn't yet shown up, who's staying a little longer than usual and not with you-know-who. That's an art, my friend, and as a detective of long standing, I have to admire it. Now give. I want some answers.'

Had Gestapo Boemelburg not warned Kohler to leave the Agence Vidocq out of things even if he and that partner of his did happen to stumble on to something—had they?

'You live with two women, Kohler. Surely you are concerned about them?'

'Is that a threat?'

'Not at all. It's merely a statement of fact.'

Giselle . . . Delaroche hadn't touched his *apéritif.* One of the girls came with cigars and automatically he started to make a se-lection only to think better of it.

'You and Judge Rouget are members of the Cercle de l'Union Interaliée, Colonel.' This wasn't known for certain but . . .

'That's no concern of yours. Surely you're not so stupid as to suspect anyone who belongs to the Interaliée?'

'We'll get to it, won't we? Vivienne Rouget hired you to watch over her Hercule. If you ask me, I think that woman knew all about his philandering but things had gotten out of hand. He was spending far too many evenings and nights away from home and not just with Élène Artur. The Folies-Bergère, the Casino de Paris, the Apollo, the Naturiste and Chez Éve—it's interesting that bare breasts keep cropping up, isn't it? Especially at La Source de Joie in Pigalle.'

The *bordel* of Régine Trudel. How had Kohler found out so much in such a short time? 'Hercule is under a great deal of stress.'

'*Président du Tribunal spécial* . . .'

'*Résistants, Terroristen.* Their sentencing. Vivienne . . .'

'Was it that Élène reminded him of a *petite amie* he'd once had?' The framed poster above the mantelpiece, the constant reminder of a stunning conquest and possession: *Une nuit à Chang-Rai, 7 March 1926, at the Magic City.* Kohler had definitely been to the flat.

'Hercule is at that age,' said Delaroche. 'The libido doesn't fade, *n'est-ce pas,* but as one grows older, one can no longer command that same stiffness nor does the *érection* last. A remedy is needed. That's all that girl ever was. A reminder of how things once were.'

'That other showgirl. The one in that poster.'

'*Oui, oui.* What has happened to Madame Artur, Kohler? Come, come, don't be so free with the insinuations and the veiled threats. Karl Oberg is a member of the Interaliée, Walter Boemelburg not quite yet, but on the list and likely to be voted in at . . .'

'*Ja. Ja, mein lieber französischer Privatdetektiv,* the avenue Foch and the rue des Saussaies are using that agency of yours and Louis and me have been told to go carefully. Point is, you'd best help us out, or is it that you want us to go right back to Boemelburg and dump the lot of what we now know into his lap?'

Kohler would do it too. Boemelburg would then have to go to Oberg and hadn't that one insisted that Hercule be totally above all such extramarital activities and hadn't Vivienne, foolish as her little outburst had been in front of this one, been only too aware of what the Höherer SS *und* Polizeiführer expected of Hercule and desperately afraid of what must happen should he not see the error of his ways and fall from favour?

Élène Artur's fitted case was set on the table, Kohler gripping its edges before springing the catches—why hadn't it been taken? Why had it been left for this one to find? 'Bob, stay. STAY, Bob. There's my soldier.'

The half of a carrot stick was found. To be fair, what with all the other smells of pâté, et cetera, around them, Bob couldn't be blamed for not refusing it and was one damn fine dog. 'Was Élène really the wife of a POW, Colonel? Let's get that straight, just for the record.'

Had the *salaud* not even known? '*Oui*, I . . . I believe she was. Did she suffer?'

No answer was given. The case was opened, Bob watching closely. A hand mirror and comb and brush were deliberately set to one side, Kohler watching, Kohler knowing that they couldn't see what was still in the case unless they got up and came round the table.

Beneath these items and such others, there would be the felt-covered pasteboard tray to which they'd been fastened. This tray was hinged and Kohler now lifted it up and out of the way.

'Judge Rouget knew that wife of his was having him followed, Colonel. Maybe it had happened before, maybe someone was kind enough to have told him. Point is, he backed off and left that girl alone. Élène didn't know what the trouble was. She knew, though, that she had done something that must have upset him, but didn't know how he could possibly have found out about it.'

'Go on. Please continue, since you seem to know everything.'

'He'd taken to giving her his little gift beforehand in the Lido here and then not showing up at that flat of his. Kept her waiting night after night. That's not good for a girl, is it?'

'Get to the point.'

'Certainly. When Lulu was taken, that daughter of his had come down here to ask if he would like a lift home, which he damned well should have done had he any sense. They argued— they must have. Maybe Élène caught sight of them and put two and two together, maybe Denise Rouget stormed the dressing room to confront the girl first. Something delayed Denise and gave Élène time to move. Germaine de Brisac got impatient and left the car running and Lulu alone in the backseat while she came here to find out what was the matter.'

'And Élène knew where that dog would be because she had seen it often enough. You should be working with us, Kohler, but I won't try to buy you off, since there is no need.'

'You let the judge know that wife of his had hired you to follow him.'

Must Kohler continue to look for trouble? 'Once I knew the extent of the problem, I felt it my duty as a friend and fellow member of the Interaliée to inform him of Vivienne's concerns. Life with Hercule hasn't been easy. That girl was but one of many.'

'But he agreed to back off?'

'For the time being, yes.'

'Are you familiar with that flat of his on the rue La Boétie?'

There must be no hesitation. 'Certainly, but are you aware that Judge Rouget has put it on the block and offered it also to our friends—your fellow countrymen? I, myself, was with him when he handed a set of keys to the estate agent.'

Louis would have appreciated the attempt. 'Which one?'

'I'll have to ask our secretary. She'll have gone home by now, but you can have it first thing on Monday.'

And no problem. 'That's good of you. I'll keep it in mind.'

A change of blouse and slip, still neatly folded and beautifully laundered by the girl's mother, were taken out of the case, a change of underwear and pair of white woollen socks, slippers, too, that Élène Artur had sometimes worn between sets and sometimes even in that flat, but had Kohler found the two thousand francs Hercule would have given her? Had the girl put it there and trusted that the others wouldn't steal it? Had she done so in haste, realizing that it had to be saved and would be taken from her?

A candy-striped tricolour leg warmer with laddered runs and holes at the heel and toe, was dragged out—something she had been too ashamed to take home to that mother of hers to mend. Bob fidgeted. Others noticed the stocking. Eyebrows were raised . . .

'It's odd, isn't it?' said Kohler. 'Detectives like Louis and myself are always searching for the little things and when we find them, we not only ask ourselves about them, but begin to look beyond the obvious. One stocking but two legs. Where's the other one?'

'*Ah, mon Dieu,* I have absolutely no idea. Stockings? How could I have?'

Louis had better not be in trouble. Louis had better be finding out all he could. 'That dressing room, Colonel. Stockings like these are always chucked out of the way when a girl's hurrying to get dressed. Frequent visitors like yourself must have seen the girls wearing them between sets if time allowed or at dance rehearsals. Bob even recognizes it, don't you, Bob?'

The head was immediately lifted. From deep within him the answer came and with it a long and mournful baying that was as much of grief as it was of anything. 'There, you see, Colonel. Bob loved her, didn't he?'

'Idiot, he's friendly with all of them. She was just one of many.'

'*Ach,* then let's use him, eh? Let's let Bob to find her other leg warmer.'

9

Again and again St-Cyr tripped the light switch. Fortunately the match didn't shower sparks as he set the open packet on Hubert Quevillon's desk, one every bit as tidy as Flavien Garnier's. Here, though, the in-tray was empty—Quevillon must have been in earlier to clean it out. The other tray held a single file folder, thin and as if waiting for more.

'The boys?' he heard himself blurt.

Sickened, he blindly groped for another match as he stared at the photo. Downcast and in tears, they were lined up on the pavement, and behind them was the house at 3 rue Laurence Savart.

Returning Sonja Remer's handbag hadn't been enough. The names of Antoine Courbet's sisters were on another slip of paper. Lovely girls Madame Courbet would never have allowed to fraternize with the enemy, Claudette, the oldest, having promised herself to a young man who was now in one of the prisoner-of-war camps.

A further note, in a different but far more professional hand, gave only, *Standartenführer Langbehn, 1000 hours Monday, avenue Foch*, the note transferred by Quevillon from his in-tray, but had Gabrielle been taken to dinner and then arrested? The note had been signed by a Jeannot Raymond whose office must be next door.

Beneath the photo there was one of Giselle le Roy who had been caught unawares yesterday while leaving Adrienne Guillaumet's building and must have been followed to the House of Madame Chabot where she'd been turned away, only to then realize she hadn't been alone.

The desk drawers were locked and he had to wonder why, since Garnier had taken no such precaution. The secretary? he had to ask.

He was running out of matches and out of time. Lighting one of the few that were left, he got down beside the chair to peer under the desk. Had she known, Suzette Dunand could easily have opened the side drawers. These could only be locked when the central drawer was completely closed and the key turned fully round and to the right in its lock. Doing so tripped two hooks, one for each pair of side drawers, dropping a locking bar into place, which could then be released if one either pushed up or pulled down on it from beneath the desk, and then pulled back on the respective bar. Sometimes one went round to the front and felt behind the central drawer, for these hooks could also be located there, but were here at the back on either side as he had suspected. The central drawer remained locked, of course, for it needed the key but this could now be opened if . . .

'Ah, *bon*, mademoiselle. Remind me to show you how this is done and what you've been missing. Hermann . . . Hermann, give me a little more time.'

The shops were closing. Soon, Suzette knew, there would only be those who were hurrying to the restaurant or leaving it much later if they had a pass. Alone with Messieurs Raymond, Garnier and Quevillon, she stood outside the Agence Vidocq. The last trains of the métro would leave at ten, the curfew was at twelve. Alone, she would be arrested for breaking the curfew, or maybe someone would follow her and, thinking she was selling herself to the Germans, grab her, beat her, tear her clothes . . .

'Messieurs,' she blurted, 'I did *nothing* but what I always do when you are not here and *Monsieur le Colonel* is out of the office and I have to close up. I put the lock on. I swear I did. The chief inspector came with me to the Champs-Élysées exit. He can't be in there. He can't!'

'*Espèce de salope, ferme-la!*' spat M. Quevillon. He had come to the flat, had slapped her hard, blurring her vision. Now he continued to twist her arm and she knew that if he ever got her alone, he would do things to her. 'Monsieur Raymond, I beg you. I wouldn't have let that Sûreté . . .'

'Hubert, see what's delaying the colonel. Flavien, go with him.'

Give me time alone with this one—Garnier knew that was what Jeannot wanted: always the right move, always that impenetrable calm. The girl was terrified of Hubert and rightly so.

M. Quevillon left in a hurry—Suzette told herself not to look at him. M. Garnier gave M. Raymond a curt nod, herself nothing but a dismissive glance. She had been changing when M. Quevillon had come to get her. She had not even been given a chance to finish buttoning her blouse or put on a skirt and shoes, had simply had her coat thrown at her.

The two of them hurried into the restaurant, brushing past the maître d'.

'You don't use cigarettes,' said M. Jeannot Raymond. 'At times like this they help.'

From a jacket pocket he took a silver flask and unscrewed its cap. 'Have a sip,' he said, and gave her that smile of his. 'It's an *eau-de-vie de poire* and really very good. Not too sweet, but sweet enough.'

A pear brandy. He lit a cigarette, left her to hold the flask and calm herself, said nothing of its exquisite engraving or of the inscription—an award for something he'd done, a scene of snowcapped mountains in the distance. She had always felt he was different from the others, that he really didn't belong with them. He had been married once, had had a beautiful wife and two young children. Two boys of six and eight perhaps, and a house in a strange country, but what had happened to them she didn't know, since all that was left seemed contained in the one photograph that never left his desk.

The *eau-de-vie* was lovely. He drew on his cigarette, seemed not the least concerned about anything but herself, let his grey eyes rest on her every now and then, knew absolutely how terrified she had been and that her cheeks must still be hurting.

'Quevillon should never have done that, Mademoiselle Dunand. He shouldn't have lost control and will definitely apologize.'

Had such things happened before? she wondered. Monsieur Raymond's smile was there again, the little toss of his head seeming to say, Everything will be all right, you'll see.

The inscription on the flask read: *À Jeannot Raymond, compagnon d'armes et pilote extraordinaire.* It was signed *Rivière** and dated *7 December 1930, Buenos Aires.*

'There, you're feeling better already.'

'*Ah, oui, oui, merci.* I really did think the chief inspector would . . .'

'Of course you did. Now don't concern yourself further.'

'He yanked Madame de Roussy's invoice from my machine and demanded that I tell him why it was for so much.'

'A round-the-clock. Flavien is still looking after that one, isn't he?'

M. Garnier. 'Yes but . . . but the inspector didn't ask this. I did tell him Monsieur de Roussy was seeing another woman twice a week, sometimes more and that . . . that she was married and the mother of three children.'

'The wife of a prisoner of war?'

'*Oui,* the chief inspector did ask that.'

'And what was it de Roussy pays this shameful *coquine*?'

'Five hundred—at least, that is what I told the inspector but also that I . . . I really didn't know. "It's only a rumour," he said of the five hundred.'

'And yourself?'

'I shrugged, I think.'

'And then?'

---

* Antoine de St-Exupéry's employer in *Vol de Nuit* (Night Flight) 1931

'He told me about a girl that had been found in the *passage* de l'Hirondelle. She'd been kicked in the face, kicked to death. Why would anyone do a thing like that?'

'These times are not easy. Now don't worry, please.'

'I had to go to the lavatory. I had to leave him alone but only for a few moments.'

'Of course, but did this St-Cyr say anything else?'

'Only that he didn't think Madame Guillaumet was going to live. Why would someone have done that to her?'

'And the other invoices, the ones that were on your desk?'

She had best tell him everything—the estimate to the Scapini Commission and to the parents of Captain Jean-Matthieu Guillaumet for a full inquiry, the invoice to Madame Morel, but . . . 'Would the inspector have gone into M. Garnier's office to find the files on that one's desk?' she hazarded. 'The one on Madame Guillaumet, the one of Madame Barrault . . .'

M. Jeannot Raymond put a finger to his lips. He was, she knew, always there in the office even when out on an investigation and often away for days on end. A presence, an anchor, he was in his late forties or early fifties, was tall and handsome, the hair black like silk but receding from a brow that was always furrowed. The lips were thin but when he softly smiled as now, they curled up gently at the corners in such an honest way.

Never once had she seen him wear a shirt and tie. Always it was the black turtleneck under the dark grey pinstripe jacket, always the long fingers without the wedding ring—why was it that he no longer wore it? His wife looked happy in that photograph, the children also.

He handled all the investigations involving the recovery of stolen property and was, with Colonel Delaroche, the one who met with the German authorities. Sometimes the illegal hoarding of food and the black market took him away; sometimes insurance fraud or embezzlement, or even labour strikes and/or prolonged absenteeism in a factory or mine. He didn't handle the troubled marriages, not since she had been with the agency. He only advised on them. After the client had met with Colonel

Delaroche and the fee had been set, such investigations were turned over to M. Garnier and, under his supervision, M. Quevillon—admittedly the bread and butter of the agency and booming now. Other investigations might briefly involve those two but only if Colonel Delaroche or Monsieur Raymond needed help, and yes there were part-time employees she never saw who didn't even come to the office, nor was any record kept of their names or wages, a puzzle for sure, but fortunately the chief inspector hadn't asked.

Lost to his thoughts, M. Raymond still took a moment to again reassure her. 'I once worked in South America,' he said. 'The Patagonia–Buenos Aires airmail service. Santiago, in Chile, too, but it was a long, long time ago.

'Ah! here they are at last.'

The desk was locked and none of its drawers would budge, though Kohler tried each of them. Bob had gone straight to the lower right-hand one and was now waiting expectantly for it to be opened. Louis shrugged.

'Bob, come,' said Delaroche, having stepped back into the corridor.

'Bob, stay.'

Uncertain, Bob looked questioningly up at this Kripo, then toward his master.

'See that this is opened, Colonel.'

'*Mon Dieu*, what is this, Kohler? You accept the hospitality that is extended while another invades the agency's premises? You do not have a magistrate's order and now you tell *me* what to do in my own offices?'

'Abélard . . .'

'Jeannot, these two have no place here. Hasn't the Höherer SS and Polizeiführer Oberg explained things to them?'

'Monday, Abélard. I haven't yet had a chance to inform them.'

'Then do so.'

'Inspectors, we've set up a meeting at . . .'

'Later,' said Kohler, his gaze taking in this Jeannot Raymond. 'I want this opened now. Whose desk is it and where's the key?'

'It's my desk but that drawer has been tightly jammed for months.'

M. Quevillon had said that. Suzette knew he was lying.

A dancer's candy-striped warm-up stocking was dangled over the desk's blotting pad to be slowly lowered to coil in on itself.

'Open it, Hubert,' said M. Jeannot Raymond.

'I can't. I left the key at home.'

St-Cyr knew that if Hermann and himself forced the issue, the agency would rightly conclude that the desk had indeed already been burgled. They would then threaten to use the photo of the boys, yet if no objections were raised and the matter meekly left, they'd believe it anyway. 'Put in a call to Walter, Hermann. Tell him we've run into a stone wall.'

'Now wait, Inspectors,' managed Delaroche. 'From time to time it's necessary for Hubert and Flavien to produce certain pieces of evidence. Things are constantly being gathered. Clients do, at times, need convincing.'

'Just like I do, eh?'

'Hermann, perhaps we should all sit down. Perhaps the restaurant could . . .'

'Colonel,' said Suzette, 'would you like me to ring through for coffee and . . .'

'A few sandwiches . . .' prompted the prompter.

A sigh was given. 'Very well. The ham that I had at noon, Mademoiselle Dunand.'

'With mustard,' went on Louis. 'The Dijon *mélange crémeux* if possible, mademoiselle. A few olives also and please forgive me for having upset you earlier and for deceiving you. I'm not usually like that and am ashamed of myself.'

The creamy mustard, but Louis had meant it too, and was bound to do something about what had happened to her as a result. Flustered, though, and glad to escape the others if only for a moment, the girl turned away and was at the phone when they reached the outer office.

'Yours, I think, Colonel,' said Hermann, indicating its totally locked door. 'If you've a bottle of cognac in there, we could all use a drink.'

'Hubert, find what the inspector was looking for and bring it to my office.'

Check that desk of yours to see if anything is missing or has been disturbed.

As the door to this inner sanctum sanctorum was unlocked and opened, Louis simply said, 'After you, Colonel,' but then he stopped in the doorway as if struck.

The painting was absolutely magnificent. Automatically it drew the gaze away from the ample leather-topped, carved French oak desk that faced out from a far corner through a scattering of armchairs. It was seen in the half-mirrored doors of an open Louis XIV Boulle armoire, was seen also in a late Renaissance Spanish mirror, the two throwing the painting's image back and forth but allowing varied perspectives of prospective clients should the colonel feel the need.

Apart from a bank of filing cabinets panelled in that same oak, the office was all but a salon in the old style. The beautifully flowered Aubusson would smother sounds. Louis XIV fauteuils and settees were strategically placed for quiet tête-à-têtes. There were bronzes—a superb copy of Boizot's *Nymph*, another of Chinard's *Apollo* . . .

'Inspectors,' said Delaroche, indicating the chairs in front of his desk, the room lighted by a rock-crystal chandelier—how had he acquired it, wondered St-Cyr, this colonel who didn't stint himself and had such an obvious passion for the finer things in life?

'This is a sixteenth-century portrait of the Magdalen as a young girl of substance, Colonel. It's breathtaking.'

Though one didn't want to dwell on it, one had best be gracious. 'Please take a closer look while I find us a little something to drink. I'd value your opinion.'

And if that wasn't pleasant, what was? The painting was worth at least 250,000 old francs. Perhaps this red-haired girl who wore a turban of the softest gold and beige had been fifteen. Penitently the eyes were downcast, she reading an illuminated breviary, a corner of whose spine rested on the smallest of beautifully carved desks before her, and hadn't the colonel found exactly the same sort of desk—not a prie-dieu—and positioned it just a little to one side so that the viewer saw the one then automatically was drawn to divert the gaze and thoughts to a similarly velum-bound breviary beside which lay an identical pomander to the one in the painting and the same gold rings whose modest cabochons of bloodstone were similar to those worn on each of her forefingers. There were no other rings in the painting.

'Droplets of the blood of Christ,' said St-Cyr, throwing the words over a shoulder. 'That's what the people of those times believed that type of stone must hold. The jewellery and garments are of the very middle of the High Renaissance, Colonel. Perhaps the year 1500, or very close to it. I commend your taste. One sees at once the sharp contrasts of colour that so delighted and intrigued with their unspoken messages. The under-sleeves are crimson and juxtaposed with the kirtle's cocoa-brown silk, whose folds have an almost metallic sheen and whose trim . . .' He would point it all out as if a buyer in a gallery or patron of the Louvre.

'Propriety is total, Colonel, modesty complete, the reformation of the fallen absolute, even of one so wealthy, but the hints of what helped to cause the trouble are definitely there all the same. Vanity, *n'est-ce pas?*'

Bob *would* be disobedient, cursed Delaroche silently. Bob *would* let him down at a time like this and sit at Kohler's feet. 'Your cognac, Inspector.'

'*Merci.* Two gold chains are about her neck. The shortest of them is beaded and that, too, would have had meaning, and from it hangs an emerald and gold pendant whose droplet pearls shed the tears that are to remind her and all who view her that when chastity or the vows of marriage are broken, the reward can only be disgrace, no matter how enjoyable or profitable the moment.'

And on and on, was that it, eh? 'It's by Adriaen Isenbrant, of the Flemish School.'

'Also given as Ysenbrant, a pupil of Gerard David. One sees

the master's influence but this is definitely a major work in its own right. She reminds me of the madrigal singer and costume designer whose murder in the Palais des Papes we unfortunately had to investigate.'

In Avignon during the last week of January. 'You and Kohler never seem to stay long in one place, do you?'

'That way we never get bored. Hermann and myself need answers and it's time we had them.'

'You have only to ask. We're here to help.'

They walked in silence. M. Jeannot Raymond said *nothing*. Did he count off the lampposts as she always did and reach out to touch them? wondered Suzette. He had no need of the pocket torch she knew he never left the agency without, had gone into his office and then that of Hubert Quevillon to see if anything had been disturbed, had stayed in there several minutes and then had come back to escort her home after first having spoken quietly with the colonel.

Everywhere along the rue de Ponthieu the blackout was complete, except for the occasional glow of a cigarette or the sudden on-and-off of a blue-shaded torch in an uncertain hand. A *vélotaxi* went by, the dimness of its taillight receding.

'It's this way,' she heard herself saying, the voice overly sharp but frail on the cold, damp air. Had she doubts about the Agence Vidocq? he must be wondering. Fears? she asked herself. Hubert Quevillon had *not* apologized and this, too, was making her nervous and when they started to cross the rue Paul Baudry, there was no hesitation on M. Raymond's part. He simply took her by the hand.

The *passage clouté*'s white marker studs were all but hidden, his fingers cold and stiff. Her street was next and when they came to the rue La Boétie, he didn't hesitate.

'Hubert will have left the lock off the flat,' he said. 'Since you haven't your handbag, I presume he didn't give it a thought.'

Ah, merde, her papers . . .

'The fifth, at the back. I'll just come up to make certain every-thing is all right.'

Did he know the building that well?

Hole for hole, laddered run for run, the warm-up stockings were compared, Hermann deliberately letting Bob smell them. Slightly built and in his mid-thirties, with small, slim hands, closely trimmed nails and no bite marks that could be seen even on the wrists, Hubert Quevillon stood looking down at him while Flavien Garnier, in his late fifties and also lacking these but with big enough hands for the Trinité assault, watched his subordinate with a grim wariness that implied he'd had to do so constantly.

'Good, Bob. There's my soldier,' said Hermann, seemingly ignoring everyone as he folded the stockings and placed them in Élène Artur's fitted case.

He scratched Bob behind the ears and under the chin. 'You're beautiful,' he went on. '*Bien sûr*, I've known a lot of dogs and loved every one of them, but never a prince like yourself. I'm envious, Colonel.'

As his hand dropped, he looked up at Hubert Quevillon, let that emptiness his partner knew only too well fill his gaze and give warning of its own. 'So how is it, my fine one, that you had that stocking in your desk?'

'Kohler . . .'

'Colonel, let him answer.'

To smirk would infuriate this Kripo the SS had marked for life, thought Quevillon, so he would do that and then tell him how it was. 'I'm constantly gathering things that might be useful.'

A smart aleck—was that it, eh? The hair was dark brown and carelessly parted so that a hank of it fell rakishly over the brow. The dark-blue eyes were hooded, the expression at once intense and looking always for signs of the mischief his words might cause, the perpetual evening shadow something the girls might or might not like, but a regular at any number of brothels so that he could make his choice and do as he liked. 'And is it that you simply stole it while that girl was hurrying to get dressed because you had told her to?'

Hermann, urged St-Cyr silently. *Don't* accuse any of them yet. Wait! 'The time, please, Agent Quevillon?'

Please . . . ? What the hell was this? 'Louis, you leave him to me.'

'Hermann, there's likely a plausible answer. Colonel, from time to time I have to remind my partner that the blitzkrieg our friends demand must still have its little pauses.'

Though taken aback, Hermann was still ready to charge blindly forward and could not be warned of what had been discovered in that desk, nor on it or under it, nor could he be told yet of what had been on and in Flavien Garnier's. For now this information, especially the sawdust and wood shavings that must have been emptied from the turn-ups of Quevillon's trousers, would have to be kept from him, since these last were identical to those encountered in the Jourdan household and the gerbils would have loved them.

These two, they were nothing but trouble, thought Delaroche. 'The time, Hubert. As close as you can give it.'

'Nine. Maybe nine ten. Élène and the other girls were hurrying to get back on stage. One of her butterfly wings wouldn't stay up so I had to help by tightening its wires.'

'*Ja, ja, mein Lieber.* And the stockings?' persisted Hermann.

'Kohler, Kohler,' interjected Delaroche. 'The girl had other such stockings that were much better. Why should it matter if Hubert, thinking it was long past its useful life, should borrow one? Why not tell us where and how you found her?'

'I thought you knew.'

'How could I possibly? Chief Inspector, please inform this colleague of yours that the Agence Vidocq is not, and never has been, engaged in murder.'

'Was she murdered, Colonel?' asked Hermann.

'If not, how then did you come by her wedding ring?'

These two would go at it now if a companionable gesture

wasn't given. 'Colonel,' said St-Cyr, 'just tell us why Agent Quevillon was in the Lido's dressing room at 2110 hours or thereabouts last Thursday.'

'Yes, please tell us. It would help, I think.'

Had Kohler been mollified by his partner and if so, why the need if not the contents of that damned desk of Quevillon's? wondered Delaroche. 'I had asked Hubert to check if any of them had heard or seen anything that might help us find Lulu. Madame de Brissac—Catherine-Élizabeth—has not long to live but the telephone is there beside her, you understand, and she was constantly using it to call me.'

'And now you're going to have to tell her what's happened,' breathed Hermann, his patience all but gone.

Delaroche studied the glowing end of his cigar. 'What did you find in the Parc Monceau? It was there, wasn't it? You must have found something of Lulu's—why else your chasing after me to Chez Bénédicte's?'

Bob barked. Bob got all excited and had to be calmed. Louis told them the remains were in the Citroën's boot and that Élène must have wanted to bury what she could where Lulu's spirit would be most content and as close to her mistress as possible.

'You'll let me have them, won't you?' asked Delaroche, ignoring the fiction of an *indochinoise* superstition—was it really fiction, wondered Kohler, and did Delaroche really feel so duty-bound? Flavien Garnier didn't seem to give a damn. He simply budgeted his cigarette as if still mired in the trenches and waiting for the tempest of fire to start up all over again.

'At 2313 hours Thursday, Colonel,' went on Louis, 'Élène Artur was forced to telephone the Commissariat of the quartier du Faubourg de Roule to alert them to the killing at the École des Officiers de la Gendamerie Nationale. Hermann and myself didn't get there until 0511 hours Friday but believe the young man, still unidentified, must have been killed at between 2000 and 2130 hours the previous evening.'

And right when Quevillon was supposed to have been helping Élène with her wings, thought Kohler, but if Garnier considered any of this important, he didn't let on. Was the expression always so grim? he wondered. A blunt man, made blunter by the blotched bald dome of his head, the greying brown fringe above and behind the ears, the heavy, dark horn-rims with the big lenses and the Hitler soup strainer. Prominent jowls reinforced the grimness, deep creases the rarely parted lips. A man of few words, was that it, eh, or one who simply knew too much and felt it best to say little? 'She had, we understand, Colonel, first been forced to let the press in on things. Bob, as you know, went straight to that telephone.'

Kohler was definitely the one who had found her. 'But of course Bob would have. All of those girls use it, as they do that staircase. The scent was old. Maybe she made a telephone call, maybe she didn't. How could any of us possibly know?'

And stubborn to the last, eh? 'Your agency was tailing three of the victims Louis and I had to encounter that evening, Colonel. Madame Guillaumet was the first, and *voilà*, what did we later find but that the press had been in to photograph her at the *Hôtel-Dieu*?'

Ah, merde, Hermann, go easy, said St-Cyr to himself. 'Colonel, we're not accusing anyone, merely trying to get at the facts.' There was a knock. '*Ah bon*, I'm famished.'

Louis had said it as if relieved.

'A little wine?' asked Delaroche. Relieved too, was he? wondered Kohler.

'If you have it, that would be perfect,' said St-Cyr, gesturing appreciatively with pipe in hand. Jeannot Raymond had still not returned from escorting Suzette Dunand home. 'The flat is just along the way,' the girl had earlier said. Then why the delay? he had to ask himself, but would have to be patient.

The lift began its journey. Suzette knew she should say something, but M. Raymond had spoken privately with the concierge about her and about the trouble she had mentioned. Monsieur Louveau had looked her over as they'd spoken—she knew he had. Even though she had instantly dropped her gaze, she had felt him doing so. A girl in an overcoat and slippers? A secretary who had been slapped hard but one who had also, he would have been told, deliberately misled a Sûreté just to keep him from this building where she lived and where there had been some terrible trouble—she knew there had.

M. Raymond didn't say anything of what had happened in the building nor of what Concierge Louveau had told him about herself. Perhaps it was that someone had been taken away. People were being arrested all the time. No restaurant, café or bar was safe, no street, but surely not here, not when two of *les Allemands* lived in the building and all the other tenants must have been given security clearances, herself included?

The lift continued making all the noises that were usual in this quietest of residences. They reached her floor and Suzette watched as he opened the cage, she faintly saying, 'It is this way.' Had she not said that very same thing to him out on the street?

He was so silent and when, at last, they did reach her door, it was ajar. M. Quevillon had not pulled it tightly closed. *Dieu merci,* her handbag was still on the little table under the oval of the Empire mirror whose mahogany gleamed because she had made certain it would.

'I'm so very lucky,' she heard herself saying, her back still to him. 'Never in a thousand years could I ever have afforded a place like this. There are so many beautiful things. A Beauvais tapestry *chinoise* that is very old, Gallé, Lotz and Lalique glass figurines and vases, and others, too, from Czechoslovakia. An absolutely magnificent vitrine has a superb collection of Sèvres porcelain.'

Had she said too much? M. Raymond was silently studying her reflection in the mirror, he having closed the door to lean back against it, but had he put the lock on? Had he sensed how uncertain she was, a girl who knew far too much? Was this why his gaze didn't waver?

'What else is there?' he asked, giving her that smile of his, she instantly grinning with relief.

'Fabulous dolls in one of the Boulle armoires. Jumeau *Parisi-*

ennes and *bébés*, Kammer and Reinhardts and those of Armand Marseille. Their party dresses are of velvet, silk and satin, their jewellery so real, it must be.'

She swallowed hard. He didn't move. 'Was I not to have touched them?' she heard herself asking. 'I know the colonel has said I'm only to use the smallest of the bedrooms and that, from time to time, he would be sending others to stay here, but . . . but there hasn't been anyone yet and if I'm to keep the flat clean, I . . . It does get lonely. One does wonder what's in a drawer or armoire . . .'

Where, please, had it all come from—wasn't this what the silly thing was wondering, but something would have to be said. 'From time to time Colonel Delaroche picks things up and keeps them here or in one of the other flats the agency has for clients who feel they have to leave home for a little. Some of them have very young children who are desperately in need of reassurance, and for each child, he tries to find what's best.'

'There's a teddy bear in my room,' Suzette heard herself saying but was he demanding she tell him everything? 'His eyes are like polished anthracite. There are little felt pads on his paws.' Pads that she kissed every night—would he wonder this? 'I . . . I keep him on the side table next to the music box I borrowed whose larks sing to me every morning when the lid is opened, after . . . after I've managed to switch off the alarm clock.'

How young and inexperienced she must seem to him—young and with a tongue that had been loosened? 'The music box is of gold and enamelled flowers and was made in Geneva in 1825, but its wind-up mechanism was stuck. I felt I might have broken it and was so very worried, but Monsieur Frères Rochat, its maker, did exceptional work, so the trouble was not his or mine but simply the dust of the years.'

The girl had taken it to a shop.

'But I really don't know much about such things,' she gushed. 'How could I, coming from where I do?'

Charenton and the house of the aunt and uncle who had taken her in before the Defeat, the father having been called up and now a prisoner of war. 'You must know the Bois de Vincennes well.'

One of the city's largest and most popular of parks. 'A little, yes. Charenton is right next to it and when I visit with my aunt and uncle on the last Sunday of every month, I . . . I sometimes go there afterwards.' Why had he asked it of her?

He said no more of this but did he know they had put themselves out to send her to secretarial school and that she was trying to pay them back and desperately needed to keep her job, that with the rationing it helped them tremendously to have her living here? He must know that *Maman* and the rest of the family, except for *Papa*, were at home in Dreux, at least eighty-five kilometres to the west of the city and that she sent money and things to them when she could but hadn't been home since coming to Paris, not with the travel restrictions and the need for *laissez-passers* and *sauf-conduits*. The cost too.

Indicating that she should show him the flat, he told her he had best look through it but didn't explain further. She took off her slippers, he his shoes, which he set neatly side by side, even to cleaning a bit of mud from the toe of one.

But had he really put the lock on? wondered Suzette. The Savonnerie carpet in the *salle de séjour* was soft and warm underfoot, the living room perfect—Louis XVI chairs and sofas she never sat in, lamps she never used, even a glazed cheval screen before a fireplace in which she had never once lighted a fire, the stove in the kitchen being hers to use. Oil paintings hung on the walls with the tapestries—landscapes, portraits, sketches—beautiful things were everywhere and worth an absolute fortune and yet . . . and yet it was but one of such flats the agency kept for its clients—hadn't that been what he'd said? Flats here, flats there. 'I . . . I don't use any of the rooms except for the kitchen and my bedroom,' she said.

Teddy was waiting. Teddy *would* look up at him. 'It does get lonely,' she said and stupidly had to shrug, was nervous too, nervous at the nearness of this man she had sometimes thought about when in bed with Teddy—would he have realized this? 'Working six days a week, I . . . I haven't had a chance to contact any of my friends from school here and am not from Paris anyway—*ah, mon Dieu,* how could I be?'

235

Which only showed how well Abélard vetted their secretaries, thought Raymond, but he wouldn't give her one of those rare smiles she welcomed, not yet. He'd make her wait for it.

The girl followed him to the kitchen, but had she realized he'd known of the teddy bear? She *would* take that music box to have its mechanism freed, a problem for sure. An offer would have been made, but had she been stunned by the value and come away only to then realize what the contents of the flat itself must be worth?

'Colonel Delaroche gives me vouchers,' she said of the kitchen. 'I use them with my ration tickets but only at certain shops. He has said my time is better spent at my desk and not in the queues, so I . . . I just hand the vouchers in and each shopkeeper takes what tickets are needed and I, in turn, take what I've been given.'

She had set the table for two and had piled books on to the chair opposite the one she would use, the day's events at the agency to then be relayed to her little friend. Thursdays, Fridays and Saturdays were meatless days, and though there must be meat available, the frying pan hadn't been taken down and set to ready on the stove. Instead, noodles were in soak. The Maréchal Pétain would have been pleased.

'Were some of the shopkeepers I go to once men under the colonel's command?' she asked. 'Most are veterans, many from Verdun. Some even wear their medals and ribbons on their smocks.'

Fear of himself, of a man and all that it must entail yet the forbidden excitement of it, too, had made her breath come quickly, but she wasn't aware of this and certainly the little fool had been taking note of far too much. 'Look, I must get back to the office. Please don't worry about Hubert. Everything will be fine.'

Pressing her forehead against the door, her fingers still on the lock, Suzette didn't hear him take the lift. He had gone down one of the staircases. A floor, two floors—on which had the trouble been and why, please, had he to check? Hadn't Concierge Louveau told him all about it?

Teddy didn't help. Teddy said, *Don't you dare!*

The side staircase was the closer, stocking feet the best, no sign of M. Jeannot Raymond in the corridor below, nor was he on the third floor, not that she could see, but one of the flats nearest to this staircase had been sealed with stickers, they having been placed both above and below the lock and covering the seam between the door and the jamb. Stickers whose eagle clutched a swastika.

' "*Zutritt verboten. Défense d'entrer,*" ' she whispered as she read the notice. ' "*Befehl der Kripo Pariser-Zentrum. Par ordre du Préfet et de la Police Judiciaire.*" '

Herr Kohler had signed the notice. The building was quieter than quiet but . . . Suzette glanced up at the ceiling—had she heard someone in that corridor?

There was no one there, and *Dieu merci,* it was the same on the fifth. The door to her flat was still tightly closed, she having silently eased it shut. Hurriedly she stepped inside, closed the door, put the lock on . . . warned herself to do so quietly.

Sighed when it was done, and pressed her forehead against the door again. 'There,' she said but couldn't find the will to turn, couldn't find her voice anymore, knew only that she wasn't alone and that he was right behind her.

The cigarette box that Hermann kept digging into on the colonel's desk was Czechoslovakian, the mid-1930s and a time when such things could still be made. It was of beautifully banded, polished malachite, whose frosted green glass lid held in relief, as if in gauze, a reclining nude, full exposure. At once it was evocative and provocative, and one had to wonder if the box had been deliberately placed there to incite further jealousy in already embittered female clients.

'You enjoy the finer things in life, Colonel. Again I commend your taste,' said St-Cyr. Quevillon, Garnier, Hermann and himself were sitting in front of the desk, the colonel behind it, his gestures effusive, the cigar hand slicing the air when emphasis was needed.

'Come, come, what is this? More suspicion? You know as well as I, the market is flooded with objects of virtu. Business has been good and when I can, I pick up what fancies me.'

Hubert Quevillon couldn't resist darting a knowing glance at his mentor, Flavien Garnier, who patently ignored his subordinate. 'Of course, I meant nothing other than that I, too, appreciate such things, Colonel.' If Hermann had any further thoughts of being incautious, he had, one hoped, now thought better of it. 'Let's get back to our discussion of the Ritz. Surely Agent Garnier must have some idea of who our Trinité victim was to have met.'

'For sex,' muttered Hubert Quevillon.

'None,' grunted Garnier, the black horn-rims lending severity to the silent warning he gave his subordinate.

'Not a *General*, a *Generalmajor*, or even a *Major*?' asked Hermann, the *Deutsch* deliberate.

Garnier tapped cigarette ash into a cupped palm, the dark brown eyes behind those specs not even having to glance down at it.

'The assistant doorman who delivered the note to the Guillaumet subject's concierge refused to tell me. His job, he said, and I must agree with him, Colonel, would not only have been jeopardized but forfeited. Decour, the head doorman of the Ritz, is an absolute bastard.'

Agent Garnier was as if of reinforced concrete, thought St-Cyr. No doubt this impersonator of himself ate his meals as though still in the trenches just as Hermann did, stolidly lump by lump while waiting for the next onslaught, but something would have to be said. 'And how, please, did you learn of her tragic assault?'

Was it to be nothing but the most inane of questions from this Sûreté? wondered Garnier. St-Cyr must have gone through that desk of Hubert's and his own but had been valiantly trying to hide the fact. 'Like everyone else, we noticed it in the newspapers.'

'She takes a good photo, doesn't she?' quipped Quevillon who seemed always to be driven to let his gaze flick from this Sûreté to Hermann, as if not just to gauge what the response might be, but to incite it if possible.

'We were as distressed as yourselves,' countered Delaroche warily.

'But none of you had the unenviable task of having to find her,

Colonel. Perhaps Agent Garnier would be so good as to tell us who else was tailing Madame Guillaumet?'

'Yes, tell us,' breathed Hermann, dragging out his notebook as Quevillon brushed crumbs from the creased knees of trousers that still had the turn-ups of the 1930s.

'You see, Colonel, your assistant may well have noticed he wasn't alone in asking questions about her,' said St-Cyr.

'Someone sure as hell knew what that "subject" of yours was up to,' added Hermann.

'Flavien, did you or Hubert . . . ?' hazarded Delaroche. 'Kohler, must you write everything down?'

There were no bite marks on the colonel's wrists or hands either, no broken-off, closely trimmed fingernails. In short, none of these three could have assaulted the Trinité victim, nor could Delaroche have been bitten by Élène Artur. 'Oh, sorry. Force of habit, I guess.'

'There were two of them, Colonel,' said Garnier levelly.

'Two?' asked Louis who had yet to accuse Garnier of impersonating a Sûreté.

'*Oui*. Both of medium height, the one much bigger about the waist than the other, who was built like a wedge, and probably as strong as an ox. They must have seen that I was on to them, for puff, they vanished.'

And how very convenient, thought St-Cyr, but something had had to be given and Garnier had done so. For each advance, first the little retreat; for each lie, the slender element of truth.

Quevillon flashed a knowing grin, but had to lose it suddenly under a scowl from the colonel. 'And when, please, was that?' asked St-Cyr.

'Yes, when?' asked Hermann.

These two would never be convinced to leave well enough alone and to cooperate, felt Garnier. 'At first I thought a competing agency must be after the same things, but then they lost interest. Colonel, how was I to have known the subject would be assaulted and robbed? How was Hubert?'

'Raped and beaten,' said Quevillon, darting an expectant

glance at each of them. 'But . . . but wasn't there something else rammed up inside the . . .'

'Hubert!' cautioned Delaroche.

'The truncheon of a *gendarme de contrôle, peut-être?*'

A traffic cop. The press hadn't known of it, thought Kohler, not even that young doctor at the *Hôtel-Dieu* had been specific, but Louis wasn't going to let on and didn't pause while repacking that pipe of his and making sure his pouch was again filled to overflowing. 'And with Madame Barrault and Gaston Morel?' he asked.

St-Cyr had not only stolen more pipe tobacco, he was like a termite with this little interview of theirs, snorted Garnier to himself. Sometimes one couldn't hear the termites in the night, sometimes they would set up such a racket, sleep was impossible but as with all such insects, it was often best to give them something to gnaw on while one got the paraffin and the match or the solution of arsenic and sugar. 'They were enjoying each other's company in secret, or so they thought.'

Hastily Hubert Quevillon pushed that hank of hair back off his brow. 'But I was able to gain access to that little nest of theirs in the Hôtel Grand and to watch the circus through a crack in the bedroom door.'

'Hubert . . .' tried Delaroche.

'*Toute nue*, the legs spread and down on her knees with Morel's *bitte* in her hands and . . .'

'HUBERT! that is enough,' snapped Garnier, impatiently flicking cigarette ash into that palm of his. 'The inspectors *asked* if you had noticed anyone else tailing the Barrault subject.'

'Yes, did you notice others were "investigating" the woman's private life?' said Hermann.

'Isn't that what an *agent privé* does?' countered Quevillon. 'Villeneuve, the manager of the Cinéma Impérial, did tell me that others had been making enquiries. With women like that it's understandable, is it not? The Barrault subject needed the part-time work and he gave her just enough of it to have the use of her and often.'

Oh and did he? asked Kohler silently. Quevillon avoided glancing at the colonel and for a moment no one could find a thing to say but was this twit of an *agent privé* confident they couldn't be touched? Delaroche, having tired of his cigar, had quickly stubbed it out, then polished off the last of the Romanée-Conti, one of the finest of Burgundies, if not the finest and once given to Louis XIV spoonful by patient spoonful, the Sun King's doctors thinking it might cure the great one's painful fistula, an outright case of gastric ulcers, no doubt.

Quevillon lit another cigarette, his fifth, or was it the sixth? 'I have the proof,' he said, tasting it too. 'Sworn statements from the cinema's staff as well as from its manager.'

'But . . . but, monsieur, these others who were tailing her?' asked Louis, gesturing companionably with that pipe hand of his. 'Could we not have . . .'

'Those others, Inspectors, also didn't maintain their surveillance,' said Garnier flatly.

'But were they the same two as with the Guillaumet investigation?' insisted Louis as if he believed every word of what had been said.

'That's correct but we didn't see them,' said Garnier. 'It was only after having been given a description of them, that Villeneuve of the Impérial became certain they were the same. We didn't expect anyone else to have been tailing the subject, Colonel. Ah! perhaps a slip-up on my part, the need always to be in more than two places at once. One of the usherettes must have let them know we'd been in and asking questions.'

'Okay, okay,' breathed Hermann, apparently jotting it all down. 'Louis and me, we'll have to check it out. Now give us what you can on . . .'

Deliberately he thumbed through his notebook, going well back into other investigations before thumbing forward just to let them know the partnership didn't fool around. 'Give us what you can on a Father Marescot.'

Had the bell of that church just sounded? wondered St-Cyr, for each of them had glanced at the others.

'The priest of the Église de Notre-Dame de Lorette, Colonel,' offered Garnier, having somehow silenced his subordinate. 'The good father couldn't tell me what the Barrault subject had revealed in the confessional she repeatedly subjects herself to out of guilt, but he did go so far as to say she had damned herself before God, as had all of the others who attend those special Masses of his and that . . . yes, yes, he had personally written to the Scapini Commission some time ago demanding that they inform the husband.'

'A prisoner of war,' said Delaroche with a sigh, sadly shaking his head. 'Far too many of their wives are simply taking advantage of their absences. Is it any wonder there has been both outcry and retaliation, especially since our boys can't defend their property or even have the use of it?'

'They're all making sluts of themselves,' said Quevillon. '*Chatte* is so common these days, one can get it for a half a cigarette the hour and more if one insists.'

The *salaud*! 'But had anyone else gone to that priest with a similar inquiry?' asked Louis, patently ignoring the use of 'property' and all the rest.

'I had no need to ask,' went on Garnier. 'Father Marescot offered the information as was his duty as a concerned citizen. Tell them, Hubert.'

'With pleasure. We weren't alone, Inspectors. "A woman comes," he said. "She is older than that one by a good twenty years and doesn't have to drag around an eight-year-old daughter." '

'Madame Morel?' asked the termite, as startled by the news as was his partner.

'Gaston is known for his affairs,' said Delaroche amicably. 'Before this Defeat of ours he employed the Barrault subject's husband as a lorry driver, clearly putting the woman in debt to him. What better a conquest than the stepsister of one's wife, especially when poverty and loneliness cause such women to do things they might not otherwise agree to.'

Like getting down on their knees for hire, was that it, eh? wondered Kohler. Sûreté that he was, Louis glanced at that wristwatch of his whose crystal had been cracked in that other war but would never be replaced, for it was at once a shining example of French frugality and constant reminder of what he had survived when so many others hadn't.

'*Ah, bon*, Colonel, for now the wrap-up, I think. Attacks are being committed all over the city. The wives and fiancées of prisoners of war, though not the only victims, are being singled out, wedding rings demanded, handbags stolen, et cetera, et cetera. Gestapo Boemelburg, at our briefing this afternoon, told us that he feels certain there is a gang at work, that the attacks are being planned and carried out with military precision backed by exceptional sources of information and that the violence is being deliberately escalated because the defeat at Stalingrad has made such criminals bolder, but with the result that Berlin has been constantly on the line demanding an immediate end to the crimes and a return to safety on the streets.'

Ach du lieber Gott, how had Louis got it all out in one breath? wondered Kohler. A cigar had best be taken, one for him too, the colonel's cigar cutter borrowed indefinitely.

These two, thought Delaroche, each was so very different yet they were the same. 'And that is why the Höherer SS Oberg has engaged the Agence Vidocq in the matter, *mes amis*, and wishes you to join us when we meet with him at 1000 hours Monday, the avenue Foch.'

'Head Office, Louis,' breathed Hermann. 'I told you but you never listen, do you? That's why I went there right away.'

'But *what* did you find and *when* did you visit Herr Oberg's office? Come, come, Inspector,' demanded Delaroche. 'Is it not time you let us in on what must have happened to Élène Artur? If we are to work together, and I am certain that is what the Standartenführer Langbehn will insist on, then it is best we know everything.'

'The Standartenführer?' blurted Louis.

St-Cyr had just been kicked in *les joyeuses* but surprise had best be registered. '*Ah, mon Dieu*, is it that you have already met?'

'Briefly. Colonel, who, exactly, is to be at that meeting?'

Such caution was admirable, but why had Jeannot not returned? Had the Dunand girl given trouble? 'Myself, my partner, Jeannot Raymond, Flavien, of course, and Hubert, yourselves also and I believe a translator, a *Blitzmädel,* Sonja Remer, who was, apparently, a victim also of this tidal wave of street violence and crime.'

Oh-oh, here it comes, thought Kohler, sighing inwardly.

'Herr Oberg is determined to punish the boys who stole the girl's handbag,' went on Delaroche. 'Flavien, were either of you able to pin down their identities? I know the bag has been returned by a devious route but it was, I believe, still missing some items.'

The termites had just choked in the darkness of their little tunnel, the one behind on the shit of the one in front. 'There's a photo of them in your out-tray, Hubert,' said Garnier.

'Get it,' said Delaroche, 'and while you're at it, if Jeannot is in his office, please ask him to join us.'

The building was silent. The lift had made no sound even after M. Jeannot Raymond had left her, but that had been some time ago, Suzette knew, and talking to Teddy simply wasn't going to help. Indeed, if others knew she did such a thing, they'd think her crazy and she should stop, would have to now anyways, but she wasn't alone in this. She couldn't be. Didn't the Occupation encourage people to retreat into illusion and cultivate their fantasies and daydreams? Wasn't that just about the only way to counter the terrible loneliness and uncertainty?

'Look, I'm sorry I didn't make us a sauce for the noodles. I was still uncertain, still agitated.'

There, she had confessed that much. He paid not the slightest attention, must really be upset with her.

'The red-lacquered Chinese gate, Teddy. You can't miss it if you're in that far corner of the Bois de Vincennes. The gate is at the entrance to the tropical garden and the Institut National d'Agronomie Coloniale and can be seen from a distance, but it . . . it's close to something else.'

Even such a hint failed to move him. 'Very well,' she said spitefully. 'I'm going to meet Monsieur Raymond there tomorrow morning at nine.'

Picked at, the noodles were cold and soggy, the slices of carrot like wood. 'The gate is near the Annamite Temple that is a memorial to the *Indochinois* who died for France in that other war. The mother of that girl who was murdered downstairs goes there to pray and to introduce her grandson to his ancestors. Monsieur Raymond said that Concierge Louveau told him the dead girl always went there to visit with her mother and little boy early on Sundays just as I go to Charenton on the last Sunday of every month.'

Still there was nothing but an ever-deepening frown from Teddy. 'Jeannot feels that someone should tell the mother what has happened, that she will have to claim the body from the city's morgue and that . . . that funeral arrangements will have to be made. Oh for sure, the daughter was prostituting herself and was the wife of a prisoner of war, but to kill her for betraying her husband was not right, he said. "What is needed is compassion." There's a restaurant nearby, on the Île de la Porte Jaune in Lac des Minimes. He has said he will take me to lunch there afterwards.'

Even this news didn't move him. He was insisting that he be told everything.

'Jeannot says there's a bronze funeral urn in the temple's courtyard and that perhaps the mother could arrange to have the daughter's ashes placed there among those of her ancestors. Then her little boy could always visit. The temple, a pagoda,* was donated to the Colonial Exhibition of 1906 in Marseille and is really called a *dinh*, he says. A large communal house that was used for worship and where the elders of the village would go to discuss important matters. Frankly, I can't understand how anyone could let such an important building be taken away but they did, and in 1917 it was moved to the Bois de Vincennes to become the memorial. Is it not good and kind of him to want to see the mother, Ted-

---

* Destroyed by fire in 1984, the *dinh* was from what is now South Vietnam.

dy, and to offer to help her financially with the funeral? A girl he didn't even know but whose mother and child shouldn't be made to suffer more than they already will? He . . . he thought that if I were with him it might make things easier for the little boy and that . . . that Colonel Delaroche would insist on our taking something from here. He was certain you could help that little boy.'

Let me have the rest of it then, said Teddy.

'Look, I'm sorry. Really I am but you'll see everything I do. There's a *passage*, Teddy. Jeannot says it's well worth a visit. All along its walls are beautiful bas-reliefs that were copied from those at Angkor Wat in Indochina. He's been there. He really has. He's seen the ruins of that great temple. He says that among our scholars there were some who at first felt that the temple at Angkor Wat was Buddhist but that there is a magnificent shrine to Vishnu, the Hindu Preserver, another to Brahma, their god of Creation, and yet another to Siva, their destroyer. I . . . I hadn't realized he would even know or care about such things. Honestly I hadn't, but . . . but people don't visit those memorials much now, so we and the mother and little boy should have the place much to ourselves.'

Teddy didn't say anything for the longest time. His feelings had, of course, been hurt and she was going to have to do something about that.

You fool, he said at last. *Wasn't this Jeannot of yours standing inside the door here when you ran back upstairs? Didn't he stop you from crying out in panic?*

'He . . . he did grab me from behind, but . . .'

He clamped a hand over your mouth and held you pinned against the door. You thought you were going to die. You did! You nearly fainted.

Teddy never missed a thing, not even that Jeannot had come back to tell her what had happened to that girl. 'When he released me, I saw that he had been badly bitten on the left wrist and thought that I'd done it in panic, but . . . but I'd only pulled the bandage off.'

It was inflamed and you stood helplessly before him in tears.

'He knew where I'd been, knew I'd followed him.'

Yet didn't accuse you of it?

'He was too polite.'

Admit it, you couldn't face him.

'All right, all right, I won't go. I won't! On Monday, when I get to the office, I'll tell him I wasn't feeling well.'

She would clear things away now, thought Suzette. She would turn her back on Teddy, wouldn't throw anything out. They would just have to eat it tomorrow for supper. 'He's not like the others at the agency, Teddy. He's decent, honest and kind, and keeps to himself. That's why he insisted we sit in the *salle de séjour* among all those lovely things, and that I drink the last of his *eau-de-vie*. He was genuinely worried about his having terrified me and held my hands. I had no need to fear him and said I would help him. I *promised*, Teddy. He'll be expecting us—he really will. I'm not to tell Concierge Louveau where we're going even if that one asks, which he will. It's . . . it's best we don't.

' "Let's keep it to ourselves," Jeannot said. His fingers trembled when he kissed me on the cheek and I felt the warmth of him. He said, "Please don't worry. Everything will be fine. It's probably best that you're not here when the coroner and the police come to remove that body." I can't have the police asking me any more questions. I can't. I know too much. I'll lose my job if they make me tell them things.'

And what about that bite you saw? Did Bob do it or some other dog like that Lulu?

'Bob wouldn't have bitten him. Not Bob. I . . . I don't know how he got the bite. I wish I did but couldn't ask.'

10

Plunged into the damp, cold darkness of the rue La Boétie at 2107 hours Berlin Time, they were moving now. They weren't wasting time, having just left the Agence Vidocq. 'It's this house, Louis. This one,' insisted Kohler.

'No it isn't. It's this one.'

'*Merde*, how the hell would you know?'

'Try me.'

The candle stub had gone out. Uncanny, that's what Louis was. 'Why *didn't* you tell me they had a photo of the boys?'

'I couldn't. There wasn't a chance.'

Jeannot Raymond hadn't been in his office. 'Have they got Giselle?'

'Later . . . We can discuss it later.'

'Garnier and Quevillon took Élène Artur. I'm certain of it.'

'Did I not say "later"?'

The door was locked. Fist to it, Louis summoned the concierge. 'Louveau?' he demanded. 'Sûreté and Kripo.'

'Messieurs . . .'

'The flat of Judge Rouget and hurry!' They didn't take the lift. They went up the spiralling main staircase two and three steps at a time, Louveau soon falling far behind.

'Armand Tremblay hasn't been in yet,' said Louis when they

got to the flat. 'The seals haven't been broken. If Jeannot Raymond paid this a visit, he must have only wanted to confirm that you had found her.'

'That still doesn't explain why he didn't come back to the agency.'

Collectively the seals were examined. Nothing could have been disturbed since Hermann's departure. Nothing.

'Boemelburg can't have let our coroner know of the body, Louis.'

'And that can only mean Oberg didn't want him to. Oberg, Hermann. Monsieur, was Jeannot Raymond here to examine these?'

The seals were indicated, Louveau taken aback. 'M. Raymond? Whatever for? He simply brought the Mademoiselle Dunand home and stayed with her awhile.'

'*Ah, Jésus,* Louis . . .'

'*Vite, vite,* monsieur, her flat!'

They took the side stairs this time. *Ach,* why hadn't they considered that the girl might live in the same building?

Louveau knocked on the door of a fifth-floor flat nearest to that staircase. 'Mademoiselle Dunand?' he quavered. Impatiently they waited. Would the detectives insist on entry? 'Monsieur Raymond told me the girl had been upset over the murder and that he had thought it best to stay to calm her, Inspectors, and to reassure her that my building was absolutely safe otherwise and that she had no need to concern herself further. He said he told her he would see her Monday morning at the office and that she was to enjoy her day off.'

'He actually came downstairs to tell you all of that?' asked Kohler.

'But certainly.'

'Your passkey, monsieur. Don't argue,' said Louis, nodding curtly at the door.

'Mademoiselle Dunand,' sang out Louveau. '*C'est moi,* your concierge. Are you all right?'

From behind the still locked door came the hesitance of, '*Oui,* I was just getting ready for bed. Is . . . is something wrong?'

'Mademoiselle, it's me, Jean-Louis St-Cyr.'

'I'M NOT DRESSED! YOU . . . YOU CAN'T COME IN! CAN'T IT WAIT?'

'Louis, leave her. She's okay.'

'Mademoiselle, what exactly did Jeannot Raymond say to you?'

'Only that I wasn't to worry about losing my job because of what you did. That . . . that Monsieur Quevillon would apologize for hitting me and that . . . that the colonel would be asked to dismiss him.'

'You lied to me, mademoiselle. You deliberately caused me to believe your flat was on the Champs-Élysées.'

'And for that, I'm sorry. It . . . it was only because I didn't know what had happened in this building, that there . . . there had been some trouble.'

'Louis, she was afraid of you. How many times must I tell you to . . .'

'Hermann, those *salauds* have out-Vidocq'd Vidocq! And tomorrow, mademoiselle?' he asked.

'I'm not even going to leave the building to go to Mass. I'm going to stay right here.'

'As she should,' muttered Kohler softly. 'There, didn't I just tell you she was okay?'

On the staircase down, Louveau ingratiatingly confided, 'She usually does her laundry on Sundays afterwards unless . . .'

'Out with it,' said Louis.

'Unless she goes to visit her relatives in Charenton but that's only on the last Sunday of the month.'

The night was like ink. Ignition switched off, the Citroën coasted up the last of the rue de Birague and into the *place* des Vosges where it could just as easily, if not better, be stolen or robbed of its tyres.

Kohler rolled down his side windscreen. Through the freezing, damp, dark, quiet of the night came the incessant cooling of the engine and the silence.

'This is crazy, Louis. You can't be serious.'

'Wood shavings, Hermann, and sawdust.'

Merde, what was he on about now?

'Sometime today, probably early in the afternoon and while sitting briefly at that desk of his, Hubert Quevillon emptied the turn-ups of his trousers. Mahogany shavings, cedar of Lebanon, French oak and walnut, also teakwood from the Far East. Certainly not the plain spruce of the no-name coffins the *Hôtel-Dieu* use for its unfortunates.'

'A carpenter's shop. A furniture repair place . . .'

'Noëlle Jourdan likes to give the gerbils she keeps something to burrow into. Matron Aurore Aumont thought the shavings must have come from the coffin shop but obviously they can't have.'

It had to be said. 'Noëlle and her father could never have owned the items she pawned.'

'Nor had a right to the stamp collection of Bernard Isaac Friedman of 14 rue des Rosiers.'

'And Delaroche must have easy access to beautiful things.'

'Some of which even that agency of his could never have afforded.'

'Judge Rouget, too, Louis? The things I saw in that vitrine of his.'

Sickened by the thought of their being led ever deeper into the morass Paris and the country had become, Kohler wiped fog from the windscreen. 'Just what did you find in that bastard's desk and please don't tell me that before this Defeat of yours he worked in La Villette.'

The largest of the city's two abattoirs and where all but 20 percent of the sheep and cattle consumed each year in the city used to be slaughtered, as well as nearly eighty thousand horses. Now, of course, little of this work was required since most of the stock was simply loaded on to railway trucks and sent to the Reich.

'Handcuffs, lipsticks, compacts, earrings and other jewellery, handbags too, some of which can no doubt be linked to victims. A spool of piano wire and clippers, a length of bloodstained sash cord and two bottles of chloroform, one of which was half-empty.'

Giselle . . . 'What else?'

'The usual photos.'

'And?'

'A jumble of negligees, brassieres, underpants and garter belts. The ticket stubs of the Cinéma Impérial—no doubt the colonel charged the expense to Madame Morel's account for the Barrault subject's investigation. Blouses that had been ripped off. Keys—lots of them. *Jetons*, too, for the telephones they might need to force some girl to use. I couldn't have let you know any of this when we were in that office. I tried to give you a hint but even that failed.'

More . . . there must be more.

'A note from Delaroche reminding Quevillon not to forget to pay his PPF dues.'

The Parti Populaire Français of Jacques Doriot whose militants, along with others, formed the backbone of the Intervention-Referat and who had eagerly assisted the nine thousand Paris police, and student police, during last year's *grande rafle*.

'Quevillon may well be the Agence Vidocq's only member, Hermann. Otherwise the colonel would, perhaps, have paid the dues himself.'

'Delaroche simply wants to give himself and the others a bit of distance yet show support. Funds will have been passed under the table. The PPF have friends in the Propaganda-Abteilung and can call on the press any time they want.'

'Especially if there's a student nurse who had best do as she's told.'

'You first, or me?'

'Me, I think, but let's hope the *agence* hasn't yet anticipated a second visit.'

'Since they'll probably have been told of the first?'

'Among other things, Flavien Garnier had a tube of Veronal in his desk and nearly fifty tobacco cards. The girl's father needs the one for the constant pain he suffers, and writes appeals to former comrades-in-arms for help; the daughter found eggs, shoes, a chocolate bar and other items for Matron Aumont's grandchildren, purchases and appeals that could perhaps only have been facilitated by the current and most popular medium of exchange.'

'You're full of surprises. I hadn't realized you could be so light-fingered.'

'Then realize that under Garnier's blotting pad there was a list of *résistants*, some of whom had ticks beside them and lines through them, and that under Quevillon's photo of the boys, was one of Giselle as she left Oona yesterday.'

Ach, where was it all to end? wondered Kohler. The PPF had been funded by the Abwehr, the counterintelligence service of the Wehrmacht, and had supplied them with the names and locations of *résistants* and other 'troublemakers' the Occupier had wanted but with the defeat at Stalingrad, everyone had started having second thoughts and, as if that weren't enough, that fanatic ex-chicken farmer and Head of the SS, the Reichsführer Himmler, had all along been jealous of the Abwehr and had sought to undermine it, and submerge it entirely within the Sicherheitsdienst.

One happy family. And guess what? he silently asked as he found the main staircase of the house at Number 25 and followed Louis up it. Given the ever-shifting sands of Paris and the Occupation, the PPF had seen the light and gone over to the SS. The Agence Vidocq must now be supplying *them* with those names and locations, Judge Rouget sentencing those taken, Oberg seeing that they were either shot as hostages for some act of 'terrorism' or shipped east to one of the camps no one wanted to mention, though everyone knew of them, especially Hercule the Smasher.

Having anticipated his thoughts, Louis was waiting for him on the second storey's landing to softly confide, 'That's not what worries me at the moment, *mon vieux*. If Oberg ordered the *agence* to take Giselle as bait for his *Mausfalle* and they failed to do so, is that not, perhaps, reason enough for rage in the killing of the *passage* de l'Hirondelle victim? To fail when working for such a one can't sit easily.'

'Giselle and two honest cops who've been getting in the way far too many times.'

'And are to be made martyrs of, in the line of duty, Hermann.'

The French loved their martyrs. 'The press will be adoring. Occupier and Occupied die in battle to clean up our streets and make them safe again.'

'I can see the smile on your corpse. Now let's deal with the Jourdan household and talk about it later. If Jeannot Raymond or anyone else from that agency has beaten us to it, he or they have either left the premises or been far quieter than ourselves.'

The tiny kitchen was a shambles. The single electric lightbulb that had hung above the plain deal table with its toppled cane chairs had been flung against the wall, its frayed cord and sliding weight yanked on.

Having escaped the prison of their overturned birdcage, the gerbils had vanished in fright, the girl having put it between herself and her assailant, but far more wood shavings had been scattered across the floor than even it would have held.

She had snatched up a knife and thrown it, then smashed the light. Under torchlight, two rabbits in the screened airing cupboard beyond the drainboard and sink, watched detective proceedings with evident alarm. The drawstring of the cloth bag Noëlle Jourdan must have earlier filled with wood shavings, was loose, the throat wide open, the bag empty.

Among the dark, nutbrown to honey-brown shavings and bits of sawdust on the floor, there were pieces of brightly coloured porcelain: the curly-haired, ash-blonde, cap-wearing head of a pretty, blue-eyed peasant girl, the loose, knee-length pantaloons of the fisher boy she had come to meet.

'Russian, Hermann. A pair of figurines from the Imperial Porcelain Manufactory.'

'Things must have seemed okay at first, Louis, the visit perhaps a little late in the day.'

'The girl in here on her own and getting tomorrow's supper ready . . .'

'The father in with whomever had come to see him.'

'But then she must have heard something.'

'That bag would have been hidden.'

'Only to then be dragged out and opened by the visitor, the figurines removed.'

'Stood side by side, the accusations given, but was she still hearing things from the other room? Was she, Louis?'

'These date from about 1825 to 1850. The porcelain is exquisite.'

'And once worth what? Ten thousand francs at least; five hundred *Reichskassenscheine*.'

'Stay here and don't pop any more of those Benzedrine pills. Let me see what has happened.'

That sympathetic, empathetic, old-soldier-understands tone of voice just couldn't be tolerated anymore. 'Confronted, Noëlle made a run for it, Louis. Since the door to the flat was wide open and she wasn't on the stairs, she may have escaped.'

'Which leaves the father and what she must have heard. Now please . . . *Ah, mon Dieu,* be sensible. He's a *grand mutilé*. He'll only bring back the memories.'

The poor bastard with the stumps and the dyed black moustache, the shrapnel scars and thinning black hair had snatched the *vase de nuit* from under the moth-eaten bed that was heaped with blankets. Somehow he had managed to get his trousers down but had collapsed on that one leg of his and had broken the chamber pot.

Christ, the constant diet of vegetables and fruit if one could get them. Ripe on the already ripe air, he had drawn that one knee up and in at a spasm and had emptied himself, had vomited as well, the reactions so swift, he hadn't known what was happening to him and had died within what?

'Less than five minutes,' said Louis. 'Remember, please, that I did warn you.'

Wearing a knitted blue toque, three pullovers, heavy cords and two socks on that one foot, Jourdan had been bundled up in bed when offered the drink and . . .

'The last half of a litre of *eau-de-vie de poire*, Hermann.'

Uncorked, the bottle stood upright on the rickety night table and next to a spent tube of Veronal, but *Jésus, merde alors*, how could Louis remain so detached?

The glass tumbler the girl must have unwittingly handed to the visitor was still on the bedside table. Under torchlight, its dregs were not like water, the smell not sweet and pleasant but stingingly pungent.

'Exposure to air and light darkens it . . .' began Louis.

'Nicotine, damn it?'

'Usually such an *eau-de-vie de poire* is either clear or a very pale yellow. This is a dark yellowish brown . . .'

'You heard me!'

'An insecticide, a fumigant?'

'Please don't try to convince me you're really serious about that little farm you keep saying you want to retire to. Worm powders also, idiot, and sheep dip. We once had to put down a neighbour's Alsatian that wouldn't stop chasing our flock and killing the lambs. *Vati* made me hold the dog while he gave it two drops. Only two.'

'Three or four are sufficient for an adult human—less than sixty milligrams, but more has been used, I think. Though oily, nicotine is soluble in most liquids. The taste is violently acrid and instantly burns the tongue and stomach, but by then it has already struck the central nervous system and most especially the sympathetic and parasympathetic ganglia, where it stops the production of acetylcholine which the nerve endings would normally produce in an attempt to counteract the poison.'

End of lecture. 'But who the hell in the *agence* uses sheep dip, if indeed that was what was used?'

'Someone like yourself who has either worked on a farm or sheep ranch, or has used it simply as an insecticide but witnessed its potential.'

'Jeannot Raymond . . . Did he go back to the *agence* to get it, while we were both in with the colonel and the others?'

'Earlier I didn't have time to look in his office. It might not even have been there.'

'And the pear brandy?'

'Enjoys it as I do on occasion, but perhaps more often. Noëlle Jourdan is of the same age and looks a lot like Giselle, Hermann.

Please remember that if we find her, it may not be Giselle. Let me be the one to look closely, not yourself.'

Duels, eyes pierced and poisons, *place* des Vosges had seen them all and too often. Number 24 had been de Vitry's *hôtel particulier* in 1617 when he'd assassinated Concino Concini, the Florentine, on the whispered orders of a sixteen-year-old boy, King Louis XIII. Concini had, of course, been his mother's probable lover and definite favourite, Marie de Medici who'd been queen of France for ten years and had been married to Henry IV, that 'chicken-in-every-peasant's-pot-every-Sunday' king who'd been stabbed to death in 1610, and certainly Concini, made maréchal de France and marquis d'Ancre by her, had been too greedy and had used his spies too often, but to behead that one's wife, Leonora Galigai, for sorcery and then to burn her at the stake?

Christ, the French; Christ, this place. Louis would be feeling it. Louis had brought him here in the autumn of 1940 and had taken him from house to house as that grandmother of his must have done. 'To understand Paris and its crime,' he had said, 'is to understand its history. Wealthy or poor, it binds each citizen, even those whose families have more lately adopted the city as their own. Though all might seem oblivious to this history, they breathe it in every day whether you think they do or not.

'Know the city like your hand, Hermann. Know its moods, its quiet places, its intricate avenues of fast retreat.'

Wise words. The courtyard of Number 2 was paved with cobblestones that had felt the centuries. Beyond it there was the stable Noëlle Jourdan must have run to, for she'd found that car of theirs and not thrown away the stained white apron she'd been wearing, but had dragged it off and hung it out as a flag for them under one of the colonnaded arches. Louis had found it and had softly said, 'This way, *mon vieux.*'

'Just tell me why the one or ones who are after her also left it out for us?'

Up from the cobblestones came the mist, down from the heavens that first sprinkling of the usual.

The stable door was open, the stench of horse piss as present as the centuries of it.

'Are you okay?' whispered Louis.

'I'll just go up its ladder. I won't be a minute.'

'Giselle, Hermann. Remember, please, that Noëlle Jourdan really does look a lot like her.'

Made of poles, hammered together with hand-forged spikes, the ladder's rungs were worn and slivered in places, and on one of these the girl had caught her skirt and had pulled a thread.

On another, she had caught the heavy, cable-stitched pullover she must have been wearing, but of course detectives can't climb such a ladder with gun and torch in hand. It's either the one or the other.

'Hermann . . . ?'

'Louis . . .'

He had reached the loft and had swung himself up on to it, the beam of that torch of his cutting a quick swath across time-darkened roof timbers.

The light was gone—Hermann knew its brightness would only destroy his night vision when needed and had switched it off. Back pressed to one of the timbered uprights, St-Cyr waited. *Merde,* it was dark. Leaking, the roof let water piddle on the stones of the floor, increasing the stench of the years.

'Louis . . .'

It wasn't a cry, wasn't even a gasp, seemed only to embody despair. 'I'm coming, Hermann. Please hold on. Watch out, too, eh? We're not alone. He . . .'

Time had no meaning. Time had suddenly evaporated. One moved only when absolutely necessary and then solely by feel. One didn't dare to show a light.

Hermann called out, 'Louis!' once again and louder. No answer was possible because none could be given. The stalls were not empty but cluttered with the parsimonious hoarding of the stable's owner or past owners, the building no longer kept under lock and key, and yet things that could have found use had been left in place. Wooden water buckets, a scythe . . . Had one of the gardeners once stored things here? Frayed rope, a shovel, another and another—the police academy killing? St-Cyr had to ask—a rake, an axe and the instant relief of having found it first.

Had the owner a son? he wondered. Though Matron Aurore Aumont had stated that she hadn't known if the girl had had any friends, Noëlle Jourdan had obviously known of the stable.

A side door gave out on to a slender *passage*, but did this lead to another courtyard, another house and then to the rue de Birague?

A breath was taken . . . *Ah, sacré nom de nom*, Hermann, our killer is standing in this *passage*, not a metre from me.

Down on his hands and knees in the loft, Kohler tried to steady himself. The blood was still hot and rushing from the throat, the wound from ear to ear. He knew her eyes would be open in shock, felt her nose, her lips. Giselle? he had to ask, for her hair had been worn short, worn just like this one's, the shoulders were just as fine, the back, the seat, that gentle mound, all still clothed, the girl lying face down in a puddle of her draining.

I'm sorry, he tried to say but knew he mustn't. Louis hadn't answered him. Louis . . .

Softly St-Cyr drew back the Lebel's hammer to full cock, knowing that this would be heard by the killer, knowing too that he had but one chance.

Plank by plank, he traced out the boards from that door to where he and the killer were standing, only the wall between them. Had the killer come alone? Had a Sûreté the right to shoot without first giving the challenge?

A breath came and he heard it, but it was closer now, much closer, and with it came another sound but . . .

'IT WASN'T A CUTTHROAT, LOUIS!'

The hammer fell on a damp, dead cartridge. The hammer had to come back and fall again. The flash of fire momentarily blinded as boards splintered, the sound of the shot rolling away . . .

'LOUIS!' cried out Kohler.

The acrid stench of spent black powder filled the air. 'I missed him, Hermann. He realized he'd been given a reprieve and took it. Those cartridges you got me from stores . . .'

Up in the loft, Louis took one look at her under torchlight and said, 'You're right, that was no cutthroat. Blood has shot a good metre from the end of that knife as he swung it away. Has he slaughtered sheep? She was on her hands and knees and trying to scramble away, was taken from behind, grabbed by the hair, the head yanked back as the throat was cut, and then . . . then was held down, clamped firmly between his knees as if on a farm or ranch until all motion had stopped.'

All quivering even. 'Otherwise she might still have run for a little.'

Good for Hermann. Such a thing was definitely possible. 'But she would never have made it down that ladder.'

'Could well have pitched off the edge of the loft.'

'He wanted us separated and realized that if she had fallen to the floor below, we wouldn't have been.'

'He's trouble, Louis.'

'Most definitely.'

'And now?'

'We must find him, but first the Jourdan flat again.'

'He might have gone back there . . .'

'Having anticipated that we would realize we had to.'

Ah, merde, trust Louis to have seen it: 'If we are ever to find out how that girl came by the things she did.'

'And what, exactly, that father of hers has been stating in his letters to former *compagnons d'armes.* Jourdan praised the girl for having let the press in to photograph Madame Guillaumet and cursed the hospital staff for admitting such women. He was all too ready to blame them for betraying their husbands.'

'Spreading the gospel, was he?'

'Enlisting support?'

'But letters only within the *zone occupée,* Louis. It's still forbidden to send anything south into the former *zone libre.*'

Even though the Occupier now occupied the whole country. 'A campaign against wandering wives and fiancées of prisoners of war.

Matron Aumont felt the girl's attitude was that of the father who had raised Noëlle from the age of five, Hermann. Apparently when asked about her mother, the girl would only state that she was dead, but such hatred on the part of the father demands answer.'

'As does everything else. Just what the hell are we really up against?'

It had best be said. 'The Einsatzstab Reichsleiter Rosenberg. Noëlle Jourdan must somehow have been getting things from one of their warehouses, as must Delaroche. Where else could that girl have picked up those figurines, where else, the colonel, that Ysen-brant painting and other *objets d'art* in his office?'

The Rosenberg Task Force, the Aktion-M squads, the plunder-ers of the household furnishings and other items of deported, transported individuals. Whole families, many of them, and cer-tainly not all had been poor. 'But why steal the stamps back?'

'Especially as we were not to have been assigned to that rob-bery.'

'Chance having been allowed to play its part, eh? Chance, Louis.'

'Fate, Hermann. Was it fate?'

'But we were told to head on over to the Restaurant Drouant.'

'Having been assigned to it and the Trinité, should assaults take place at both, which they definitely did.'

'The Agence Vidocq must have learned of Boemelburg's assign-ing us to blackout crime even before we did, Louis.'

'They're very well connected and have more than adequate sources of information . . .'

'Boemelburg has always kept us busy and has so far been able to counter SS and Gestapo rank-and-file hatred of us, simply be-cause he has to display some semblance of law and order but now Berlin aren't just being adamant. They're demanding his recall should he fail.'

'Oberg wants an end to us and hires the *agence* to work with Sonja Remer, using Giselle as bait . . .'

'But she doesn't let them take her, Louis. She wouldn't have. I'm certain of it.'

Hermann was no more certain than himself, felt St-Cyr, but shouldn't be contradicted. 'Berlin want the streets safe and an end to this plague of assaults . . .'

'Otherwise it's bad for the image. Even the Swiss are citing Paris as an example of how bad things can become, so the chief does what he always does.'

'He unwittingly assigns us to the task.'

'Not knowing what Oberg really wants because that one hasn't quite told him.'

'And Oberg might well want the POW wives to be targeted, Hermann, since they're being held responsible for the huge increase in venereal disease the Oberkommando der Wehrmacht have been bitching about.'

'And the Reichsführer Himmler wants to impress the Führer *and* the High Command so that it and the army, like everything else can be put better under an SS thumb.'

'And Oberg wants to take over complete control of the French and Paris police. What better way, then, than to prove them utterly incapable of controlling the streets at night?'

'He also wants Judge Rouget taught a damned good lesson, Louis.'

'And hires the Agence Vidocq to take care of the matter?'

'Or did he? Couldn't the *agence* have had another reason?'

'Élène Artur is forced to make a phone call concerning the police academy victim, indicating that the *agence* is responsible for both.'

'But why kill her in a building you've a flat in, one you let your secretary use, unless there *is* another reason? Why not simply kill Élène out on the streets where some would say she had definitely belonged?'

'Some like Vivienne Rouget?'

'I think so.'

'We're going to have to keep an eye on Mademoiselle Dunand, Hermann.'

'And on Oona and Giselle, if we can find her before it's too late, eh? And on Adrienne Guillaumet and her kids, and on

Marie-Léon Barrault and her daughter. Gaston Morel can take care of himself.'

'Come on, then. Me first, Hermann.'

'No, me, and that's an order simply because I'm better at it than you.'

'Then let's not become separated, for I think we are dealing with one who will not hesitate because he and the others can't afford to.'

'And that's what Oberg really wants.'

'An end to us.'

The house at Number 25 was far quieter even than when they had first encountered it. Rainwater, piddled on the lower stairs, glistened under torchlight but didn't leak from above. Shoulders rubbed as they touched each other, first Hermann going ahead, felt St-Cyr, and then himself, the one hesitating and then the other. Landing by landing, and not a sound. No further sign of the rainwater on the third floor except for that from themselves. Had this killer realized the splashes would give warning and removed his shoes and coat, even to rolling up his trouser legs to stop the leakage?

The door to the Jourdan flat was closed but hadn't been left that way by them. The string was loosely looped around its nail, but this could easily have been done from inside and then the door closed.

Hermann fingered the string—had their killer a gun? he'd be wondering. The SS might have supplied the Agence Vidocq with them; alternatively such weapons could simply have not been turned in after the 1914–1918 war; alternatively, too, they could be purchased on the black market, either from one of the Occupier or from any number of others—the German troops on leave were notorious for selling things. Hence Sonja Remer's Tokarev TT-33 could just as easily have come by that route but would have been bought with a purpose. Always there would be a purpose behind such an acquisition by the SS.

The string was teased from around the nail, the door given but the slightest of nudges.

'He's in there, Louis,' said Hermann, his lips moving silently under finger-shielded torchlight. 'We split. We have to even things up.'

Showing a light only meant showing a target and yes, there was little enough furniture to contend with. The table at which Jourdan had written his letters and neatly stacked them for the daughter to post was empty of all but its ink bottle, pen, blank paper, blank envelopes and loose stamps. A gerbil scurried across the floor and one could hear it rooting around in a tin box, but then even that sound ceased. Now only the rain hitting the windows could be heard.

Kohler knew, from the feel of it, that he was in the girl's bedroom and not alone, but had the son of a bitch wanted to separate him from Louis again or had he been unable to lay his hands on what he'd not wanted them to find?

The blackout drapes were of doubled burlap, dyed black no doubt and with a dyed sheet behind them next to windows that would overlook the gardens. Along from the curtains, in a far corner against the wall, there was an armoire whose doors were open. Clothes had been scattered as if the search had been in haste and desperate.

A thin cardboard gift box had been discovered but had fallen to scatter its contents and tempt the unwary.

The throw rug under this debris had been made of woven rags.

He lifted the Walther P38 and took aim, the darkness all around them and complete.

'He's gone, Hermann. As quickly and decisively as he came.'

Noëlle Jourdan hadn't had a lot. The mirrored doors of the armoire were losing their backing and gave reflections that appeared as if silver filings were being thrown at the viewer. The lower drawer had been yanked out and gone through, the box uncovered.

'What was he after, Louis?'

'Something that girl would have hidden from her father.'

It wasn't under her pillows or under the mattress or in it, nor was it under the rug or behind the armoire. It was on top of this last and hidden behind the trim of a scalloped moulding.

The envelope was of plain brown kraft and when shaken out, gave photos of Jourdan and the girl's mother at their wedding, 10 July 1914, in Nancy. There was another of the couple taken at the Gare du Nord on Jourdan's return from being a POW, the sergeant evidently still in a lot of pain but proudly wearing his Croix de guerre and Médaille militaire.

'His Légion d'honneur also, Hermann.'

Louis found the red ribbon he'd recovered from the police academy killing and momentarily put the two together as an old soldier should.

'Did one of them borrow or buy it from her?'

'She'd not have sold it, even if threatened, Hermann, but told me that one of the building's children must have been in and taken it, and that she'd get it back.'

'And the boy, the young man in these?'

At the age of seven and that of nine perhaps, Noëlle and her friend had been photographed by someone in front of the stable; at the age of ten and twelve they'd used one of the Photomaton booths at the Bon Marché to catch themselves holding hands, Noëlle not grinning, not smiling, the boy doing so and thinking it all a lark.

At the age of fifteen and seventeen, they'd kissed and recorded the event in secret; at the age of nineteen and twenty-one the young man had found himself a camera and film and had photographed her both alone and with himself last autumn in front of that same stable.

He'd money. He'd a good job by the look and yes, he'd not been called up, hadn't become a POW. 'Our academy victim, Hermann?'

'The loft, then, for another look.'

'Just give me a moment with Jourdan.'

Louis could examine a corpse for the longest time.

'His papers are missing, Hermann. They weren't in the right

trouser pocket or his shirt pockets, nor under him, nor on the night table or in the overcoat the daughter would have had to help him into.'

'Was he searched?'

'I'm certain of it.'

'Then he's very thorough, this killer of ours, very quick thinking and . . .'

'Wants definitely to keep us from seeing something.'

'But *what*? We know they're supposed to be working for Boemelburg and Oberg, know they're supposed to be helping us put a stop to things.'

'Yet are the cause of them, Hermann. It begs answer.'

'Jourdan obviously would have been a member of the *Grands Mutilés*.'

The association of them. 'But that, in itself, is no reason to take his papers. Flavien Garnier is a member of the Union Nationale des Combattants, which is ultraconservative and has within it a very right-wing, reactionary, collaborationist faction.'

'Who would like to see the wives and fiancées of certain POWs punished?'

In the South, in the former Free Zone, and in spite of stiff opposition to their doing so, Pétain and his government had banned all previous veterans' organizations and had squeezed them into one, the Légion Française des Combattants, but in the north, in the former and still 'Occupied' Zone, the Occupier had seen such a single group as a decided threat and had banned it but allowed all the others to remain much to Vichy's displeasure and consternation.

'Is it that the Agence Vidocq has its own agenda, Hermann?'

Neither that of the SS and Gestapo, nor even of Berlin and the Occupier at large, but themselves. 'And with their former commanding officer again telling them what to do?'

'Perhaps, but *ah, mais alors, alors,* Hermann, in the South, the far right of the Légion Française des Combattants is also known for similar attitudes and denunciations.'

'Especially if hidden valuables are involved, and women are to behave themselves, aren't they?' said Kohler. 'They're to stay at home where they belong, with the children no matter how tough things get.'

'Most of us veterans wouldn't be a party to targeting anyone, but many would, I think, find it difficult to forgive the wife who strays even after what has become such a prolonged absence.'

Every request by Pétain and his government in Vichy to let those million-and-a-half POWs return to France had fallen on stone-deaf ears. 'A popular cause, then?'

'One that would at least engender the tacit approval from many if nothing else. Noëlle Jourdan could call on shopkeepers, some of whom were veterans and probably fellow UNCs.'

'Her father wrote to others and *voilà* not only are his papers missing but his most recent letters.'

'Unless earlier posted by the daughter.'

'And Adrienne Guillaumet is the wife of an officer, Louis.'

'Whereas Madame Barrault is that of a common soldier, the Agence Vidocq making sure that we would be assigned to both.'

'But why the Tokarev? Why not a Luger, a Lebel or any other?'

'Why, indeed, unless such a weapon, having easily been obtained on the black market, and later left at the scene of yet another assault and murder, would definitely point the finger of blame at the Communists.'

The Francs-Tireurs et Partisans . 'Along with the bodies of two honest detectives.'

There were a number of upright wine barrels in the loft, and among them one whose lid, when removed, yielded wood shavings and sawdust that were to protect the rest of the contents and give comfort to gerbils. 'A terra-cotta nymph, dated 1784, Hermann, and signed by Joseph-Charles Marin. The boy in those photos with Noëlle Jourdan had good taste.'

'A silver breadbasket, Louis. Russian, I think.'

'Gilded and enamelled to give the appearance of its having been woven.'

'A Fabergé egg.'

And another. 'Jewellery, Hermann. Earrings, bracelets . . . No diamonds that I can see, only trinkets perhaps, but . . .'

'Good goods all the same.'

And stolen.

The concierge of Number 2 place des Vosges was bundled up in pink kneesocks, pompom slippers and housecoat, and not about to be forthcoming.

'WHY DO YOU ASK?' she shrilled when shown one of the most recent snapshots of Noëlle Jourdan and friend.

The cat was clutched. Turning on the charm with this one wasn't going to work, thought Kohler, but he'd try it anyway. 'Look, it's only a general inquiry.'

'AT THIS HOUR?'

Incredulous at such a thought, she tossed the mangled heap of auburn curls with their bedtime twists of paper and threw still heavily made-up eyes to the ceiling. The damp fag end that clung to her lower lip miraculously remained in place. 'Here, have one of these.'

A light was also offered but such politeness from the police should not be viewed with anything but suspicion, though the generosity was that of one of *les Allemands,* it was true, and he *did* speak French. 'What is it you really want, Inspector? Has my little Max done something he shouldn't?'

Max. 'No, not at all.'

Had he done things in the past—was this what the inspector was now wondering? 'He's away in any case. In Lyon, on another pickup.'

Lyon. 'It's the girl we want to question, madame . . . ?'

'Auger, Nina. And the madame is really quite immaterial since I was fool enough to have married him and mine went to his maker when that one was five years old.'

As did Noëlle Jourdan's mother. The things one learned. 'Life is never easy, is it?'

'WHAT'S SHE DONE?'

'Let some nosy photographer take some pictures.'

The *Hôtel-Dieu.* 'Ah! I thought so. You didn't find her with that father of hers?'

'He said she'd gone out.'

'With the curfew coming at us like an express train?'

Louis should have heard her but was arranging for the district's iron man to photograph the victims and the local *flics* to secure the sites.

'She's a tease, you know,' said Nina, flicking ash away from the cat that was now draped across the claw-frayed back of an armchair that should have been thrown out years ago. 'Always the promise,' she went on, 'never the little capital. That father of hers would have killed her too, I think, if she'd let my boy have her.'

Gott im Himmel, she was a treasure, just like Bénédicte Mailloux, but a conspiratorial tone had best be used. 'What, exactly, happened to her mother?'

'Ah! who knows? Who can blame her for straying from such a man? The screams in the night, the agony of the shelling relived at the slightest bump and hour by hour. Mine was made of better stuff perhaps. Who's to say? One day she had a fall and so did my Henri. Two places. The first in that house at Number 25, the second here in the stable out back and a little later. An *accident*, both of them.'

'And the boy?'

'Finally has a good job that pays well and has a future. The colonel saw to it. My husband's colonel. Things are better now that *les Allemands* are here, of course, yourself included.'

Two further Gauloises bleues were laid on the slim oak counter of the *loge* she had 'inherited' from Henri, who'd been fucking Madame Mariette Jourdan up in that stable's loft. Everyone had known of it. Everyone. Noëlle least of all.

'Your son, madame. When do you think he'll be back?'

'Not for a few days. He's often away on a job.'

'A pickup, you said?'

'Did I?'

'*Zut alors*, I'm only trying to fill things in. My partner will ask. He's a stickler for details.'

A partner . . . 'Furniture and other household items. It's a furniture company, isn't it?'

'Which one?'

'The Lévitan. Very classy, you understand, very expensive in the old days, but a little something for everyone. Business must still be good.'

'Furniture?'

'That is just what I said, is it not?'

The Lévitan store was in the Faubourg Saint-Martin, in the Tenth, huge and with several warehouses and shops like carpentry ones, ah yes! 'It was good of your son to come by and let you know he'd be away. Parents always worry, don't they? Oh for sure, a mother most of all, but fathers too. I know I did.'

Did . . . 'You have children?'

'Had. Two boys, Jurgen and Hans, but . . . but they were both killed at Stalingrad.'

Hurriedly Nina crossed herself and kissed her fingertips but did this one with the terrible slash and the faded, warm blue eyes want more from her? 'The boy didn't come by. Always he is told at work if he is to be away, and I never hear of it until he's back and worry just as you've said, but . . .'

He waited, this one. Gently he held D'Artagnan under the chin to look at him and then scratched him behind the ears as a cat lover does. 'But Colonel Delaroche was passing by and thought to come in to tell me.'

'Today?'

Why should it matter? 'On Thursday afternoon. This last Thursday.'

Noëlle would have been at work. 'That was good of him. Colonels are usually a bitch to put up with where I come from. Mine certainly were.'

He'd a nice smile, this inspector. Had he still a wife back home in that country of his? Was he lonely for her like so many of them were?

'*Merci,* madame. You've been most helpful. I'd leave you some of my matches but am nearly out.'

'And don't have a lighter?'

'You wouldn't know where I could get one, would you?'

'For a price, yes.'

'And full of good fluid, not that black-market crap that singes the eyebrows and torches the clouds?'

'*Oui.*'

'How much?'

There would be no sense in this one's haggling and he obviously knew the system well enough not to bother, but was offering to purchase, not threatening to steal. And weren't friends needed, especially at such times as these?

Max wouldn't mind, not really. Max would find her another. 'Five hundred, I think.'

It was from Cartier's, was easily worth thirty or forty times that and she knew it too, or knew something of it. 'Here, take a thousand just to be on the safe side.'

Lost in thought, Louis fingered the lighter as they shared a cigarette in the Citroën, the darkness of *place* des Vosges all around them. The *flics* were taking their time in getting here and most probably were checking in with their headquarters at the Préfecture de Paris who would then check in with the rue des Saussaies, who would then do so with the avenue Foch, who would then notify the Höherer SS Oberg and maybe wake him up.

'Did you tell her about her son, Hermann?'

'I couldn't. She deserves better, has had a hard life.'

'Yes, yes, but . . .'

'*Verdammt,* we needed information not tears. And as for her having earlier heard that shot of yours, forget it. That one would only have shrugged if asked, and sucked on her fag. You know as well as I that these days everyone clams up and no one admits to having heard a thing.'

'Or seen anything.'

'Why kill him if he was working for them?'

'Them being the Einsatzstab Reichleiter Rosenberg, Hermann.'

'You know what I mean.'

'The Aktion-M squads? One of those furniture squads that go around the city and the country raiding the houses of its citizens?'

'And clearing them out, even of their Jewish toothbrushes and long-handled shovels, this last if not borrowed from that stable? All right, I admit he must have broken the rules and could no longer be trusted, but why kill him in such a fashion and then let the press know of it?'

Hermann was far from being naïve and knew the answer well enough but was blaming himself for the sins of his *confrères* and desperately needed support. 'To set an example for others, especially as the Agence Vidocq must use part-timers, but still, you're right. To have killed him in such a rage begs answer just as it did with the *passage* de l'Hirondelle victim.'

'Max Auger took the stamps, Louis, and must have shown them to Noëlle Jourdan.'

'Who then took them to Félix Picard of Au Philatéliste Savant.'

'Having first sized up the shop.'

'Which can only mean that the girl was working with Max as his partner and fence, Hermann. If not the shop, then Ma Tante, but gradually so as not to arouse suspicion.'

'Except that someone went looking for the collection and noticed that the stamps were no longer in the Lévitan's former furniture store.'

'Where the Aktion-M squads deposit the furnishings of countless homes for further sorting, packing, repairs, if necessary, and shipment.'

'To the Reich, to party officials who've been bombed out or to others of them who are setting up house in the eastern territories.'

The first such shipment had been made in April of 1941, the second in October of that year, but in July of 1940, the Maréchal Pétain and his government in Vichy had passed a law *allowing* the sale of such confiscated property after six months had passed. All proceeds were then to have gone to the Secours National, which, in spite of continued protests from Pétain and others, hadn't yet received a sou, nor would it. But Hermann would never taunt his partner with such complicity and collaboration on the part of this country's government. Hermann was just too conscious of his partner's feelings, especially at times like this.

'We have to face it, Louis. The Agence Vidocq aren't just working for themselves and Oberg, but also for the ERR.'

'As are others, each supplying the ERR with targets.'

'As well as giving the SS the names and locations of *résistants*.'

'Business must be really good.'

'And we've stepped right into it.'

A late supper was in progress, the Tour d'Argent that epitome of culinary majesty. *Ach, mein Gott,* how the other half lives, thought Kohler, taking it all in from behind the grill of the *patron's* cash desk and head waiter's stand. Uniforms everywhere, beautiful *Parisiennes* too. BOFs, of course, in suits and ties, and *Bonzen* sporting their Nazi Party pins and gongs. Paris-based administrative types too . . . Dr. Karl Epting of the Deutsche Institut no less, with wife Alice, a Swiss, the legendary hostess entertaining another crowd of writers, artists and musicians: the latest going-away exchange group that would tour the Reich in the name of *Kultur*, not forced labour or worse, and no ration tickets needed here. Absolutely none. Would Epting even have heard that one of his part-time teachers had been savagely raped and beaten?

'Messieurs . . .' began the maître d'.

'St-Cyr, Sûreté. Just go about your business and leave us to ours.'

'But . . .'

'No buts. Kohler, Kripo, Paris-Central. Is this the register you keep the duck numbers in?'

It was. Pages dated from 1890 when the great Frédéric Delair had bought the place and started smothering six-week-old ducks brought all the way from the Vendée market at Challans. Every last one of them had been given a number. His *canard à la presse ou canard au sang*. Both the same. Pressed duck or duck with blood.

'Hermann . . .'

A battery of silver presses was available, the front row tables next to the heavily draped windows best for viewing as sous-chefs screwed the briefly roasted creatures down. 'Twenty minutes in a hot oven, Louis. Slice the filets thinly, then squeeze hell out of the carcass to catch the blood. Add a dash of lemon juice, if such is still available, a little salt and pepper, spices—only the current chef knows the alchemy of those—the mashed raw liver of yet another duck, though, and a touch of Madeira, a glass of good port—nothing but the best champagne *aussi*, the Heidsieck perhaps, or the Dom Pérignon—and cook for another . . .'

'Yes, yes, Hermann. Twenty-five minutes and don't you dare take any more of that Benzedrine.'

'Serve piping hot from a silver plate, but don't boil the juice. Look, Louis. The Grand Duke Vladimir of Russia ate number 6,043 in 1900; King Alfonso XIII of Spain bit into number 40,362 in 1914 just as we were pulling on our boots and saying our prayers and good-byes to loved ones. Hirohito, Emperor of Japan, had number 53,211 in June of 1921, so why is he now an ally of the Reich?'

'HERMANN . . .'

'Franklin Delano Roosevelt ate number 112,151,* though, in 1929. I hope he enjoyed it. Göring . . . The Reichsmarschall and head of the Luftwaffe had numbers . . . *Ach*, I always wondered how many times that one had caused young ducks to be smothered. Ten . . . fifteen . . . Surely a trencherman and avid art buyer like Göring wouldn't have passed this place up?'

'HERMANN, WE SIMPLY HAVEN'T TIME!'

The restaurant would have been taken over had the owners refused to cooperate and closed the place back in June of 1940. 'Oh, sorry, Chief. I was just curious and trying to keep myself sane and not worry about Giselle. Found them, have you?'

---

* The Toronto *Globe and Mail* of 4 May 2003 reported that the millionth had been served. Unfortunately Göring's numbers weren't listed in the article, nor were those of any other of the Occupier.

'Table thirty. Monsieur . . .' Louis turned to the maître d'. 'If you or any of your staff so much as clear away, I will personally empty my revolver into the ceiling. This is a murder inquiry and my partner and myself have had it up to here.'

'With bodies,' confided Kohler, pulling down his lower left eyelid to buttonhole the starched shirt and tails. 'Young girls who had all of their lives ahead of them, *grands mutilés*, dancers, boys. Bring us two chairs and hurry.'

'But . . . but, please, Inspectors. Madame Rouget has a bad heart. Could it not wait a little? Surely they can have nothing whatsoever to do with . . .'

Louis let him have it. 'They have *everything* to do with our inquiries.'

'But it is *Monsieur le Juge*'s birthday celebration?'

'Then that makes it even better.'

Not bothering to remove that fedora or overcoat, Louis started in among the tables, a dark-blue, gold-lettered Vuitton leather secretarial case tucked under each arm like a government accountant on a tax fraud. Records . . . case histories that Denise Rouget had brought home from work and that the judge's sleepy-eyed little maid of all work, having been awakened, had not been able to prevent them from 'borrowing' from the entrance hall's table when they had called at the house to find that he was here.

'Judge Rouget? Judge Hercule Rouget?'

Others were taking notice. 'What is the meaning of this?'

Stung, Louis tossed that head of his. 'The meaning? There's the body of a dancer in that flat you keep on the rue La Boétie, Judge. We understand that you knew her well.'

'How dare you?'

'Élène Artur . . .' gasped Vivienne Rouget, unable to prevent the name from escaping.

Quickly the daughter laid a hand over that of her mother, Germaine de Brisac—it must be her, thought Kohler—taking the other. Two very well-dressed, beautiful girls in their mid- to late thirties. Friends for life, ardent social workers. The first, brown-eyed like the father, but not mud-brown, the second with fabulous green eyes and absolutely perfect reddish-blonde hair and what else? he asked and had to admit, she's uncertain and damned afraid.

'A few questions, Judge. Nothing difficult. We'll save those for later,' said Louis, clearing the plates and glasses aside to set down the cases. 'But first, Mademoiselle Denise Rouget, I gather from questioning the family's maid that it was your custom to bring such records home.'

'My daughter's caseload is heavy, Inspector. Would you not want her to go over things in the evening in preparation for each following day's interviews?'

A cool one when the chips were down. '*Ah! Bien sûr,* madame. It's perfectly understandable. It's just that . . .'

'Well?'

'May I? It helps the thoughts and makes what I have to say easier.'

Pipe, tobacco pouch and matches came out. Ignored, the judge was far from happy but conscious of the Walther P38 that had been laid on the table and was pointing at him.

'Hermann, be so good as to check on our Trinité victim. The *Hôtel-Dieu* is just along the quai de la Tournelle and across the pont de l'Archevêché. Take the first turning to your left when you are on the Île de la Cité. That will lead you quickly to *place* du Parvis and the hospital. It's dark outside, but . . . Ah! I hate to ask it, Mademoiselle de Brisac, but would you be so kind as to show him the way? A few moments of your time. Nothing much, I assure you.'

'But required of me, is that it?'

Must beauty come in so many forms? '*Oui,* and please don't bother to argue, Judge. This party of yours is now over.'

Louis had seen it too. The judge's birthday present.

11

The folio was also from Vuitton and of dark-blue leather like the secretarial cases. Imprinted in gold leaf, a boldly handwritten flourish gave *Juge Hercule Rouget*, and below this, in somewhat smaller writing, *Président du Tribunal Spécial du Département de la Seine.*

The night-action courts.

It would be best to let the fingers of an apparent envy caress the folio. 'May I?' asked St-Cyr—he wouldn't set the pipe aside, would simply clench its stem between the teeth. Unaware of what she'd done as the daughter had released her hand, Vivienne Rouget had gripped the dessert spoon she had been using when so rudely interrupted.

'IT HAS NOTHING TO DO WITH THAT SLUT!' she spat, crashing the spoon down flat on the table to disturb the adjacent diners.

'VIVIENNE!' hissed the judge.

'Of course the death of Élène Artur has apparently nothing to do with this, madame, but as I once collected stamps, I would appreciate the opportunity. Judge?'

'Look if you must, but it will be your last.'

The cloud, the hurricane, the fierceness were all there as if on the bench. 'She was cut open, that mistress of yours, Judge. Deliberately disembowelled and allowed to run—ah! forgive me, Madame Rouget, mademoiselle. The detective in me slips up from time to time.'

'Cut open . . .' blanched the daughter, throwing wounded eyes at her mother who savoured the news only to realize this Sûreté had seen beyond such an impulse to its harder truth.

'*Ah, mon Dieu,* Judge, the 1849 to 1850s twenty-centime black. The blue also, though it was never issued. The Vervelle, the colonials . . . A stunning collection. Perfect if donated—is it to be donated to the Nation on your death?'

'Inspector . . .'

'Madame, this collection, except for its rebinding, matches entirely one that was stolen at between twelve twenty and twelve thirty a.m., Friday, but it's curious, I must admit. You see, though my partner and I were definitely not to have investigated that crime, the gold louis that were also in the safe were not taken by the thief or thieves. A simple smash-and-grab one would otherwise have thought, but done to order. It must have been, that little something left as hush money.'

Everyone said St-Cyr was despicable, thought Vivienne, a cuckold who would gladly have forgiven that wife of his if he could have. A seeker of truth with the holier-than-thou attitude of a martyr!

But when met and held, the deep-brown eyes registered neither condemnation nor forgiveness and understanding, only an inherent curiosity. 'If you *think* I am about to inquire as to how it is you have concluded such a thing, Inspector, you are very much mistaken. I purchased that collection from a very reputable source, and only after much deliberation.'

'I'm sure you did, but please bear with me. You see, those gold louis were borrowed by the *flic* who was first on the scene.'

'The fool! Did you arrest him?' demanded Rouget.

'Judge, don't look for sparrows among the crumbs. Leave such things to the hawks of a reformed conscience since the *flic*, though tempted, has a family and he put the louis back next day for me to find when I called on Monsieur Félix Picard of Au Philatéliste Savant in the *passage* Jouffroy.'

'Denise, take your mother to the *toilettes* for a tidy-up.'

'Judge, you are under instruction. Please don't be difficult. We'll get to Élène Artur and the child she was carrying soon enough.'

'*ESPÈCE DE SALAUD! LÉCHEUR DE CHATTE!*'

Fucking bastard; cunt-licker . . . 'HERCULE, NOT IN PUBLIC!'

'*MAMAN*, LOWER YOUR VOICE!'

All conversation ceased in this culinary paradise, all eyes were on the table. Some stood for a better look, among them the Standartenführer Langbehn, who let his napkin fall to the floor and then cautioned a waiter not to pick it up.

'Judge, before that one reaches us, it's my considered belief that Élène Artur was disembowelled to find the fetus she was carrying and dispose of it. Fortunately my partner recovered the body of what would have been your son.'

Kohler let the match flame linger as a shiver ran through Germaine de Brisac, green eyes wincing as she drew on the cigarette he'd given her. '*Merci,*' she muttered—guilty, was she, of knowing too much? Damned afraid, in any case. He'd make her sit here in the car on *place* du Parvis, would let her feel the pitch-dark silhouette of the *Hôtel-Dieu,* would let her freeze in that woven shawl with its threads of burnished copper-gold that set off the colour of her hair and eyes, the Schiaparelli dress, silk stockings, high heels and brand-new camel-hair overcoat with its broad lapels and turn-down flaps, her perfume exquisite. A woman of exceptional taste, with emerald drop earrings from Cartier to catch the last of the match's flame, and so much for the cigarette lighter that had recently been acquired. He'd take his time with her until she realized he wasn't going to get out from behind the Citroën's wheel until he had squeezed every last little thing out of her.

Then he'd make her visit Adrienne Guillaumet. 'So, tell me about Lulu. On the evening of Monday, January eleventh, you left your mother's Irish Terrier in the car outside Chez Bénédicte at about six thirty and went down into the Lido to find out what was delaying Denise Rouget.'

Did he know everything? '*Maman* worshipped that dog. When one is dying, Inspector, a companion such as Lulu means all the more. Lulu gave my mother life. To have stolen her . . . to have killed and *eaten* her was to have . . .'

'You knew she'd been eaten?'

Ah, merde! 'We assumed she had. Don't those people *eat* dogs?'

Deliberately Herr Kohler gave her a moment to calm herself.

'Correct me, Mademoiselle de Brisac, but wasn't Colonel Delaroche still looking for Lulu? If so, how is it that you knew Lulu had ended up in the soup pot? It's probably a culinary delicacy, just as was horse meat here in France before this lousy Occupation.'

' "Lousy," is it?'

'Just tell me.'

'I didn't know. I . . . I only assumed.' Ah *Sainte-Mère, Sainte-Mère*, why had *Monsieur le Juge* not insisted Denise accompany her?

'You knew, mademoiselle. You have just stated it as if you did, which can only mean . . .'

Must he pause like this and make her catch a breath in fear of what was to come? 'All right, damn you! Abélard also knew or suspected it but didn't want to tell Mother such a thing.'

'A good friend of the family, is he?'

'The best! Like a father. Always there for Mother when needed, always interested in how I'm getting along. Mine was killed in action. He . . . Colonel Abélard-Armand Delaroche tried his best to take that place for Mother and me. I was only eight years old when we got the news about Papa, nine when Abélard was first able to come home to see how we were.'

'But he didn't think to confront Madame Élène Artur with the theft?'

'WHY SHOULD HE HAVE? HE . . .'

'Had other plans for her?'

'I . . . I don't know what you wish to imply, Inspector. I really don't. Abélard would not have harmed that girl. He was only asked to have her followed.'

'But I thought he was looking for Lulu? Surely he wasn't told to follow Élène?'

'You know very well what I said. Mother and . . .'

'And whom?'

It would do no good to lie since he must already know, but it would be best, as with such men, to let him think her spirit had been broken. 'Mother and Vivienne hired him.'

Hired not *asked.*

'Must you sigh like that?'

'Vivienne knew all about the judge and Élène and didn't like it one bit, did she?'

'Should she have? That bitch wasn't the first but the latest of many. *La syphilis, la blennorragie*—the clap to you, *la chaude-pisse* that burns, *n'est-ce pas*? To have had to live in terror of his contracting such . . . such filthy diseases and then giving them to her as he did time and again? Is that not reason enough?'

'And he has a taste for the exotic, hasn't he?'

'If you wish to call it that, I don't! The wife of a prisoner of war? The mother of a child she should have been home looking after yet who constantly flaunted herself naked on stage and sold herself to the highest bidder while her husband languished behind barbed wire? How could she have done such a thing?'

'Here, have another of these. That one will only spoil your nail polish.'

She should flick the butt into Herr Kohler's face, but mustn't. 'Vivienne is a patriot. She does what she can. No one could do more.'

'And your mother?'

'Can't do much, poor thing.'

'But offer to help pay for things and is her confidante, as is Colonel Delaroche?'

'Isn't that what lifelong friends become? These bitches have to be stopped. They can't be allowed to betray their husbands like others did in the last war. They've got to be taught a . . .'

Irritably Germaine de Brisac drew on her cigarette and turned to stare out her side windscreen. 'I . . . I didn't mean to say any of that.'

'I think you did. I think your late husband fooled around a lot

before he was killed during the blitzkrieg. You had already peti-
tioned the courts to let you divorce him.'

Avoiding it would do no good. 'And now I no longer use my
married name. Oh, for sure, I've reason enough, just as Mother
had before me. Fortunately for her, *Papa* didn't return from the
fighting, and fortunately for myself, neither did my husband.'

'And when you went down into the Lido having left Lulu ripe
for . . .'

'Listen, you, I have blamed myself enough already and have
asked countless times why I didn't simply take her with me.'

'You were worried about your friend. Lulu would have thrown
herself at the judge and . . .'

'All right, all right, I *knew* I couldn't. Does that satisfy you?
Monsieur le juge was besotted with that *salope indochinoise*. She was
always in heat for him, always did things poor Vivienne couldn't
bring herself to do or submit to. Denise *begged* him to come home
and never see the girl again but . . .'

'He wouldn't agree. He had made up his mind to see her again,
hadn't he? Men like the judge don't just have urges. They've the
erection of a constant, ego-driven need to conquer and an arro-
gance that can and does lead them into trouble. Last October,
Élène asked him to meet her in the Parc Monceau. My partner
and I believe she was going to tell him of the child she was carrying, and likely she did because when Lulu found them, the judge
kicked hell out of that terrier.'

Fornicateur that he was himself, or so Denise had been told by
her mother, Herr Kohler held on to the cigarette he had placed
between her lips, making her tremble at the nearness of him, at
the musk such men exuded. 'Well?' he demanded.

'Denise was in tears when I found them at that table of his in
the Lido. He had two thousand francs in the fist he had thrust at
her, his daughter! She gripped my hand and held it to her lips. I
felt her tears. I . . . I told her we'd best leave, that the car was running. So many of the women we have to deal with have no morals
just like Élène Artur. They try to deny it to our faces when confronted with the evidence. Marie-Léon Barrault is the same. We've

photos of her in the Hôtel Grand, waiting for the lift. Photos with Gaston Morel, sometimes the two of them even with her daughter, Inspector. A child of eight! Just what must Annette be thinking at such times, a mother who disappears upstairs in a huge hotel like that? A mother who . . .'

'*La fellation?*'

'Isn't that what such men always want from such women?' *Ah, Jésus . . . cher Jésus,* why had she let him drive her to say such a thing? 'I didn't mean that either. I really didn't. Annette Barrault is very worried about her mother and missing her dear *papa* terribly just as I did my own.'

'You've interviewed her separately from the mother?'

Did he know *nothing* of social work? 'We always do that. It helps to get the children off by themselves. Things the mother won't admit are then sometimes revealed.'

'Just like detectives—the real ones anyway. Divide and conquer, eh? So when did it all begin, Denise taking client case files home and that mother of hers going through them?'

'I don't know. How could I?'

'You and Denise are as close as your mother and Vivienne Rouget, if not closer.'

'HOW DARE YOU?'

'Sorry.'

'I'm cold. Could we not go in and get this little visit of yours over?'

'Adrienne Guillaumet has two lovely children who desperately need her.'

'Then why *didn't* she control herself? Why did she deliberately arrange to have an assignation with a man who was not her husband? Why hire a *vélo-taxi* to pick her up at an agreed upon time and the shouts of her name from another who would guide her to it?'

'You knew there were two men waiting for her?'

'I . . . I just assumed. It's very dark on the rue Conté at that time of night outside the École Centrale. There's always a rush after classes.'

And two men had been waiting for her—this was what Herr Kohler was now thinking as he pinched out his cigarette and added it to his little collection. 'This precious Madame Guillaumet of yours had already sold a good deal of her clothing. What better, then, than to sell the use of herself?'

'To whom?'

Ah, bon! 'A general. Why not go right to the top, if you're from a class that aspires to it and can speak the language fluently?'

'A general . . .'

'*Oui.* At the Ritz.'

She and Denise Rouget had checked it out. They must have. 'His name? Just for the record.'

'Schiller. Hans-Friedrich, from Baden-Baden and a very old and well-established family. The youngest of four brothers and an architect before the call-up.'

'A lonely man?'

Must Herr Kohler still taunt her? 'Why else his wanting the use of a woman? Oh don't get the idea Denise and I have met or even spoken to him. It simply took a phone call to the desk and a little name dropping. Admit it, Inspector, the bitch was having trouble paying the rent and wouldn't listen to our advice on how to budget more carefully. She could have gone to her in-laws and begged them to forgive her for stupidly having not asked her father-in-law's permission while her husband was away. A holiday in Deauville she just had to have before the children were born? The husband's parents would have gladly helped her now, had she but humbled herself, but . . .'

'Adrienne didn't want to listen.'

And got exactly what she deserved—was this what Herr Kohler wanted most to hear? 'We tried, Inspector. We really did. Henriette Morel . . .'

'Put up the money and you and Denise hired the Agence Vidocq to follow Madame Guillaumet and find the proof.'

'That is correct.'

'And with Marie-Léon Barrault and others it was the same.'

Did he have to hear that, too? 'But fortunately she wasn't hurt so badly. With some of the others, it . . .' *Ah, merde, merde,* he had done it again!

'Yet, if I understand things clearly, Mademoiselle de Brisac, her offences were even worse?' Gaston Morel repeatedly; the manager of the Cinéma Impérial also—enough for some dark-minded little priest to write letters about her to the Scapini Commission.'

'Filth, and worse, yes, but is the sin of the one really any different than that of the other?'

'Or that of Élène Artur?'

'I believe so, yes.'

And really uptight about it. 'But neither you nor Denise thought to ask Madame Morel to pay for having that one followed?'

'Vivienne . . .'

'Was behind it all, wasn't she? The rapes, the beatings, the punishment. A little campaign that got out of hand.'

Standartenführer Langbehn was in mufti. Tall, handsome—polished, *ah mais certainement,* thought St-Cyr. The successful businessman or banker perhaps, the greying, dark hair close-cropped in military style, the forehead high, face thin, eyes iron-grey and always noting things but giving very little away, the lips wide and full, the expression sardonic, the chin sharp and closely shaven. Not a medal on him or a wound badge, only the SS-Dienstauszeichnung with runes and ribbon, the long-fingered hands with their meticulously pared nails and broad gold wedding band perusing the stamp collection of Monsieur Bernard Isaac Friedman, no doubt a guest of the SS-Totenkopfverbände if still alive.

All around them the Tour d'Argent had settled back into the heads-in-the-sand of its *bons vivants.* Oh for sure the SS and their Sicherheitsdienst would have made a point of knowing exactly where Judge Rouget was at all times, especially on his birthday. Langbehn had probably only intended to offer congratulations in public while reminding the judge and family of that one's duties by bringing the Fräulein Remer along, but now the unexpected intrusion of this Sûreté would have to be dealt with.

Grinning, the Standartenführer leaned back to consider each of the family before saying, 'It's a splendid collection, Madame Rouget. My compliments. Judge, you'll be the envy of all such collectors and must be immensely proud of this dear lady of yours.'

Coffee, cigars and cognac had been brought from Langbehn's table. But what of this girl of the Belgian barley sheaves and handbag theft, this stalwart liar in an immaculately pressed, made-over *Blitzmädchen* uniform? wondered St-Cyr. The expression was one of cold appraisal, the look in those china-blue eyes one of what? Of the threat of 'I dare you to try to stop me from condemning those four neighbourhood boys of yours to death or deportation along with every member of their families?' After all, a uniform had been disgraced and the Germans . . . *ah, mon Dieu*, but they loved theirs.

'That collection was stolen, as I've stated, Standartenführer. Since it is a key link in a long chain of murders and assaults, it must be held by me as evidence.'

'Judge, lock it up,' chuckled Langbehn as he handed it back to Rouget.

'Standartenführer . . .' One had to try.

Langbehn reached for his cognac in salute. Sonja Remer didn't waver, but sipped only water, Denise Rouget all but knocking her glass over, Vivienne softly saying, 'Hercule.'

'A speech, then, Judge. Begin, please, by telling me the names of all who had access to and the use of that flat of yours on the rue La Boétie. "Important people," Concierge Louveau has stated. Former military men, the latest of which, some five weeks ago, was a retired general who . . . *Ah, excusez-moi un moment*, the notebook—so many items are collected on these investigations. Little things that are carelessly left behind. The red ribbon of a Légion d'honneur, Judge. Ah! here is the note I want.'

He'd give them a moment now to set their glasses down, as had the Fräulein Remer, whose regulation black leather handbag couldn't help but be seen since it was on the table next to her left hand.

' "A general with the snow-white moustache and hair just like the Maréchal Pétain." '

'I know nothing of this. Abélard . . .'

'Judge, this is not a courtroom yet. Colonel Delaroche has a key to that flat, has he not?'

Had that idiot of a concierge actually told St-Cyr this or was he simply assuming it?

'WELL?'

Élène's keys could just as easily have been used, and St-Cyr must know this, but to admit that Abélard had one might be useful. 'I let him use the flat as often as he wishes. Surely there is no harm in that?'

Rouget knitted those thick fingers of his together as if on the bench and condemning this Sûreté to bite the tongue while dangling by the neck. 'Harm? Perhaps not, but first this general who enjoys cigars as much as you and the Standartenführer.'

'They all do!' scoffed Langbehn. 'Show me a general relaxing and I'll show you a cigar smoker.'

'Relaxing with an auburn-haired prostitute who was no older than the Fräulein Remer, Standartenführer?'

'A whore . . .' breathed Vivienne Rouget. 'Married, too, was she, to one who is absent and can do nothing whatsoever to stop her from debasing herself with another man?'

Madame Rouget had best be ignored to prod her into saying something else. 'Judge, is it that you allow Colonel Delaroche to let former French army officers use that flat? Remember, please, that you're a member of the Cercle de l'Union Interaliée, as is the colonel.'

'You leave the Interaliée out of this. Fail to do so and you will pay for it.'

'But not with cash, eh, as this general and others paid the girls they used in that flat, yourself included?'

'*Maudit salaud,* must you rant on and on about my fucking that cunt. She was nothing but a bit of fun, a . . .'

'Hercule, Hercule . . .'

'Vivienne, *ferme-la*! Don't, and I will shut it for you. Denise . . .'

'No, Judge. They're to remain. Now answer, please, as you are required by law, if there is *any* law left in this nation of ours.'

'*Salaud,* of course I let Abélard use the flat, and others, too, of the Interaliée. It helps with the rent. Am I not free to do as I please with my own property?'

'Inspector . . .'

'Standartenführer, this is a murder inquiry.'

The Fräulein Remer would kill St-Cyr and Kohler, and if not her, the Agence Vidocq. That had all been arranged. The matter of this one and his 'partner' would then be closed.

'Very well, proceed.'

'*Ah, bon.* You see, Judge, two men were involved in the murder of Élène Artur. Just why they chose to kill her in that flat of yours, and not in some darkened *passage*, is another matter my partner and I will eventually get to, but for now, one of the assailants knew that flat of yours very well and took care of it even after what they had done. Perhaps he held her down, Madame Rouget, while the other raped her, slashed her breast and shoulder, for they'd torn her clothes from her, and then—and we are not certain yet which of them did this but now must think it the same person as committed a recent murder—cut her open and let her go so that she ran from them, trying desperately to hold her intestines in and . . .'

'That is enough, Inspector!'

'Judge, murder is murder, the details never pleasant. After all, she was a person you kept seeing, one to whom you paid at least two thousand francs a visit and who did things . . .'

'Inspector, this really has gone far enough.'

'It's Chief Inspector, Standartenführer, and before you start interfering again, pause to consider that my partner and myself were assigned to this matter by Gestapo Boemelburg and that the Kommandant von Gross-Paris ordered my partner to provide him with up-to-the-minute progress reports.' This wasn't exactly true, but what else could have been done in such circumstances? 'Hermann will have taken care of this even as we speak. That's why I sent him away. He will, of course, have placed our latest synopsis on the Kommandant's desk so as to have it ready for him at 0700 hours. He's an early riser, our Kommandant. We both know him well, Standartenführer, and know, too, that he will tolerate absolutely no interference and that everything that is being done by us will and must be done to make the streets safe again.'

'Even for those who would sell the use of themselves, Inspector?'

'Vivienne . . .'

'Hercule, that is the crux of this matter. Women who betray their husbands or fiancées who cannot, because of circumstance, carry out the punishment themselves but must hope and pray that others will see to it for them.'

The room was empty, the bed empty, the *Hôtel-Dieu* in a crisis and short-staffed. In panic, Kohler ran his gaze over the stark sterility. The kids . . . her Henri and Louisette . . . Just how the hell was he to tell them their mother hadn't made it? They'd *hate* him for the rest of their lives, would hate every last one of the Occupier no matter what.

'Come on you,' he demanded.

Green eyes rebelled. 'I'm not going anywhere further with you.'

Grabbing her by the wrist, he yanked her after him, would go down the staircase three steps at a time, would catch her up as she tripped and had to pull off those high heels of hers, would make her follow and ruin those silk stockings, would teach her *not* to treat others the way she and Denise Rouget had. 'I want answers, damn you,' he called out as the stench of overworked drains, disinfectant and cold, no-soap, eau-de-Javelled laundry hit them.

Dimly lit, the *Hôtel-Dieu*'s morgue was in the cellars.

'Monsieur . . .'

'Kohler, Kripo, Paris-Central. The body of Adrienne Guillaumet.'

'Guillaumet . . .?' muttered Martin Thibodeau, blinking to clear the eyes of much-needed sleep, not that this Kripo or the one that was with him would care in the slightest.

'Thirty-two years old,' said Germaine de Brisac. 'Residence: 131 rue Saint-Dominique in Gros-Caillou. No wedding ring. That was stolen along with her handbag.'

'*Merci*, madame. Such information as you have so succinctly imparted is of inestimable value.'

A man of big words at a time like this!

'Badly bruised,' she went on.

'That, too,' clucked Thibodeau. He would toss the head, to indicate knowledge of the terrible injuries sustained. 'She's the one. We'll soon find her.'

A drawer was pulled, and then another, the shrouds flicked to half-mast, an old man, a teenaged boy . . . a traffic accident? 'Autopsy?' asked Thibodeau. 'Sometimes the doctors still do them, but with the suspension of all medical studies late last year and now the threat of the forced labour, the students have left for the hills and the *maquis* or gone into hiding elsewhere, or been sent into that same forced labour.'

The green-eyed one was startled by such an evident affront to the status quo but looking pale, the Gestapo about to regurgitate. 'This way, please. I think they must have cut her open but let's hope she's been stitched.'

Kohler knew he had paled at the thought and had almost turned away, for this socialite who played at being a social worker was now smirking. Louis would have forced her to view the corpse from head to toe. Louis would have told her they weren't just concerned with Madame Guillaumet but with Giselle who had been followed by those bastards she and her friend and their mothers had hired. He'd say, my partner is sick with worry about this Mademoiselle le Roy, *moi-même aussi* since we haven't yet been able to find her.

He'd make this 'parasite' tell him everything she could about Colonel Abélard Delaroche and company.

Somehow a cigarette was found, somehow lighted, but he was all but crying, this giant of a Kripo, thought Germaine. He was standing before her in this examining room with its pallets and drains and bottles of preserved organs and collection of fetuses in all stages and he didn't know what to say, flung down that cigarette of his in disgust, was as quivering custard, the attendant puzzled, alarmed and looking back at them, having completely removed a shroud.

'Her kids!' blurted Herr Kohler. 'Not only will they *not* have the father who gave their dear *maman* such a hard time and made her keep everything in the flat exactly as he wanted it kept, they *won't* have the mother who understood them so well she made a special place for them anyway. A room of their very own.'

One must be calm, must have dignity in the face of such an outburst. 'She was an officer's wife, Inspector, was of that class and had a duty to live up to but wouldn't listen when reminded.'

'The top and the bottom of the heap, eh? That why the difference between her punishment and that of Marie-Léon Barrault?'

'Yes. I . . . I believe so. Abélard . . . Colonel Delaroche is—was— an officer himself.'

'And when Vivienne and your mother raised the issue of these delinquent wives?'

'He offered a solution.

'Correction: He suggested he could put together the necessary manpower since he was already using some of them and helping others. *Grands mutilés* and their daughters, shopkeepers who were former servicemen under him and with axes to grind.'

And prejudices—it was clear that this was meant, and all the rest of it, the need for collaboration, for France to take her rightful place in the new Europe, the need to blame those responsible for the Defeat and to ensure that only those who had actually fought in this one would be considered as true veterans.

Ashen, he bleated, 'Are there still others who are involved?'

Merde, but one wanted to smile! 'Other veterans, Inspector? Those perhaps who are among *les égoutiers*?'

The municipal sewer workers . . .

It felt good to get the better of Herr Kohler, but perhaps the message should be reinforced. 'Men you will find almost impossible to apprehend, Inspector. Oh, there aren't that many, probably. Denise and myself really don't know much about what's been going on. Abélard has always been very close with his business dealings and keeps them even from *Maman* and Vivienne with whom we've talked a little about it, but . . . but these men, they are down there wading in the shit all the time, isn't that so, and can come up anywhere they please.'

'To rob a shop that sells used postage stamps and leave a wad of clay to silence an alarm?'

Had she startled him? 'If necessary, I suppose, but why not ask Abélard yourself?'

This one was tougher than she looked and kept glancing past him to the body. 'I will. How much are Vivienne and your mother paying that agency of his?'

Was Kohler too afraid to turn towards the corpse? 'The work is by the piece. The more who are dealt with, the more the Agence Vidocq is paid.'

Was she really this cold? 'But it's gone far beyond your mother and Vivienne Rouget going through yours and Denise's caseload files at home, hasn't it? Others are now feeding that agency targets of their own, still others no doubt putting up the cash.'

Should she tell him that ten such men met regularly at the Cercle de l'Union Interaliée? A retired general with white hair and Pétain moustache, other former military officers, Préfet Talbotte, two industrialists, one the owner of . . .

'That colonel you worshipped as a child suddenly realized he was on to a good thing, didn't he?'

She said nothing. She just stood there looking up at him, he still unable to turn towards the body. 'Judge Rouget is among the backers, isn't he? Come on, tell me, damn you!'

All right, she would, and derive satisfaction from doing so. 'How better, Inspector, to hide from others that which you are still keeping, or were until recently?'

He'd best sigh as he said it, thought Kohler. 'The wife of a POW herself. But why kill her in that flat of his unless paid to do so?'

The lift began its journey. There had been no sign of Concierge Louveau, no sign of anyone else in this former *hôtel particulier* on the rue La Boétie, no other sound but that of the cage as it rose and the memory of saying, as they had crowded into the foyer, 'Permit me, please, *Monsieur le Juge*, but I'd best go first.' There hadn't been room for all six of them.

Standartenführer Langbehn stood to one side in the cage, the Fräulein Remer to the other. Had she no thought but to win her little piece of this war regardless of the cost to others? wondered St-Cyr. So little had been said in the car en route from the Tour d'Argent, one had to think the worst. She neither smiled nor frowned.

They passed the first floor. *Merde,* but these old lifts could take their time. They reached the second, Sonja Remer having never taken her gaze from him. A *Mausefalle,* Rudi had told them, *une souricière* with Giselle le Roy as its bait. A narrow *passage* and SS floodlights suddenly coming on to help her target two honest detectives.

She would know that he and Hermann would have been told her version of the 'attack' as she had recounted it to Judge Rouget in front of the Butcher of Poland, would know, too, that they had had the boys' version of the same, since the Sicherheitsdienst would have paid Rudi a visit to question him and his sister most thoroughly as to exactly how it was possible that this *Blitz's* handbag should have turned up at the restaurant.

In Deutsch, he said, 'I understand, Fräulein, that your fiancé was killed in Norway during the invasion. Please accept my condolences.'

Did this *verfluchter Franzose* think to engage her in conversation to soften her resolve? wondered Sonja. The Standartenführer gave her the curtest of nods and she must do exactly as indicated, responding curtly as ordered but not in *Deutsch*. 'Oui, mon Erich.'

Nothing else. The lift stopped, the cage door was opened by Langbehn who indicated the corridor.

The seals were all there, but Hermann had a system. Sometimes a hair would be placed across the crease between the door and the jamb and exactly two centimetres below the lowest hinge, sometimes a clot of household dust or pocket lint and with only a touch protruding, sometimes the tiniest bit of paper.

Never white or brightly coloured, this last was there but much, much closer to that hinge than it should have been.

Uncertain still of what to expect from this Kripo, Thibodeau indicated the corpse on its pallet in the morgue of the *Hôtel-Dieu*.

She had been wearing a hospital gown, but such things must be in very short supply and she'd not have needed it in any case, had been beaten to hell. The left shoulder and wrist, Kohler knew, had been badly sprained but not broken. There'd been blood on her lips and chin when Louis had taken her from that taxi and this Kripo had had to carry her to the car, she having passed out.

The lips were now a deep, dark plum-purple and slack, no rigor yet. An upper front incisor had been broken, the rest all stained by nicotine, a heavy smoker . . .

'A fingernail was recovered,' he heard himself mutter, and then, as Louis would have done, 'Forgive me, madame, but I have to look more closely.'

She was cold, smelled of death and of the cheap, ersatz perfume with which she had regularly dosed herself. The skin of the right hip didn't rebound, of course, when pressure from his fingers was released after having nudged her side up a little.

The forehead had been opened in a five-centimetre gash but what the hell had done it? Blood would have blinded her in that eye. The nose had been broken, the bony, pasty knees and thighs badly scraped. Fibres from her skirt or coat were still glued to the legs, black hairs also, black pubic hairs . . .

'TAKE A LOOK AT HER, DAMN YOU,' he cried. 'COME ON. SEE FOR YOURSELF WHAT YOU AND DENISE ROUGET AND THOSE MOTHERS OF YOURS HAVE HELPED TO CAUSE!'

Germaine de Brisac turned away and had to be caught. Dragged back and forced to look, she gagged. Madame Guillaumet's eyes hadn't yet been closed, the darkness of the lips matching that of the bruises on the neck of this . . . this officer's wife who would sell herself to another, her head forced back as the rapist had . . .

She coughed, she cried, she threw up the *pommes d'amour flambées à l'Amaretto,* the *salade d'endives de Belgique, canard à la presse, caviar russe malossol et bisque de homard à l'armagnac et huitres à la florentine,* the Romanée-Conti also, or Nuits-Saint-Georges and the champagne, mustn't forget that, thought Kohler. They'd a fabulous cellar at the Tour d'Argent. Legendary, Louis had once said, though he'd never been able to afford such a place.

Her throat still stinging and eyes still watering, Germaine could see that the woman's mascara had been smeared by the rain and the rapist's fingers. The pencilled eyebrows were grotesquely crooked. There were scars from two Caesarean births, that of an appendectomy. Moles, warts, the red blotch of a nasty birthmark . . . *Ah, Sainte-Mère,* what the hell was this?

'Smell her,' demanded Kohler.

'No! I refuse!'

'INSPECTOR!' shouted Thibodeau. 'PLEASE EXHIBIT SOME RESPECT!'

'I am.'

'Inspector, *please.* I beg you . . .'

Herr Kohler grabbed the corpse's toe tag and she heard him reading it out. 'Location: Pigalle, eh? Date: the thirteenth; Time: 1020 hours? This isn't—I repeat, isn't—the body of Adrienne Guillaumet, you idiot, so tell us where the hell she is and don't keep us in suspense any longer?'

'Not her? But . . .' managed Thibodeau. Something would have to be said, some rational explanation given. 'Since her name was known, Inspector, the remains must have been consigned to the funeral home of the next-of-kin's choice or . . .'

'Cremated—is that what you're saying?'

'There is no necessity to raise the voice!'

Ach, mein Gott, the French sometimes! 'There is every right, *mein Lieber,* but just tell me. I thought the *Hôtel-Dieu* put them into no-name coffins.'

'*Ah, oui, oui, certainement,* especially those without known names, and certainly bureaucratic mistakes are unfortunately made from time to time, and certainly the earth will, perhaps, be frozen or soaking wet and inopportune for such excavations. As a consequence, and with due process, I assure you, some are despatched to a crematorium.'

Ach, mein Gott, Louis should have heard him! 'Which one?'

To suggest something close would not be wise. 'La Villette's. I have it on good authority that there is one there, I think. The greater the distance from the city centre, the greater the economies, since the state and taxpayer must . . .'

'La Villette.'

'Oui.'

And out by the abattoir and just to the northeast of the Parc des Buttes Chaumont, home territory to the boys on that street of Louis's. 'Would the family have been notified?'

'Of course.'

Oona would really need him, if only for a few minutes. 'Come on, you, and don't argue.'

'I won't,' managed Germaine, her lower lip still quivering. 'I . . . I've seen enough not to.'

'Good. Then you can be the one to tell her kids who was responsible.'

The others had gone on ahead in this flat, this place Denise knew she had heard so much about over the years but never seen until now, but why had the chief inspector not wanted to follow? Surely he must realize she would be needed? *Maman* would continue to say things that must never be said. *Maman* would tell *Papa* to look closely at that dead lover of his and understand what he had caused her to have done, that she could no longer have lived with his philandering and squandering her family's fortune, that he had to stop if for no other reason than his own safety and position but that he must also think about those he ought to love and protect. Things could not continue as they had. These days one had to be so very careful.

'No sound comes from that innermost bedroom, does it?' said this Sûreté. Having deliberately packed that pipe of his, he now lit it but watched her closely through the smoke before saying, 'Sit down, Mademoiselle Rouget.'

Must he stand in front of the mantelpiece so as to further draw attention to the framed poster of that . . . that dancer *Papa* had been so infatuated with, he would have had children by her had it not been for *Maman*'s having had the slut arrested and convicted of theft? *Une nuit à Chang-Rai, 7 Mai 1926* at the Magic City. Chantelle Auclair, 'Didi' to her friends. *'Une sacré bonne baise,'* *Papa* had yelled at mother once too often: a damned good fuck! A handbag containing jewellery and banknotes to the tune of 250,000 old francs had been found in this 'Didi's' dressing room, found, *ah, oui, oui,* by Colonel Delaroche and then by the police he had summoned. Prison hadn't been good for the career, and the long absence of even those three years had put an end to the affair, especially as brief encounters had been readily found for *Papa* by that same colonel.

But the inspector would know none of this. At last he waved out the match and, having wetted it with spittle, tucked it away in a jacket pocket—a creature of habit? she had to wonder.

To ask if Élène Artur had suffered more than he had already stated would only invite his, Why not go and see for yourself? To ask if there was blood everywhere in that room would elicit but, Can you not smell the carbolic?

She could give him only what he wanted. Nothing else would suffice.

'A few small questions, mademoiselle. Nothing difficult, I assure you.'

How could he be so calm?

'The forensic staff and our coroner will be able to pin things down,' he said, indicating the bedroom. 'That stamp collection, Mademoiselle Denise Rouget.'

'Actually it is Catherine Denise Rouget, Inspector.'

'After your mother's lifelong friend.'

'That is correct.'

The wavy, permed, thick auburn hair, carefully made-up, chiselled face and big brown eyes that could, at times, be soft perhaps, were there but so was the strain. *'Ah, bon*, mademoiselle. One tries, doesn't one? While at the Tour d'Argent your mother stated that she had purchased the stamps only after much deliberation and from a very reputable source. Her statement indicates that she viewed the collection on more than one occasion.'

Must he be so pedantically precise?

'Well?' he asked.

'That, too, is correct.'

Companionably the pipe-hand lifted. 'You helped her to choose it?'

Ah, merde! 'Oui.'

'From whom, please?'

'I . . . I'd rather not say.'

'Then let me remind you, mademoiselle. To not answer is to . . .'

'The Baron Kurt von Behr. He and Colonel Delaroche are friends—good friends. More than acquaintances, you understand.'

And wasn't that a cosy way of putting it? From Mecklenburg and speaking fluent French, this son of an aristocratic family was totally unscrupulous and as a consequence, had recouped the family's fortune tenfold. 'The Baron . . .'

'Oui. Colonel Delaroche . . . Abélard put us in touch with him.'

But she and her mother and Germaine de Brisac and others would have met von Behr at any number of the socialite parties that had been thrown for his benefit and that of his British wife, or thrown by them, since extravagance was their style and everyone who was anyone always said that people should see what Von Behr was up to. 'You first viewed the collection where?'

'At an office on the avenue d'Iéna.'

And but a short stroll from the SS and the avenue Foch. 'Number fifty-four?'

Did he have to hear it from her? 'Yes!'

Head Office of the French branch of the Reich's Ministry for the Occupied Territories, but one must be pleasant. 'And then?'

'Again, but . . . but at a large warehouse on the . . .'

'A former store whose owners once specialized in making furniture?'

And whose large, once neon-lit letters atop the building hadn't been removed but simply overhung by a huge swastika. Once again the chief inspector was making her say things. '*Oui*. In . . . in the rue du Faubourg Saint-Martin.'

'The Lévitan?'

'If you know, Inspector, why force me to admit it?'

'Because, Mademoiselle Rouget, you and your mother must have known you were buying stolen goods.'

'It wasn't stolen! It had been legally expropriated!'

The day of reckoning would come—one had to believe this, otherwise what hope was there? 'Look on it any way you like. This reputable source of your mother's is none other than the director of that office you went to. Until last month, though, the Baron Kurt von Behr was also deputy director of the Einsatzstab Reichlieter Rosenberg to which he will have retained close ties since he is a much-valued associate of the Reichsmarschall Göring, for whom he often finds important works of art.'

Paintings, Old Masters, porcelains, coins and tapestries, thought Denise, all of which had been 'stolen' and to whom, everyone who was anyone knew, Von Behr and his wife had gone to Berlin last year on 12 January, the forty-ninth birthday of Göring, to present to him the original of the Treaty of Versailles with all its signatures.

'A letter to Napoléon III from Richard Wagner was also included, mademoiselle,' said St-Cyr, having read her thoughts. 'He moves in nothing but the highest of circles, this reputable source of your mother's. Oh please don't trouble yourself about the mess in that bedroom and what is delaying your parents. The Standartenführer is patiently explaining to them that they must understand that the Höherer SS *und* Polizeiführer Oberg has only their best interests at heart and that the Sicherheitsdienst are watching over them at all times, even to having tidied things up so as to deny my partner and myself the victim's corpse as proof and to allow that father of yours to continue to pronounce nothing but the stiffest of sentences.'

'The night-action courts . . .'

'And those trials of juvenile delinquents, mademoiselle, that come before him, the littlest of black marketeers also, and un-licenced prostitutes, especially those unfortunate enough to be married to absent prisoners of war. The price of the stamps was negotiated, wasn't it?'

'Colonel Delaroche . . .'

'How much did your mother give him to deliver to the Baron von Behr?'

'Three hundred and fifty thousand francs.'

'Old ones?'

'New ones. Mother . . . Mother had me count them for her since . . .'

'You had contributed your share.'

Must he continue to blame herself?

It could only be said with sadness but one had best sigh heavily and then let her have it. 'A new folio was ordered but the stamps went missing and the colonel discovered who must have taken them.'

'Please, I . . . I don't understand?'

'Of course you don't, but for now that is all I want from you.'

Through the rain and darkness, the headlamps shone fully on the Fountain of Mars. Kohler rubbed away the fog that kept collect-ing on the inside of the front windscreen. Germaine de Brisac was cold and soaked through yet hadn't complained, had kept silent since the *Hôtel-Dieu* except for having guided them through a city that had shut down so hard, they'd met but one patrol and had had no further difficulty. Simply empty streets at 0221 hours Sun-day and not a soul.

'Hygeia,' he said of the fountain as if relieved to have found it at last.

'Inspector, do I really have to apologize to those children of

Madame Guillaumet's? I've two of my own and know how they must be feeling.'

'Nothing worthwhile is ever easy, is it? My partner brought me here in the autumn of 1940. He was "educating" me, showing me a city he said I had not only to get to know, but also love, and even after everything the two of us have had to go through, I still did until now.'

'It is beautiful. It doesn't always rain.'

'Old soldiers counted most for us then and still do, since we'd both had enough of war and of this one also.'

Old soldiers . . . 'Former *compagnons d'armes*?'

'Former enemies, Mademoiselle de Brisac. Stay here, then, but I'll have to switch off the headlamps and the engine, and take the key.'

He didn't trust her. He got out of the car and left her for what seemed with each passing minute to take longer and longer. She would say nothing further to him, because she had already said far too much. What should have been a simple assault, a lesson, a rape, yes! had turned into the murder of Adrienne Guillaumet, and Denise and herself were as guilty as any since they'd both known Vivienne and *Maman* had gone through the case files to find names for Abélard to deal with and then . . . yes, then, Denise and she had hired the Agence Vidocq themselves for Madame Morel.

'I'm a murderess,' she softly said to herself. 'I've allowed my hatred of a dead husband and my yearning for a father I hardly knew but blamed for betraying Mother come to this, and my children will learn of it if I don't do something.'

What could she do to stop Kohler and St-Cyr? What would Denise advise? Denise, without whom life would have no meaning.

Germaine got out of the car and let the rain hit her. Quickly she crossed over and took the rue de l'Exposition, would go down it until she reached the rue de Grenelle, which would lead her out to the boulevard de la Tour-Maubourg and the esplanade des Invalides. Herr Kohler would never find her if he chose to drive round and round searching for her. She wouldn't be followed by anyone, not at this time of night.

Dieu merci, her shoes didn't make that horrible clip-clopping of the wooden-soled hinged ones most had to wear these days since there were no others available to them. Hers were of leather but they *did* squeak and would give her away—was someone following her?

Step by step she became more certain of being followed but when she turned suddenly and started back defiantly, there was no one.

'I KNOW YOU'RE THERE!' she heard herself shrill. 'LISTEN, YOU. I'M A WAR WIDOW. MY HUSBAND WAS KILLED DURING THE INVASION.'

There was no answer. Was there more than one of them? Denise . . . Denise, my love . . . *'Please,'* she heard herself saying. 'I have two children.'

She waited.

'Listen, you, I'm one of Abélard's people. You can have my jewellery and handbag, just don't hurt me or cut off my hair. I won't resist.'

Again he said nothing. Again she wasn't even sure he was there.

Retracing her steps, Germaine at last found the car still parked beside the fountain. Forced by nature to urinate, she did so in the gutter like a common prostitute, had never had to do such a thing before, was both ashamed and embarrassed.

The smoke from a Gauloise bleue filled the car. Herr Kohler was sitting behind the wheel.

'Get in and behave yourself.'

'Please, I . . . I didn't think. I should have. It's . . . it's horrible out there on those streets.'

'Just tell me everything you can about Jeannot Raymond and the others. Leave anything out and you really will be finding your own way back.'

He'd do it too. She knew this.

'They came and they took Oona, mademoiselle. Maybe it's that they couldn't find Giselle le Roy and needed Oona as bait, maybe it's that they've the two of them, but they took the woman those kids of Madame Guillaumet's had come to depend on as I knew Henri and Louisette would because they needed her desperately.'

They didn't use the lift in this house on the rue La Boétie where Denise's father kept a flat, had been told by the maître d' at the Tour d'Argent that this is where they had best go. Germaine winced when she saw the broken seals around the door. She knew it was a reaction she couldn't have avoided. Herr Kohler noticed it, as he did everything. He didn't remove the handcuff that bound her to him as a common criminal.

'You're hurting my wrist, damn you.'

'Be quiet. Speak only when spoken to.'

He checked his gun, said, 'Don't make me use it.' Was very upset and worried about this Oona Van der Lynn but wouldn't let such concerns interfere in the slightest with what he had to do.

He opened the door and made her walk in front of him, nudging her when she paused to pry off her shoes. 'My coat,' she said. It now dangled from that wrist. Her dress was ruined, her hair, her everything. How could he do this to her? Did he not *know* who she was?

Abruptly he stopped her in the entrance to the *salle de séjour* and she knew he would not let her go any further until he wanted her to. He must be looking around the room at everyone, must be taking it all in.

Broken glass littered the carpet at Louis's feet amid the shattered wreckage of the mantel's theatre poster. Denise Rouget had looked up suddenly, the daughter sitting tensely on the edge of a distant settee with that mother of hers whose hands were bandaged but who showed every sign of being about to leap up and smash something else—the vitrine? wondered Kohler.

Judge Rouget couldn't find the will to even notice green eyes or this Kripo or that wife of his, nor was he enjoying the cigar whose smoke must cloud the thoughts when clear thinking was demanded. He'd been told exactly where things stood and hadn't liked what he'd heard. Undying loyalty to the Führer and the

Reich even if things were beginning to look doubtful and the Allies might just possibly invade en masse as so many were now hoping.

The Standartenführer Langbehn simply remained supremely confident with knees crossed and cigarette in hand. Sonja Remer, having gone into the kitchen to get herself one of those chairs, sat by that exit with handbag in lap, intently watching the proceedings without expression beyond a blankness that unsettled because one had still to ask, as always, was there *nothing* that could be done to change her mind?

'Hermann . . .'

'Louis, this one told me Madame Rouget arranged and paid for the killing of Élène Artur.'

'I did no such thing,' spat Vivienne, sucking in a breath and darting a look at everyone but her daughter.

'Kohler . . .'

'Standartenführer, don't get in the way of a police officer exercising his duties.'

'A moment, *mon vieux* . . .'

'Not now, Louis. Just let me handle this.'

'There is no body, Hermann.'

'Cleaned it up, did they?'

'Kohler . . .'

'Be quiet, you. An SS-Gestapo *Mausefalle*, eh, and two honest detectives dead because of the marksmanship of this one? Try it and see what happens, Standartenführer. Madame Rouget? Madame Vivienne Rouget of the rue Henri Rochefort?'

Hermann gave the house number and said that his partner would take down her *procès-verbal,* her statement.

'I arranged nothing. You have no proof, not now.'

'*Ach,* but I have.'

'Let's see it, then,' she said in French.

'*Aber natürlich. Bitte,* though . . . *Merci, un moment.*'

Hermann was flying on Benzedrine—taunting her with that mix of languages. Nudging Germaine de Brisac ahead of him, he went over to the *Blitz* and took the handbag from her at gunpoint, tossing it on to the carpet some distance from her. 'That's to even things up,' he said and nudged her with the Walther P38. 'Just try to get it, *mein Schatz*, and you'll never try another thing.'

Tucking his pistol away, he dug deeply into a pocket, had to finally release the Mademoiselle de Brisac but told her, as only he could, not to sit down. Fist clenched and then opened, he let Vivienne Roget look at what had, no doubt, been promised her by the killers but hadn't been found until later.

'Have you a collection of them?' he asked. She didn't answer but only glared. 'I'll give it to you later, then. For now it's all the evidence we need since my report is on the Kommandant von Gross-Paris's desk, awaiting his perusal at an hour you wouldn't understand.'

Grâce à Dieu, Hermann had realized that his partner would have used just such a lie, but had they grown so close, their lives, their very beings were now welded into one?

Squeezed, Louis, Hermann would have said. Like *canards à la presse.*

'Mademoiselle Germaine de Brisac?' he said, using his Gestapo voice.

Terrified, she looked at Hermann, who continued. 'Tell them what you told me of Jeannot Raymond.'

Her overcoat fell to the carpet, her wrist was favoured. Alone before them, she knew her dress clung to her, that she mustn't pluck at it, mustn't even try to tidy the hair that was plastered to her brow, that to do such would only be considered unseemly of her, betraying a cowardice she didn't wish to expose.

'Abélard knew him from before the Defeat, from that other war, I think. The victory then. The Cercle de l'Union Interaliée, too, in the early thirties when he . . . he was living there and Monsieur Raymond had come home from Argentina to stay.'

'But always the cool one, that right?' prompted Herr Kohler, nudging her, she drawing away from him sharply. 'Never anything else,' he continued. 'Dangerous—wasn't that what you said when I asked it of you? Damned dangerous?'

Again he touched her. Again she pulled away. 'Well?' he demanded.

'Dangerous and brave. When flying over the Andes Mountains, he and . . . and the other pilots of that airmail service he worked for had to draw their own charts and make their own repairs if forced down by bad weather or engine failure.'

'Or walk out, Louis.'

'He . . . he had two ranches. The one much nearer to Buenos Aires was for cattle and horses, while the one far to the southwest in Patagonia was for sheep. He . . .'

'Had a wife and two children,' said Madame Rouget, sucking in a breath and waiting to see their reactions. 'A wife who betrayed him.'

Had she tasted it? wondered Kohler, Louis too.

'*Maman*, that is only a rumour,' blurted Denise. 'You know he mightn't have done what Abélard told you and Madame de Brisac.'

'He did! He didn't make that night flight he was supposed to, but returned to his cattle ranch, Inspectors, and took care of that wife and the lover she had taken behind his back!'

'He . . . he cut Rivière's throat first as that one slept and then . . . then made her watch as he cut those of the children,' said Denise, unable to keep the sadness from her voice, the heartache of it, thought Germaine. 'Rivière was his boss. Only then did Monsieur Raymond cut her throat and burn the hacienda to the ground.'

'She . . . she had repeatedly begged him to let her and the children return to France, was terribly lonely and didn't even speak Spanish, but he . . . he wouldn't listen,' said Germaine emptily.

It was Denise who said, 'He refused to give up everything for her.'

'A rancher, Louis. Sheep and cattle. Successful and then broke, a naturalized Argentinian who had adopted the country as his own and then had to run because he was unable to stay.'

'And what of Flavien Garnier, mademoiselle, and Hubert Quevillon?'

Had this Sûreté asked it thinking the worst of her, having seen it so clearly? 'I felt more comfortable with Garnier than with his subordinate. Garnier is very direct, very thorough and business-like. He . . . he doesn't try to force himself on a woman, has a wife and grown children, is very professional and is not in any way . . .'

'Threatening?' prompted Louis gently.

Denise leaped to her feet, the look she gave pleading with her not to say anything, thought Germaine.

'We know,' grunted Rouget, tossing his cigar hand in dismissal. 'What you two do in private is disgusting, in public . . .'

'Hercule . . .'

'Vivienne, that daughter of yours had best deny it right now. No men in her life beyond those first few unfortunate and fleeting attempts at normality? Mixed swimming parties and afternoon dances she didn't want to attend and was mortified when she had to suffer through them and was pawed by some boy who only wanted to get his fingers sticky? Did you actually believe I wouldn't notice her tears? A daughter of mine?'

'*Papa* . . .'

A fist was clenched, the cigar stubbed out. 'Just deny it. Don't and I will disown you.'

Homosexuality wasn't only against the law but a definite no-no, especially if admitted in front of an SS. 'Garnier's not like Quevillon, Louis, but is a veteran like the others. So where has the Agence Vidocq got Oona Van der Lynn, Standartenführer, or are we to read about it in the press?'

Kohler's attitude would never change. 'That you will have to find out for yourselves on Monday at 1000 hours, the avenue Foch.'

12

They were now alone in the judge's flat. 'Oona, Louis,' said Hermann. 'The boys on your street. Your boys, mine too.'

They had perhaps a day, didn't even know where any of the Agence Vidocq lived. *Bien sûr,* Delaroche must have been told by Oberg to take Giselle, and when Garnier and Quevillon had failed—if they really had—Oona had been necessary.

'Let me have that Sûreté blunderbuss of yours and the spares. Don't argue.'

Fingers were impatiently snapped. Clearing things away on the judge's coffee table, Hermann broke the Lebel and emptied it *and* the 'brand-new' packet of 11 mm, black-powder 1873s whose cartridges rolled about until silent. Spreading them, he muttered, 'Verdigris. No wonder you people lost this war.'

It wasn't a moment in which to disagree. It was 0422 hours Sunday, 14 February 1943 and they had until 1000 hours Monday. Shoving most of the cartridges to one side, Hermann chose six to reload and that . . . why that, of course, left only five as spares. A folded handkerchief was produced, a girl's, a woman's—clean, white, ironed and decorated with a diligent bouquet of beginner's needlework.

'Lupins,' he said, smoothing it out. 'Oona dropped this in the foyer of Madame Guillaumet's building. She left it for me, Louis. Deliberately.'

It was the handkerchief her two children had presented to her on her birthday, days before the Luftwaffe's Stukas had repeatedly bombed Rotterdam on 14 May 1940. 'You're in love with her and deeply, I think.'

'Just don't relay that to Giselle if we find her. *If,* Louis. Germaine de Brisac let it slip that there had been two involved in the kidnapping of Adrienne Guillaumet outside the École Centrale. One to wait with the bicycle taxi and, though she didn't say it, to later commit that assault, and one to call out Adrienne's name as classes were let out and to lead her through the crowd to that very taxi.'

'Two at *place* de l'Opéra and now another two, one of which was common to both.'

'That one having a wedge of shoulders and big hands. She also made a point of telling me that Delaroche could call on some of the municipal sewer workers.'

'Most of whom are decent, hardworking men who consider themselves a breed apart, but the Church of Saint-Nicholas des Champs is very near to the École Centrale and opposite it, one of the main entrances to the sewer system. Boats can be hired . . .'

'Men can come up and go down at will and later rob a stamp store, eh? Two and two and two, Louis, the one down under the streets gathering a little mud while the other one was attacking Adrienne Guillaumet in the *passage* de la Trinité. Old soldiers, admit it!'

'With another to undertake the Drouant mugging, having first assisted with the taxi theft. Veterans, yes, it's quite possible, but I don't think the two who isolated the owner of Take Me in *place* de l'Opéra's street urinal and then stole that taxi were sewer workers. They'd have had their waterproofed suits and hats and have had no need of using fish-oil margarine.'

'Unless wanting to keep their identities to themselves.'

'Walter uses the Agence Vidocq from time to time, not knowing they've been working against him and are on their own agenda.'

'But does Oberg now know what they've been up to?'

'Has he offered them absolution if they get rid of us?'

'The Fräulein Remer now being nothing but insurance, Louis, Standartenführer Langbehn having been told only so much?'

'And the agency absolutely confident nothing will be pinned on them, they having the protection of the SS, as does the judge.'

Suzette Dunand heard them leave. Clutching Teddy, she had run to the door, had stood before the two detectives in her nightdress, ashamed, terrified and embarrassed until Herr Kohler had said, 'Please don't cry. We're here to help.'

They hadn't stayed more than a few minutes. She had told them everything she could about Jeannot Raymond, most especially that he was the one who always handled the recovery of stolen property and was often away from the office for days on end.

'The Einsatzstab Reichsleiter Rosenberg, Hermann,' the Sûreté had said. 'Jeannot Raymond is the one who hunts down the owners of that property and then the *agence* help themselves.'

'Flats are kept for clients who need a place to stay,' she had said.

'Four, five—how many?' the one called St-Cyr had asked, they both dismayed to find she didn't even know where any of them were other than this one and the one downstairs.

Admit it, said Teddy. *You couldn't stop thinking about your date with this Jeannot Raymond. Nine o'clock this morning, Suzette? Isn't that a little early if you are then to be taken to lunch?*

'The Chinese gate. I . . . I had thought perhaps a walk afterwards through the Institut National d'Agronomie Coloniale.'

And now? he demanded.

'I was wrong. He . . . he was going to kill me.'

Hiking the hem of her nightdress, she blew her nose and wiped her eyes, must be brave, must do exactly as the detectives had told her.

Fortunately her tears hadn't splashed the *laissez-passer* and *sauf-conduit* Herr Kohler had given her, he glancing at the one from the Sûreté for further agreement before filling in her name and the town of Dreux, the chief inspector saying, 'Hurry, Hermann,' but had a part of them been lost? Had the passes been for someone else?

'Pack a few things, mademoiselle,' he had said. 'A small suitcase. Carry a shopping bag with whatever food you can gather for the journey and a little extra to help out at home—not too much, though. Bringing food into Paris is illegal and contrary to the rationing, so taking it out with all the shortages will only raise eyebrows.'

'Remember that you haven't been home since the Defeat,' Herr Kohler had said, 'and that you're very worried about your mother and how she's managing without your dear *papa.*'

'Make sure you emphasize he's a prisoner of war and an excellent garage mechanic and that he has found lots of work in the camp and is pleased. Tell them how many brothers and sisters you have. Has your mother a medal?'

'The silver,' she had said, their advice coming so fast it had been as if spoken by one.

'*Ah, bon*, there are eight of them, Hermann. Be brave, mademoiselle. Open your suitcase only when asked by the control. Try to remember to say, *"Jawohl, Herr Hauptmann,"* especially if he's a private. They like it when a little *Deutsch* is used and they've been flattered.'

'Put in some extra underwear,' Herr Kohler had said. 'If he fingers it, don't worry.'

'Just look away, as if embarrassed.'

'If he steals it, let him. Underwear is in short supply at home and is valued most.'

And then? asked Teddy as the bottle of cognac Herr Kohler had brought from the flat downstairs and reluctantly parted with went into the shopping bag.

'You and the cognac will be seen, Teddy. If they take the one, I'm to say nothing.'

And if they should also take me? he asked.

'I will kiss you good-bye, as the friend you've been, and will walk on through the control to the train. I won't be able to look back. I mustn't. I'm not to hurry, am to walk steadily away and then step up into the carriage.'

She was to leave the flat well before nine and to take the earliest possible train, was to give herself time but not too much. 'You don't want to be noticed hanging around the station,' the one from the Sûreté had said. 'Act naturally. You've the necessary papers. Be positive about them. They're good and have come from the very best of sources.'

'Don't even think of them as being false,' Herr Kohler had said and given her five hundred francs in small bills. 'I'd give you more but we don't want it attracting attention. Split it up. Keep only two hundred in your handbag, the rest in pockets but not those of your overcoat.'

St-Cyr had said to make sure she bought a return ticket; Herr Kohler, that she was to use her looks if necessary but wasn't to go so far as to hesitantly touch her throat or plead with her eyes. 'Those people on the wickets can be bastards,' he had said. 'Some of them are in the pay of *les Allemands* and can, by pushing a little button under the counter or giving some other signal, summon help.'

'For cash,' St-Cyr had said. 'Yours especially.'

At 5.00 a.m., 4.00 the old, the rue Laurence Savart began to stir but they had no time to watch it come alive even though parked and sharing a cigarette outside the house at Number 3. 'We had to do it, Louis. We had no other choice.'

Oona and Giselle, if the latter was alive and if the two could be rescued, wouldn't get their *laissez-passers* and *sauf-conduits*, nor would Gabrielle and her son or even Hermann. Antoine Courbet and Dédé Labelle would leave the city via the Gare Saint-Lazare to begin what would be the longest journey of their lives, to the farm of Madame Courbet's sister. *Bien sûr*, their destination was near Rouen, which was being bombed repeatedly by the RAF. There'd be incendiaries and high explosives. Certainly the boys would be fascinated but . . .

A drag was taken, the cigarette returned. 'Admit it, Louis. They couldn't have stayed here.'

The boys were to 'help with the spring planting' and had been 'excused from school.'

Hervé Desrochers and Guy Vachon would travel south to a farm near Dijon, they leaving the city via the Gare de Lyon and bearing a similar, officially handwritten letter that had been signed by the Kommandant von Gross-Paris and forged by Hermann. And didn't the Occupier love to have his pieces of paper, and didn't one hope that Von Schaumburg wouldn't discover the forgery and that no one would question its not having been written on official letterhead?

That the boys might never come back was one thing, that they were only ten years old, another, and that they had had to grow up overnight, yet another.

'Suzette Dunand, Hermann. That girl still worries me because she knows far too much.'

Though she hadn't been able to tell them much about Jeannot Raymond, what she had said had confirmed their worst fears. In October 1940 there had been at least 150,000 Jewish people living and working in Paris, nearly half of all those in the country. Only a quarter had been of French descent and citizens, but with the continued arrests and deportations, that total had since plummeted to around seventy thousand.

Elsewhere in the country, it was approximately the same. The pecking order that had been initiated at Vichy's request had focused first on the immigrants, especially those who had been refugees from the Reich, but now it was directed at those who were left, the French citizens, many of whom had been veterans of that other war, as had many of the immigrants.

Citizen or not, Jewish or not, for there were also many other unfortunates, *résistants* among them, it hadn't and wouldn't matter to the ERR's Aktion-M squads, and yes, Jeannot Raymond and the Agence Vidocq were not the only ones helping themselves. 'But as flats and houses here in the city are emptied, Hermann, Delaroche must be having his pick of them.'

'Which he then furnishes to his taste and at absolutely no cost or very little.'

'Thereby setting aside an ever-growing store of wealth few if any will know about.'

'And when the Occupier has to leave?' asked Hermann.

The cigarette was taken, ash flicked to one side. 'The *agence*'s targeting of delinquent POW wives will put them in favour with the sympathies of many.'

'Admit it, Delaroche will claim they've been secretly working for the Résistance.'

'Having just as secretly betrayed many of them.'

Hermann took a deep drag. 'And enough, probably, to have silenced all disclaimers.'

'But Walter can't know of their having targeted those wives and fiancées.'

'And Oona could be in any of those flats or houses, Louis.'

'*Ah, oui, oui,* but isn't it more likely that she has to be held somewhere that is absolutely secure and where no one, no concierge no matter how much in the pay or how loyal to the cause, will question her having been brought there or say anything of it later?'

'The Lévitan furniture store in the rue du Faubourg Saint-Martin is huge. There'll be guards and not just a few of them, dogs, too.'

And 0900 hours at the Chinese gate would come soon enough and couldn't be missed.

Birdcages, dishes, pots, pans, sheets, beds, blankets, furniture of all kinds . . . 'Clocks, Louis. *Jésus, merde alors,* look at them!'

They went *tick-tock, tick-tock,* rang if off the hour or were silent, but didn't just line the many aisles in regiments. Categorized, sorted as to species, they were stacked on shelves to the once white-painted, embossed tin-plate sheathing of a ceiling that fell to pseudo–Louis XIV plaster cornices before descending to a floor whose stained tongue-and-groove was store-worn.

'Philippe had needed a crib,' Louis had said as they'd sat a moment in the car—it had just been one of those dumb things a partner would say before taking the plunge, any plunge into the unknown. 'Marianne wanted me to make the choice for her, but I had to work, so I made her take care of it.'

Had Louis the sudden need to get it all off his chest? That boy, that little son of his, had grown and had then to have a bed, a chest of drawers and, perhaps, if the money could be found, a little table and chair of his own. Always there had been money problems, the wages for defying death next to nothing, just like in the army. 'But again she wouldn't choose them herself, Hermann. That wouldn't have been right of her, she had felt, like so many of our women, and had insisted that, as "head of the household" I must make that decision for her.'

This war, this Occupation, had made a lot of them change their minds about that and change them quickly. Louis had ordered the stuff from the Lévitan, spring of 1940, but would the memories and the loss of that second wife and their little boy haunt him to his dying day?

They had entered the Lévitan through a door next to the loading docks, had smelled the rank soot from the Gare de l'Est and heard its locomotives beyond the usual high wire fence all such places were supposed to have. There'd not been a light anywhere out there in the darkness of that railway yard and but a stone's throw away, nor had there been anyone on that door, the place apparently wide open yet that couldn't be, but they'd gone up the stairs anyway so as to keep out of sight.

Kitchen stoves were also on this third floor and Kohler had to wonder at the logic of this since most were of cast iron and heavy. Sinks, washbasins, bathtubs, bidets, mirrored medicine cabinets and toilets were here, too, as were iceboxes and tennis rackets, ironing boards, steamer trunks and suitcases still with their travel stickers, ladies' hats, fur coats, dresses, suits, corsets . . .

'Candlesticks,' breathed Louis. 'God has deserted us, Hermann. There are thousands of them.'

The escalators, installed in the thirties but now frozen in time to save power, were to be used simply as staircases of another kind. 'Oona, if she's here, must be in the cellars.'

Lamps were on the fourth floor and seen to the horizon's walls, wireless set, too, and gramophones with heaps of black Bakelite recordings.

'Mendelssohn,' breathed Louis. 'The Violin Concerto—it's magnificent. A Deutsche Grammophon. Nothing but the finest.'

Though Mendelssohn was a definite no-no at home and even here in France.

Sheet music, tied in half-metre-thick bundles, made its ramparts but there were no pianos. Those had been taken by the Sonderstab Musik and were stored elsewhere in three large warehouses just to the north of the city. Numbered, certainly—how the hell else were they to have kept track of them, seeing as their legs, bearing those same numbers, had been removed to make the carcasses easier to ship?

But there were piano benches, delivered here by mistake. A teenager's note, when found, said only, and in her native *Deutsch*:

Herr Kaufmann, if we are to meet in secret even for coffee and the cakes you love so much, my father would never forgive me. You would then be out of a necessary employment and would, in addition to your extremely modest fee, no longer receive the generous tips that are his great pleasure to present to you when such progress has been deemed entirely evident, even to ears that cannot, and never could, to my knowledge, hold a tune or keep the voice on key, due entirely, it must be admitted, to the noises of the foundry he owns and tirelessly manages so that my younger sister and myself may experience the finer things of life from such a talented instructor as your kind and diligent self.

A mouthful.

'Let's go downstairs, Hermann. Maybe they're waiting for us there.'

Clothing racks held men's suits. Shoes, sorted from their mountains, were piled on shelves. Some had even been polished.

Lists of the contents of each house or flat would have been made, sometimes by the owners if time allowed, most often by the ERR with Germanic thoroughness though done most likely by a French employee and overseer, since virtually all of the Aktion-M boys were locals, and sure, they had needed the jobs just like Max Auger.

Jewellery, china, books—whole libraries of them—desks, family photos by the spill and heap, were accompanied by military decorations, and why hadn't Colonel Delaroche simply taken a Légion d'honneur ribbon from here? Too Jewish, too tainted, or simply, unlike Max, goods that had best not be taken unless paid for, even if only a little and especially as one had a hold on a fellow veteran who would have had to agree to letting him have the use of his own?

Personal things even letters and tax records, the lot had been gathered. First the fist or truncheons at the door, then the arrest and the stick-on seals to tidy things unless the neighbours were able to dash in and grab whatever they could, but this would have happened anywhere, Kohler knew. The Netherlands was still seeing it, Poland too, even the Channel Islands. Wherever people were arrested and deported.

'Legalized, officially sanctioned robbery, Hermann.'

'And then murder, Louis. We both know those "work camps" they're being sent to aren't just for work.'

Once sorted, catalogued, cleaned and repaired if necessary, the loot would be packed up and either sent to the Reich and the Eastern Territories, or to another depot for later transhipment.

Deliberately they had avoided the ground floor, had chosen instead to make the briefest of reconnaissances up here first. Seen from the head of one of the escalators, though, the ground floor had its riches—billions of francs worth of loot. Aghast at the display, Kohler hesitated. Savonnerie and Aubusson carpets were spread out, Turkish ones, too, and Persian. Tapestries—Flemish, Beauvais and Aubusson—were there, paintings . . . family portraits by the look, hundreds and hundreds of them on the floor, piled and leaning against each other while above them hung the richly carved, water-gilded empty frames of still others whose subjects had been cut away and trashed—they must have been—even those dating back a century or two or three.

'Louis . . .' he managed.

'Hermann,' came the reply.

Descending a few more steps, he again paused. There were aisles and aisles, a maze in which the contents of the *grandes salles* and *salons* of châteaux, *maisons de maître, hôtels particuliers* and *appartements* had been emptied and some of them hastily reassembled, though totally depopulated. Among the contents there were gorgeous bouquets and splashes of flowers that, even when seen from such a distance, still took the breath away. 'Henri Fantin-Latour, Hermann. Pierre-Joseph Redouté . . .'

Egyptian alabaster vases, Greek sculptures, Boulle armoires, vitrines full of enamelled silver and/or gold music boxes, snuffboxes, jewellery boxes, Augsburg silver tureens and silver-gilt pilgrim bottles, Sèvres porcelain and Meissen figurines, Régence mirrors, lacquered Chinese screens and those whose many-coloured silk birds seemed to fly up into the electric light from above . . .

'And no one about, Hermann. Not a soul but ourselves.'

'It isn't right, Louis.'

'Are we not expected?'

Could they be so lucky? 'What's that smell?'

There wasn't time to answer. Gallé glass figurines, vases and bowls, with Daum, Lalique and other pieces made a floor-to-ceiling rainbow through which stared the silent ebony and teakwood faces of African sculptures, absolutely exquisite works beyond which, they having reached the ground floor at last to be hidden by its contents, were rock-crystal, Baccarat and Venetian chandeliers that hung as if from a gallows or lay draped over Louis XIV and XV settees and sofas, or prostrate at the feet.

'Velum-bound illuminated Renaissance books of hours with their calendar pages from the early 1500s, Hermann. Old-Master sketches . . . *Pour l'amour de Dieu*, how the hell could Pétain or anyone else in Vichy or Berlin have sanctioned such robbery?'

'Coins, Louis. Drawers and drawers of Roman coins.'

'Used postage stamps?'

'Most certainly.' And this was only a portion of the loot that was constantly being gathered. Roll-topped desks and others, still with their fountain pens and inkstands, waited in long rows, their letters and account books still evident. 'A marriage licence,' said Louis. 'The deed to a flat in Passy. Another in Auteuil.'

Swords, matched pairs of pistols in their velvet-lined cases, battle-axes . . . There was still no sound other than the careful passage of themselves, the time 5.57 a.m.

Bedroom suites gave the dressing tables of the once-wealthy, blonde hairs still clinging to a hairbrush and comb, a spill of rings and earrings as if but taken off and left frozen in time but scattered deliberately, for the piece and its chair and mirror couldn't have been moved otherwise and brought here from wherever.

'Set out again, Louis, even with the silk sheath of a nightdress so as to amuse and intrigue those who come to see what the Baron von Behr and the ERR are up to.'

That one and his British wife often did bring their after-dinner, after-theatre parties here and for just such a purpose and to sell items on the side. 'Far too much is at stake for us to be allowed to interfere, Hermann.'

'We'll try talking to them anyway. We'll lay out our cards and see what theirs are.'

'What cards?'

They entered a ground-floor carpentry shop where pieces awaited further repairs, found wood shavings and sawdust in plenty, hardwoods of various kinds. Tapestries were awaiting further restoration in another room, laundry its ironing in yet another, carpets their cleaning in yet another.

'And the stuff they use for packing, even the wood shavings, returned, Louis, to be used again and again.'

It wasn't a brass gong that rang, nor some relic that had been brought back from the Far East, but a washtub that was being beaten furiously by a soup ladle. At once there was commotion from underfoot—shouting, grumbling, moaning, swearing in Yiddish, Hebrew, Spanish, Polish, German, French, Russian and

Czech—Hungarian too, until silence of a sort was restored, the shrieks of, *'RAUS! RAUS! SCHNELL! ALLES!'* echoing. *'ZUM AP-PELL!'* Roll-call, too, and then . . . then, *'EINS, ZWEI, DREI . . .'*

They took the back stairs down, the stench of toasted, burned, sour black bread and ersatz tea of boiled hay, weeds, roots and other things mingling with those of the washed, the still unwashed and the latrines.

The cellars were a prison. Timber-held wire mesh ran from the floor to a bricked and ogive ceiling, and in this fetid cage which stretched on and on, one hundred and fifty ... two hundred souls slept on tiered, grey blanket-draped bunks whose mattresses leaked sawdust and wood shavings as the prisoners stood to greet the dim electric light of day by lining up to be counted and then given their breakfast.

Men, women, old, young, middle-aged mostly, some in the stiff, still heavy black woollen suits and broad-brimmed black felt hats of the Marais, many not, some of the men even wearing their yarmulkes, defying the guards to snatch them off.

A spatula-wad of stiff grey-white grease—margarine, *verdammt*—from a galvanized bucket, was being slapped on to each thick slab of black bread to be finger spread later on. The canteen trolley was one of the Wehrmacht's mobile soup kitchens, but the three behind it were not in uniform, the one with the ham cheeks and gut of a big bass drum, the resident cook among his other tasks, and wasn't it interesting that the sous-chef immediately beside him was also of medium height and built like a wedge whose big hands must have lost part of a fingernail?

'Fish oil, Louis. If only Marie-Léon Barrault and Gaston Morel could see that cook and Adrienne Guillaumet, the one in the middle. Steal the taxi, collect the victim and take her to the *passage* de la Trinité while the big one heads for the Drouant.'

'And the other one, the second of the sous-chefs, having called out her name as if to help her to that taxi, then sinks his fists into the mud.'

'With a certain safe in mind and Au Philatéliste Savant not far a walk.'

'And with time enough for the one in the middle to have come from the Trinité attack to make sure those stamps were recovered.'

Five Wehrmacht guards were behind them, two with shouldered Schmeissers, a sergeant, a Lagerfeldwebel, in charge. 'It's Sunday, Louis. They've toasted the bread as a little treat to make it taste better. They must have given the prisoners an extra hour of sleep.'

They didn't talk, these sorters, shippers, needlewomen, laundresses, tailors, carpenters, furniture restorers and other artisans, some no doubt former Lévitan employees. Each awaited his or her turn until all the bunks but one were empty. 'Oona . . .'

She was sitting on the edge of a lower bunk, was clutching herself tightly by the shoulders and rocking back and forth, had been badly beaten. 'Hermann, *don't* say anything.'

'You to the right, Louis. I'll go left. We'll cut this lot loose and see what happens.'

'*Ah, merde*, don't be an idiot! They've nowhere else to go without a great deal of outside help and you know it. Aren't concierges who look the other way in short supply? Aren't flats that are now empty and might be used if a cooperative concierge could be found, too often having neighbours who would simply report such new occupants? Too many would be killed in any case, or wounded. Besides, they're hungry.'

'Don't argue.'

'Then listen to me. We've *not* been expected, not yet.'

'Oona's clothes are torn. Was she . . .'

Hermann couldn't bring himself to say it, but Hubert Quevillon was standing to one side of the machine pistols and so was Flavien Garnier.

The first was amused by the roll call, the second couldn't have cared less, but when seen through this mesh of wire and its crowd of faded yellow stars and grey-striped shirts and trousers on some, dresses of the same on others, it was enough.

'A waterproofing compound, Louis, when there are raincoats, capes and boots in plenty in this place.'

'Unlike Max Auger, they know enough not to take anything.'

'Hubert Quevillon having been later told all the lurid details of Madame Guillaumet's attack and that of the Drouant. If he's raped Oona, I'll kill him.'

'That's for the courts to decide and you know it.'

'What courts? Hercule the Smasher's? If we're going down, we're going down hard.'

'Then be so good as to back me up.'

'Remembering always that we've an appointment to keep at 0900 hours.'

The Bois de Vincennes, the Chinese gate. 'Suzette Dunand, Hermann. Have we missed something we should have anticipated?'

The detectives, Suzette knew, had warned her not to get to the station too soon, but the waiting in this flat was terrible. Clothes that would be impossible to replace, would just have to be left. She was to take only a little and had been ready for hours, had told herself over and over again that if arrested, she must never reveal the identities of the detectives who had given her the false papers, must simply say she had purchased them on the black market, an additional crime, oh for sure, but one the police or the Germans might eagerly latch on to and overlook the other.

And the letter they will find in your handbag that is signed by Colonel Delaroche stating that you have been designated an essential worker and must not be taken for the Service du Travail Obligatoire? What will these arresting police or Germans do should they find it among your papers? asked Teddy.

'They'll telephone him. He . . . he'll send someone for me or will come himself.'

With that dog of his?

'*Oui*, but I can't leave that letter, Teddy. It has to be with me at all times, otherwise . . .'

You're crying again. Must you give yourself away so easily?

'I'm sorry. I just can't help it.'

Won't the métro be crowded? Won't we be jostled if the police or the Gestapo or the German soldiers don't stop you first?

How could he do this to her? Everyone had to face a ridership that had gone from two million a day to nearly four million. Whenever people could, especially on Sundays, they packed the trains very early on to head out into the surrounding countryside to forage the farms for food, taking things to barter and, if successful, then risking arrest at the controls on return.

You'll have trouble getting us a ticket, said Teddy spitefully.

'The change,' she gasped. '*Ah, Sainte-Mère,* I had forgotten.' Exact fares were required. So scarce were small coins, the German soldiers always taking them away as souvenirs or simply forgetting them in a pocket, one now, and for nearly the past year and a half, had had to have the precise amount. The line-ups were terrible. 'We'll take the Concorde station. Oh for sure it will be crowded, but this can help us if necessary.'

Is it that we'll have a need to hide? he demanded.

'I . . . I don't know. I'm just being careful. The number one, the Château de Vincennes–Porte Maillot Line from the Concorde runs straight out to the Bois de Vincennes. If someone is following us . . .'

He'll think that's where we're going, but . . .

'Will see what I'm carrying and think I'm taking a few things to my aunt and uncle, a little laundry also.'

Teddy just looked at her like he always did when wanting to tell her she was wrong.

'We'll get off at the Châtelet station. It's one before the Hôtel de Ville. We'll wait until the very last moment to step off the train, then catch a number four but . . . but take it only to the Gare Montparnasse station, walking up and over from there to its Gare du Maine Départ.'

Leaving him on the other train like in the films? A killer, Suzette? M. Jeannot Raymond and a girl who knows far too much about him and the Agence Vidocq?

'We have to try. We can't stay here.'

*   *   *

Torchlight fled urgently over the prisoners. Some were momentarily caught wolfing the last of their bread, others draining the rusty tins they used for mugs. It hit the tiers of bunks. Searching always, it fled along the corridor that surrounded the cage, casting wire-meshed shadows and settling at last on the main breaker box.

Fuses that would have been a stiff hand span in length, with thumb-sized copper contact bars protruding at each end and umpteen volts, were not easily pulled, especially if in darkness and haste.

'And yet they have been,' breathed Helmut Meyer.

'Lagerfeldwebel,' came the oft-excitable voice of Grenadier Willi Keppler. 'There are no spares. They were always kept on top of the box but are no longer here.'

Keppler was the youngest of the men—barely nineteen—and eager, yet requiring almost constant attention. Meyer looked back along the corridor past the boy and then at the prisoners who were waiting. Schmeissers were being trained on them by Bochmann and Ullrich, so that was good, since those two, in their late forties but still looking like grandfathers, were the most able and could, one hoped, be entrusted with such reissued weapons.

Krass, having found his Mauser rifle, had fixed its bayonet in place and was standing at the ready next to the cell's gate. That, too, was as it should be, though Krass was still far from being 100 percent. Russia had done things to each of them.

Steam billowed from the canteen trolley whose cook had carefully set his ladle aside to take up one of the long-bladed knives. Flavien Garnier and Hubert Quevillon were standing very still, the latter no longer amused but afraid he was about to be taken to task for what he'd done to the Dutch woman the two of them had brought in earlier.

'Put the people back in the lock-up,' Meyer heard himself calling out.

'It's the one we had you put in that cage,' said Garnier, his voice carrying on the damp, cold air. 'Kohler and St-Cyr have come for her.'

Had Garnier not liked his use of 'people' for the *Juden*? wondered Meyer. 'Then take her out and give her to them.'

'*Ach*, Lagerfeldwebel, we can't do that,' objected Garnier. 'The Höherer SS . . .'

'Orders are orders, my friend. Yours, mine, those of others. Sometimes they conflict and this is one of those times, since I have received none and merely agreed to your hasty and unusual request, coming as it did in the earliest of hours.'

'We'll take her with us. Just escort us to our car.'

'*Ach*, there could be trouble. Aren't these detectives you are concerned about armed?'

'They won't shoot at . . .'

'Won't return fire should we start it—not myself, you understand, but these men of mine? Certainly these boys haven't seen the front in nearly a year but must I remind you that we are here in Paris to recover from battle fatigue? Can you not also understand that a posting such as this is highly valued and that they wouldn't wish to lose such a cushy job even though one or more of them might be convinced to shoot, out of nervousness only, of course.'

Meyer was just pushing things, felt Garnier. 'Let us take her, then, and leave.'

'That would, under ordinary circumstances, be appropriate, but once locked up, always locked up until I have the order to release her.'

Ah, merde, the *salaud*! 'Fifty thousand.'

'*Reichskassenscheine?*'

'If you wish them,' said the Frenchman gruffly.

'One hundred thousand of those to be split among my men, and a further one hundred thou' for myself, for the expenses and unnecessary delays of production, which you will understand have to be reported in my log and perhaps even verbally explained.'

'Two hundred thousand it is, then.'

'And no trouble but if there should be . . .'

'There won't be.'

'That woman, Herr Garnier. Was she raped by the one that is with you?'

'Not raped. I stopped him.'

'Caught him in the act, did you?'

'But in time. Now listen, there won't be any trouble.'

'Because, my friend, these men of mine will not fire on those two detectives. The General von Schaumburg and others of the Oberkommando der Wehrmacht, who are our commanding officers, don't exactly like what has been going on here at the Lévitan and elsewhere in the country they occupy and for whose order, and plundering, I must emphasize, they are ultimately responsible. Hence, it is best that myself and those under my command proceed with caution.'

'Three hundred thousand.'

'That is a little better but still I have ordered— Men, did you all hear this?' he called out.

Like parrots, their replies came in rank by rank.

'I have ordered them to withhold all fire once the prisoners are again locked up and the one you wish has been released into your custody.'

'The Baron von . . .'

'Behr? He will not want any of these beautiful things of his to be damaged by the thoughtlessness of an exchange of fire that need not have happened, especially as such a disturbance would most certainly bring further attention down on what he and the ERR have been up to, yourselves and others as well, I understand.'

Must everything have its price? swore Garnier silently. 'Four hundred thousand.'

Eight million francs. 'It's a lot, Louis,' whispered Kohler. 'I'd no idea our boys were so corrupt.'

'Of course you did, but can they be corrupted further?'

'If offered the fuses they need?'

Like most big stores, the Lévitan had a pneumatic system for the cash, cheques and paperwork each floor had to send to the head office which was here at the back of the ground floor.

Hermann had been going to feed the fuses into it for safekeeping when voices had been heard, thanks, no doubt, to one of the prisoners holding a portal open, or had it been the Lagerfeldwebel himself?

'Garnier and Quevillon can't be armed, Louis.'

Inevitably the Occupier was reluctant to arm even its most fanatically loyal supporters. The Agence Vidocq might work for Boemelburg *and* Oberg but that didn't mean they had powers of arrest, even if hunting down *résistants,* and in any case, they could be armed on the spot, if felt necessary.

'I'll try to negotiate,' said Hermann.

This wouldn't go well, St-Cyr was certain, but the tube was blown into. '*Achtung, achtung,* Lagerfeldwebel. Kohler, Kripo, Paris-Central. Release Madame Van der Lynn and tell her we're here. Garnier and Quevillon, and those three behind the trolley, are all under arrest. Lock them up and we'll let the Kommandant von Gross-Paris know that good German boys have helped with their capture. He wants them, *meine lieben Herren.* Our orders come straight from him.'

'And not from Gestapo Boemelburg?' shouted Garnier, his voice muffled by distance.

'From the chief also.'

'But not from the Höherer SS Oberg who wants to be rid of the two of you.'

'*Eine kleine Mausefalle,* eh?'

'What does it matter, then, how that happens?'

Garnier had a point, but why would he waste time talking about it . . . 'WATCH HIM, LAGERFELDWEBEL!'

The warning was too late. A burst from a Schmeisser raked the air, screams, shouts and commands pouring from the tube. 'YOU, YOU AND YOU, INTO THE LOCKUP NOW. YOUR PISTOL, LAGERFELDWEBEL. *VITE! VITE!*'

'AND IF I REFUSE.'

'YOU WON'T!'

'I might just as well.'

'*Idiot,* no one need know. Just leave us to deal with those two and we'll give you back your weapons.'

'Bochmann, since you were foolish enough to have lost yours to this one, please go and release the prisoner into their custody.'

'He snatched it away from me, Lagerfeldwebel. I wasn't expecting . . .'

'Yes, yes. It's all right, Bochmann. We'll do as we have to and deal with it later.'

'Russia . . . They'll send me back, Lagerfeldwebel.'

'I know, but it can't be helped. Kohler, the fuses, where are they?'

A sensible man. 'Lying here on the former director's desk. Let the prisoners go to their work stations and ask among them for someone to show you the way, if needed.'

Angry shouting followed, then silence, then a whispered, 'Kohler, the woman has managed to run from them. Garnier and the others have taken our torches but have not, I think, yet found her.'

'Louis, did you hear that?'

There was no answer. He had already left.

Crouched, half-hidden, St-Cyr eased the Lebel's hammer fully back. Garnier and the others—the cook, his two helpers and Quevillon—weren't just shining their torches into and along each aisle. They had spread out in a line, aisle by aisle, room display by display, and were crossing the ground floor in unison, moving inevitably towards the director's office and Hermann, who might not yet know this but might anticipate it.

Garnier had dropped right back into being the sergeant he'd been in that other war. The cook and sous-chefs were also veterans—one had but to glance at them to see this. The former now carried a Schmeisser, the latter two had the Lagerfeldwebel's Luger and the rifle.

Alone of them, Hubert Quevillon had been allocated the cook's knife and relegated to the farthest aisle and immediately to Garnier's right, that one still wanting to keep an eye on his subordinate or better still, to use that weakest link to advantage.

Looking down from the first floor at the head of the escalator he had somehow found in the dark, St-Cyr knew Garnier was being thorough. That one would use everything he could including, especially, that Oona had gone to ground.

Torchlight from the cook raced along the row of Boulle armoires but came back quickly to settle on one of them and then on another and another. One of the doors to this last hadn't quite been closed. Had he found her?

Gingerly this cook teased it open. Caught in the mirror, the torchlight momentarily threw back its reflections. Blinking, he jabbed the muzzle of the Schmeisser deeply into the armoire. He didn't call out, this man with the stomach of a barrel. Though one had at first felt he might have done, the soldier within him was too ingrained and brought only silence.

The line advanced. Its having all but reached the halfway point, *Monsieur le Chef de Cuisine* would have to hurry if he was to keep up. He showed no concern.

A torn piece of the lining from Oona's woollen dress was fingered, the cook looking back along the aisle into darkness before teasing it out. He shone the light into the first of the vitrines whose curved glass doors and contents gave back their glints. He tried the next armoire but suddenly decided to retrace his steps.

He was counting off the armoires and when, at last, he came to the one next to where the torn fabric had been found, its doors were tightly shut. Perhaps it was a game to him, perhaps it had its sexual overtones. Harshly on the air came the pungency of the black bread he and the other two had toasted for the prisoners, burning, caramelizing what sugars there were in those round, hard loaves. The smell of too many Gauloises bleues was here, too, that of anise and sweat and garlic and pomade. A heavy man. A man of this Sûreté's height and close now, very close. A little more . . . only a little and then the bracelets, that bit of cloth stuffed into the mouth to guarantee silence.

Oona's right shoulder had been laid bare and had been badly bruised by Hubert Quevillon. There were bruises on the slender throat. Her lips had been split, her cheeks revealing where she'd been struck. She didn't cry out but blinked at the light, dismay registering in those bluest of eyes, was all but bent double, would have difficulty getting out of the armoire.

'*Un moment,*' she softly said, the accent still there as it always would be, the memories of the Exodus from Rotterdam constantly with her, the loss, the endless days, weeks, months, years of never really knowing if her children would be found alive or in some hastily dug, unmarked grave a farmer might accidentally come upon years later.

She didn't look past this cook who had found her. She stood before him, he shining the light over her. 'My hair,' she said. 'It's come loose. Please give me a moment, monsieur.'

The pudgy cheeks with their glazed-over nicks from a morning's dull razor, their shadowed hairy moles and warts and aftershave, tightened. The Schmeisser lifted. Its muzzle was now pressed firmly against her stomach, Oona . . . Oona looking only at the cook, she watching that one's eyes closely, too closely . . . . *Ah, merde,* Hermann. HERMANN, ME, I DIDN'T REALIZE SHE WOULD WANT HIM TO KILL HER!

The silence hurt like hell, the sense of loss was total. Over and over again Kohler silently said, 'Louis, why couldn't you have waited?' He *knew* Louis had gone to find Oona for him. Louis would do something like that. Louis.

The trickle of another rain of porcelain trailed itself away. Another large wedge of vitrine glass or mirror collapsed. The stench of cordite was all too evident, the ears still rang with the emptying of a Schmeisser's box magazine, all thirty-two rounds at five hundred a minute.

There were no torchlights. These had instantly gone out with the firing. There'd been no shouts—nothing like that from Garnier or any of the others. Nor had there been a sound from below them, from the cellars.

Quevillon had pissed himself and was still quivering. The

butcher knife and torch he'd held when found were lying on the floor at his feet, the urge to kill him all too . . .

'Hubert?' came a whisper at last from out of the surrounding darkness, calm, though Kohler nudged the back of Quevillon's neck with the Walther P38's muzzle.

'FLAVIEN, WHAT HAS HAPPENED?'

Must Hubert be so shrill? thought Garnier with a snort. Blindly, gingerly he felt his way forward. He had to find a gap in all this rubbish, had to get through to Quevillon's corridor before Kohler realized what was happening.

'Flavien?' hazarded one of the sous-chefs some distance from him.

Again there was no answer.

'Eugène, are you okay?' whispered that sous-chef. Kohler was certain of it. Had Louis found Oona? Had they both been killed?

Instinctively Garnier knew he had reached the far end of the aisle. There was that sense of openness, of being free of things. Stretching out his left arm, torch in that hand, Schmeisser in the other, he would take a silent, tentative step forward, would hurry yet chance nothing.

He had to make his way well around Hubert, couldn't let Kohler realize this. Had it not been for that burst of firing, Kohler would have been taken, but now . . . now that Kripo must have Hubert. Eugène Roulleau would see that things weren't good and would retrace his steps to find out what had happened to Claude Beaupré, the cook. Victor Denault would hold his position. Those three had often worked together but never at anything like this since Verdun.

The dressing table had its chair. Kohler nudged Quevillon into it. Louis wouldn't have shot this *agent privé* or anyone else, not unless absolutely forced to in self-defence. Louis simply wasn't like that.

A wrist was taken and pulled back behind the chair, the other one, too, Quevillon not objecting but waiting only for help—was that it, eh?

Metal clicked against metal and clicked again. Instantly

Garnier knew the bracelets had been applied but Kohler wouldn't hang around. And what of St-Cyr? he wondered.

Claude Beaupré must have found the woman, but had that Sûreté found the cook with her? It wasn't like Claude to have emptied that gun. Had the finger of a dying man been jammed against its trigger? Had the woman been killed?

When he found Hubert, Garnier felt the silken nightdress that Kohler had crammed into that one's mouth. He waited. Vehemently Hubert shook his head but had Kohler done the unexpected and hung around?

Only the soft fluttering of the silk as it moved in and out at its corners with each attempted whisper came to him. There was no other motion now, simply a stiffness in Hubert that gave warning enough.

Kohler . . . Where was he? Near, so near—watching through the darkness? Waiting for what—the torch to come on, the Schmeisser to be swung away from Hubert and what must be beyond him? Did Kohler actually believe he would spare that little shit?

A wash of perfume had been released on to the dressing table in front of Hubert, the flacon lying on its side but with the stopper deliberately set upright, the scent that of a woman of exceptional taste—was this what Kohler wanted to suggest? A Jewess? A wife, mother, daughter, mistress, the perfume still flooding from its little bottle?

The folding mirror under hand was in three panels. Hubert would see himself in it when the lights came on. Was this what Kohler had had in mind?

Blood, brains and bits of bone had been sprayed across the floor and over the nearby armoires and vitrines with their bullet-shattered doors and broken glass. It didn't need a light for one to realize this, thought Eugène Roulleau. The cook had been hit in the back of the head at very close range, the slug racing around in there before tearing away much of the forehead and the eyes on exit.

One of the old Lebels, he silently swore. The fingers that had found the wound were wet and greasy. The Schmeisser Claude had held might have slid away but he doubted this and couldn't recall having heard the clatter it should have made.

Merde, this wasn't good. What the hell had the colonel got them into? *Bien sûr,* the odd job at night. It had been right of them to take care of those bitches, to teach them lessons their husbands couldn't give. The schoolteacher, an officer's wife, had been given hers hard, the stamps had then been recovered but . . .

There was no sign of St-Cyr, nor of the Dutch woman. With the Schmeisser's burst there had been no sounds other than the terrified shriek she had given.

Wasn't there an escalator nearby? Of course there was.

The muzzle of a Lebel has a signature all its own and much different from that of a Schmeisser or Luger. Sometimes warm, often cold, all are individuals when one has experienced such things, and all mean the same. Would a nod suffice?

The Luger was teased away. Roulleau waited. One didn't think St-Cyr would shoot—Claude had been unavoidable and maybe the woman *was* dead and lying crumpled up in one of the armoires.

One would just have to try to duck aside or bend the knees on impact so as to soften the blow. Those old revolvers weighed a tonne. He'd have a king-sized lump.

Garnier heard the blow and the gasp it brought before the body collapsed. Stiffening, he looked away through the pitch-darkness towards where Claude Beaupré must have been, knew that Eugène Roulleau, the one who had raped the Guillaumet woman, had been taken, wanted to call out to Victor Denault of other such attacks and the robbery, with Roulleau, of Au Philatéliste Savant, but stopped himself, wanted to use the torch but found he couldn't.

'Gently,' breathed Kohler, taking the Schmeisser from him. 'We wouldn't want to ruin anything else, now would we?'

In the cold, grey light of dawn they shared a cigarette but would it be their last? wondered Kohler. What they had uncovered wasn't good. Too many in high places were being threatened; all would flock together, none would let two dumb *Schweinebullen* continue to interfere as they had most definitely. Jeannot Raymond might well arrive thinking to find Suzette Dunand waiting for him, but what of Delaroche, or of Sonja Remer and the Standartenführer Langbehn?

What of Oberg and even of von Behr, who wasn't going to like the problem they had left on that Lévitan doorstep?

What of Judge Rouget and Vivienne, of the others too, that still shadowy and probably never-to-be-named group of men of influence who met at the Cercle de l'Union Interaliée to finance and advise Delaroche's campaign of teaching POW wives and fiancées not to misbehave?

'Too much is at stake, Hermann, too many are threatened.'

The cigarette was returned, the time, the moment, one of silence.

Caught between the Marne and the Seine, the Bois de Vincennes stretched bare branches up into the fog. Immediately beyond the Lac des Minimes, the keep, the donjon of the Château de Vincennes, all 52 metres (about 170 feet) of it could barely be seen, rising as it did higher and higher to a turret at each of the four corners, one of which carried a swastika every bit as huge as that atop the Eiffel Tower and not a breath of wind.

'Six hundred, a thousand, Hermann. Two thousand? How many men garrison that stronghold?'

'I'd worry about what the Wehrmacht have got stored under that keep.'

High explosives, artillery shells and ammunition.* They had left Oona at the *Hôtel-Dieu*, had asked for Matron Aurore Aumont if possible and had said they'd be back soon, a lie of course but . . . 'Oona's the one for you, Hermann. Stop all this talk of a little place on the Costa del Sol with Giselle tending the bar and having babies Oona will take care of. You need her desperately and she needs you now more than ever.'

---

* On 24 August 1944, at the close of the Occupation, some of these were used, causing considerable damage to the Château and adjacent buildings.

Hermann had held her all the way there. 'And Giselle?' he asked.

'We'll find her. I promise.'

'I just wish I had your confidence.'

A Peugeot four-door sedan, dark green under the fog's sweat, was parked outside 45 bis avenue de la Belle-Gabrielle not far from the Château's keep but looking damned lonely as such would these days. Kohler used a fist to clear side windscreen. 'Ah, Christ, Louis,' he said, that sinking feeling in him all too evident. They should have had plenty of time to get in place but now had none.

A teddy bear, torn from Suzette Dunand's grasp, lay on the backseat. On the floor there was a small suitcase, beside this, a shopping bag that had toppled over as its cognac bottle had been grabbed and taken away.

'I should have seen it, Hermann. I knew we should have been more careful with that girl. This place . . . It's freely open to the public only on Thursday afternoons from 1400 to 1600 hours. At all other times permission must be obtained.'

No casual visitors. 'And now you tell me.'

Gilded fleurs-de-lis surmounted the tall, wrought-iron gates which, partly open, looked as if having been unlocked by an attendant who had had no wish to hang around and yet had had to do as bidden. Louis wasn't happy about it. 'Adrienne Guillaumet's husband spent an extended tour of duty in Indochina. He and that father of his would be known to several other officers and men, one or more of whom could be involved.'

'And there are veterans and veterans from that other war.'

'I was here in 1920 when the memorial to the Annamite dead was consecrated. Brave men, good men. That temple, pagoda, *dinh* or communal house whose red tiled roofs so beautifully point towards heaven at their corners, is magnificent. There are rooms you wouldn't expect, ironwood pillars—I counted at least sixty. Carvings that are exquisite, individual memorials to many of the fallen, altars to the gods of this and that, as well as to the Buddha.'

'Let's just hope we're not too late.'

'They can't have let that girl live.'

There was no one waiting under the Chinese gate. How could there have been? One could wish for another time to cross this courtyard or walk through a garden which, in summer, would be tropical, not under blankets of last autumn's leaves or wrapped in layers of burlap sacking, its monuments and statues to the fallen looking not just damned lonely but eerie in a silence that was broken only by the sound of gravel underfoot.

'Hermann, there's a *passage* that runs beside the temple. Two-metre-high sandstone bas-reliefs, copied from those in the avenue at Angkor Wat, line this. You'll find them strange and frightening if coming upon them suddenly. Battle scenes from the holy books and epics of the Hindu. Remember, please, that not only will you be driven to feel as one with those men, you'll be distracted. It can't be helped, not after Verdun and all the rest we had to face in that other war.'

Everyone listened but no sound was heard, Suzette was certain. Dragons in dark, highly polished wood, their bulging eyes glistening as they watched her and waited, were coiled about the pillars or lying stretched along the rafters as if but awakened to what was happening and going to happen to her. Brightly painted terra-cotta unicorns tensely waited with phoenixes and turtles and they, too, seemed to listen and to watch. A polychrome Buddha waited, sitting on a lotus blossom. Spiralled incense coils—tall, open, white-ribbed cones—waited as they hung above the altar of this crowded shrine whose joss sticks the colonel had lit to smoulder constantly before the ash urns of the dead behind which were the framed photographs in glass of their owners, all of whom were in uniform.

Though there had been no sound that could have been heard, Bob had given warning and rigidly watched the block-printed red silk hangings that formed a screen over the doorway to this shrine. Colonel Delaroche had carefully redoubled his hold on the leash, Jeannot Raymond stood behind her, waiting too, as did the dead of that other war to whom relatives had burned further joss sticks before each photograph and had left offerings of money. Banknotes that had been printed in France in 1939 and never sent out, the colonel had said to Jeannot Raymond, who had caught her as she had hurried down the steps of the Concorde station and had forced her to come with him after first telephoning the colonel.

Bob didn't move. Bob was very still, the two of them watching him and not herself, but would it matter, could it? Her hands were tied tightly behind her back. They had stuffed a kerchief into her mouth. The knife that would be used was still lying on the table before her and, among the reflections from its black lacquer, she could clearly see those of the incense coils and the dragons. 'An old friend,' Jeannot Raymond had said of that knife he had brought from Argentina. A gaucho's knife with a long and shallow groove on either side and almost the whole length of the blade to hold and drain away the blood—her blood—once the throat had been slashed. He would simply pick it up, grab her by the hair, yank her head back and cut her throat as he'd done to others, she was certain of this. A knife whose blade was twenty centimetres long at least, two in width at the top and razor sharp, with a flattened, S-shaped guard, the handle beautifully embossed with what looked to be hammered, coppery-silver designs of crisscrossed triangles, curves, ridges and countless patterns.

'One kills to feel it,' Colonel Delaroche had said to her before Bob had stiffened. 'Though the time of the gauchos was long ago, Jeannot employed only those who could prove they were descendants.'

'The only honest human beings,' that one had said. 'Whenever possible they would use no other weapon than the *facón* each carried at the waist in its sheath, behind the back.'

Perhaps that knife weighed two hundred grams. Certainly it must be light for such a length. 'The *gavilán*,' he had said of it in Argentinian Spanish. 'The balance has to be absolutely perfect. This one's short by a good ten centimetres because I wanted it that way.'

Wanted it . . .

Bob fidgeted. It wasn't that he didn't like the smell of the burning joss, it was, Suzette was certain, that their scent reminded him of someone and that this then made him uneasy.

Again and again it came to them: the softest rustling—rats? wondered Kohler. Was it backup Delaroche had called in? Curtained doorways to niche memorials had been deliberately drawn, others left open. Bongs, gongs, drums, funeral biers, flags, bowls and urns—*lieber Christus im Himmel,* the bloody crap was bound to get in the way. A life-sized bronze Buddha sat behind the main altar, glowing softly in the ever-subdued light, waiting, it seemed, for something to happen. Others of wood were seated about in shades of dark varying to a light rose-amber, one with a hand raised in caution—was it caution—all eyes closed, the expressions beatific?

Merde, the rustling was stronger now. Louis hadn't moved from where he was standing just inside the main entrance. Backlit by the growing light of day, he was a perfect target.

Now louder, the rustling put one on edge. Louis jabbed with the Lebel to indicate something off to the side in front of him. An altar. Joss sticks, bowls, urns, rows and rows of short strips of thin, reddish-purple paper with vertical lines of writing on them—hundreds and hundreds of these hung directly above one another from horizontally mounted bamboo rods, forming a panel maybe a metre-and-a-half wide by two in height. 'Token offerings,' he whispered, all but mouthing the words. Promises to the dead, for when times get better, wondered Kohler; items given, even with the shortages; good deeds done in the eternal quest to influence one's karma?

The fog must be clearing. Air was moving through the *dinh* and, as each gust passed by, it lifted the loose ends of the paper offerings, one after another, row with row, and carried joss smoke up from behind a curtained door halfway along that side.

'Don't kill her, Colonel. Let's talk.'

There was no answer.

Curtains of block-printed red silk were parted. 'Colonel . . .'

'Put that gun down, Kohler. Don't and she dies,' said Delaroche.

Jeannot Raymond had a knife like no other at her throat, the kid in tears.

The Walther P38 made its sound as it struck the glossy-black lacquer of the table. 'Louis,' he called, throwing the name over a shoulder, 'the bastards have got me.' There'd been nothing else he could have done. Nothing.

'Join us, St-Cyr,' called out Delaroche.

'He must have gone to check that *passage*,' offered Hermann.

'Then we'll wait. You two . . . Why couldn't you have done what you were supposed to?'

'Find the Trinité victim and then those of the Restaurant Drouant but nothing else, not the killing of Max Auger at the police academy and that of Élène Artur, or those of Noëlle Jourdan and her dear *papa*?'

'Kohler, Kohler, why the hell couldn't you simply have agreed to Herr Oberg's request? A simple enough thing, a freshly baited little trap he still has in mind.'

'Perhaps.'

'False papers—did you really think Jeannot wouldn't anticipate your trying to get this girl away from us? These are good, by the way. Proof enough of what you two are capable of. Boemelburg will have to see them.'

A little squeeze, was that it? 'Don't even bother, my fine one. I often pick them up on the black market to show the chief how the quality is always improving.'

'Lie if you wish, but join us.'

'With a French army MAS 1935A pointing at me? Eight of the 7.65 Long in the box and one up the spout? More than enough fire power to counter a Lebel 1873 with those old cartridges, eh, as this one must know?'

The shot when it came, filled the *dinh* with its sound. St-Cyr caught his chest, cried out, HERMANN! silently and said, a whisper, 'Forgive me, *mon vieux*. I should have seen what they'd do because we gave them no other choice.'

Bob had been startled by the shot and had hunkered down

beside that master of his, but now lifted woeful eyes as a hand was extended. Tentatively he sniffed at it, rejoiced, licked it eagerly and let his ears and chin be gently fondled.

'Colonel, tell that son of a bitch to take that knife away from her throat and pull the gag before she chokes on her vomit.'

St-Cyr had still not come. 'We also have the Van der Lynn woman, Kohler.'

'Oona?'

That had startled Kohler. 'Taken yesterday, but surely you were aware of this?'

The one with the knife hadn't let up, but was it that these two still didn't know what had happened at the Lévitan? In too much of a hurry to grab the girl and get here? No time, then. No time. 'We looked for Oona but couldn't find her, Colonel.'

Then why not ask where she was being held? Instead, Kohler warily glanced from Jeannot to himself as if uncertain of where things would now lead, and in the end, again reached out to Bob.

'Believe me, Kohler, we really do have that woman of yours.'

'Just the one—is that it?'

'Unfortunately, yes.'

'The *passage* de l'Hirondelle killing a mistake?'

'Giselle le Roy will be found and will pay for it.'

His cape thrown back, that mustard-yellow scarf worn loose, Delaroche's free hand was still wrapped tightly about Bob's lead. Jeannot Raymond's watchful grey eyes were expressionless, the black overcoat open, the black turtleneck pullover and dark grey pinstripe jacket, black hair and high if furrowed brow not those of a worried man but of one who knew exactly what he had to do and would, no matter what. Much taller than the girl, who was being held tightly from behind, his chin didn't even touch the top of her blonde head. His reactions would be instinctive, no matter what. That blade would slice deeply as it was drawn from left to right, the girl's eyes registering shock first, then panic, then loss as life faded. Could nothing be done?

'The Lévitan, Colonel? Is that where you think you've got Oona?'

'*Salaud,* what have you done?'

'And not happy about it, eh?'

'Must I remind you I'm the one with the gun? What went wrong?'

'It being a Sunday, Colonel, the Komandant von Gross-Paris will still be at 26 avenue Raphaël, the villa the Wehrmacht requisitioned for him. Every morning it's the horseback ride first in the Bois de Boulogne, rain, snow or shine. Then it's breakfast. Always the *café noir avec les croissants chauds* and the plum jam, no other, then it's off to work, but on Sundays, I have to tell you, he stays at that villa a little longer. Sundays are always his bath days. No one is ever allowed to bother him. I hated to interrupt but . . .'

There was still no sign of St-Cyr. 'I'm waiting, Kohler.'

'As is that "partner" of yours?'

'Get on with it, damn you!'

'*Mais certainement.* Not only was a Wehrmacht guard detail disarmed and their weapons used against them, their uniforms were disgraced. The only possible recourse, since I was under his orders, was to send the perpetrators, minus one, to the villa under arrest and with Lagerfeldwebel Meyer bearing a note from me detailing the reasons. You and that Agence Vidocq of yours are for it, my friend. *Bonne chance.*'

Kohler would have done it, as would St-Cyr. 'Bob, stay. Bob, sit.'

'He's upset, Colonel. Missing Élène, are you, Bob? Got the scent of the joss she used to burn here?'

'And what of these four?' asked Delaroche, indicating the boys on Louis's street, the photograph and its negative.

Had the son of a bitch thought to barter? 'They've already left town.'

'Using false papers? Really, you do surprise me, Kohler. They'll be hounded down and brought back. The Höherer SS will be as definite about them as he will be about our showing up at that meeting tomorrow morning with the two of you and Giselle le Roy or Oona Van der Lynn. It won't much matter which is used, will it?'

'There are meetings and meetings, Colonel, papers and papers, uniforms and uniforms. This Occupier of yours has a thing about all of them, hasn't he? Afraid of what Oberg's going to do when he finds out what you and that agency have been up to behind his back and those of Von Schaumburg and Gestapo Boemelburg? Terrorizing the streets after dark? Making the Führer gnash his teeth over it? Killing people, raping some of them first and raping others, too? They did, Bob. They really did. That one with the knife held Élène down while this one . . .'

'Kohler, don't even bother to try to unsettle Jeannot. Vivienne insisted that we take care of Élène in the manner and place she wished. We did what we had to.'

Louis . . . what the hell was keeping Louis? 'And with Max Auger?'

'The boy had disobeyed me. An example had to be set.'

'And the mistake in the *passage* de l'Hirondelle? Hobnailed boots again, Colonel? *Ach,* don't you French ever throw anything out, especially after all the wars you've been in? I couldn't get rid of mine fast enough. Rage, Colonel, that's what it suggests to me. Uncontrollable rage, just as with Max and Élène. A very troubled mind that was, and still is, very afraid of what Oberg really will do when he hears about everything you've been up to behind his back. The Cercle de l'Union Interaliée and an inner circle who advise you on which targets to use as examples, Hercule the Smasher being one of those advisors? Men who gladly fed you far more names than Denise Rouget or Germaine de Brisac could ever have provided. POW wives and fiancées who needed lessons those bastards then financed.'

It would do no good to even say it, but . . . 'Please try to understand that we're fighting a war on the home front. Préfet Talbotte is one of that inner circle.'

'Heroes are you, to veterans and others who believe it's right to punish such women? Then listen hard. You're a fence sitter and we can prove it. You work for the SS nailing *résistants* and others they and Von Behr and the ERR want, but at the same time you've been covering your ass for later, when the Occupier has to go home. Garnering support from as many as you can while filling vacated residences with the *objets d'art* and other things of the deported? Cash from double and triple billing the clients, from the sale of wanted names and from contract killings—that's what Élène was, Bob. Cash you then hide in real estate and probably gold and diamonds, even though it's illegal for you or anyone else to buy and hold these last. Already you must have built yourself quite a bankroll.'

There would be no sense in trying to bribe Kohler. 'Tell St-Cyr to join us.'

'Not until you tell me what makes a man like that one tick.'

'Jeannot? He discovered that the woman he adored and would have done anything for had betrayed him not once but several times.'

'And you, Colonel? Did you discover what he'd done and then get him to work for you?'

'Jeannot and myself are equal partners, fellow members, yes, of the Interaliée, which is where I first met him. This Occupation affords so many opportunities and now, of course, the Argentina he came to love and want to help to build is on the best of terms with the Reich* and has agreed that, again, he can be accepted as a citizen, especially as he has sufficient capital to buy back and enlarge his ranches.'

'Travel by submarine?'

'Perhaps. Now tell St-Cyr to stop whatever he thinks he's doing and join us.'

'Me? You still haven't got it, have you? Louis is the one who usually does all this wrap-up stuff and has a mind of his own.'

Would the cartridges be damp and useless? wondered St-Cyr. Would Jeannot Raymond's reactions be too swift even then? Would the colonel shoot Hermann?

There was only one way of finding out. He looked at the Lebel in his hand, but to say to it, Don't fail me again, seemed senseless. Hermann would still have wanted him to try. If not success-

---

* this was still possible but eventually under U.S. pressure, Argentina broke off relations with the Third Reich on 26 January 1944

ful, at least he'd know that this partner and friend of his had made the attempt.

All the matches in the packet he'd brought from the car would be needed—*merde*, they were so hard to get. The black powder from two of the cartridges Hermann had okayed, but should have bitten first and wiggled, was added, as were paper token offerings whose loss the dead would not object to and joss sticks, the shoes and socks left to one side. Bare feet would be best. The rosewood planks in the floor had been lovingly honed and polished so that they glistened.

The four-legged turtle urn he had chosen was large enough to contain the fire and not burn the temple down. The matches flared, the powder took, the paper strips igniting as the joss began at once to burn.

Incense billowed up to be caught by the latest gust and carried to them, but would they be distracted by it, Hermann intuitively realizing what his partner was up to and becoming a part of it?

'Bob, there's my soldier,' sang out Kohler. 'He's really missing Élène, Colonel. These what you're after in my jacket pocket, Bob? The white, lace-trimmed pongee step-ins I used when I found her wedding ring?'

Eagerly Bob tugged at the briefs, pulling Delaroche off-balance. Joss smoke was everywhere . . .

Smashed in the forehead, the shot reverberating, Jeannot Raymond released his grip on the knife as he fell. 'COLONEL, DON'T!' yelled Louis.

Hermann leaped. The pistol was grabbed, wrenched away, Delaroche hit and hit hard with it until he, too, dropped, Bob looking puzzled now, the briefs dangling from his mouth, Suzette Dunand trying to steady herself.

'*Ah, bon,*' said Louis with a sigh. 'It's over, Hermann.'

'Delaroche won't sing and you know it.'

'But will be asked to.'

'Though not by us.'

*　　*　　*

Up through the woods, the sounds from the industrial suburb of Suresnes came to mark an end to the day. Wet through and cold, pneumonia was bound to set in. Louis handed him the cognac bottle. 'It's safe,' he said, having downed a goodly measure and found no nicotine. How could he have been so sure?

'I wasn't,' he confessed. 'I just assumed it since the cork had been bunged home and leaded sixty-seven years ago.'

Below them, prudence had demanded that they leave the Citroën tucked in against the base of an oak that, for some reason, hadn't been logged, burned or sawn up for lumber in 1871. 'The Prussians must have felt they needed its shade,' Louis had mused. Those people had found the fort up there on Mont-Valérien empty. In that distant war, they hadn't even had to shell that dismal pentagon of buttressed grey stonework at the end of this rutted, boulder-strewn lane. On 29 January of that year they had marched in without a shot having been fired, the strongest of the seventeen such forts in the defence of Paris.

And now? Kohler had to ask and answer, Why now they're back in it again.

'Sixty-nine-and-a-half years later,' said Louis drolly, having calculated it to the Defeat of June 1940. 'He won't wait for us, Hermann.'

It was still Sunday 14 February 1943 and they'd been run off their feet. Giselle had remembered Louis's singing the praises of his friends on *place Vendôme* and their shop, Enchantment, and had managed to reach it. Taken in by Muriel Barteaux, of Mirage perfume fame, and Chantal Grenier, her partner, both well into their seventies and lifelong companions, she'd been 'assessed. *Complètement nue*, my Hermann,' and now was one of their lingerie mannequins. Good goods, very high class. 'Another profession,' she had said and given him a peck on the cheek. 'Safer, too, I think, than keeping house for one who doesn't need a housekeeper.'

As if she had ever done that. And Oona? he asked. Oona had found Adrienne Guillaumet, who had been moved to another floor in the *Hôtel-Dieu*. She'd gone to tell Henri and Louisette that their dear *maman* would soon be rejoining them and that, for a little, she would need some help.

Oona would stay with her in the flat on the rue Saint-Dominique. A shy and hesitant touch on the arm, that's all he'd been able to give her, she the same with him. A lingering last look? he wondered.

The boys had got safely away and would work on their respective farms until after the autumn harvest at least. The street would be lonely for Louis but then, he was hardly ever home and not likely to be in the near future.

They continued on up the hill. At least the rain had quit.

'You forgot something, Hermann. The Ritz.'

And right next door to the shop Enchantment. Adrienne Guillaumet hadn't been about to sell the use of her self but rather the Biedermeier furniture her husband treasured. They had negotiated the sale to the General Schiller from Baden-Baden. At least it wouldn't be stolen, and she'd got a fair price, *Reichskassenscheine*, too, all of fifty thousand of them, a million francs. She would divorce the husband if the courts would let her, would leave him in any case and never wanted to see him again, was thinking of Spain and the Costa del Sol, of a seaside lodging house perhaps, but only because Oona had suggested it. Deauville had been an alternate, though for later, when this Occupation was over.

'And Marie-Léon Barrault?' asked Louis.

'Innocent too.' It had all been lies and they'd made damned sure the Scapini Commission in Berlin learned of it, since they'd had that sour little priest, Father Marescot of the Notre-Dame de Lorette, write the letter.

When Gaston Morel had told her to take the lift in the Hôtel Grand, and she'd been photographed doing so, she had gone up to the fourth floor, to a room where one of the *Bonzen* dabbled on the side in the black market and had aspirins, cough syrup and other medicines for sale. Good stuff, too. Things one could trust, Annette having had a bad cold at the time, a temperature, and the only occasion in which her mother had accepted money from Morel. And as for the manager of the Cinéma Impérial trying to get her to have sex with him, one word had been enough, and the muzzle of Louis's Lebel.

Suzette Dunand they had safely seen on to her train. She might be home by now and would have lots to say when she got there.

'Which leaves only us, Hermann.'

It didn't, not quite, but no matter. 'My boots are leaking again.'

'You'll think of something.'

Together they entered the fort within whose cells, it having been built between 1830 and 1848 during the reign of Louis Philippe, languished *résistants* and others Judge Hercule Rouget had condemned to death but not this late-afternoon's quota.

The posts were occupied, the blindfolds in place, the volley harsh-sounding on the damp air but brief.

Tall, rheumy-eyed, ramrod stiff in greatcoat and cap, an Iron Cross First Class at the throat, Von Schaumburg had but a few words for them. 'Your witnessing this won't look good for either of you, Kohler, but understand that is precisely why I've summoned you.'

Maybe 1,500 had been executed so far, maybe more in this most feared of places and buried in its surrounding woods. The Résistance would, of course, be bound to get the wrong message and think this partnership had been present at any number of executions; the Occupier, its SS and Gestapo particularly, would know this wasn't so, but think the worst of them in any case.

Oberg wasn't happy and neither was Boemelburg but then, neither were often happy. The Standartenführer Langbehn had been recalled. Sonja Remer hadn't been able to do what she had most wanted but wouldn't be leaving the avenue Foch in the near future, so would always be on hand should Oberg take another notion to get rid of them.

Gabrielle was fine, or so it appeared. Safe for the moment, but there'd been no time for her and Louis to spend together.

The bodies were being freed, the blindfolds and ropes to be used again and again, the colonel's first and then those of the one who had attacked Adrienne Guillaumet so savagely and then had hustled to the *passage* Jouffroy to rob the stamp shop with the other sous-chef, who now lay beside him.

'There's no need for either of you to sign the death notices,' said Von Schaumburg. 'My office, and it alone, will take care of that.'

Garnier and Quevillon had also been executed, Berlin pacified. Gradually the streets would return to relative safety. Vivienne Rouget had committed a crime of passion and would never see the inside of a cell or face the breadbasket. Hercule the Smasher was just too valuable to the Occupier, as were those of the Interaliée who had backed the Agence Vidocq. Louis and he would just have to leave it.

'Until spring comes, Hermann,' he muttered.

'Walk with me to my car,' said Von Schaumburg, ignoring the muted outburst. 'I've something for you.'

Their train would leave at 2000 hours. Vittel was in the Vosges and still in the grip of winter.

'The Kommandant went to school with me, Kohler. Give him my regards.'

Ach, another Prussian of the old school!

'And the problem?' hazarded Louis.

'Something about a ringer of bells who ought to know, or have known, better. The line wasn't clear.'

Only when they reached the Citroën did Hermann say, 'Bell-ringer, Louis. It has a good ring to it.'

'Idiot, we're to get the hell out of Paris and you know it. Wasn't Talbotte a member of that inner circle?'

A last look uphill was just that, the Kommandant von Gross-Paris's car heading straight for them as they stepped aside.

'I'll drive, Louis. It's better for you if I'm seen to.'

They got in, were crowded, greeted and licked as if they'd been absent for an eternity. *'Pour l'amour de Dieu,* Hermann, get that animal away from me!'

'He's lonely. You'll get use to him. He's good for the image.'

'Ours is tarnished enough!'

Bob was persistent; Bob needed his friends. Finally Louis settled back in defeat to place a hand on Bob's head, which had somehow found its way into his lap.

'Do you think the backseat would be better for the two of you?' offered Kohler. There was no answer. 'Bellringer, Louis. It must have something to do with a monk or priest, or novice or one or the other. Bob's going to love it. He'll feel right at home. It'll be good for him.'

Hermann always had to have the last word. In a way, the Occupier in him demanded it but some philosophical thing at least should be said just to put him off stride and make him think.

A sigh would be best, and then, 'There are no endings, Hermann, only beginnings.'

THE ST-CYR AND KOHLER MYSTERIES

FROM MYSTERIOUSPRESS.COM
AND OPEN ROAD MEDIA

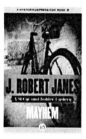
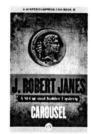
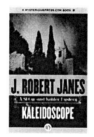
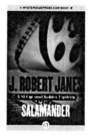
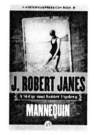

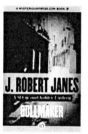
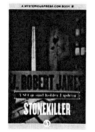
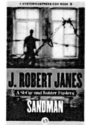
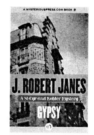
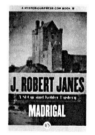

Available wherever ebooks are sold

MYSTERIOUSPRESS.COM

MYSTERIOUSPRESS.COM

Otto Penzler, owner of the Mysterious Bookshop in Manhattan, founded the Mysterious Press in 1975. Penzler quickly became known for his outstanding selection of mystery, crime, and suspense books, both from his imprint and in his store. The imprint was devoted to printing the best books in these genres, using fine paper and top dust-jacket artists, as well as offering many limited, signed editions.

Now the Mysterious Press has gone digital, publishing ebooks through **MysteriousPress.com**.

MysteriousPress.com offers readers essential noir and suspense fiction, hard-boiled crime novels, and the latest thrillers from both debut authors and mystery masters. Discover classics and new voices, all from one legendary source.

FIND OUT MORE AT

WWW.MYSTERIOUSPRESS.COM

FOLLOW US:

@emysteries and Facebook.com/MysteriousPressCom

MysteriousPress.com is one of a select group of publishing pa 3 1170 01069 0000 ated Media, Inc.